Ārambha

Celebrating
30 Years of Publishing
in India

Ārambha

The Birth of Vijayanagara

Buchi Ramagopal

HarperCollins *Publishers* India

First published in India by HarperCollins *Publishers* 2023
4th Floor, Tower A, Building No 10, DLF Cyber City,
DLF Phase II, Gurugram, Haryana – 122002
www.harpercollins.co.in

2 4 6 8 10 9 7 5 3 1

P-ISBN: 978-93-5629-668-8
E-ISBN: 978-93-5629-679-4

Typeset in 11/14 Adobe Garamond at
Manipal Technologies Limited, Manipal

Printed and bound at
Replika Press Pvt. Ltd.

MIX
Paper from
responsible sources
FSC® C016779

This book is produced from independently certified FSC® paper to ensure
responsible forest management.

For

Mily and Govi

'The two stars in my life'

ನನ್ನ ಜೀವನದಲ್ಲಿ ಎರಡು ನಕ್ಷತ್ರಗಳಿಗೆ
(Nanna jīvanadalli eradu naksatragaḷige)

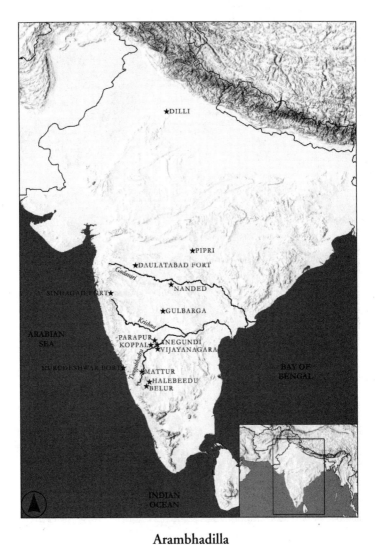

Arambhadilla

(Locations and places of interest between 1327-1328)
Artistic Rendition. Maps are not drawn to scale.

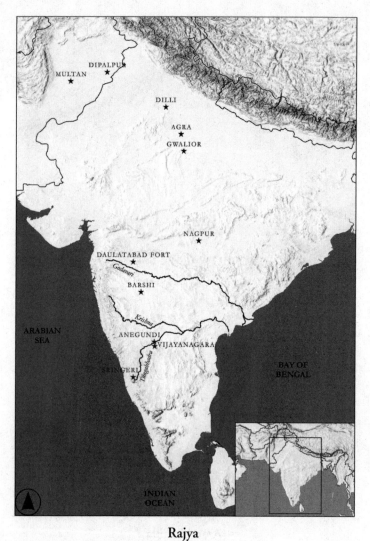

Rajya
(Locations and places of interest between 1331-1337)
Artistic Rendition. Maps are not drawn to scale.

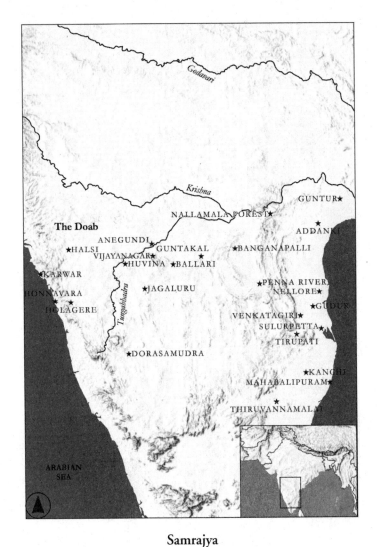

Samrajya
(Locations and places of interest between 1341-1346)
Artistic Rendition. Maps are not drawn to scale.

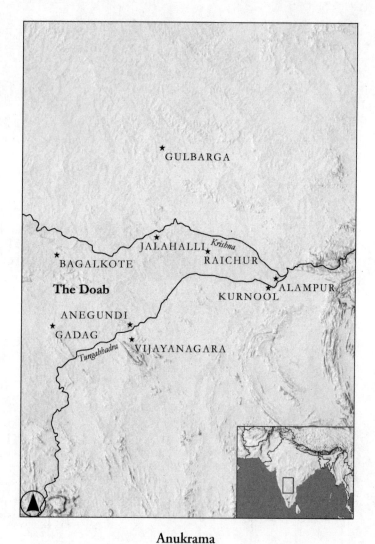

Anukrama

(Locations and places of interest between 1357-1374)
Artistic Rendition. Maps are not drawn to scale.

Contents

Book 4
Anukrama: Succession

Book 1

Arambhadilla: Initially

1

Is this the end?

(1327: Anegundi Fort and marching towards the sultan's new capital, Daulatabad)

Few outcomes are random

It seemed like they were walking through a sandstorm. In fact, it was the two thousand captured soldiers and a hundred of the sultan's guards marching with them who were kicking up all the dust. The sun was beginning to set and it gave the clouds of dust an eerie, infernal glow. Perhaps, he thought, it's just preparation for what hell will truly be like: blistering heat, pain, a demoralized soul and heart-wrenching loss.

'Keep moving!' It was the bellicose voice of one of the Turkish or Afghani soldiers of fortune that the sultan of the North hired in droves for his expeditions of plunder. He spoke some more gibberish in an alien tongue, and Bukka could not care less what he said. Better to get put down now rather than face the wretched prospects awaiting him and his wounded brother (whom he was supporting on his shoulder), and the two thousand defeated soldiers ahead of them. Dragging his feet, he kept moving. Bukka had that rancid taste of defeat in his mouth along with the grit from the dust they were inhaling. It struck him that the taste was becoming familiar.

The man riding on the horse to his right was Abu Ibn Faraj. He had been put in charge of getting the prisoners to Daulatabad, a five-hundred-mile journey to the sultan Muhammad-bin-Tughlaq's new capital. Bukka glanced sideways and noticed the finely tooled saddle and beautiful sword. He surmised Faraj must be from a prominent family at court: relatively young, arrogant, and completely absorbed by the responsibility. Surviving the next few days would depend completely on how this apparently clueless young man could be managed.

It felt like they were walking aimlessly. No direction, no plan, just monotonous marching. His own body hurt, and half-carrying his older brother Hakka was getting to be virtually impossible. Hakka had a broken arm, a few bad gashes where he had been sliced by a sword in battle and a raging fever. Just as Bukka was about to slip into the monotony of dragging both himself and his brother along, Faraj's horse suddenly and violently reared up. It threw the young man off the saddle, but his leg was caught up in one stirrup. The horse, sensing she had not lost her rider, started to buck viciously to get loose. Bukka shoved his brother onto the soldier to his left, lurched over and caught the horse by the bridle. Faraj barely missed getting kicked in the head.

Bukka held the bridle firmly and calmed the horse down at the same time. He'd always had the ability to manage a horse and understand it. It was clear to Bukka that the horse was hurt. Faraj was still lying on the ground in a daze, having hit his head hard on the fall. Bukka disentangled his leg from the stirrup and helped him up. A few of the sultan's soldiers just ahead thought he was the aggressor and pulled their swords. Faraj, fortunately, was coming out of his daze and waved them away. One of the soldiers helped him up and he looked at Bukka with grudging gratitude. It was not good for a soldier to get thrown off his horse, much less in front of a horde of prisoners and his own men. He motioned for Bukka to go back and the soldiers were only too happy to push him back into the line.

Faraj then decided to take matters into his own hands and whip the horse. The poor animal tried to back off but then decided to rear up and run up towards him. Bukka raised his hand and shouted 'Don't!'. One of the three soldiers shoved him, and another asked him why.

'The horse is injured. If you don't take care of her right now, you'll lose her, just the way you are going to lose all these prisoners and treasure as you try and transport them to the sultan.'

'You idol-worshipping shit!' Faraj bellowed as he threw the reins and the whip to one of three soldiers and walked away.

The soldier holding the horse could speak some Hindi and asked what was wrong with the horse. 'Someone with a semblance of an ability to think,' Bukka observed. He pointed to the horse's left foreleg below the knee, but the man did not notice at first. Then Bukka went over, knelt, rubbed the horse's leg and gently pressed down on the swollen part. The horse pulled her leg away and whinnied.

'It's either sprained or cracked,' he said.

'What do we do?' the soldier asked, this time with a bit more respect in his voice.

'First, you cannot ride her for a while,' Bukka replied. 'Next, the leg needs to be massaged a few times a day. Finally, if you can bandage it with some camphor, she will heal.'

'But where will I get some camphor?' the soldier wondered aloud.

'If we continue to go north, we should be in a small village in an hour or so. You can get some in the village for one or two silver tankas.'

The soldier asked if he would lead the horse for him. This was a first. Bukka was a general and here was a sipahi (soldier) asking him to do his job. Now he had two lame charges: his brother and the horse. He took off his shirt, tore off both sleeves and used them to bind the horse's leg up after vigorously rubbing it, and she snorted with satisfaction. Bukka had Hakka placed between himself and another Kampili soldier, arms round their shoulders for support. He gathered the mare's reins in his free hand and they set off.

It would not be long before the sun set, and as they dragged along, Bukka recognized the landscape: they were approaching a small village in hilly terrain right by Gunderi Lake and halfway to Holakere. Bukka's mind was whirling with possibilities. Should he get word out to the troops to make a break for it once they got to the hills? The risk in fleeing was that Malik Zada, the sultan's general, was to their south. Once he knew they'd escaped, he was likely to inflict a harsh reprisal. And the Hoysalas still further south, even if they made it that far, would be less than welcoming. The only likely alternative was to somehow get Faraj to think about the risks he might face. It could be the one way to save this situation.

For whatever reason, the procession of bedraggled and demoralized soldiers came to a stop. Bukka heard a horse galloping towards him and soon noticed that it was being ridden by the soldier he had been talking to earlier.

'The commander wants to see you,' he announced.

'And where is your commander?' Bukka asked.

'Follow me,' the messenger said, and they started walking away from the convoy. After a few minutes he could see Faraj sitting on a rock, surrounded by a few soldiers.

Bukka went before Faraj, who was clearly attempting to wear an air of authority and asked in a lordly tone:

'Are you Hakka the general?'

'No, I am his brother, Bukka, and second in command. Besides, his name is Harihara. We call him Hakka.' Faraj nodded and then ordered all the soldiers to move away except the interpreter and another who seemed to be a bodyguard. He asked Bukka to come closer before looking at the interpreter.

'Why did you say I was going to lose all these prisoners and treasure when you spoke to me earlier?'

Bukka paused, contemplating whether to plunge in. Then he spoke:

'I can tell you are not a military man and have not fought in many battles. Have you ever transported a large number of prisoners and treasure over such a long distance? You have thirty-five horses and about one hundred men, and very few of them are well trained. You have two thousand prisoners and five bullock carts packed with gold that you are taking back to the sultan. If you lose it, or provoke a prisoner rebellion, or both, your career is not going to fare well.'

Faraj stared at the translator to absorb what he was saying.

'Are you threatening me with rebellion?'

'If I were planning one,' Bukka replied, 'I would not have told you. I'd have waited till we were in the hills and then made it happen.'

'Then what do you want?'

Bukka asked if he might sit. Faraj nodded.

'What you want is to get the treasure and prisoners back to the sultan,' Bukka said. 'I can help you do that. But I can only do that if you take care of your prisoners, for we could help you find a safe way back. We know the way through the hills but you will have to spend two small sacks of gold to buy provisions for yourselves, the prisoners and horses, as well as organize the march more methodically. Otherwise, you risk losing everything. You lack organization now and that will be dangerous if you continue for even another day.'

'Why another day?'

'Because we are in deserted country and pretty soon the bandits will start following you and will make a play for the treasure and the horses.'

'They would not attack such a large number of soldiers. It would be suicide!'

'Not expecting them to—that would be suicide. They are tough fighters and will hit hard, inflicting significant damage before you can recover. You are not prepared. If they raid you once, they will come back in larger numbers again, and there will be mayhem.'

'So, what would you do to organize this situation?' Faraj enquired with a smirk on his face.

'Three things,' Bukka replied. 'First, less than half a mile away there is a lake at Gunderi. Settle the men there for the night. Second, send scouts out to Holakere, about five miles to the north, and see what provisions you can purchase for the horses and men. Buy some basic herbs to treat the wounded men and your horse. Third, plan how to defend yourself should there be an attack. The bandits usually come in the early morning hours, so there is enough time to get some basic defences set up.'

'You make it sound like war.'

'It is. Just more difficult. Everyone is exhausted and most are defenceless. Finally, if you do not show leadership, your men and your prisoners are going to be impossible to control. Be careful, Faraj, you are travelling with a lot of gold. Loyalty flies away like a bird.'

'Take him back!' Faraj commanded.

'Well,' Bukka thought, 'if he listens to half of what I said, there may be a chance.' Yet he was sceptical. He hobbled back and over the next few hours he noticed a few changes. The sultan's guards were ordered to tie up all the horses and bullock carts together at one spot under a clump of trees fifty yards from the water. Later that night the Hindi-speaking soldier found Bukka and provided him with the four things he had asked for: camphor, turmeric, neem leaves and neem oil.

Bukka went to work on Hakka's injury. He mixed a paste of oil and turmeric and applied a thick layer on the open wounds. He found a few sturdy twigs, tore up more shirts, and while six men held the screaming Hakka down, Bukka set his arm and quickly bound it up in neem leaves and neem oil.

Next Bukka asked if he could tend to the horse. 'Al'ahmaq [fool]!' yelled one of the guards and pushed him back. Deciding it was easier to bypass him, Bukka called out to Faraj who immediately rode over, irritated.

'What is so special about this horse?' Faraj enquired, throwing up his hands in annoyance.

'You will need every horse for the trip north if you want to carry your treasure.' Only then did it dawn on the young man that the bullock carts would soon be useless. Faraj grunted and rode away. Bukka worked on the horse, washing its leg in the lake, massaging it and binding it with some of the camphor he had. Leading it back to the group of other horses, he checked in on Hakka, who was fast asleep. His brother's fever had broken.

Bukka quietly sent word to his men about the possibility of being attacked by bandits that night. Four groups were set up to keep watch over the next eight hours. The men quietly picked up strong lengths of driftwood when collecting firewood, which they kept by their side. After dinner, Bukka lay down to sleep wondering how this was going to end.

A few hours later, he felt a nudge and immediately woke up. Achappa, his sergeant, was a seasoned soldier, sharp and wily in any altercation.

'They're here, the lazy idiots,' he whispered. 'They just followed us and did not even go round the lake to add an element of surprise.'

'Where?' Bukka asked. Achappa pointed in two directions: about fifty of them to the right of the trees and some creeping up to the camp horses and the carts with the gold. A few others held about fifteen of their own horses.

Shamshed loomed in the darkness and Bukka whispered instructions. He crept after his men to get behind the bandits trying to get hold of the treasure and horses and caught them unawares. It was amazing to see the impact that the driftwood had on them.

Stunned, they were relieved of their weapons and held down, but not without creating some noise. Bukka ordered some of his men to stand guard over the bandits, while others took possession of their swords and their horses.

The noises had awakened Faraj and his men who had been asleep—clearly not all Bukka had advised Faraj had registered. They now joined in the fighting. Soon, a fierce skirmish was raging.

Bukka noticed Faraj had been slashed on the right arm. He jumped onto one of the horses, grabbed a sword, and galloped toward Faraj just in time to save him from a charging bandit. Coming from behind, Bukka slashed the attacker's neck. He pulled Faraj onto his own horse. Bukka rode away and signalled to one of the soldiers to take Faraj. He then returned to the fight. To his surprise, however, it was over. Seven bandits had been captured. The others had been killed. Recognizing the altercation was over, Bukka roared out 'nillisi' (stop) in Kannada to his men.

He thought this was a reverse robbery. With fifteen new horses, the bandits had in fact brought them a gift. Still, Faraj had lost six men, and nine of them were wounded to varying degrees. Fortunately for Bukka, none of his men had suffered any casualties. Faraj had broken his hand and was badly cut on the shoulder. They ministered to him and bound up his wound. It would be a day or two before he came out of the fog of pain. Bukka decided they would rest for a day or two—a welcome reprieve for the first time.

As they helped the wounded, a glint of dawn broke, bringing some light. He ordered his men to tender their weapons to the sultan's soldiers and fall back.

Faraj ran a high temperature for two days, oblivious to the world, so Bukka took it upon himself to organize the group. The sultan's guards were enlisted men, used to taking orders from officers. In Faraj's absence, they instinctively turned to Bukka, a general who had shown his mettle, which gave him free rein to organize the camp and the soldiers. He had provisions bought from the next village, set up a camp kitchen, arranged for the campsite to be securely guarded, and the horses fed and cared for. The chain of command in his group was re-established.

Hakka recovered from his fever and was walking unaided now. After three days, Faraj came to. Once he was lucid, it was agreed the camp should prepare to move out the next day.

Having eaten first thing in the morning, the group of rested but bedraggled soldiers began their journey once more. Bukka insisted that Hakka ride while he trudged along on foot. He led the wounded mare along, who was also perceptibly better. Another day or two and they would know if she had cracked a bone and whether she could handle the weight of a rider. The swelling in her foot was nearly gone. With the organization he had put in place, they were progressing at a reasonable pace. Faraj was ahead with the carts of gold that Malik Zada had looted from the treasury at Anegundi Fort. Hakka and Bukka followed behind and it gave them a chance to talk about what had been a gruesome month.

An egregious sacrifice

'Is that all they have?' asked Hakka, referring to the treasure. His voice was getting stronger.

'Yes,' replied Bukka.

'But that was—' Hakka began.

'Stop, Hakka!' Bukka hissed. 'The two of us are the only people alive here who know about the rest.' But Hakka insisted on continuing, though he made no reference to the carts in question.

'Just imagine, Bukka,' he sighed, 'a pittance for what we lost, my brother.' Bukka went quiet. It was clear to Hakka that his younger brother was still coming to terms with what had transpired over the last month. Clearheaded and pragmatic,

Bukka was a deeply caring person. He did not take loss easily. It was worse when it was of those he loved.

After walking for an hour or two in perfect silence, Bukka finally spoke up:

'Did it have to end that way, Hakka?' Hakka was fully aware that the conversation would hurt more than his wound. It would wrench their insides, yet there was no avoiding it. If they did not come to terms with what had happened, they would just become decrepit souls—not that raking over past events made living any easier. Still, maybe facing up to the wretchedness was part of the grieving process.

They both fell back into the searing cauldron of their memories, recalling what happened. Bukka raised the subject once more.

'Hakka, why were you not more forceful in your point with the maharaja? Why did you not urge the military commander to consider the flanking action? We could have come out of the other entrance to the fort. A flanking action would have distracted Malik Zada enough to force him to give up the siege of the fortress, and our men would have lived to fight another day.'

Bukka was ambling along, remembering. The sultan's troops attacked them at the fort in Anegundi with little warning. At the time they had been at the southern border, engaged in skirmishes with the Hoysalas, the vast kingdom to their south, news arrived about the sultan's troops marching on the kingdom of Kampili. On the commander's orders, they withdrew to Anegundi Fort, Kampili's capital. For a frantic week they had gathered all the supplies and provisions they could find. Villages were emptying out and the inhabitants were fleeing south to avoid the rumoured attack by the sultan's army. They were not to blame, as they fully expected this crop of marauders, like others before them, would likely pillage, plunder, rape and kill senselessly.

Despite the panic migration, a reasonable amount of food supplies and materials were accumulated. As with any siege, however, it was difficult to gauge how much might be needed. How long could troops in the fort be fed? How badly did their enemy want the fort? How long was he willing to press on with a siege? Crucially, could the fort hold out long enough against a sustained assault?

The answer was clear after a month. Food and water ran out, with no sign of the siege being lifted. 'You could literally look into the eyes of the bastards,' Bukka thought. It was clear they were not giving up anytime soon. With a good supply train to back them up and cognizant of the situation inside the fort, the attackers had the upper hand.

He remembered during a lull in the hostilities, an Afghani soldier shouted out and his words were translated by one of the Musalmans in the maharaja's army: 'You must be starving; there is no shit coming out of the fort.' They knew.

The maharaja, Kampiladeva, called for his advisors to take stock before deciding how soon they should succumb to the inevitable. Today, tomorrow or the following day? He sent for the army commanders, who included Hakka and Bukka. Once they heard the decision, the pressing question was how they would break out of the fort. Bukka remembered being baffled by the answer: the decision was to open the main gate and fight their way out.

Away from the king's ear, both Hakka and Bukka confronted the commander-in-chief, Devaraja, about the potentially calamitous plans. Devaraja's response was that the king wanted to go down fighting honourably.

'What about the chance that he might still be able to squeeze out a victory?' Hakka said. Devaraja asked them how they thought it could possibly be achieved.

'Split the men in two, with one group larger than the other. The smaller band of men will break out from the main gate to distract their opponents, while the larger group comes out of the back gate and surprises the attackers on their flank.'

'You think you can accomplish that with the four thousand men we have?'

'Nayaka [general],' Hakka replied, 'it's better than heading out in line to get slaughtered.' His proposal was greeted with a monosyllable: 'No.'

The plan was to hit the enemy in the afternoon of the following day to allow time for preparation. 'How do you prepare for certain death brought on by an attack of stupidity?' he remembered thinking. Bukka asked his brother, who was the senior officer, to intercede with the king.

'That would be insubordination, Bukka, and you know it.'

Bukka pushed him even more.

'We are not confronted with a normal situation. Breaking out of a fort is rarely successful, and this plan makes the odds worse. Go see him; he will give you an audience. You have enough credibility and have done enough for him, so he should at least hear you out.'

Hakka instead pleaded with Devaraja to go with him to present his case to the king but was instructed to follow orders. Hakka made repeated attempts to change Devaraja's mind but only irritated the commander more, and he finally looked

Hakka in the eye and said, 'Just prepare to go down fighting honourably. That's a soldier's credo.'

Under normal circumstances the maharaja would have spoken to him and the other senior commanders again before the battle. Yet the mood had suddenly changed, and there was a sense of gracious resignation to what seemed like an inevitable outcome.

'Hakka, there appears to be a collective madness at work. They might as well surrender, and perhaps the result would be better.'

'Ah, but that would not be honourable,' Hakka replied.

'Honour may be a currency you and I use, but why should the poor soldiers pay for this idiocy? They have no reason to consider how history will view them; rather, they worry about getting back to their families. Let's at least give them an intelligent fight,' Bukka implored.

'And what would that involve?'

'I will let you know when I have the answer,' Bukka said as he hurried away.

Bukka stood on the ramparts and surveyed the fort and the configuration of the enemy. Then, gathering his colonels, Shamshed and Karthikeya, they discussed how they might get the better of the enemy the next day. 'There is a way to keep losses down,' he said, as he pulled his thoughts and plan together.

Achappa was asked to summon four of his lieutenants. For half an hour there was a torrent of detailed instructions. They were told to assemble their teams to put Bukka's plan in place. Bukka was going to do his best to make sure that nobody died needlessly.

He spent the next morning organizing his men, working at a furious pace for he had very little time to prepare. Hakka's orders from his commander-in-chief were merely to follow him and the king. That left Bukka with enough leeway to plan a more innovative and, hopefully, decisive exit. While he was partially aware that soldiers were gathering firewood and anything else that might burn, he was consumed with getting his plan in place.

It was approaching noon when he came up from the bowels of the fort. He was shocked at the scene in front of him. On one side of the grounds, four thousand men were ready to move. On the other side was a hill of firewood that had been set alight. He could feel the searing heat even standing at a distance. And then he went speechless. The queen, her daughters and noblewomen started to jump into the fire in a jauhar. He had heard about this but had never witnessed it. Before he could react, he learned that Shveta was already consumed by the inferno. Shveta was the king's youngest daughter.

Bukka screamed until his lungs hurt. Hakka and a few of his men grabbed him and held him down. All he could remember repeating to himself was, 'How desperate can people get?' When Hakka released him, Bukka screamed at his brother: 'Why didn't we just surrender?'

Hakka was harsh in his response: 'And have the women raped by those filthy bastards? They decided to do this of their own volition. So, make your peace with it, and now focus on saving your life.'

'Can we lead the charge?' Bukka pleaded with Hakka.

'No, our orders are to follow Devaraja's group and the king in the second wave'

'Can I lead your group?' he pleaded. 'No,' was the answer again. Bukka told his brother that he had a plan and it would help if he led the final group.

Maybe it was pity. Maybe Hakka felt he needed to cover the rear. Anyway, he relented and Bukka got his plan moving.

It was time for his contingent to move.

'First,' he told Hakka, 'I will lead my men out to the left from the gate, so we hit the fringes of the enemy forces there. We'll be moving on ground that slopes downward from the gateway. Their horses and men don't stand a chance against an attack from above. That will leave our left flank clear as they will be to our right. We'll form a defensive wall to our right against the enemy forces and so create an open path. Just follow this channel that we'll have carved out and your men can come straight through. Then we can hit the right flank of the enemy.'

'And what makes you think you can carve a channel?' enquired Hakka.

As they started to move, Bukka yelled out: 'For once, just follow!'

He asked Achappa to fetch the dogs and he called for the many palace doors that he had had removed and modified after he had made his plan. Bukka distributed them with instructions.

As the Kampili army emerged from the fort, the carnage Bukka expected played out. Maharaja Kampiladeva was killed, as was Devaraja. Bukka raised the battle cry of 'Kampili!' and as they charged out of the gate to face the sultan's troops, he ordered the dogs to be released. He knew this would cause chaos. The Musalman had an aversion to dogs and would do anything to avoid them. The dogs went after the horses, creating disorder and confusion in the frontline of their opponents. The dogs weaved in and out, biting the horses' legs, toppling riders before moving on. As the formation loosened up, Bukka moved his men.

Doors from the fort buildings had been fashioned into shields, each of which was held up by three men, and they advanced quickly. To their right, they held off the sultan's soldiers using their door shields. The sultan's soldiers were pushed down the slope towards the deep moat and did not have a chance. Hakka's contingent had made it out, unscathed, through the channel.

Regrouping, they now rushed at their opponent's right flank. The dogs attacked the cavalry—the Kampili men even managed to get a few horses to mount for themselves. Bukka had positioned archers to provide covering fire as they attacked. Surging forward, they initially sliced through with little resistance.

Realizing what was happening, the enemy regrouped and held off Hakka's charge, managing to hold Hakka and his men back at first. Hakka ordered his men forward and led an audacious charge into the enemy's flank, pushing them back. Hakka was on foot and refused a horse. Suddenly a cavalryman came galloping through, having identified Hakka as a general because the bannerman was next to him. Just as the cavalryman was closing in on Hakka, a dog intervened. Losing control, he fell from his horse and a lancer got him squarely in the chest. However, he had his sword out and the momentum gave him the chance to slash out at Hakka. Hakka might have been killed had it not been for one of his men who grabbed him by his collar and pulled him back. He ordered one of the men to take care of Hakka and his wound. It appeared he had also broken his arm badly.

Bukka realized that the advantage of numbers was now helping the enemy. He decided it was pointless to continue.

Looking around, Bukka realized that his brother was incapable of managing the situation. Standing up on his stirrups, he shouted out to the bannerman to come closer, and then he loudly announced he was in charge.

He ordered the bannermen get on a horse and signal surrender.

The bedlam slowly came to a stop.

While the battle had ended, no one seemed to be responding to Bukka's demand to speak to a commander. 'What is taking these barbarians so long?' Bukka asked Karthikeya, more as a rhetorical question, as they waited for someone to come and officially accept their surrender.

'Their generals don't fight like you and your brother, semanya … They stay safely in the rear and drink sherbet and give orders. But they are first in line to try and find gold and treasure.'

Just then, they saw the horde in front of them giving way to someone on a white horse. The rider, possibly a general, was wearing elegant clothes, with a colourful turban with a large bejewelled brooch. His tunic was made of silk, and his scabbard was shining silver studded with gems.

Bukka found this kind of ostentation disgusting. 'What a peacock,' he thought.

As he came closer, he saw that the man appeared to be in his early forties, short and fat. He looked Persian.

Accompanying him was an Afghani soldier. The soldier spoke first, in Kannada.

'What is your name and what position do you hold in the army?'

Bukka answered him and added that the senior surviving commander was his brother but was incapacitated. He was standing in for him. The fat little Persian mumbled unintelligibly to the Afghani translator, who then said:

'This is the great general, Malik Zada, sent by Sultan Muhammad-bin-Tughlaq to add the southern country to his empire.'

'How many men did you lose?' Malik Zada enquired.

'Too many,' Bukka replied.

'How many did you lose, because I know how many there were in total,' the general said testily.

'I'd estimate about two thousand,' Bukka said.

'Do you know how many of my men you killed?' Malik Zada asked.

'Not exactly, but maybe six hundred.'

'We've lost three thousand men to your part of the attack. I have two things to say to you. First, if you were going to surrender, why didn't the whole army do it earlier? Second, where did a young man like you learn to fight and to command an army?'

Bukka felt he needed to be clever in his response. This fat little fellow was shrewd and inquisitive. He seemed different from the usual mould of Afghani, Turkish or Persian generals the sultan employed in his army. Was he just sly or was he intelligent?

'The plan to surrender during the fight was mine, and the decision not to surrender earlier was not mine. I was trained and taught by my brother, General Harihara.'

Malik Zada shook his head and continued staring at him. It was as if he were piecing together an intricate puzzle. Raising his hand, he yelled out a few names. Three men rushed up and he barked out orders to them. Malik Zada turned his horse around and instructed him to follow. Bukka quickly gave Karthikeya some directions before departing. He wiped his face with his scarf and scraped off blood, flesh and grime.

As he followed Malik Zada, Bukka was surrounded by ten horsemen who stayed more than a sword's length away. They were Afghani: big, strong and bearded, with steely blue eyes. He offered to hand over his sword to one of them but the soldier refused, instead pointing in the direction of Malik Zada. Not far ahead he saw a large and flamboyant tent that had been hidden from the fort's line of sight. He observed Malik Zada dismount and settle into a chair that was brought out for him. Bukka was told to approach the general.

Malik Zada asked for his full name.

'Bukka,' his captive proclaimed, offering his sword.

'I will take it as a symbol, and not because I think you will attack.'

'How can you be so sure, Malik Zada?' he asked.

'On the battlefield, you could have slaughtered at least another thousand of my men and not lost many of yours. But you understood the pointlessness of it. You are with honour, Bukka.'

'Does that mean my stuffed head does not go to the sultan?'

Malik Zada laughed. 'I think you should be sent to the sultan—alive. Let him decide how he might use you and your brother.'

'What about my soldiers,' Bukka pursued.

'Take them with you to Daulatabad. They might be useful.'

As fast as Bukka's mind was racing, he realized he'd encountered someone whose thought process was quick as lightning. Malik Zada made spot decisions about whom he could trust, although it could also change in an instant. He waved to one of the soldiers to take Bukka's sword.

'Let the sultan return it to you when he sees fit,' he declared. He ordered a chair and asked Bukka to sit.

Malik Zada moved uncomfortably close. He peered at his opponent, preparing to broach a question.

'How do we get to the treasury?'

Bukka decided this was not the time to prevaricate.

'I know the location and if we search amongst the bodies, we might be able to find the keys.'

'You know who would have it?' Malik Zada asked sharply.

'There are two keys. I only know of one who might have it.'

'Bring us water,' Malik Zada commanded. The general had noticed Bukka's voice was growing hoarse; his throat was parched as they had run out of water in the fort that morning. He drank from a big silver tumbler, an unusual object for an army laying siege on a fort. But the sultan's men played the game differently. After a few minutes of quiet, Malik Zada called out again and all Bukka could understand was the name 'Altaf'. Altaf was presumably one of his senior officers, who appeared immediately from inside the tent. Malik Zada spoke to him for a few minutes. Then he turned to Bukka, and speaking through the interpreter, ordered him to 'go find the key': a task as wretched as it was painful. Still, their lives were dependent on finding Devaraja, the army commander-in-chief who had one of the keys. Bukka mounted the horse that was led up to him, and left with his escort to search among the shambles of the battlefield.

He was perplexed: the fighting, the mindless loss of the women and the idiocy of not hitting the attackers with the best they could muster. What they had done was commit mass suicide. On the battlefield and in the fort lay all the hapless victims of the whims of a few leaders. If they were looking for a perch somewhere in the annals of history, he wished they would all be labelled cowards.

When Bukka neared the fort, he dismounted and threw up. Altaf approached him, offering water from a sheepskin.

Taking a swig, Bukka rinsed his mouth and wrapped most of his face with a scarf. He walked to where he thought the first group coming out of the fort might be. The bodies were three deep.

He identified the spot. As he moved the bodies, he saw Devaraja's golden turban, then the general's corpse, which was lying next to the king's body. A soldier helped him move the bodies and Bukka saw Devaraja had been cleanly killed by a single arrow. Too kind an end for someone who did not even put up a fight. Bukka felt about the midriff, and under Devaraja's belt was a string with a set of keys attached. He asked for a knife to cut it off.

He then attended to the king's body. The only thing he wanted to memorialize this wretched battle was the king's ring, which was usually the royal seal. He asked Altaf if he wanted it. Altaf waved him off, indicating he should keep it.

He suddenly noticed Malik Zada was standing just behind him. Obviously, Zada had followed them. Through the interpreter, Malik Zada said, 'Let's go to the khazana.' 'Principles and people be damned,' thought Bukka, 'this is all about plunder.' So now Malik Zada wanted to see what he could find in the treasury.

Bukka held his feelings in check as they walked into the fort. He found himself shivering and presumed it was because he had not eaten for two days. It did not help that he had seen them behead the king's body a moment ago.

They walked down three levels and the steps were steep. Malik Zada was right behind him, followed by four fierce-looking soldiers. At the end of the staircase was the first door. Bukka got out the first key, and went through the process of opening the lock: he turned it twice to the right, twice to the left, and then pressed a button at the back which was camouflaged as a rivet, after which the huge lock opened. He repeated the action at two more doors. He felt sick and exhausted but managed to push through to reveal four small rooms. Malik Zada shoved him aside. Passing into the rooms, surveying the gold and silver objects, and sacks of coins, he scratched his crotch and grunted to himself. It was like watching a ferocious animal that was satisfied its dead prey had some meat on the bone.

'Lock it up,' he instructed Bukka, after all the men had left the room. Malik Zada was not a person who trusted even his most loyal soldiers. Bukka wondered how Malik Zada would buy their silence. The price would depend on how much he sent north to the sultan. Maybe these soldiers had earned themselves a place on the frontline of the next battle.

Malik Zada was the last one to emerge from the treasury. He watched Bukka lock it up, all the while monitoring him closely. As they got to the ground level, Malik Zada put out his hand for the keys. With them firmly in his grasp, he yelled out the name of Zafar. Bukka identified him as the translator.

'Tomorrow after sunrise I want thirty men to load up all the carts with the contents of the treasury. Bukka, you will open the locks, and once the treasure has been loaded on to the carts, you and the prisoners will march to Daulatabad.'

They returned to the encampment and Bukka enquired if he should join his men. 'No, you will spend the night under guard by my tent,' and with that, Malik Zada went into his tent followed by three of his generals. Bukka lay down on the ground and dozed off. Not long into his sleep, he was woken by the blunt end of a spear. A plate of food was placed near him.

'Will my men be fed?' he asked. He heard a growl from behind. The translator strode round in front of him, drew his sword and swore at him. The message was crystal clear:

'You are in no position to be making demands, infidel.'

The loud hissing voice of Malik Zada emerged from his tent. 'What is the reason for this commotion, Altaf?'

Altaf spoke to his general. Bukka guessed what he said from his tone. He stood up, turned to the interpreter and retorted:

'Let the general know it was not a demand, rather a question. I cannot eat if my men are not going to be fed.' Zafar sullenly translated. Malik Zada looked at Bukka and suddenly he sensed something about their relationship had changed.

Malik Zada returned to his tent and, in his imperious way, gestured for Bukka to follow him. He paused before calling for the interpreter. Altaf followed with his sword still drawn but Malik Zada barked an order and he sheathed his sword. Bukka entered the tent and all he could see was opulence. It was large enough to accommodate four rooms in the royal section of the Anegundi fort and full of fine furniture, beautiful fabrics, and gleaming utensils. The wealth on display drew awe as well as questions in his mind as to what Malik Zada's connection was to the sultan.

The chairs were laid out in an oval. At the head was a luxurious seat piled with many cushions, leaving no doubt who it was for. Malik Zada settled himself, before snapping his fingers. Two attendants came over, one with a towel and a bowl of water, the other with a gold cup. Malik Zada washed and dried his hands and face, then raised the cup while the servant poured wine. Bukka thought, 'Here is a Musalman with an appreciation for the finer things in life.

Malik Zada called out, 'Bukka,' and pointed to the chair next to him. Bukka confidently sat down. Malik Zada clapped his hands, summoning two of his officers to join. Malik Zada looked at them and said:

'A general, even though he is a prisoner, will not eat if his men are not fed. *Ya Allah mazbooth* [Allah, how excellent].' He raised his cup to Bukka, and the two other men smiled reluctantly. Both were hulking men. 'He fights in the front, leads his men, so you can see why not one of his men would let any of your cavalry close to him, Hussein. And he won't eat without his men eating.'

Whatever redeeming value Malik Zada saw in him, Bukka did not want to get on the wrong side of these two villainous-looking men. His saving grace was that he was the only one who could open the treasury. The servants came round with cups of wine for the three men. Bukka stood up, raised his glass to Malik Zada and then to the other two men. He bowed, just slightly, acknowledging how well the siege was managed and how well his opponents prevented any escape or counterattack. He did not expect any response but for the first time the two Afghanis looked at him with approval.

'Abu!' Malik Zada bellowed, and when there was no response, he roared out the name again. The man came rushing through the entrance of the tent.

'Your eminence,' said the young man, who seemed to be cut from a very different cloth from the two louts sitting there. He was slender, tall, fair and did not appear to have been sullied by the action on the battlefield earlier that day.

'This is Bukka, the general,' Malik Zada announced. Bukka shook his head and said to the translator, 'Just a soldier.' It prompted a wry smile from Malik Zada, who now ordered the two Afghanis to leave and rest.

'This is Abu Ibn Faraj, who helps plan my strategy and manages supplies,' Malik Zada said through the interpreter. 'He will accompany you back to Daulatabad and present you to the sultan. Perhaps they will find some use for you and your brother at court. I will be going south on the orders of the sultan. You and your brother will be expected to manage your soldiers and maintain discipline. You seem trustworthy and, as a man of honour, I expect you to follow Abu's orders.'

Faraj was crestfallen. He had obviously hoped that he would stay for the campaign to the south. He began to speak but Malik Zada cut him short.

'The sultan will be happy that you brought him both treasure and two generals he can use. Execute this assignment and you will catch his attention. This is not going to be easy for you, so cover every detail to get this done right. The alternative will not be pleasant. You leave in the morning after your carts have been loaded with gifts for the sultan.' Faraj was then excused.

Malik Zada sat there, drinking more wine while deep in thought. He would occasionally glance at Bukka. He clearly liked to keep people guessing. A little later, Bukka was shown a space where a mat had been laid out for him to sleep. His plate of uneaten food was next to it, along with a glass of water. Drinking a mouthful, he went to sleep.

The loud call of the buq-al-nafir (a long straight trumpet) in the morning woke him up and immediately the camp came to life.

Bukka refused the food they brought him, again. He was roughly told to eat: his men had all been fed. He went and checked; it was true. Bukka devoured the bread and meat waiting for him.

Not long after, Malik Zada came out of the tent and gestured to him to follow. They went to the treasury and the contents were loaded onto carts, covered and secured. There were sixteen cartloads of gold and silver. Only five were to go to the sultan.

Bukka could guess to whom the rest was going. Whoever did an accounting for the spoils of war?

Progressing to unknown outcomes

It was a few days after the bandit attack. Bukka was encouraged not only by Hakka gaining strength but also the sight of his men maintaining a decent pace as they trudged forward. Then he heard barking. Turning back, he noticed a few dogs chasing them. It puzzled him since the area was not known for wild dogs. Bukka fell back and heard Hakka mumble:

'Be careful, don't let your stupid love of animals get the better of you so you get bitten as a result.' There was something about the barking that sounded familiar. Seven of the dogs ran towards him, and he realized they were his. The ones he had trained since they were puppies at the Anegundi Fort. They had survived the battle, and had caught his scent and followed. He bent down to welcome the dogs and they knocked him down, licking and frolicking. He was suddenly debilitated with grief, thinking about the two dogs that did not make it, the wretched waste he'd witnessed, and the senseless loss of Shveta.

He felt a hand on his shoulder and the rich, reassuring voice of Hakka.

'Paravagilla [it's okay].'

Bukka stood up, touching one of the dogs nuzzling up against him. Holding on to Hakka's good shoulder, he started walking and muttered, 'It's not good for a soldier to be seen sobbing.' Hakka, however, never seemed short of an appropriate response.

'Soldiers grieve too,' he reassured Bukka. He added, staring at the dogs, 'What are we going to do with your zoo?'

'They'll take care of themselves, and perhaps even take care of us as they did at the battle at Anegundi.'

It's what soldiers do

Dhum, two, three, four. Dhum, two, three, four. Dhum, two, three, four. There were two drums playing, sounding out a beat for the long line of marching soldiers. They were halfway on the five-hundred-mile journey to Daulatabad, the sultan's new capital. Both Bukka and Hakka were conscious that more uncertainty awaited them.

The drums were beaten to ensure the convoy of soldiers kept moving at a reasonable pace. It helped that the men had been getting rest and receiving more food. Bukka was responsible for the organization of medical assistance, making sure security was in place and keeping morale up. Gradually, as Hakka got better, Bukka sought direction and enquired whether Hakka had any orders for him. His brother just said:

'Manage the march north, and if you think I need to be consulted, do so. However, give up your modesty and get a good horse to ride. You're going to be more effective to all of us if you can get around faster. Get our senior commanders, Karthikeya, Shamshed and Achappa, on horses as well. This march is going to be challenging, and it's best you have the resources to get us prepared.'

Bukka asked one of the sultan's soldiers to surrender his horse. He refused; the days of peace after the dacoit attacked had made the soldiers complacent. Bukka raised his voice and commanded him to dismount. He swung off the horse in an instant, drew his sword and went for Bukka. Two of Bukka's men tried to restrain him.

It was time to set an example. All the sultan's soldiers nearby had gathered out of curiosity. The soldier had his sword held in front and was about to charge. Bukka lunged forward. Grabbing his arm, Bukka wrenched the sword from him, and used the flat side to swipe him on the side of the head. As he fell to the ground, for good measure Bukka kicked him in the crotch.

Throwing his sword down on him, Bukka asked the men to continue marching. The man lay on the ground writhing in pain. Some of the sultan's soldiers wanted to help the man. Bukka forbade it. Speaking on behalf of a senior officer, the translator asked, 'What should we do with him?'

'Leave the pig there to die. If it can walk and join us, we can decide how to deal with the disrespectful animal,' was Bukka's reply.

Mounting the horse, he looked at the translator and said, 'Take his sword from him.'

While the men kept marching, there was congratulatory murmuring amongst the Kampili soldiers. The sultan's military were unaccustomed to seeing senior generals take part in combat, much less witnessing an encounter. Bukka started to ride up the column and passed Hakka, who said, 'Nothing like credibility to establish authority.'

Bukka established that the front of the column was moving along at a decent speed, and made sure the injured men were in reasonable shape as they rode the horses seized from the bandits. The five carts of treasure were moving with increasing difficulty as they were now going uphill. Bukka asked his men to help by pushing from behind. Something had to be done soon, as the poor animals were struggling with the load. He then cantered back to Hakka, who was close to the rear.

Suddenly a lance swung out of the column as an Afghani cavalryman intercepted him.

'Faraj wants to see you. Now.' He held the lance pointed at him maliciously, and grimaced. There was no mistaking this was meant as an insult.

'Where is he? Ask him to come and join my brother farther down the column.' And with that, Bukka began to move towards the rear, fully anticipating an attack from behind. He had barely completed the thought when he heard the cry, '*Allahu akbar* [Allah is great]!' The lancer started towards him, lance out, crouching in his saddle as he tried to gain speed but he did not have enough room for the horse to even break into a gallop.

At a full gallop, a capable lancer could wreak havoc—if he had the ability. This one was clumsy and slow. As he approached, Bukka slipped off the saddle to the far side of his horse and pulled out a dagger tied to the saddle. The lancer missed and shot ahead. As he turned to attack again, Bukka held up a hand, shouting, 'Nillisi [stop]!' The soldier did not slow down. Bukka screamed, '*Taayi Durga!*' and released his dagger. Blood spurted between the rider's eyes, the dagger embedded to the hilt. The rider fell and was dragged before the horse halted.

Bukka walked up to the soldier hanging from the stirrup. He picked up the lance and looked at the dumbstruck Faraj who had ridden over. Raising the lance in both hands, Bukka screamed the battle cry 'Kampili' and plunged it into the dying lancer. As he stared at the soldiers, he raised his face skyward and roared, '*Gauravavannu torisi* [show us respect]!' He mounted his horse and trotted back to where Hakka was in the formation.

'Munde! [forward!],' he ordered, as he fell in next to Hakka.

Dhum, dhum, dhum, the beat of the drum got the convoy moving once more.

'Nice work, soldier,' Hakka said in a dry tone as marching resumed. They both knew this was not the end of the events of the day.

It was not long before Faraj, accompanied by five of the sultan's soldiers on horseback, rode towards them at a furious pace.

'Shaitan, Bukka!' Faraj screamed. 'You will be punished for killing one of my men and wounding another. The only question is whether I should put your head on a spike, like your king's, and deliver it to the sultan.'

Bukka contemplated the raging youth silently, he glanced at Hakka, deferring to him. Hakka's left eyebrow twitched when he was angry, and this time it was nearly fluttering. In an imperious tone, he advised Faraj to take this conversation away from the convoy.

'You do not tell me what to do, infidel!' Faraj screamed at Hakka.

Hakka stayed quiet, indicating once more that they move apart for a private conversation. Faraj made the mistake of drawing his sword.

'Haraami!' he screamed at Hakka. He had gone a step too far. Bukka nodded at Achappa, and in a smooth manoeuvre, the whole convoy transformed. In a flash, two thousand men surrounded the sultan's troops.

'It's best that the three of us have a conversation. While we talk, your men can get a feeling of what it is like to be prisoners of the imprisoned. It may teach them some modesty.'

The sultan's soldiers gave way as Hakka rode out of their encircled ranks. Faraj and Bukka followed. When they were a few hundred yards away, Hakka told Faraj to put his sword down. Angrily, Faraj raised his sword again—and felt the tip of a lance at his neck. Bukka made sure to draw a bit of blood for effect.

'Faraj, put your sword down!' Hakka commanded. This time there was docile compliance on Faraj's part. Bukka, unsure of the young man's mental state, gestured to him to drop his sword to the ground, which he did. Hakka dismounted, with Faraj doing likewise. A bit of pressure from the lance was all it had taken.

Once the two men were facing each other, with Bukka's lance at his opponent's neck, Hakka asked:

'When did we disrespect you to deserve treatment like this from you and your soldiers?'

Faraj looked sullenly at Hakka.

'What respect do prisoners deserve?' he replied. 'I would recommend to the sultan that he have all of you beheaded when we get to Daulatabad.'

Hakka stared at him, feeling their conversation was pointless. Faraj failed to realize that he had lost the deference and goodwill exhibited by the Kampili soldiers.

'Listen up, you idiot,' Hakka hissed, 'you are now our prisoner, along with your men. My brother gave his word to Malik Zada that we would go meet the sultan, and that we would do so without incident. And that is what we are going to do. From today you will be treated like one of my men, fed like them, with the same privileges. The same goes for your men as well. Any bad behaviour and it will be seen as an act against the sultan and punished appropriately. If you behave for the remainder of the trip, I may let you present us to the sultan.

Otherwise, I will do so myself, and let him know that you had designs on his treasure. Now start walking back.'

Hakka and Bukka followed Faraj back to the waiting soldiers. Bukka ordered all the sultan's soldiers to disarm, and those on horses to dismount. With the exception of three of their officers, the others were instructed to walk. The two brothers now had a large number of horses to deploy for the needs of the convoy.

At noon, when the convoy usually stopped for a break to avoid the scorching sun, they transferred the treasure onto the backs of the horses, who had an easier time carrying a lighter load than a man. They kept a few horses spare to allow them to rest in turns.

The march began to pick up tempo. Bukka and Hakka rode off to the side away from the convoy with the dogs accompanying Bukka. He did not want them getting the sultan's horses nervous since they were unaccustomed to being around dogs.

The sultan's soldiers were split in groups of ten and each group was interspersed amongst one hundred Kampili soldiers. All the horses carrying treasure were in the middle of the pack.

Hakka laid out his route to Bukka.

'Onward to Koppal and we'll be at the border of the Kampili kingdom. Once past Koppal, the incline up to the rocky country and no man's land will begin as we make our way to Gulbarga. Once past Gulbarga, we will cross the edges of the famous Maratha fiefdoms. They are not quick to take offense, but let us be careful not to give any. The route from Gulbarga to Nanded is rocky and hilly country so we will have to take care that our horses are handled with care. I always worry about anyone trying to rush a horse when they are on rocky terrain—many a poor animal has been lost to carelessness. Once in Nanded we will be due west of Daulatabad. Hopefully this route will minimize contact with the sultan's soldiers, who might interfere. The high country is less troubled than the terrain closer to the coast, though that would be the easier route.' The course had been charted and they started to move towards the hills in a northeasterly direction.

Once the arrangements and assigned responsibilities were made, the beating of the drum resumed and the convoy started moving once more. The march to an uncertain outcome had begun.

The prisoner army

Bukka gradually left the handling of the larger issues of direction and outcomes to his brother. He shifted his attention to managing the army and its welfare. A small contingent of scouts formed and went ahead on horses to make sure the route was clear. Food was a critical issue; they made sure to buy supplies when the opportunity arose. Fortunately, the monsoons had been good and there was surplus to be had. They organized a camp kitchen that could cook for all. The stablemen made sure the animals were fed and cared for. Bukka was in his element: organizing, anticipating and making the most of the limited resources.

Hakka had once told the raja of Kampili that they had been able to thwart the forces of the sultan twice only because of Bukka's ability to plan. Hakka also warned them that good armies could only handle sudden attacks a few times, after which rebuilding had to take place. He had cautioned them after the second attack on the Kampili kingdom, pointing to the need to focus on a defensive position rather than spread out thinly. This time, Hakka fully intended giving Bukka all the resources and opportunities necessary to rebuild this small army even though they were on a forced march. At least now the march was on their terms.

Over the next few days, they made good time approaching Koppal. Scouts occasionally spotted the sultan's supply train but they managed to keep a good distance from it and were not noticed. Bukka realized Koppal might be their final chance in familiar territory where they could get items they would need. He darted about, coordinating every last detail for the next phase, which would be demanding.

Hakka was absorbed, sitting ramrod straight in his saddle, occasionally making sure his men were monitoring Faraj. When his brother came by the next time, it was clear he had a few things on his mind.

'We should think about some of our plans carefully, Bukka. Neither you nor I, or the men for that matter, should be unprepared.'

Bukka nodded.

'Let's use this time to get the men trained and in good condition,' Hakka went on. 'Otherwise, their minds will dwell on apprehensions and it won't help morale. The next thing to consider is, what can we expect at the other end? What is it like at court? Who are the influential courtiers? And, crucially, how do we curry favour with the sultan?' Hakka paused before adding: 'I do not want us to sell our souls. I might be willing to lend it for a while, for the sake of surviving.' That prompted a wry smile from Bukka.

'Whom do we exploit at the other end?' asked Bukka. 'There are no connections and the old network that the kingdom of Kampili once had has perhaps evaporated after the news of the defeat.'

'Not all, Bukka,' his brother replied. 'It might be worth trying to remind them of debts owed. There must have been a reason Malik Zada did not execute us. The question is how might the brilliant and brutal sultan find us useful? Military insights perhaps? Now that he's moved his capital south, does he want advice on how to consolidate in the southern region? We just need to get some insight into the thinking at court to make sure that we start out on the right foot. You know full well that the force of the initial attack can change outcomes, even when the odds are against you.'

Over the course of the next few days, Hakka asked Bukka about how events had transpired in the aftermath of their surrender. They went through this inquisition a dozen times. Hakka wanted to know about all of Bukka's interactions with Malik Zada: the various conversations he had with him, Malik Zada's expressions, and any other people involved. Then Hakka would recite them back to Bukka. This was just the way Hakka worked, grinding through a report to make sure he had a complete understanding. Then he went quiet for a while before quizzing his brother.

'Bukka, he must have sent a courier. Otherwise, there are too many missing pieces. How will the sultan know what to do with us? Unless he wants to make a spectacle of beheading two thousand people, which Malik Zada could have done in Anegundi and saved a lot of trouble and expense. So, Malik Zada must have decided to send a courier with a letter that will get to Daulatabad before us, which is easy, as the courier would travel faster. He would use that to set the stage for what our collective fate will be. And Malik Zada was willing to take the risk of sending so few soldiers to guard us, as well as a nobleman with an empty gourd for a brain to manage this transport. That was a test to see if you, or we, would keep our word. So, if we show up in Daulatabad, we pass the first test. The rest is a puzzle that needs to be solved.'

2

To the new capital

(1327–1328: From the fort at Anegundi to the sultan's fort at Daulatabad)

'Badshah ke yahaan!'

To the emperor's house! With that salutation, which sounded like a war cry, six uniformed horsemen, the sultan's couriers, were off on a hard ride to Daulatabad. At least once a week, Malik Zada would dispatch them with long missives to the emperor to apprise him of the campaign's progress. He'd sent off the ragtag group of prisoners yesterday to Daulatabad, accompanying the spoils. After he saw off the courier he walked back into his tent and shouted out for some wine.

Darkness was approaching; he was feeling satisfied and felt he deserved to indulge himself. A beautiful slave woman bearing a tray entered and poured him a cup of wine. She demurely walked backwards and out of the main area of the tent. Malik

40

Zada took a mouthful and considered his plan for what would come next.

The move to subjugate the Hoysala kingdom in the south, and its capital of Doorsamudra, was going to be more challenging than Kampili. But that was only because the Hoysala kingdom was larger and had more resources. However, based on the reports of his spies, it was unclear to him whether there were any generals in the Hoysala army who possessed the skill and ability of the two brothers he had encountered only three days previously on the battlefield. A chill went down his spine as he thought about it. Had Bukka continued fighting and not surrendered, there would have been a bloodbath. Malik Zada might have been able to overcome them but at a huge cost. If Bukka and Hakka led the charge out of the fort, the encounter might have ended differently altogether. He shuddered to think of the outcome. They could have broken through. Watching from afar, he had been struck with the pace, Bukka's ingenuity and the ferocity and the tactical backup from his brother when they came out of the fort.

Despite the fact that he was the emperor's confidant, trusted advisor and military commander, Malik Zada had survived only because he could read people. In the two brothers he saw what was unusual. They were both men of honour, and competent, fierce and intelligent generals. Most of all, they were thinking generals unlike the ferrets he had in his camp who just bit at the first thing that came their way and lacked the sagacity of these two young men. Hakka and Bukka had bested him twice when he attacked this little kingdom, and had nearly done so again a few days ago.

Malik Zada's mind began to wander. He thought about his recent letter to Sultan Muhammad-bin-Tughlaq, or Jauna as he

called him in private. He was careful to make sure that none of
it could be misinterpreted. While few would have access to his
communications with the sultan, those that did could create
enough mischief.

Malik Zada shouted to call for the scribe to bring back one
of the copies of the letter he had just sent, with a warning that
the document might still be damp with ink and might smudge.
It was dark outside and he saw the silhouette of the beautiful
young slave woman coming round to light the lamps. 'Yet
another good find,' he thought. 'She satisfies all of my appetites
and needs.' He held up the letter and started to read aloud as
if his intonation might smooth over the inaccuracies or sharp
edges of his rendition of events.

My dear Sultan, emperor of all and divine beneficiary
of Allah's wisdom,

With God's grace, we finally defeated the infidels at
the fort of Anegundi two days ago. We did not lose
too many men and, in what was an act of suicide,
King Kampiladeva rode out from the fort to his death.
However, in a rearguard action, two of his generals
nearly broke through. Thanks to our foresight but also
their intelligence, they decided to surrender along with
two thousand of their men.

Of what I have found in their treasury, I have sent
the most valuable gems and coins to you. It is my
estimation that it weighs about sixty manns. The
remainder of the gold in idols and items used by locals
in prayer will be melted down to pay for supplies and
the upkeep of the soldiers.

Among the most important prisoners are two brothers. The older one is Harihara, and his younger brother is Bukka. In my estimation, they are truly exceptional generals. They are accompanied by Faraj, the young orphan who is being trained by our mudaris [teacher], Qutlugh Khan. By the time they get to Daulatabad, I expect the two brothers to have taken control of the march and the army. However, they will, I think, keep their word and present themselves to you, along with the treasure.

My Emperor, I hope that you will look kindly on these two men. They will likely give us an understanding of the region, what potential it has and how it might be administered. They will also give our military an understanding of how to overcome the enemy when the odds are not in our favour.

I will continue to pursue your plans and move the battle to the kingdom of the Hoysalas in the south. With God's grace I will be able to bring back the traitor Baha-ud-din to you, preferably alive. And along with him, I hope to bring you the prize of the kingdom of the Hoysalas and their ruler, Ballala III.

Al-mujahia fi sabil Allah,
Malik Zada

Malik dismissed the scribe, satisfied that he had given the sultan enough information.

Jauna, as he always thought of him, was an incredibly astute person, and given their long relationship, he knew exactly what the sultan would do with the two brothers. He was convinced that he had found two very capable locals whom he, and the sultan, could use to their benefit.

Most of all, they seemed to possess that rare quality of integrity, over and above their other distinctive characteristics. Malik Zada mused at how he had set up the march back. It was going to be a test at many levels. First, he did not expect Faraj to maintain leadership of the group, especially with the two skilled generals and their small-statured but well-trained soldiers. They would overwhelm Faraj's soldiers. Still, he fully expected that they would not be harmed, however events played out. The young man was not trained and did not have enough savvy to understand what he was up against.

A forced march with prisoners was difficult, particularly when the prisoners outnumbered the guards. It was going to be a long march which would require skill in terms of planning, making sure they took a sensible route and, of course, the scourge of every general: logistics. Two thousand men can eat a lot of food. Feeling his sense of excitement rise as to how this would unfold, he wagered to himself that the brothers would be in command before long.

Hakka and Bukka would get to Daulatabad in record time and present themselves to the sultan with a full account of all they had spent. If those conditions were met, Malik Zada would once again have picked two winning horses, two men he could trust and delegate to, and so become even more effective in his military pursuits.

He shouted for some more wine. The slave girl came back and filled his glass. She was about to leave when he slipped his arms around her legs. He liked the Indian slave girls. They were attractive, robust and willing to serve. Getting up, he walked to his sleeping area where she followed him.

In the morning he would have to start planning the next stage and get the army moving south.

Dooradrishti or foresight

'Column! Stop!' The loud and sharp command came from Achappa.

'Dismount!' All who were on horses immediately jumped off their horses, which included Hakka and Bukka as well. From this point onward they would walk alongside their mounts.

'Faraj,' Hakka called out, 'do you realize you are the only one that is still on a horse?' Faraj dropped to his feet sullenly.

'Commence march!'

The dhum, dhum, dhum of the drum began again. Both Hakka and Bukka were happy with the pace the last few days. The gradient increased and they were now moving to higher ground while the surface was getting rocky. Now that they had dismounted and were walking, Hakka teased Bukka about being worried his sisugaḷu, his babies, might get injured. He fully appreciated how possible it was, as this was the kind of terrain where horses could easily get hurt. The horses were valuable. If they were attacked or needed to get anything done with speed, the animals would be critical.

Once they started climbing, the convoy regained its pace. Hakka called out:

'Bukka, Karthikeya, Shamshed, Achappa.'

They were all within earshot and moved over to him. Bukka knew that they were going to get a slew of orders.

'Our speed is getting better every day and if we can keep this up, we could be in Gulbarga in ten to twelve days.'

Shamshed's jaw dropped.

'What is it?' Hakka enquired.

'Semanya, we are on rocky terrain and the men are not used to walking at such a speed.'

'Shamshed, I am not asking the convoy to run,' Hakka answered bluntly. Then he threw in an incentive. 'Here's a wager: if we get to Gulbarga in twelve days or less, you win and I will order a rest for three days. The forests around there are good for hunting deer. We'll send a party out and we can feast, drink some kallu and rest up. Shamshed, that is your challenge. Make sure you follow Bukka's directions and let's advance.'

Hakka turned to other pressing matters and spoke to the others.

'Achappa, we need two men to take three bags of the mohurs that we retrieved on the way from our hidden stash in Mattur, and hand them to Pattu in Anegundi discreetly.' He corrected himself and said, 'to Ramaswamy Mudaliar,' as Pattu was his nickname and nobody except Bukka would know it here. 'I want him to use the money to provide food for the families of our soldiers. He will know how to arrange it. We just need to make sure that he has a list of names. Since they all come from ten villages, it ought to be easy to get them what they need. Hopefully, it will be enough to feed the families for a year. And then ...' He paused. 'We'll take care of the rest when we get there. I will write to Pattu. But, Achappa, we need someone like Kempayya or Devayya for a task like this, unless you have a better choice. They need to leave today, as Eeswara [God] only knows how these families have been managing.

'Karthikeya, I would like you to ride ahead with Altaf and Haneef to Daulatabad. Bukka will give you detailed directions on whom to meet. You will be with Altaf and Haneef for a week. Gather what information you can and meet us as we progress onward to Nanded. Bukka will give you a sack of our gold mohurs, which you can use to persuade some locals to give us information and to prepare for our arrival. Maybe the three of you should pretend to be horse merchants. Try and get close to the stables, as that is where you will likely obtain information on the comings and goings of the nobility. I will give you the names of three people that you should meet. All of you should travel as civilians, so buy clothes that will let you blend in with the locals. Karthikeya, I expect you to return in less than two weeks. Bukka will give you more detailed instructions.

'Finally, Achappa, we need to distribute the lances and swords that we confiscated from the bandits to the men. Starting tomorrow morning we will go through our exercises and practice. The men have eaten well for a few days during the march, and have recuperated from battle. It's time we began training again.'

Hakka dismissed them all. He handed his horse to a soldier close by and did what he always did: walk with the soldiers as they went on long marches. 'Know your men' was his refrain to his officers. And he made sure he did. Morale improved as a result, and he would come away with better information and ideas. Today he was going to march with the sultan's contingent from the village of Gubbi, a small group of survivors who had been saved in the battle by Bukka and his men. This was his way of finding out how they were coping after the horror of war. Of course, he was keen to know the effectiveness of Malik Zada's troops. He was increasingly convinced by Bukka's assessment that the sultan's troops were poorly trained in comparison to his own. Changing places with soldiers to make sure the formation was not disrupted, he marched with them all day.

The convoy arrived at Shorapur, leaving behind the hilly terrain to their relief. Scouts were bringing back advice on the best route. They managed to find enough food and Faraj seemed to have healed from the wounds inflicted by the bandits. His disposition was improving, too. The new regiment set up by Hakka was working well and the scouts told him that Gulbarga was just a two-day journey away. They were making good time. Shamshed would win the bet. Bukka established a good location by a lake. Occasionally, the convoy broke out in chorus singing village songs customary in Hakka's army.

It was late in the afternoon when the last group in the convoy got to the lake. The formation stood to order with Hakka on horseback. Raising his hand, he voiced his satisfaction: 'Good work!' The men broke out in applause and began chanting, 'Jai Hakka, jai Bukka, jai Kampili.' Hakka was relieved the men had regained their spirit. Word spread that Hakka had made provisions for their families for the next year. For that there was a great deal of gratitude. It was very much a case of loyalty earned.

Later that evening, the camp was bustling as guards were set up, the perimeter was secured, with a group of soldiers on standby; cooking fires sent up smoke and the fragrance of cooking wafted in the air. Hakka and Bukka were drinking some kallu, satisfied they had made the most out of what had been a terrible situation. Bukka was still grieving and it would be a while yet before the pain receded.

There were three places Hakka lived in contemporaneously: the yesterday, the present and the tomorrow. The yesterday was always a lesson waiting to be squeezed for meaning and implication. Today was his canvas, which he would paint in as vivid a fashion as he could. The tomorrow was a prospect he wanted to divine, discern its contours and fashion into a situation that was mostly better for all he cared about.

News from Anegundi

'Nillisi [halt]!' came the shouts of the guard at the outskirts of the encampment. Even at this distance it was difficult to miss hearing the horses come to an abrupt stop. Within a few minutes, the sound of a horse walking towards them grew louder. It was Farshan, a young man who had enrolled in the army against his father's wishes. His father ran a small weaving business in Anegundi. He appeared bedraggled and the horse was worse for the wear.

Jumping off the horse, he hit his clenched fist over his heart in the Kampili salute, and bowed to Hakka and Bukka.

'From the mudaliar. He gave us two additional fresh horses so we could get to you as quickly as possible.' He offered a pouch.

Hakka called for a torch to be brought closer to them as he unpacked the contents of the pouch. Inside was a sealed letter, a packet and two amulets. The packet, marked with Bukka's name, contained kardantu, a sweet native to the area from which their mother came.

'I always knew she liked you more,' Hakka roared out, laughing. Judging by the aroma, it had been made by their mother, Sangama. As Bukka reached out for the packet, Hakka, in an instinctive move from their childhood, snatched it away, and doubled over, laughing.

Opening the letter, the two brothers hunched over it in the limited light from the torch.

My dear brothers Hakkappa and Bukappa,

I heard that after the battle at the fort of Anegundi, the two of you survived. I was also informed that Hakkappa was seriously injured. We were anxious about him after you were all taken prisoner. Given the conditions, we feared the worst, even though we knew Bukappa would do his best to tend to his wounds. Getting news from the two of you and hearing stories from your courier has allayed many of our concerns.

Your old habit of taking command of any situation does not seem to have abandoned either of you. Your courier tells me how the prisoners have taken over their captors. While it should not surprise me, I am always amazed by your capacity to turn situations to your benefit. My prayer is that you never become traders like me, as I would likely be left a pauper dealing with the two of you!

Your mother, Sangama, and your three brothers are well and are shortly going with me to the pepper plantation in the hills. It should give us some safety from the forthcoming onslaught by Malik Zada. Sultans and their soldiers look for gold to plunder, not pepper to trade. The arrival of the courier has allayed many of your mother's concerns, but has not put all of them to rest. Of course, even if you were here with her, she would find new worries to harbour.

Now, to the issues that you want me to address. First, all of the surviving soldiers and their families will be taken care of. I will use the mohurs you sent me and when you are back in the near future, we can find a way to make a reckoning of how much I owe you. Along with your couriers are two of mine as well, as I would like your answers to some questions. Some of the king's monies are with me. If you can tell me the names of the soldiers lost in battle, I can identify the bereaved families and use some of these funds to help them. What King Kampiladeva left with me ought to be enough to help these families through their hardship.

While I will not question your resourcefulness, I do have people who can help in Daulatabad. I buy horses from Persian and Arab traders and sell our urukku swords and pepper to them when they come to the port in Murdeswar, which supplies the sultan's cavalry in Surat. They know people at court in Daulatabad and other traders in case you need funds. My credit is good with these people. And should you want to get to the coast fast, they will offer you a supply of horses and get you on a boat to come home. There is a lot of this boat traffic coming south as King Ballala of the Hoysalas has been buying military supplies and horses since Malik Zada is expected to come south now that he has overthrown Kampili. However, it is expected that Ballala will feed the monster a few tasty morsels that meet his satisfaction.

Once in Daulatabad, you will be met by Kazi Rahim Rahmatullah. He is a good friend and trader whom I have known for a long time. His parents were weavers and moved south in search of work. Kazi will approach you with the question, 'Do you like the weather in Daulatabad?' Along with your other sources, Kazi will be able to give you any piece of information you are looking for. He will also make sure you have all that you need. That will be his priority.

Hakkappa, please do not take any unnecessary risks and, as always, my advice to the two of you is: you do not have to conquer the world this year. It can wait!

May Hanuman give you both strength and fortitude, and shield you from harm. That will be my prayer to the Long-tailed One every day.

Forever in your debt,
ᆸᆫᆫᆫ (Pattu)

Calling the riders from Anegundi, Hakka and Bukka gave them short, cryptic messages that Pattu alone would understand. The couriers also described the route they had taken and what they saw. Malik Zada's supply train never seemed to end, as they rode north. His army was marching south in two prongs to Belur and Halebidu, the two important cities in the Hoysala kingdom. The only pressing question was just how long it would be before he attacked.

Bukka made sure that the riders were provisioned for their ride back, along with a small gift for having made such good time. As soon as they were gone, Bukka discussed how this would play out.

'Hakka, Ballala does not have the stomach to fight and he'll hand over Baha-ud-Din, whom King Kampiladeva sent to him for safety. He'll give Malik Zada a few young women, several sacks of gold and throw in a few elephants. To end the dastardly feast, Ballala will sing a song of how he will remain a loyal vassal of the great sultan. If I were to guess, that will satisfy Malik.'

'Will that satisfy his appetite?' asked Hakka.

'It will be just enough to show the sultan that Malik Zada had accomplished all the Emperor wanted, be able to pocket some change, bring home some gifts to entertain the court and, most of all, he will get back to court. I think he is loath to be away, as he is insecure about what happens when he's absent. Besides, he hates living in a tent on the road.'

'In that case, we will not be alone in Daulatabad for too long, dear brother,' Hakka answered. 'And does that change the algebra of survival for us and our men? Should we add speed to how soon we ingratiate ourselves to the sultan, and subtract what impact Malik Zada might have? Or should we change what we add and what we subtract?'

By the river Godavari

The water was warm and pleasant to swim in. Nearly all the soldiers were having a bath or swimming in the wide but shallow stretch of the river where they had set up camp. One more day and they would begin marching to Daulatabad, which the scouts said would take about twelve days to reach. The march to Nanded had been uneventful. They trained, and marched with purpose, led by two men whose ability and caring evoked loyalty.

Bukka swam lazily. Hakka, however, swam back and forth frenetically to expend as much energy as he could. Hakka was also making sure that the left arm he had injured was healing. Bukka anticipated what was likely to happen next. Catching his breath, Hakka would be full of ideas and plans. Anyway, Bukka felt rested, like all of the men, and they were ready for whatever Hakka planned. They'd managed to find good food, lots of drink and the weather had permitted them to sleep well. That was not bad for soldiers on a long march.

Bukka dried himself as he stared over at Hakka. His brother was sitting on a rock as a local ayurvedic physician gave his arms a vigorous massage. He noticed Hakka cock his head, motioning him to come over.

'I've missed having a nice young woman over the last few days,' Hakka said. Bukka squinted to warn him they were not alone. There were times he had to restrain Hakka's lust for life. With that thought barely completed, Hakka dismissed the physician.

'Slowly but surely,' Hakka said, 'things are going to start moving now. And I keep wondering about what we need to anticipate and be prepared for.'

'Fifteen or twenty,' Bukka responded.

'What do you mean?' Hakka asked.

'Fifteen or twenty questions you have to make sure we're prepared, and directions to anticipate what might come our way.'

Hakka started to laugh. 'Only questions for now, General Bukka.'

Bukka knew that this was the cue for a monologue from his brother. Yet this variant was going to be a long train of questions, attached to facts with all of the attendant implications laid out. These answers, known to both, were often supplied by Bukka, so actually it was a duologue. It was Hakka's way of thinking out loud and he knew that when the reasoning was flawed, Bukka would stop him. He'd done this since they were children playing gulli-danda and kabaddi, or after wrestling matches in the village. He'd want to know what had gone wrong or what he could do better. Only now the stakes were much higher.

'Bukka,' he began, 'we know the sultan is deeply intelligent. He speaks at least three languages, writes very well, is a hafiz, and knows the Hadith. Added to that, he is a fearless soldier and a very effective general. His father said he was the best general he'd ever had.

'But here is what is undeniable ... all of his successes are attributable to when his father was around. When his father was not by his side, he made a mess of all his campaigns. Take Warangal as an example. His army deserted him. And he has not had a single military success in recent times other than those you can attribute to Malik Zada. He is kind and generous to a fault, loves his mother and family deeply, but at the same time he can be outlandishly cruel. Does the lack of success fuel this sultan to behave so erratically? Nothing he plans works out. This is a matter that we need to understand in order to survive, Bukka.'

Hakka had been pacing back and forth on the sand as he spoke, while Bukka leaned against a large rock as the monologue continued.

'What are the answers to this puzzle of a man, Bukka?' Hakka asked, as he threw up his hands in front of Bukka.

'Two useful observations, Hakka. One, he was always successful when his father Ghias-ud-din Tughlaq was present to temper his decisions. Now, as sultan, he has no one to question his decisions other than his mother, and, to some extent, Malik Zada who grew up with him. So, he lashes out when others are unable to do his bidding. And two, he is not cunning enough.'

'What do you mean, Bukka?'

'Think of a few examples we know and the information we have gathered so far. His courtiers are for the most part the old men who served his father. Circumstances have changed, yet they still cling to his father's ways that were successful in his time. So, when the sultan wants to do something new, they thwart his plans overtly or covertly because it is not the way things were done. His instincts are often right on the nail, but he is not tactical in his approach.'

'But how is it that a highly intelligent man like him has not studied his mistakes and how might being cunning have helped him? We need to understand this better,' Hakka said.

'Then let's think about what we know,' Bukka replied. 'With each initiative, he wants to do the whole thing, as opposed to planning in pieces. He decides to go to Persia with a view to conquer the region. So, he starts to build an army of four hundred thousand soldiers for his Khorasan expedition and is bled dry because it takes too long. He does this as his rear flank is also engaged in operations spearheaded by Malik Zada. Take another example: while he wants to be a lenient leader and is accepting of all other faiths, he is unwilling to include the ulema in his plans. So, they thwart any attempt at tolerance. Here's one more: in reforming his system of coins, he fails to realize that it might be easy to counterfeit them. He is impatient, never thinks about the ramifications of his actions and fails to outwit the opposition to his initiatives.'

'Okay, then,' agreed Hakka. 'The conclusion is that he tries to do too much, too soon, with too little support and too little planning. Then the question is, why has he not been deposed or why has the empire not collapsed?'

'Empires are like forts. They are hard to crush. You do realize that he is not a total failure. He has a good administrative structure established by his father and one that still operates fairly effectively. His treasury still gets filled despite his poor planning. However, it's not a good state of affairs. Perhaps he could be more successful than he is, although that would be a fearsome prospect for us.'

'What does he need? What does he want?' Hakka was pacing again.

Bukka was silent for a while before answering.

'Let his mother and wife take care of what he needs. We must look at what he wants, which is more pressing.' He added, 'The simple answer to all of this might be that he requires good generals with trustworthy and effective administrators.'

'Where? And for what?' Hakka continued to grill his brother.

'Well, that is only going to be revealed when the sultan moves his pieces on the chaturanga mat. For us, Hakka, there are three questions. First, how is the chaturanga mat laid out: who is in what position? Second, are we to think of ourselves as ashva [horse or knight], or gaja [elephant or bishop]? Finally, while it may not be important, whose turn is it to move a piece on the mat?'

'Aha!' Hakka exclaimed. 'The last point is the most important, Bukka. Both sides will want to move first. The raja in this case will not see the first move. But the others involved will see it, and that will resolve if you are seen as an ashva or a gaja. We will have to take the initiative. So, it turns out there is just one question that remains: what is the positioning on the mat?'

'It just seems ironic,' Bukka remarked, 'that the prisoners are planning on making the first move.'

Hakka was quick to respond. 'We need to move away from preconceptions and assumptions about who we are. Just remember the story of Alexander and Porus. When asked by Alexander, who defeated him, how he wanted to be treated, Porus answered, "Like a king!" We need to remember that we all bring with us special abilities and we need to make sure they are appreciated.'

I've failed

Shamshed was perhaps the first to notice the change in attitude in Faraj. The arrogance had worn off and the sullen behaviour seemed to have dissipated. He passed on his observation to Bukka.

'Faraj is coming to terms with his new situation and, who knows, he might even become a useful ally.' Bukka made a note of it and let it pass. There were too many other pressing issues to deal with, as they were on the final stretch to Daulatabad, which was less than a week away. Karthikeya had yet to return with information. Moreover, they had not solved the conundrum of whom they would engage with once they got there.

Hakka had astutely observed: they would only be treated well if they engaged with someone of the same rank as Malik Zada, in the sultan's inner circle. Otherwise, they would be considered another artifact of the Kampili campaign and left to the devices and whims of some officer, with no control of their fate.

This morning, Faraj was walking just ahead of Bukka. He looked back and asked Bukka if he could walk by his side. Hakka was somewhere in the column, talking to the men and getting the pulse of their mood. He never stopped doing this and Bukka knew his brother had never forgotten how he started his life as a foot soldier, before quickly rising up the ranks. Also, Hakka was looking for new talent. It was his ability to guarantee the well-being of the men that set him apart from other high-ranking officers.

Faraj fell back alongside Bukka with the interpreter, though over the last two months they had come to understand each other, even if only at a rudimentary level.

'I am thankful and grateful to you, Bukka,' Faraj said.

Bukka was taken aback and wondered if the translation was correct.

'What are you grateful for?' he said.

'You've saved my life. And both you and your brother have treated my men and me as your equals. I have learned a lot during this march, and the experience has influenced me deeply. At the beginning, I did not behave with honour. Now I understand.'

Bukka heard him out, then asked a slew of questions: 'How old are you? Where do you come from? How long have you been at court, and how did you come to work for Malik Zada?'

The story of Faraj began in Balochistan, where he was born. His father was a soldier in the army, and related to the vali, a local governor. The vali had sent him to Dilli with introductions to the vazir. Faraj's family was butchered by the Mongols on the way to India. When Faraj finally made it to Dilli, the vazir placed him with Malik Zada. He was now twenty and had been working with Malik Zada as an aide-de-camp for less than a year.

'Have you had any military training?' Bukka asked Faraj, despite knowing the answer.

'No, though I wish I had.'

'Then find an opportunity to get some, or you will forever be doing Malik Zada's dirty work,' Bukka advised.

'But I have failed, and will not be given another chance by Malik Zada,' Faraj responded.

'You were meant to fail, Faraj. This was not a test for you but a test for us. Malik Zada wanted to see if I would keep my word by coming to Daulatabad and presenting ourselves to the sultan. The question is what happens to us once we pass the test.'

'What happens to me then?' Faraj blurted out. The moment he said it he realized he had shown his hand.

Bukka stayed quiet. They were coming to the end of the march for the day. The sun was going down and they needed to set up camp. He noticed the scouts had met the front of the column and were guiding them to a campsite.

Faraj, hesitantly, spoke up again.

'Will you train me, Bukka?'

'If Malik Zada finds this request acceptable, then we can return to the conversation. You could write to him once you reach Daulatabad, detail your experience and ask his permission. And make sure you speak to the vazir as well. You can then consider whether it is a workable plan.'

Bukka advised Faraj to think about their conversation; then, calling for a horse, Bukka went to join Hakka at the head of the column. The scouts had found a small lake about a mile away from their route with a good view of the path to Daulatabad. They were now less than two days away from the fort at Daulatabad, close to a small hamlet called Pipri.

What is Daulatabad like?

'I'd have expected to get spotted by their scouts sooner than a two-day march to the capital city,' Hakka remarked.

'Maybe it's arrogance, maybe they have good intelligence and already know, or maybe they are disorganized after moving to a new capital,' Bukka suggested.

The drums signalled dinner was ready. Standard repast on the road was millet balls and, if they were lucky, some pickle or cooked vegetables. 'Oh, Sangama, when will I ever eat in your kitchen next?' groaned Bukka; he was missing his mother. Just as they headed off to get their rations for the night, the scouts drew their attention with a low-pitched whistle. It was someone they knew, presumably Karthikeya coming back from the capital. Even at a distance they could hear the snort of a horse as it made its way up to the camp from the rough-hewn road to Daulatabad. The rider dismounted, leading the horses up the path.

It took a while before Karthikeya got through the two perimeters of security. He unsaddled the horse, removed its bridle and saddle, and gave it some water. Hakka smiled to himself. Bukka had trained Karthikeya and many men like him. All of them had learnt how to deal with their animals with care and affection. Once he'd taken care of his mount, Karthikeya joined Hakka and Bukka, who had settled down for dinner. Karthikeya brought packages, and was helped by another young soldier as he trudged up the pathway. He broke into a big smile upon seeing the generals and saluted them, addressing them as Semenya (General) Hakka and Semenya Bukka. They sent for Shamshed and Achappa to hear the news too, instead of Karthikeya having to repeat himself.

The brothers were both sitting cross-legged in a clear open space, with Shamshed and Achappa standing to Hakka's right as Karthikeya related what he had discovered on his trip to Daulatabad.

'Semenya and adhikarigalu (officers), the most important news is that Malik Zada is coming back to Daulatabad after King Ballala sued for peace. Rumour has it that Ballala gave up Baha-ud-din to Malik Zada. And, as a peace offering, he has given Malik Zada seventy-five elephants, two hundred horses and one hundred manns of gold. He is supposed to have added a hundred slaves as part of the deal. He promised to pay a tithe to the sultan every year which will include twenty-five elephants, fifty manns of gold and a hundred horses. Additionally, he has guaranteed soldiers if the sultan wishes to go further south to the land of Ma'bar (the land of the Tamils) or seeks to conquer the territory of Calicut.'

To Hakka it seemed like King Ballala had paid a higher price than he had anticipated.

'Daulatabad feels a lot like a tent city,' Karthikeya continued. 'There is much building going on but it does not come close to what is needed for people to live. Our connections were able to provide us with news from the court. Malik Zada sent a letter to the sultan in which he speaks very highly of both of you, semenyas. From what we are able to tell, based on the informants in the vazir's administration, the sultan would like to personally meet the two of you. There is no mention about being treated like prisoners. The vazir has asked for an area to be set up as a camp for the Kampilis, along with provisions.

'Altaf and Haneef have found quarters with a cobbler's family. This is situated close to the stables. We were able to connect with the three people you suggested. However, there was something strange. We were approached by a trader who told us his name was Kazi Rahim Rahmatullah. He showed us a gold mohur with the crest of the king of Kampili to identify himself as someone who was connected with Kampili. His message was, "I'd like to know what the semanyas think about the weather in Daulatabad." He repeatedly asked if we needed supplies, money or any other information. He invited us to have a meal with him but we refused, not knowing him or his connections.'

'What else did you see that was different and what more should we know, Karthikeya?' Hakka asked.

'Semenya, there are soldiers everywhere as well as nobility. Never before have I seen so much wealth. Everything is shining with gold, silver and gems on people's clothes.

'On two occasions, we went inside the fort. Kazi Rahim Rahmatullah got us inside and he appears to know a lot of very influential officials. We went to sell high-quality mares at the weekly purchase. It is a fort that can only be described as incredible, and so big that it could fit the Kampili capital of Anegundi within it with room to spare. But the fort, semenya, is built to deceive. If you planned to attack it but did not know the layout, once you got inside, you'd be lost. Outside the walls is a large moat that is full of crocodiles and snakes. The walls are at least fifty feet high, and the fort, which is in the shape of a triangle, is on a hill. I cannot imagine how anyone would be able to conquer it. Even for the semenyas it would be a military puzzle. On one occasion when we were outside the fort, we saw the sultan on his elephant.

'There is one last thing, semenya,' Karthikeya concluded. 'I ate food that I have not tasted before. The flavours and the taste are nothing I have experienced. I brought back a sweetmeat made of milk, called a peta.' With that, he brought out a small wooden box and offered it to Hakka. There was silence for a while as they ate and absorbed the unusual taste and texture. 'Semenya, I kept telling Altaf and Haneef that I hope we are not walking into the devil's den of temptation.'

Karthikeya's description had them in splits of laughter. It left the young man feeling sheepish, which was not common for someone so sure of himself.

'That was good work, Karthikeya,' Hakka said. 'Now, are you sure that Altaf and Haneef will be safe?'

'Semenya, I have asked them not to trade in horses until we reach Daulatabad. The ruse I designed for them is that they are waiting for the next shipment of four fine Arabian steeds that they will pick up from Surat next month. In the meanwhile, they will keep watch over the prices of the horses being bought, gather information on the comings and goings at court, and refrain from drawing the attention of spies or officials. I've told them to stay away from the fort and only connect with our contacts on the outside. They will obey their instructions, semenya, and God willing, they will stay out of trouble until we arrive in a day or two.'

With that, Karthikeya gave the sack of gold mohurs back to Bukka and said:

'If it were not for Kazi Rahim Rahmatullah, we would have had trouble with money, if we had tried to spend large quantities of gold that was not stamped with the sultan's mark. He immediately gave us ten gold mohurs' worth of silver coins so we would be less conspicuous. He would not take the gold mohurs from us in exchange. Instead, he repeatedly said there was an arrangement you had in Anegundi and that this was not something to concern ourselves with.

'Before we left, we insisted on giving him something in exchange as a deposit. Kazi Rahim Rahmatullah recommended the best thing for us to do was to instead leave fifty mohurs with Altaf and Haneef. He would give them the equivalent in gold mohurs with the stamp of the sultan so it could be used in the market or to buy things. So, we agreed, semenya. He seems to have very large resources but disguises the fact that he is rich, even though he has money for everything. All three of us kept wondering if we were making a big mistake but we had plenty to eat, pay for the horses we traded, pay for three months' rent for Altaf and Haneef, to buy new clothes and eat a lot of peta!' They all laughed before helping themselves to more of it.

A curious entrance

'We are going to make a very unusual entrance,' Bukka remarked to Karthikeya.

'Why, semenya?' he asked.

'Look at us. No one has had his hair cut in two months, everyone is sporting a long beard, our uniforms are tattered, and the only ones who look clean and well-tended are the horses and dogs. We look like an army of beggars, Karthikeya.'

'But there was never such a good army of beggars,' Karthikeya replied. 'Whatever can be cleaned and polished has been addressed. The horses' bridles and the dogs' collars shine, semenya. All the scabbards and the belts are well polished and the weapons sharp. So, we will present ourselves with pride, however we might look like to the sultan's army. Fancy clothes are for parades and those who don't fight wars. We are a fearsome group and that's the most important thing for an army.'

'Well said, Karthikeya,' Bukka said. 'Now, have the scouts move in a little closer or they might bump into the sultan's scouts or his forward battalions very shortly. We should be in Daulatabad by late afternoon. Let's see what happens next. Tell Shamshed to ride with Hakka and myself. Oh, and make sure the dogs are at the end of the column as the Musalman can get very agitated by them. Then ride through the column and inform the platoon captains to be on the alert. Remember they must be alert to protect the treasure we are transporting. How many horses are carrying the gold?'

'I will pass on your orders, semenya. We have forty-two horses hauling the gold,' Karthikeya said.

'How many men on horseback do we have today?'

'Twenty-nine, semenya,' Karthikeya replied, who was accustomed to the cross- examination.

'Okay, keep five at the rear of the column and make sure they have lances. There are nine officers on horses, so the remaining horses should flank both sides of the column evenly. When I tell you what formation to set up, the men and the horses must fall into their positions. That's all for now, Karthikeya.'

'Yes, semenya,' he responded and saluted in the manner of a Kampili soldier, with his fist over his heart. He marched off to get the column prepared.

Bukka rode the mare that had thrown off Faraj at the beginning of the march. She had healed and gradually grown able to take more weight, with the result that she became one of the horses carrying the gold. But she was now Bukka's horse. He decided to call her Chetana, or 'spirited one'. It was a pleasure to see her at full potential and in good health.

He cantered to the head of the column to Hakka, Shamshed and Faraj. Hakka suggested two of them lead the column with the bannerman carrying the Kampili standard to their side. Shamshed was to follow closely as he might be able to act as translator. He was their bridge to Faraj and the sultan's soldiers, and coped sufficiently well with the smattering of Arabic he had learned when he sailed on the trading dhows to Muscat and Jask.

It was early afternoon when they heard the scouts signal the movement of a column of soldiers half a mile away. They estimated roughly forty of them with seemingly no other reinforcements. Neither were there any formations to the south, the east or the west. Hakka breathed a little easier. He spoke quietly to Bukka.

'The sultan needs help and Malik Zada is betting we can help him. The only question now is what, precisely, does he want us to do?' He added, 'I think I will buy you some peta after dinner tonight,' and broke into a loud laugh.

Bukka responded with a wry smile. 'Hakka, optimism is a luxury that we still cannot afford, so stiffen your back and prepare for the worst.'

They were riding down a long stretch of road when they saw the company of cavalrymen approach with a bannerman carrying the sultan's colours. They were a small group of helmeted soldiers on fine horses, briskly trotting in good formation. The column was four across and about twenty-five deep. Would they be asked to stop and wait? Or would they be accompanied to a secluded spot for some egregious act of treachery where they would get mowed down? Or perhaps they might even be escorted into Daulatabad? Pretty soon the pieces on the chaturanga mat were going to start moving once more.

The sultan's soldiers had barely stopped when Hakka whipped into action.

'Division! Halt!' Two thousand pairs of feet thumped the ground as they stopped and stood in place.

At the head of the sultan's column was a regal-looking soldier in a splendid uniform, seated on a horse with equally fine accoutrements. He appeared surprised. Hakka proclaimed:

'I am Hakka, general of the army of Kampili and we are marching to see Sultan Muhammad-bin-Tughlaq to lay down our arms in surrender, as required by Malik Zada.' Hakka waited for Shamshed to translate. Before the soldier could reply, Hakka went on:

'Malik Zada's representative, Faraj, has accompanied us on the march from the Anegundi Fort. Please let us know how you would like us to proceed.' The soldier at the head of the sultan's platoon appeared overwhelmed by the force of Hakka's introduction, especially when he heard the translation. Hakka motioned for Faraj to come up to the front.

'Subhanallah. The great Malik Zada asked me to present these warriors from Kampili to our sultan, Allah be praised, Muhammad-bin-Tughlaq,' Faraj said. The man at the head of the sultan's platoon seemed to relax a bit at this. He replied to Faraj, who translated in a rapid mutter to Shamshed.

'The vazir of Sultan Muhammad-bin-Tughlaq, Vazir Khwaja Jahan, has asked the Sultan's Guard to escort you to your quarters that have been prepared for your arrival in Daulatabad.' Shamshed, in turn, translated to Hakka and Bukka.

'Then ask him to please lead us there,' Hakka boomed. Shamshed translated while Faraj reaffirmed the command.

The soldier ordered his men to turn around and start riding back. Bukka gave the order to follow.

On the left, rising from the haze of dust, was a steep hill topped by a hulking black fort. Even at a distance it was imposing and seemed like an insurmountable obstacle to anyone with plans to lay siege.

By early evening they arrived at what appeared to be a city at the foot of the hill. A large crowd of curious onlookers stared at them: women, children, soldiers and vendors in the market. As they walked through, they could see that some of the buildings seemed hastily constructed to meet the needs of the sultan's edict to move his capital from Dilli to Daulatabad.

Finally, they were led into a large encampment surrounded by a high fence, with guards posted at the entrance. The man who had headed the sultan's guards spoke to Shamshed and Faraj.

'This is the camp to which you are assigned. There is a house for the generals and tents for the men. A kitchen has been built at the rear with supplies to feed the men. I will leave a messenger behind and you can ask for anything else that might be required. This is on the orders of the vazir. In case there are messages for you, a runner from my guard battalion will bring them to you. You should not expect any messages for a day or maybe two.'

It was a well-organized military encampment with tents for the men, troughs to feed and water the horses, and a large house on one side. A young servant pointed to it and the interpreter let Bukka and Hakka know that it was meant for them.

Bukka rode around the camp with Karthikeya, Shamshed and Faraj, and delivered a volley of orders to settle the men and animals in the camp. He then went into a courtyard where Hakka was sitting on a comfortable divan, sipping a drink.

'Welcome to my simple home in captivity, brother. I hope you will stay a while!' Hakka and Bukka started laughing, joined by the others.

Once the other three had gone to their quarters, Hakka leaned over to speak in Bukka's ear.

'The stakes are higher than I imagined. I just hope we're prepared to play it at this level.'

Bukka joined his hands, looked upward and said, '*Eeswaro rakshatoo.*' May God protect us.

Teacher, advisor or lieutenant?

He was a tall man, very tall indeed. As Hakka and Bukka walked into the garden, he looked as if he towered over everything.

The two brothers had been sent for and escorted to one of the palaces of Daulatabad that morning. The bodyguards stepped away as the tall old man came closer. Standing before him, both Bukka and Hakka had to crane their necks to look him in the eye. He was a Muslim, as his garb showed. He was dressed in a long, white silk tunic with a bright-green waistcoat, with his sword slung at his side. Bukka noticed the telltale signs: the sword's scabbard was scuffed and dented. It was no ceremonial artifact and the owner clearly knew how to use it.

He was a courtly man, graceful, with an aura of confidence and wisdom. He greeted them and said, 'Hamdullilah,' accompanied with an adaab: he raised the cupped palm of his right hand up to his face. Both Hakka and Bukka responded with a traditional namaskaram, or namaste.

Qutlugh Khan was accompanied by an elderly man who stood by the side. Since he held a book in his hand, it suggested he was a scribe. He was the interpreter. Qutlugh Khan spoke and the scribe translated. He spoke Kannada, the tongue spoken in Kampili, which surprised the brothers.

'My name is Qutlugh Khan and I have been Emperor Muhammad-bin-Tughlaq's teacher since he was a young boy. I previously worked as a malik (general) for his father, Ghias-ud-din Tughlaq, even before he became the emperor, may his soul rest in peace. I welcome you, Malik Hakka and Malik Bukka, to Daulatabad.'

He then pointed down the broad pathway to an immaculate garden in which stood a gazebo with benches. He walked with an easy gait; it was difficult to miss the power that emanated from this man. Though his hair was grey, Qutlugh Khan had large, sinewy hands and was clearly still fit and muscular. 'Was he the emperor's teacher of the martial arts?' thought Bukka. In the gazebo, the seats were set out in a close circle. Their host invited them to sit down. The translator remained standing.

'Since the time you maliks worked for King Prataparudra of the Kakatiya kingdom, we have been aware of your abilities on the battlefield. In fact, we'd always hoped you would not be part of any engagement against us,' Qutlugh Khan said with a smile.

'When the two of you were given increased responsibilities in Kampili, your names would frequently be part of military discussions. You beat us twice in Kampili and nearly a third time. If your soldiers had not been starved due to the siege, it is likely that the sultan's soldiers would have encountered a very different outcome. But then, of course, we would not be here and perhaps would never have met.'

Waving to someone they could not see, Qutlugh Khan summoned servitors. The brothers were instantly surrounded by attendants bearing trays of food and drink. He offered them mango and lime cordials and water, which the attendants served them in gold tumblers. He encouraged them to help themselves to the fruit and other choice viands on the golden trays. They had never seen anything resembling the pastries and other titbits before them, some of which were covered with what looked like a film of silver. The flavours were such as they had never encountered before. Bukka smiled to himself: 'I just hope the glutton Hakka does not lose self-control.'

This was opulence of an order that not even the king of Kampili could afford, much less be able to conjure up such grand elegance.

'Moving on,' Qutlugh Khan continued, after he had ensured his guests were served, 'the emperor is always interested in informing himself of capable and talented generals, whether they are from Khorasan, Kabul or Kampili. Because, as you know, in the craft that emperors practise, today's enemy could be tomorrow's ally.'

He leaned over to pick up a pomegranate, gently breaking it in half. He brought it close to his nose to savour the fragrance before he put it to his mouth and began noisily sucking on it, slurping appreciatively. An attendant handed him a towel. Handing Bukka the other half, Qutlugh Khan invited him to try it.

'It's a shame that we will not be having many of those for a while. They were the last few that we got from Dilli. When I grew up in Baluchistan, we lived on these fruits all summer long. I miss them. Yes, I am a Baluchi by birth, but I've have been in the service of the Tughlaq family for a long time now.

'But, Malik Hakka and Malik Bukka, getting back to what I was saying earlier, occasionally one is able to spot exceptional generals. Yet, there are even fewer generals whose integrity is beyond question and who can be relied upon to conduct themselves with honour. The two of you, it appears, are such people.'

Uncomfortable with the praise being ladled out, Hakka thought, 'Is this marinade we soak in, before we get cooked?' He began by thanking Qutlugh Khan for his hospitality. With his typical bluntness, he added, 'I expected us to lay down our arms and be consigned to prison. Instead, we have excellent quarters, no sight of a heavy presence of guards and we are still in possession of the treasure from the fort of Anegundi.'

'You are not prisoners, Malik Hakka, but guests of the emperor. And perhaps you will stay with us a while, as we learn from you and you learn from us. Please make yourselves comfortable and ask for anything that you might need. While I myself do not drink, I understand you and your soldiers do, and I will make sure that some of our wine is made available.'

As this conversation progressed, Hakka just felt that there were too many questions being left unanswered.

'Malik Hakka, did you meet Malik Zada?' Qutlugh Khan asked. Hakka replied that he had been wounded during the battle of Anegundi and it was Bukka who had interacted with Malik Zada.

'It's a shame that you were not presented with the opportunity. The emperor and Malik Zada were both students of mine. I have been with them since they were seven years of age. I first taught them the Quran and the Hadith. Some might say too well,' he chuckled.

'Why?" enquired Bukka.

'They are now both hafiz. And whenever there is a discussion or debate, there are few others who win, as they have total mastery of the texts and can recall any verse or verses as the finest hafiz would.'

Qutlugh Khan laughed again as he recalled the memories. 'As young boys, there was no desire to sit for hours at a time learning the holy book. Yet, that is the time of your life when your mind is fresh and absorbs easily what must be learnt.' He proceeded to quote a sura:

So, follow what has been revealed to you by your Lord.
There is no god but He! And turn away from those who
assign partners to Him. (6:102–106)

'However,' he continued, 'the boys would balk and sometimes make a fuss, or say they were sick and their stomachs hurt.' He chuckled to himself once more. 'I rewarded them with burfis when they learned their lessons, or took them horse riding. I also used a cane to punish them. At times they complained to the emperor, who would cane them for complaining. By the age of twelve, they were accomplished in every aspect of the religion. They were both hafiz and could debate and recite the Hadith and the Sunnah and the ulema would always find it difficult to argue with the young boys. Then I taught them how to become accomplished riders and how to use a sword and lance. The finer parts of conducting war they learned from the master, Emperor Ghias-ud-din Tughlaq, who was graced by God with talent. There was not a single battle he fought or war he waged that he ever lost.

'And since they are now grown men, I've given myself over to helping with tasks, small and large.'

Hakka was getting impatient.

'What should we do in the meantime?'

Qutlugh Khan stood up. 'Malik Hakka and Malik Bukka, you are free to arrange your business as you see fit. There are no restrictions on you.'

'May we use the grounds by the camp to exercise the troops and make sure they continue their daily practice?' Hakka asked.

'Of course,' Qutlugh Khan said. As he prepared to leave, he said, 'Two things: please stay and eat some of the food that was cooked for you. I recommend the sambusas, the halwas and the burfis. They are the best in the world. Second, I will have the basith [messenger] bring a tailor tomorrow to measure you for suits that are worthy of maliks.'

'Subhanallah,' he said as he stood up and walked a few steps to a beautiful black steed that had been led up for him. He offered them an adaab and the brothers stood up and repeated their namaskarams as Qutlugh Khan rode away with his bodyguards.

'That man does not need a contingent of bodyguards,' observed Hakka. 'He is as strong as an elephant and I would be loath to meet him in a sword fight.'

'I am not sure he wants to meet you in a sword fight either,' replied Bukka.

Unwilling to respond to his brother's comments, Hakka simply muttered, '*Irali bidi.* [let it be].'

They wiped the trays clean, enjoying the experience of new flavours and the textures of the food. Hakka smacked his lips, licked his fingers and closed his eyes as he relished the sapidity of everything on offer. The basith, who had brought them to the garden, accompanied them back. Firdoos Shah was the translator who had been assigned to them.

While they had ridden to the garden, they decided to walk back. The only comment that Bukka made on the long walk back to the camp was, 'Gaja [elephant or bishop] or ratha [chariot or rook]?' Without hesitation, Hakka replied: 'Gaja.'

Golden cage

As promised, the basith came along with the tailors the next afternoon. He asked if Firdoos Shah could join them so the tailors did not misinterpret their instructions. The tailors had come with bolts of cloth including expensive silks and satins. Hakka jumped into the sartorial fray and spoke to Firdoos:

'We just want to be able to wear the same uniforms as we have now, which are made of cotton. Otherwise, we will look like strange men leading our own army. It has to be the same uniform. Can the tailors do that?'

'But that is not what a malik wears,' was the head tailor's reaction, who had come with a small retinue.

Hakka held himself back, but he stood firm.

'For now, janaab, please make us a copy of our uniforms.' They were rough tan cotton, with a loose upper jacket and loose trousers made of the same cloth. They had belts to hold their swords, in contrast to Malik Zada and Qutlugh Khan: each wore a cummerbund about his waist and a belt across the torso, from which hung a sword at the hip.

Two weeks went by, and with every passing day, Hakka drove himself and the men harder. They practised their sword work; they marched; they practised with their lances on horseback. They were visibly tired from their exertions, so Bukka protested at further drills and demanded a day off to rest.

Both the brothers were mingling with the soldiers after a large midday meal. Suddenly they noticed beautiful horses approaching the camp with one of the riders carrying a flag with a coat of arms. A loud voice announced at the gateway of the camp:

'From the vazir of the Emperor Muhammad-bin-Tughlaq, a message for Malik Hakka and Malik Bukka.'

The brothers walked over, followed by Shamshed, Karthikeya and the interpreter Firdoos Shah. Firdoos Shah identified the brothers and spoke to the messenger, who handed over a golden tube with a scroll rolled up and sealed inside. Bukka broke the seal and unrolled the missive but was unable to read it. The interpreter read out and translated the brief note:

Malik Hakka and Malik Bukka,

You are asked to present yourselves and your men at the Diwan-i-Aam tomorrow.

The time of your appearance is scheduled for the hour before noon.

From
Vazir Khwaja Jahan

With a shouted salutation, the messenger mounted his horse and departed. Hardly had the messenger left when six large carts arrived at the entrance, headed by the tailor. All of the Kampili regiment had new uniforms. Bukka tried his on and was pleased with it. Though it raised morale around the camp, Hakka wryly quizzed his brother:

'What price will we have to pay for all of this, Bukka?'

Hakka could barely sit still for the remainder of the day. There was a torrent of issues raised and whenever Bukka was present, he resorted to his rhetorical device of thinking out aloud with a never-ending stream of questions. By the end of the evening, he had worn himself out, albeit satisfied that he had addressed every intricate detail. At least he thought he had.

Attending the grand durbar

The two thousand Kampili soldiers formed twenty companies of a hundred men each, ordered into twenty-five rows and four columns. To Bukka's eyes, they looked crisp, and he was satisfied with how effectively they presented themselves. They were being led by soldiers of the Emperor's Guard, who were escorting them. In comparison to these guards' resplendent livery, the troops' uniforms looked dull but severe, and it highlighted to the observer that these men meant business.

The frills had all been eschewed for a simple presence that caught everyone's attention.

At the gate to the fort, Hakka dismounted and asked all those riding to dismount as well. However, he instructed the severely injured soldiers to remain on their horses. All thirty-eight of them rode at the end of the column.

The captain of the Emperor's Guard asked why they had dismounted.

'When you go to see the emperor of the army that defeated you, you behave appropriately,' Hakka said simply. The man looked at him quizzically.

Looking around, Hakka observed that the fort was built on a hill that was between five hundred and six hundred feet high. The first defence was a deep moat with crocodiles, with plenty of them in plain sight. The second was the hill whose sides had been shaved off to make it difficult to attack. They were going to cross it on a narrow bridge that would allow only two persons walking abreast. It seemed the fort had only one entrance. As they passed through the gates, he saw large spikes set in them, which would prevent an enemy from using elephants as battering rams. This was not a fort that could be easily overwhelmed, if at all.

After a long and steep walk upward, they came into an open space. The view was spectacular. This was the area where the emperor held his durbar. The splendour of the decorations and the lines of men and animals inspired awe.

At least twenty elephants, all beautifully caparisoned in bright silks, stood in the large oval space. The horsemen were all on jet-black horses wearing impressive deep-green uniforms.

They filed in and formed ranks ready for inspection. Hakka stood with Bukka at the head of the formation; behind them stood Shamshed and Karthikeya.

At one end of the durbar space was a large platform sheltered by a shamiana, a large open tent made of wide stripes of white and green silk. A magnificent golden throne on a stepped dais dominated the platform. Before it, at a lower level on the platform, were arranged about ten chairs.

At five minutes before the hour, they heard drummers. Hakka called his men to attention. Preceded and followed by soldiers wearing the uniform of the Emperor's Guard, ten men rode in. One of them was Qutlugh Khan. Handing over their horses, they all walked up to the platform and sat down at prearranged spots. Two divans were placed close to the steps leading up to the throne, and Qutlugh Khan sat on one of them. It was hardly a hundred feet from where Hakka and Bukka were standing, and they could see these men's faces clearly. They all wore bright clothes and a turban. They had necklaces of jewels, and their turbans had large precious stones in them. The men from Kampili were amazed at the extravagance of the display; the whole situation symbolized power and wealth.

They heard the drummers start to beat a loud and rapid beat, followed by trumpets and horns. A crier announced:

'*Allahu akbar*, we now announce the arrival of Emperor Muhammad.' In a minute, they could hear the horses, and ten horsemen rode in.

Behind them was the most beautiful white mare Bukka had ever seen. A man of medium height, wearing rich clothing, was riding it. He was followed by another horseman holding over him a parasol of gold and green silk. The man on the white mare rode up to the platform, and gracefully slipped off the horse. Before moving away, he stopped for an instant and rubbed the horse's forehead and spoke to it.

Handing over the reins to a servitor, Muhammad-bin-Tughlaq briskly walked up the steps to the platform.

All ten men were standing, waiting for him. He stopped and greeted each in turn, and quickly walked up to the throne, sat down, and turned to the man closest to him.

'Vazir Khwaja Jahan,' he said, 'What is the order of business today?'

'*Allahu akbar*,' the vazir proclaimed and it was echoed by all the men on the platform. 'My emperor, your request was to have this Diwan-i-Aam dedicated to Malik Zada's prisoners of war.'

'So I did,' the emperor replied in a voice that was strong and clear, and though not loud, carried far. Here was authority without arrogance. 'You may proceed with business, then,' he said.

The vazir turned to face all of them. At the same time, the emperor said something softly, and Qutlugh Khan walked up to him and stood to his right. Firdoos Shah, the translator, came and stood at the bottom of the steps to the throne. The vazir called out:

'Hakka, commander of the defeated forces of Kampili, please walk up.'

Hakka marched up to within five feet of the steps of the platform and stood to attention. He offered a namaskaram.

The emperor sat erect and looked him in the eye, and said: 'What do you have to say?'

'Chakravarti Muhammad, I have three orders of business. I request your permission to proceed with them.'

'You are at liberty to do so,' Tughlaq said.

'My first order of business is to lay down arms,' Hakka declared, and, not waiting for an answer, he swivelled on his heel and marched smartly back to the formation. When he was a few feet away from Bukka, he stopped. In a thunderous voice, he commanded:

'Brigade! Present arms.'

The sound of two thousand swords being unsheathed simultaneously made a ringing noise. Each soldier held his sword up erect before him.

'Surrender arms,' Hakka then commanded, and all of them, in perfectly synchronized fashion, knelt, put their swords down on the ground in front of them and stood at attention. Hakka, drew his sword, raised it and let out his battle cry of 'Jai Kampili!' There was a roar as they all repeated it in unison. He turned, walked back to the platform, stood at attention, knelt like all the others had, put his sword on the ground, and stood back up. Bringing his fist above his heart, the salute of Kampili soldiers, Hakka said:

'Chakravarti Muhammad, we declare ourselves prisoners of war and put ouselves at your mercy.'

'What is your second order of business?'

'Chakravarti, I have a task to complete that Malik Zada had asked my deputy commander to carry out.'

'Proceed.'

Hakka again turned around and stood at attention.

'Present supplies!' he bellowed. Bukka now took command and gave another set of orders. A formation of twenty-nine horses led by Kampili soldiers came forward.

'And what is your third order of business?' the emperor went on. Hakka hesitated for a moment and then looked up.

'Chakravarti, it is a Kampili tradition to provide the best care possible for those wounded in battle. We have thirty-eight men, whom you still see on horses, who have been severely wounded. It will take a long time for them to heal, if at all.' At this point, he went down on his knee, looked up at the emperor and said, 'I request your help in taking care of my wounded men.'

The ensuing silence felt ominous. The emperor turned to Qutlugh Khan and spoke to him. He then turned back to Hakka and said:

'It is a tradition that will be honoured, and my teacher and qazi, Qutlugh Khan, will make sure they are seen by the hakeems and taken care of.'

The emperor then called for the vazir, and the three of them—Qutlugh Khan, the vazir and the emperor—went into a huddle and had a short discussion. The two went back to their seats.

Leaning forward, the emperor looked at Hakka.

'As for your first order of business, you and your soldiers are not prisoners of war. You will remain active soldiers, but will be incorporated into my army, as my brigade from Kampili. Therefore, you may keep your arms. Please ask your soldiers to arm themselves again.' He waited.

Hakka went through the routine and commanded, 'Collect arms,' which was accomplished in an instant.

He turned to face the emperor again.

'Your third order of business has been addressed,' Tughlaq said, 'as my hakeems have been ordered to attend to your wounded. So now for the business of the treasury. This is what Malik Zada had predicted would happen. I am happy that his prediction has been realized.' He spoke privately to his two advisors again.

Looking at Hakka, the emperor spoke again.

'Malik Hakka you may dismiss your men.'

Hakka marched back and issued the command to dismiss them and and send them back to the camp. As they prepared to march out, Karthikeya, who was leading them, raised his sword and bellowed:

'Chakravarti Muhammad!'

Two thousand voices roared back, 'Chakravarti Muhammad!' and the soldiers of Kampili marched out.

The vazir then came up to the edge of the platform and declared the end of the Diwan-i-Aam. Hakka was standing facing him and the emperor. Behind him was Bukka who, according to protocol, had not been dismissed. The vazir now announced that they would adjourn to the more secluded Diwan-i-Khaas.

'Malik Hakka is what my qazi calls you, so I will do the same,' said the emperor. 'Please join me at the Diwan-i-Khaas along with Malik Bukka.' The emperor arose, walked down quickly and got astride his horse. The others filed down and did the same. Qutlugh Khan was the last to come down. He walked over to the two brothers.

'Come, my dear maliks, let's walk to the Diwan-i-Khaas, which is nearby.'

Even when he was walking at a slow pace his strides were long. They kept pace, but it was unsettling to have to scurry to keep up.

'You have now seen the ten men closest to the emperor. Of the nine who were there whom you have not met as yet, the vazir, the oldest malik and the senior member of the ulema are very conservative. You should be aware that they are very old-fashioned, and believe in Islam as the core of everything.

'Further, they do not like the idea that there are quite a few Hindus whom the emperor does depend upon, like some of his generals and governors of states. At every point, the three will directly or, sometimes in insidious ways, thwart the emperor or those who do not fit the mould. Their mould, that is. I say this because you will soon find opposition to any assignment given to you by the emperor. This may be direct opposition, which is easy to confront. Frequently it is indirect, when it can be dangerous. I will make sure that you know when the dangers might be severe enough that you need to exercise care.'

They were at the entrance of a large building built of stone and like a fortress within a fortress. It was surrounded by immaculately tended gardens. It was very heavily guarded and as they walked up to the entrance, two large men walked up to Qutlugh Khan and asked if Hakka and Bukka were accompanying him into the palace. When he said yes, they asked for their swords and other weapons they may be carrying.

'They have been invited by the emperor and they come at my own recognizance,' Qutlugh said. The guards bowed and retreated.

Most noticeable was the fragrance of burning incense as they walked into a vast hallway. There were huge carpets on the floor, vases of flowers and fine furniture, and gold ornaments adorning the walls. Bukka was struck by the sheer magnificence and scale, and was looking about him wide-eyed, when he felt a massive hand on his shoulder.

'I also was born and grew up in a mud hut,' Qutlugh said softly. 'You never grow used to it. And if you do, I will have to put you to the sword.' He smiled, and the three of them started to laugh.

Leading them through three more entrances, finally they were facing a massive door that was swung open gradually. Walking in, they saw the emperor seated at the end of the room. Sitting up erect, he faced divans to his left and right, with the three empty seats closest to him at his right. Sitting closest to him at his left was the vazir. The emperor nodded slightly, and Qutlugh indicated that the brothers should sit down in the empty seats. Hakka and Bukka removed their swords, walked over to the emperor, bowed and placed them before him.

'You may keep your swords, maliks,' the emperor said. It was Bukka who spoke up this time and said:

'Chakravarti, our tradition mandates we present to you everything we have. It is a tradition that will be difficult for us to change. We ask for your indulgence.'

The emperor nodded. The brothers went and sat at the edge of their divans unlike the others who were sitting back quite comfortably.

The emperor now spoke.

'There is a lot that I know about Kampili, about your army and about the two of you. So, if you are wondering why you have not met the fate that is usually the lot of the captured, the answer has a few parts.

'My army has never been as effective as it should be, especially in campaigns south of Daulatabad. Our administration has also not been good at understanding the people of the south and how we might administer them more effectively and benevolently. And now that I am in Daulatabad, I would like to make sure that the south of the country is entirely under my control.

'I intend to start with the subjugation of the Koli kingdom of King Naga Nayaka, which lies immediately to my south.'

Pausing for a moment, he went on, 'My mudaris [teacher] and my yarshud [guide], Qutlugh Khan and Malik Zada, advise me that you both can help with these tasks.' He stopped for a moment. He tilted his head a bit to his right, and asked: 'Can you?' His voice was a little louder, as if he wanted all the others to hear him.

Hakka stood up, folded his hands in a namaskaram and spoke to the emperor, but also made it a point to look at the others as well.

'As your soldiers, my brother and I are your subjects. And Chakravarti, if these are the tasks you have for us, we will accomplish them to your satisfaction.'

The emperor looked at him and Bukka straight in the eye. He said to Hakka, Bukka and Qutlugh Khan:

'In the few weeks you have before Malik Zada returns, you can work on preparing for all these tasks. And when he returns, we can meet again. We can then hear how you will build the military campaign against the Kolis. You can also guide us to better understand what we should do in this area of the empire to be effective patrons of the people.' He looked at Qutlugh Khan and nodded.

'I wish you have the blessings of your gods in completing these tasks. We will meet again in a few weeks and, until then, Qutlugh Khan will be your rafiq [companion]. *Allahu akbar!*'

Everyone in the room stood up and repeated *Allahu akbar* after him. He then said, 'Hamdulillah,' stood up, nodded at them again and walked out of the room, followed by all the courtiers. Qutlugh Khan left the hall with Hakka and Bukka.

When they got outside, the man holding Qutlugh Khan's horse was Faraj. He greeted them with a graceful 'Subhanallah,

Malik Hakka and Malik Bukka.' Looking at the expression on Bukka's face, Qutlugh Khan smiled.

'Faraj is going to be my musaeid [assistant] for now. Take a rest for the remainder of the day, and I will send Faraj or a basith with a message. If it is not Faraj who brings the message, the basith will bring my signet ring for identification.' He showed them a big golden ring on his left ring finger, turned inward. When he turned it round they saw a large emerald.

'Jauna gave this to me when he ascended the throne of Dilli,' he said. He swung onto his horse and rode off.

3

Nishthavanta (Loyalty)

1328: Daulatabad and Sinhagad Fort

How good can they be?

Thada-thud. Thada-thud. Thada-thud. Thada-thud. Thada-thud. Thada-thud. The thunder of hooves came from the vast grassy field where the sultan's soldiers practised their horsemanship and did their training. Horses were galloping in a straight line, one after another.

The spectacle today had two thousand Kampili soldiers on one side of the field and approximately three thousand of the emperor's soldiers on the other. Four hundred yards separated them. Qutlugh Khan, on Bukka's suggestion, had decided to see which side was better trained by proposing a competition. Only then, Bukka suggested, would they know what each side was capable of. On the emperor's side the soldiers were led by Malik Zandvakili, a close confidant of the vazir.

To start, they agreed to an event called 'tent pegging'. In a battlefield situation there was a scenario before an attack where a few cavalrymen would gallop through a camp using their swords or lances to remove tent pegs. Frequently, they targeted the tents of senior officers.

The rider charged at full gallop, screaming a war cry, and attempted to pierce or knock off as many of the tent pegs as he could before riding away. The tents would collapse on the sleeping officers and men, creating confusion and lowering morale. This competition attempted to re-enact such circumstances. Consequently, each rider was to ride down a straight line, about a furrow's length, set with twenty tent pegs. The goal was to knock out as many pegs as possible. If ever there were a true test of horsemanship, this was one. Speed, balance and the unerring ability to guide a galloping horse while managing a lance tested the ability of a rider like nothing else.

Ten riders from either side were picked at random in addition to ten of their best riders, adding up to twenty attempts by each side. The emperor's cavalry, on beautiful and powerful horses, galloped down the stretch screaming *'Allahu akbar!'* while attacking the pegs in the ground. Then came the Kampili soldiers who thundered down the same path, shouting, 'Kali Devi!' The thudding of the hooves, the shouting of the men and the snorting of the horses were almost deafening.

In just over two hours, the two teams had completed their runs. The results were noted by the sultan's representative; he seemed surprised.

Sword fighting was the next challenge. Zandvakili and Bukka chose a hundred men each for their respective sides. The men used blunt swords with red dye; there were ten duels at a time lasting five minutes each in front of a judge. It took two hours to complete.

The final challenge consisted of a group of one hundred foot soldiers who would confront a charge by a hundred cavalry. Opposing sides presented their foot soldiers and cavalry, with the engagement timed for an hour. Each team used blunt swords and lances with no tips, all dipped in red to mark each hit.

Unknown to anyone, Qutlugh Khan sat on top of a slope with an excellent view of the field. The emperor's cavalry went first. As they attacked the Kampili soldiers, the latter quickly formed a cluster with their shields facing outward, like a tortoise in its shell, and warded off the initial charge. When the horsemen charged again, the Kampilis split up to surround all the cavalrymen. There were some tussles but the cavalry was hemmed in. It was over in fifteen minutes.

Next it was the turn of the Kampili cavalry who attacked the front of the emperor's company. The Kampilis pushed hard, took some losses, but the pushing was so intense that the emperor's soldiers fell back. On this occasion, the trial was over in ten minutes.

Qutlugh Khan stroked his beard and asked Faraj to fetch him some water. A horseman galloped up and presented him with the results. In the tent-pegging exercise, the Kampili cavalrymen took twenty-six pegs against the emperor's men's eleven. In the sword fight, ninety Kampili soldiers had 'blooded' the Emperor's soldiers well before the time limit. As for the cavalry charge, the results were plain to see. Qutlugh Khan mused about how Malik Zada was right. If it had not been for the fact that the Kampili soldiers were weak with hunger, they would have beaten the emperor's men at Anegundi. He attributed it to the skill of the brothers and their ability to train relentlessly and lead their men from the front.

It was pleasantly surprising, he thought, how Hakka and Bukka were so similar to the emperor and Malik Zada. Though he had to concede that Hakka and Bukka were arguably better at doing more with considerably less, it forced a smile. Malik Zada had always been able to pick winners and was unerringly right.

Thinking about it, the final piece now fell into place. The only reason Malik Zada won in Anegundi was because King Kampiladeva was demoralized and the army was hungry. They tried to break out of the fort without much drive and for whatever reason (perhaps because the brothers opposed parts of the plan), both Hakka and Bukka brought up the rear of the column. Despite fighting with a group of starved soldiers, they very nearly broke through. Luck was with Malik Zada that day. The greatest prize he unearthed that day was when he captured the two brothers. Qutlugh Khan reminisced for a moment about what the emperor's father—Emperor Ghias-ud-din-Tughlaq—used to say:

'My greatest treasure is not in the treasury. All of it sits in my Privy Council.'

There was a reason the emperor had proposed the tasks at the last meeting. He was using them as a tool to get the two brothers incorporated into a structure ready for a campaign. Yet there was more to it. The emperor, Sultan Muhammad-bin-Tughlaq, was an intelligent man and he, Qutlugh Khan, could vouch for that. But if he asked Qutlugh Khan to be their teacher, to incorporate the brothers into the imperial structure, he was plainly thinking of bigger plans. The emperor depended on Malik Zada's recommendation, given his implicit trust in his general and childhood friend, even if they did not always agree.

Qutlugh Khan departed the grounds where the military games had taken place. He was working with capable men and for that he was grateful. The brothers were undoubtedly exceptional generals. They left little to chance, and whatever surprise they encountered, they were adept at innovating. Bukka was a little more reserved than his elder brother but both were men he would trust. He had an ability to see through personalities and he trusted his instinct on this. All that Faraj had told him was confirmed by his own eyes. The brothers complemented each other like Jauna (as Muhammad-bin-Tughlaq was called by those close to him) and Malik Zada when they were young boys. Still, he kept wrestling with his task.

It was clear to him that he was dealing with two exceptional generals. He had seen this before, and he had the ability to identify that undefinable skill in exceptional generals. Ghias-ud-din-Tughlaq had it, the emperor had it, and Malik Zada had it. In their own way, they would take measure of the enemy and the battlefield, and wrest a victory out of rapidly changing circumstances.

He could recommend that the brothers be given command of an army right away. While he expected Jauna to accept his recommendation, what worried him was the faction of almuminin bihaqin, the so-called true believers. In their minds, all the emperor's actions ought to be about the glorification of Islam—of which they were the self-proclaimed arbiters. Amongst this group, he had to make sure the vipers, the vazir and Malik Zandvakili, did not get to use the two brothers as an excuse to thwart the sultan again. Giving the brothers the command of an army too soon would do just that.

No, for now, the brothers would act as advisors and help prepare for the upcoming campaign. He would prepare them for the future and the opportunities it would invariably bring. And, once the needs of the campaign were clear for everyone to see, he would be able to override the opposition of the almuminin bihaqin and bring them in. He was satisfied with his decision.

Many other voices

'I must see the brothers,' the man insisted. The guards were not going to let him enter the camp until he told them the nature of his business. Relenting, he finally told them, 'I need to ask them how they like the weather in Daulatabad.' The guards doubled over, howling with laughter.

'They like it just fine, Mr Merchant, so you can leave.'

Soon there was a small crowd of soldiers who were laughing at the expense of the poor man. Shamshed was supervising horses having their shoes replaced when he noticed the gathering and came up to see what the commotion was about. The soldiers stiffened up, but had grins on their faces.

'Meladhikari (boss), there is a man who wants to ask the semanyas if they like the weather in Daulatabad.' Something seemed amiss, and Shamshed enquired as to the man's business. He claimed he traded horses. Only then did Shamshed realize that this might be the person Karthikeya had met when he was previously in Daulatabad. He asked the trader to accompany him to Bukka and Hakka. When he saw the brothers, the man introduced himself at Kazi Rahim Rahmatullah, before repeating his enquiry about the weather in Daulatabad.

Recognizing him as the contact mentioned by Pattu, they quickly attended to business. He gave the brothers what news he had. Pattu had taken care of their requests and all was well with the men's families. He was going to bring a sack of mohurs that he had converted from Kampili coins to those minted by the sultan. The men in the various outposts were doing well. News from the couriers was that Malik Zada would be in Daulatabad in a week. He was riding with a small group of men and making good time. In a hushed tone, he said he heard from the vazir's officers that there was a concern that the brothers were going to be given command of the campaign against the Koli kingdom and the minister of defence felt he was losing control. They were actively considering how to prevent such an outcome, preferring one of their maliks to lead the effort instead.

'It seems like they are looking for ways to make sure that Malik Zada's victories are minimized,' Kazi Rahim Rahmatullah warned.

'Minimized in what way?' Hakka asked. Kazi Rahim Rahmatullah had enquired but could get no more information from his source.

Makhduma-i-Jahan (Mistress of the World)

When Qutlugh Khan started to work for the emperor's father, who was then the governor of a small fiefdom, he had come to know the dowager queen. A Jat from the Punjab, she was the first wife of Ghias-ud-din-Tughlaq and came from straitened circumstances, just like him. All through his life, she was a wife who was a partner, and he always sought her counsel. As a person she was gregarious but shrewd. With his long acquaintance, Qutlugh Khan had been accepted into the family and was allowed to visit the harem. Qutlugh had lost his wife many years ago and dedicated himself to the service of the family: first as a general, then as a close advisor to Ghias-ud-din, the first Tughlaq emperor, and finally as the teacher of the heir apparent. Even now, though she was older than him, they enjoyed meeting and conversing about the well-being of the emperor.

The attraction of being able to eat at the kitchen managed by the dowager queen was another reason he visited frequently. There were few places in the world where he could have eaten better food. When she drank her sherbet in the afternoon, there would usually be sweets and savouries on offer. Qutlugh Khan walked through the large entrance into the harem and noticed she was speaking to a large number of women and handing out clothes. When he spoke to the guards, the dowager queen immediately recognized his voice and greeted him, 'Subhanallah, Qutlugh Bhai, come in.' She dismissed the women and asked them to come back later. With Qutlugh Khan by her side, the two walked into a large courtyard. She had flowers in vases all over the harem. It was strange how a blind woman was so drawn to beauty.

As they were deep in conversation the maids in the harem began bringing in the usual procession of delicacies. Qutlugh Khan was not going to be disappointed: sambusas, pakoras, halwas and chiwdas were all on offer. He kept helping himself although he knew he had to leave shortly. As they ate, she leaned over and whispered, 'Have you been hearing the rumours?'

'What in particular, sahiba?' he replied in a soft voice.

'The vazir is stirring up the ulema because he thinks Jauna might be in a weak position. And, of course, it all relates to how Jauna is too complaisant about the idol-worshippers.'

'Sahiba, that is an old one he's tried before.'

'Qutlugh, Jauna is weak and has used up a lot of his political capital, so I worry that he is vulnerable.'

'I will watch out and let you know what I find,' Qutlugh Khan reassured her.

He stood up, offered his adaab to her and thanked her for the treats. She giggled and said, 'I know the way you time your visits, Qutlugh.' Both of them began to laugh. 'At least when Ghias-ud-din-Tughlaq was alive, you ate every meal with us. Now I do not get to see you so much, especially after coming to Daulatabad. You must promise to come and see me more regularly.'

'I will, Makhduma-i-Jahan,' he promised.

'Qutlugh, it was a request,' she said.

'Of course. I know. It's just so easy to tease you, sahiba.' As he was about to depart, there was a flurry of bodyguards securing the space in the courtyard. The emperor entered with his usual relaxed gait and walked over.

'*Ya eazizi almaelim* [my dear teacher]!' the emperor exclaimed as he bent down and touched his feet and offered an adaab. Only then did they embrace.

'Isn't it about time you gave up this practice?' Qutlugh suggested.

'Ammi would complain that I was getting arrogant if I did not,' Jauna replied, smiling. This was a window into their relationship very few ever got to see.

'Why are you leaving?' Jauna asked.

'To attend to business that must be taken care of, my emperor.'

'Well then, let's have dinner together soon: Ammi, my family and Ahmad [Malik Zada Ahmad-bin-Aiyaz] and his family, when he is back next week.'

'As you wish,' Qutlugh said with a smile.

'Now, let me eat some food from my mother's kitchen and get some of the more recent gossip, including what I am sure you've passed on,' the emperor joked. She was the most well-informed person in the land.

Cornucopia

Just as news came that Malik Zada was going to arrive in the city the next day, a basith arrived. Bukka recognized him because he was wearing the regalia of Malik Zada's corps of command: a green vest with a purple headdress. The basith rode in with a contingent of the sultan's guards. The message stated that the general would be occupied for the next three days attending to the emperor and spending time with his family. On the fourth day, he invited the brothers and their generals to attend a gathering at his palace. The guards would come two hours before sunset to escort them.

'I like the grandiosity of it all,' Hakka remarked. 'Being a king, with a big harem and lots of gatherings, would suit my disposition well.' With that he lay back against a tree in the garden. Since it was a day of rest (taken every tenth day), he was drinking kallu. Bukka laughed.

'Why is that funny?' quizzed Hakka.

'Because managing a harem is not what I think you would be good at. It's not the same as managing an army,' quipped Bukka.

Hakka doubled over, laughing, and said, 'I'll leave you to manage the harem, that way I will not deal with the problems!' He roared out loud. Bukka was glad to see him relaxed and in a good frame of mind.

On the fourth day, an escort arrived. Along with the guards, Faraj had come to accompany them. They greeted each other with the camaraderie of soldiers who had endured harrowing experiences together. The palace they rode to was in the city and not in the fort where Malik Zada lived with his family. Malik Zada used the opportunity to have the generals and senior courtiers meet Hakka and Bukka and their officers. Two exceptional singers from Dilli were going to provide the entertainment and Hakka was already excited in anticipation of the proceedings. Never one to be diffident, he asked, 'Will there be any kallu?'

'Semenya Hakka, Malik Zada would not live a day without a good quantity of wine. So, yes, there will be very good wine, and lots of it,' Faraj replied. Hakka looked forward to the prospect of good music and lots of wine. He wondered if there would be fine young women in attendance.

When they reached the entrance of the palace, Malik Zada greeted the brothers as they dismounted from their horses. He put his hands around their shoulders and also welcomed Shamshed and Karthikeya, before ushering them up the steps to the large reception hall. They were given towels to wipe their hands, cotton coverings for their feet after they had taken off their shoes, and each of them was presented with a golden cup that was filled with sherbet by a beautiful young slave woman. There were thick cushions laid out in a rectangle around the room that was filled with the smell of incense and jasmine. He accompanied the men to their seats and sat down beside Hakka and Bukka, with the translator sitting right behind. The singers that evening were Sarabanu Begum and Mian Tanras Khan.

Just as they sat down, they noticed Qutlugh Khan sitting opposite them. Nodding his head in acknowledgement, he gave an adaab. Trays full of golden tumblers were brought over and

Malik Zada explained the three kinds of wine on offer that evening. It was a small and exclusive gathering with drinking being a key part of the event.

'If you are ready, we will start,' Malik Zada said to Hakka and Bukka. He stood up and welcomed everyone, pausing briefly as he looked at Qutlugh Khan. Raising both his hands up, bent at the elbow with the palms upwards, he announced to his guests:

'That my *ya eazizi almaelim* is here to enjoy this makes me happy, especially since his understanding of music is so deep and it is something that touches his soul. Alhamdulillah [praise be to God].' Just then a tall lady dressed in a red ghagra with a diaphanous shawl draped over her head, walked to the side of the rectangle where three musicians were seated. She was about fifty years of age, beautiful and elegant.

Noticing their awe, Malik Zada whispered, 'Her voice is even more seductive than she is.' The lady sat down and spoke quietly to the musicians. She told the audience she was from the 'Qawwal Bacchon Gharana' or the Dilli school of Hindustani classical music. Looking at Malik Zada and Qutlugh Khan, she softly asked if she might begin. They nodded, to which she subsequently raised her hands with her palms held up and said, 'Subhanallah.' She informed the audience that she would start her first piece in the raag malkauns, the oldest of the raagas.

Nobody moved for the two hours she performed. When she finished, her audience stood up and clapped enthusiastically with the customary vaah-vaah (bravo). Malik Zada presented her with a large gold tray heaped with clothes and fruits; draped over the clothes was a beautiful necklace that was once worn by the queen of Kampili.

Neither of the brothers missed that detail.

Hakka requested another drink. He told himself that getting emotional in the raw world of power, where victors of wars were the arbiters, was pointless. Bukka added one more comment to his impression of Malik Zada: brazen.

Mian Tanras Khan was markedly different from the first singer. Short and rotund to the point where he measured more sideways, he waddled into the hall to take his seat. Going through similar greetings and introductions, he began singing. His voice had the character of a huge banyan tree. It was rich, incredibly deep, and he sang with a fierce devotion. Yet again, the audience was enthralled except this time only their ears were involved.

Immediately after the music, Qutlugh Khan left. Malik Zada said he came only for the music. He never stayed for anything that might smack of impropriety. It was only when the dowager queen invited him that he stayed longer.

The attendees sat at dinner under a huge gazebo in the gardens. The pilafs, the roasted meats, and the many-flavoured vegetables were an experience that transcended even the rich fare at the palace in Kampili. Hakka, whose sweet tooth got the better of him, insisted on trying everything.

Lest this get out of hand, Bukka insisted that they leave after dinner, despite requests from Malik Zada to stay a while. As they prepared to depart, the horses were brought over. Hakka looked Malik Zada in the eye and said:

'Your opposition is gathering information on you and they will likely use it sometime soon.'

Malik Zada stopped in his tracks. His eyes grew wide.

'Your abilities impress me. I do thank you for your warning.'

As the brothers left with the guard that had accompanied them, along with Faraj, Shamshed and Karthikeya, they pulled back from the contingent so they could speak quietly to one another.

'I am not sure if he will be a good ally,' Hakka muttered, 'but he's the best we have, for now. Given the circumstances, it makes sense to protect your ally for the time being.'

Being tested at a trial

Just how relative the word 'soon' was, became immediately obvious. Early next morning, Faraj rode to the camp. He was perturbed. The men were awake and getting ready for a day of work. The emperor's guards accompanied him, which raised the tension. Hakka and Bukka were ordered to present themselves to the Diwan-e-Khaas at ten o'clock in the morning.

Faraj relayed the bad news.

'The qanuni [law enforcement officials] have come with me and they are under the instructions of the emperor to see if you have hidden any valuables in the camp.'

Bukka noticed Hakka's brows beginning to knot up and decided to take the initiative.

'I will take them to our quarters and show them all we have.' The qanuni were a severe looking group, wearing black uniforms. Bukka motioned them towards the quarters. They immediately surrounded him with their swords drawn. His men saw this and reacted in kind. Suddenly the emperor's guards, the qanuni, along with Faraj, Hakka and Bukka, were all surrounded by a few hundred Kampili soldiers. Bukka paused for a moment before commanding his men with the word 'birali' or let it be. He told them to put their weapons away, which they did. But he refused to tell them to disperse, so that he controlled the situation.

Walking into his quarters, accompanied by Hakka, Faraj and the qanuni, Bukka called out for Shamshed.

'Bring us all of the gold we have, Shamshed.' He asked the qanuni to accompany Shamshed so they did not get the impression there was anything to hide. They came back with the sacks of gold.

A tall officer aggressively confronted Bukka and said to the translator, 'How do we know this is all of it?'

Bukka smiled.

'You have a donkey's ass for a brain. If we were going to hide some of it, we would not tell you. If you think there is more, go work for it, you lazy dolt.'

Bukka invited him to search the whole camp. No more was found. Once that was done, he demanded all the gold be counted with a declaration and witnesses attesting how much gold was found and handed over willingly. The man respectfully agreed. Bukka let him proceed with his search, leaving Shamshed to supervise.

It was time for them to ride up to the fort for their meeting with the emperor. Surprisingly, Faraj was told they could ride up to the Diwan-i-Khaas. With a few minutes to spare, they were ushered in and passed Malik Zandvakili, who looked smug as he sailed past them. Both Hakka and Bukka were shown to a small room next to the hall. It was heavily guarded as if to intimidate them. They were asked to wait for the vazir. The brothers glanced at each other and knew what was likely to transpire.

It was not long before a few guards came into the room with a scribe and an accountant, led by the vazir. There was no exchange of greetings. Instead, he quickly got to the point.

'There are suspicions that you might have appropriated gold from the treasury at Anegundi or, for that matter, appropriated gold from Malik Zada. We request a list of everything you remember in the treasury. I will leave you with the accountant and the scribe who will take notes. You are expected to finish this task in an hour, after which your evidence will be presented to the emperor.' He left abruptly.

The brothers sat for a while and then Bukka called for the translator. As they were waiting, he looked at Hakka.

'Two-tenths or three-tenths?' he murmured, meaning the portion Malik Zada probably kept for himself out of the eleven carts they left behind.

'Three parts seems more likely. The man is not a saint,' Hakka replied.

Even as a child, Bukka used to be teased for his prodigious memory. Since the treasury and its contents had been his responsibility, he was easily able to remember the contents. He divided them up into categories: gold and silver coins, large gold objects, gold bars, silver bars and jewellery.

For each of these categories, he estimated the weights. He had loaded up about five manns of gold in each of the five bullock carts and the rest they left behind for Malik Zada. The total left behind came to eighty manns; Bukka decided on declaring a total of sixty-four manns, and dictated accordingly.

Walking into the Diwan-i-Khaas, Hakka and Bukka were told to approach the emperor. Malik Zada, who was visibly angry, joined the brothers. Qutlugh Khan was present too and took his seat.

The emperor spoke.

'I have never questioned my maliks about the plunder taken in war. If I trust them with my army, then I trust them to return to the empire what they find.' He smiled and added, 'Sometimes a few mohurs get lost, don't they, Malik Zandvakili? However, the vazir raised a serious charge that had been brought to him. I have asked the vazir to bring this case in front of us so the Privy Council can render a verdict for me to judge.'

'My emperor,' the vazir began, 'many reports have come to us after the capture of Kampili. Among those are claims that Malik Zada appropriated a major portion of the treasure in the Anegundi treasury. So, as a first test, I had men measure the amounts that Malik Zada personally delivered to you and that delivered by Hakka.'

'To you, vazir, he is a malik,' the emperor interjected. The Vazir bowed.

'I then asked the other malik,' the vazir went on with elaborate punctiliousness, 'for an estimate of what he thought they left behind after emptying the treasury. My accountants have given me an account of the treasure tendered in this scroll, and here,' the vazir held another scroll aloft, 'I possess the other estimate by Bukka.'

'Well then, tell us how your calculation compares with Malik Bukka's estimate. If you have not seen the second estimate in the scroll, please give it to me. Go ahead and tell us what you have.'

'My emperor, the two lots of gold amount to seventy manns.'

The second scroll was handed to a scribe at the foot of the throne. The emperor ordered the scribe open the scroll and he read out Bukka's estimate of sixty-four manns. 'It appears we owe Malik Zada some gold, then,' the emperor said. This seemed to unsettle the vazir. Not to be distracted from his objective of cutting Malik Zada down, he revealed that he had additional information.

'Then go ahead!' barked the emperor.

'When the qanuni searched the Kampili camp, they found nearly a mann of gold that the Kampilis seem to have kept for themselves. The guards tell me that they have just brought it over.'

'Then have it brought in.'

'Have the bothers really failed the test?' wondered Qutlugh Khan. He considered this problem for a moment but was convinced there was likely to be a good explanation.

It took two guards to bring the five bags of gold. Hakka noticed Malik Zada's forehead knotting up.

'Explain to us where you got this gold, Malik Hakka,' the vazir asked in a contemptuous tone. 'Does this not belong to the emperor? Should you not have handed over this as well? Instead, it seems you decided to keep some of this treasure for yourself.' He glanced at a doorway and two glowering giants of the vazir's police force appeared behind Hakka, ready to lay hands on him.

Qutlugh Khan stood up and was about to speak when the emperor leaned over to the vazir and spoke to him softly:

'Perhaps we let him answer before you decide to put him to the sword, vazir?'

This caught the vazir off guard again. There was silence as he tried to regain his composure. He had hoped that the emperor's habitual impatience might give him the upper hand in the argument, or at least dent the credibility of the brothers, since he was unable to dent Malik Zada's bona fides.

'Please come up and explain,' the vazir said pointing aggressively at Hakka. The two policemen melted away.

Bukka stood up.

'I was responsible for the treasury at Anegundi. When the treasure was transferred to Malik Zada, my brother was suffering from a battlefield wound and was not there at the handover.'

'If that is indeed the case, malik, where did this gold come from?' the vazir's harsh voice rang out.

'Vazir Khwaja Jahan, we picked up this gold and silver at Mattur. There were hidden supplies and gold in a few locations around the kingdom.'

'That is a convenient ruse you seem to have created,' the vazir sneered.

'Actually not, dear vazir,' Bukka replied confidently, knowing he had the argument under control. He was going to use it to discredit the vazir.

'Do you have any of the gold coins that Malik Zada brought or those that Malik Hakka handed over to the emperor?' Bukka asked the vazir in a soft, respectful tone. He made sure to look at the emperor, Malik Zada, Qutlugh Khan and the others in the Privy Council.

The emperor gestured to one of the guards to bring one of the sacks Hakka had willingly surrendered at the Diwan-i-Aam. It was opened and the vazir pulled out a coin.

'So, what does this prove?' he enquired.

'If you were to get a coin from the other sack, we can make a comparison,' said Bukka.

With both coins in the vazir's possession, Bukka asked, 'Vazir Khwaja Jahan, what is the difference?'

'None!' he declared with contempt. He then burst out: 'You are wasting the time of the emperor and the Privy Council.'

'This will just take a few more minutes,' Bukka said persuasively. 'Now, if you compare these coins, what differences do you see?' It now felt as though the vazir was the one being interrogated.

'The ones from the camp are smaller,' he stated, still unaware of the path Bukka was leading him down.

'What about the dates on the coins,' questioned Bukka. The vazir inspected the coins.

'The dates on the coins from the camp are from twenty years ago, while the coins Malik Zada and Hakka brought over are from three years ago.'

'Thank you,' said Bukka. He stopped for a moment and then asked another question. 'Do the small coins from the camp have any marking other than the date?'

'No,' the vazir replied.

'And what markings do the larger coins have?'

The vazir shrugged his shoulders and said, 'Kampili, of course.'

Bukka looked at the emperor and said:

'My sultan, I think this shows that the coins in the camp were not from the treasury. None of the coins that we delivered to you, or those that Malik Zada brought, are similar to the coins found at the camp. Thus, if they are different, it proves we did not take it from the treasury in Anegundi.'

The vazir interrupted as he stood up, 'You knew which coins were in which sack and you just picked those off and made up this clever explanation. That hardly exonerates you or your brother.'

'Vazir Khwaja Jahan, I was not in the treasury when the gold was packed. I was a good distance away from the carts when they were loaded. The sacks were all sealed with Malik Zada's insignia. Furthermore, the only sack that we opened was for expenses prior to recovering the other coins. Between the soldiers doing the loading and those that were guarding us before we set off for Daulatabad, there were at least a few hundred witnesses. I hope this shows you these were not coins from the treasury that someone alleged we took. And that is all, my sultan.' Bukka performed a namaskaram, bowed and stepped back.

'Come forward, Malik Bukka,' the emperor commanded. Bukka walked to where the vazir was. The emperor was stroking his beard and his eyes were thoughtful. 'Why did you have these coins in Mattur, and what proof do you have in Mattur? You do know we could establish that quite easily.'

'My sultan, your first question was about why we had these coins in Mattur. It is a matter concerning military tactics that the king of Kampili and Hakka decided to have a cache of weapons and gold in a few locations in the kingdom. Just in case we were forced to retreat after an engagement, it was necessary to have arms and funds elsewhere to regroup. I did not know the location of the Mattur cache, my sultan. It was only the king, the minister of the army and General Hakka who knew the location and what was available.'

'Malik Hakka, where exactly is this in Mattur, so we can put the vazir's investigation to rest?'

'Mattur is a few miles beyond a ford on the Tungabhadra River; it is a village your men can find easily. Exactly two miles to the west, there is a small collection of huts. It looks like a small settlement that a large farmer might have. While some soldiers with a few animals are stationed there, no one else ever goes there. Should anyone plan to visit the site, I will have to give them a means to identify themselves, as the soldiers are tasked with protecting the site. It should be clear to see that inside one of the huts the floor has been dug up.'

The emperor was curious by now.

'How many of these locations do you have, Malik Hakka?'

'Five in all, my sultan.'

'And you know the location of all these places?'

'Yes, my sultan. Every one of them. A small army needs to be nimble and have resources for contingency plans. Most of these little encampments are run by reliable scouts who take turns to be on the lookout. However, none of them know what exactly is cached there.'

'Vazir Khwaja Jahan, obviously you must complete your investigation,' the emperor declared as he sat back on the cushions of his divan. 'You will get all the information you need about the location of Mattur and the other camps he talked about, and have the soldiers bring back the coins and supplies they find. I expect that the coins are going to match. Your men will be accompanied by an officer from Malik Zada's army and an officer from the Kampili army. Once we have determined the outcome, you have one last task.'

There was a silence that seemed interminably long. Stroking his beard, the emperor announced:

'Your task is that you identify those that brought forward this frivolous complaint. I will have an independent set of qanuni conduct the inquiry. Once that is done, and it confirms what we know, the troublemakers will be put to the sword at the Diwan-i-Aam.'

Yet again a thick pall of silence fell on the room.

The emperor looked at Qutlugh Khan and said:

'You know, qazi, the coins are smaller and they have no markings except for the year they were minted. It makes sense—if you are a retreating army and have to move into alien territory, or if you want to make sure you do not put your people in danger when they use the money, then these coins would be perfect. If such coins are found on someone, they have no identification marks and are from a long time ago. The person can always say the coins were part of a family inheritance. Look at them: they all appear old. There is a lot we can learn about planning from Malik Hakka and Malik Bukka.'

He turned to the assembly.

'The inconvenience to Malik Hakka, Malik Bukka and Malik Zada is regretted,' the emperor declared as he stood up and concluded the discussion.

In between

Qutlugh Khan was a regular visitor over the next few months, coming to see the brothers at the camp and the training grounds. Occasionally he would invite them back to the garden where they had first met. He saw them once or twice a week, usually arriving unannounced. Malik Zada would send them letters to check that the brothers and their men were taken care of. Over this period, Qutlugh Khan asked them to increase their training efforts. The number of men they were now training was close to ten thousand. A few large camps were set up close to their own. It was, in effect, a little city in its own right.

There were rumours aplenty. Needless to say, their primary source of information was Kazi Rahim Rahmatullah, Pattu's contact. To the surprise of the brothers, it was accurate and frequent. The king of Kampili's informants at the sultan's court had run dry, and after a while they were cut off. But Kazi Rahim Rahmatullah never failed to amaze them.

Whenever Hakka and Bukka enquired about the cost of his services, he merely said that he was indebted to Pattu and this was his way of expressing his thanks. It was only now they began to realize that Pattu had in fact built his own commercial empire and collecting information was crucial to the way he did business. The question that lingered was, how extensive was this empire? It was also intriguing because Pattu was a part of their extended family. He came from deprived circumstances and had lost his own family when he was a young boy. Sangama (Hakka's and Bukka's mother) had taken him in and always treated him as one of her own. The tables had now turned, and over the last few years it was Pattu always making sure that they had the resources they needed. He was their eyes and ears. Now his informant, Kazi Rahim Rahmatullah, was the one who was keeping the brothers abreast of developments.

Three days had passed since Kazi Rahim Rahmatullah visited them. He reappeared on their rest day, after dark, bringing some fine kallu, with news of home and the happenings in court. He was quickly becoming a welcome guest. Sitting on the divans with Hakka and Bukka in the courtyard of their house, he gave a vivid description of what had passed.

The inspection at Mattur panned out as expected. All the directions and details Hakka had provided were found to be true, which enhanced the brothers' stature in the eyes of the sultan. The vazir was under pressure because he had to reveal his source and since it was all made up by him and his cronies, he was in a bind. That was exactly what the sultan wanted.

Malik Zada was being considered for a governorship in one of the twenty-three provinces but had requested an assignment at court. It was believed he might replace Malik Zandvakili as the head of the sultan's army but many in the Privy Council opposed this as they saw his behaviour as bordering on apostasy. How could somebody like Malik Zada be a true defender of the faith? That seemed to be the argument being presented by the conservatives in the Privy Council.

Meanwhile, the sultan was getting intermittent reports that the Mongols might be planning another attack in the north, though he had been hearing these reports for a while and nothing had transpired.

The last issue of which Kazi Rahim apprised them was very consequential. The campaign against the kingdom of the Kolis with the objective of defeating King Naga Nayaka, which the sultan had mentioned, was now being planned.

'Do you have any information as to how soon they want to proceed?' enquired Bukka.

'Semenya, what I hear is that decisions are being delayed by various factions at court. They are also waiting to see the progress of the men in training and whether they are ready for war. So, to answer your question, perhaps it will be three months before soldiers will be required for action.'

Kazi Rahim Rahmatullah finished his kallu and departed.

The brothers remained quiet for a while, sipping their drink. Hakka was the first to speak.

'This raises so many questions about how we should proceed.'

'Actually, much has been resolved, if all the information he gave us is accurate,' was Bukka's response. Hakka looked at him quizzically. Bukka explained his reasoning.

'Undoubtedly, the sultan wants to subjugate the Kolis, but there is a potential threat from the north and that has always taken precedence over all other issues. It makes sense that the sultan will wait to get better information about the north, and then decide about us.

'Then he is likely to deal with the faction that thwarts his plans. He has to do that, given the fact that he needs people to get things done. And the one person who gets his plans executed, Malik Zada, is also the one the conservative faction dislikes. The sultan will clip the wings of the vazir, and maybe he will do that by making Malik Zada the minister of defence.

But it will depend on how much he can push the true believers. It's no coincidence so far that Malik Zada is constantly sent out on campaigns: it's the best outcome for the sultan. That way he keeps Malik Zada out of sight of the conservative faction. All of his shenanigans are away from the eyes of the "true believers", or at least they're not so obvious.

'Yet, if he was at court, to what extent would the sultan have to temper Malik Zada's behaviour and, more importantly, can Malik Zada temper himself to take on the responsibility? And then, to manage and govern a large army is different from leading a campaign out in the field. Once the sultan commits to having him in court, reversing the decision will only cause him to lose political capital.

'Malik Zada's love of luxury is another issue. He likes a lavish lifestyle and can afford it on campaigns. At close quarters, it will become glaringly obvious and how would he finance it? Even in this case, it was only because you forewarned him that he was able to cover for any shortfalls. Hakka, without Kazi Rahim Rahmatullah forewarning us, the situation could have become truly dangerous for him and for us,' Bukka said.

'This makes it clear that we had better be ready for a campaign,' Hakka observed. 'The question will be, who leads it? Are we going to be taken along and made to do the dirty work? Could it be true that they might allow us a free hand with the conduct of war?' Hakka stopped as he mulled over the endless possibilities.

'It all depends on what we are being tested for,' his brother responded. 'Learning what we have to teach them is only part of it. Qutlugh Khan has something in mind, and perhaps Malik Zada too. It cannot be that they want us just to be involved in the campaign against the Koli kingdom. And what's more, is subjugation of the Kolis enough? For whatever reason, are they thinking of overwhelming *all* their opponents? They need to realize that the Marathas are fearsome warriors and independent-minded—with that lot, it could be a bloodbath.'

Hakka's face was no longer pensive and thoughtful.

'To some extent, they know what they are up against, Bukka, which is why they went around the Koli kingdom and took on the kingdom of Kampili first. Remember, we were smaller and they knew that whore Ballala would keep harassing us from behind. I am convinced that was part of the deal they made with him: harass us from the rear while they got ready to attack us at Anegundi and catch us off guard. After he was no longer useful, they pursued him and the Hoysala kingdom, which was light work.

'Malik Zada was clever enough to realize that once he had the Kolis isolated and exposed from all sides, the odds would be significantly better. Now that he has the conditions set up, he needs help to put the final piece in place.'

'Is that all, Hakka?'

'For now, there are two things they want to know,' Hakka said. 'First, are we truly capable of doing bigger things? Though we gave them a beating in Kummata on two occasions, they overran us in the end at Anegundi. I realize that even on the third encounter we gave them a scare, but defeating the Kolis will be more important because Malik Zada can show the beautiful tapestry he has woven together for the sultan in the southern part of India. Of course, it is the sultan's plan but it would be Malik Zada who achieved it. It will also end the criticism about moving to Daulatabad and will help enhance the emperor's stature at court. It's the final piece, and Malik Zada also needs a victory to secure himself against his enemies.'

'And what is the second?' asked Bukka.

'We need to demonstrate that we can be trusted and will be loyal.'

'And what is the second?' Bukka asked again jokingly, wondering if his brother might have had a little too much kallu. Loyalty seemed a given, if they were going to be trusted with an army under their command.

Hakka laughed, guessing at his brother's thoughts.

'Despite the kallu, Bukka, I am still keeping track of all the moving pieces. The second conundrum is something I can only guess: if the first issue works out to their satisfaction, they will want to use us for something else. At least that is what Qutlugh Khan has in mind. While Malik Zada can only think two steps ahead, Qutlugh Khan plans well in advance. For him, the major question will always be how he can put the empire on a secure foundation for the sultan. That has and always will depend on the people surrounding the sultan. That is why they need long-term loyalty from us. So, the first matter is mostly about Malik Zada and second piece of the puzzle is reliant on Qutlugh Khan.'

The air had turned dry and cool. It was getting late but both realized that they needed a deep understanding of what was likely to happen and be as prepared as possible.

'At the very least,' said Bukka, 'we need to start gathering intelligence about the Kolis and make sure that we have a clear idea of how their army is set up. It will also require an ear to the ground to know of developments at King Naga Nayaka's court. It's time for us to send Karthikeya's scouts to the kingdom. I'll order a group to collect any information that's readily available so we can start working with the hard facts. Then another group will infiltrate the capital, establish contact with our old connections and learn about their training techniques. We already have a decent knowledge of their military commanders. The only way we can win is to outwit them. Otherwise, it will be a bloodbath as they will not give in easily.'

Hakka nodded in agreement and gave his approval.

Over the next few weeks, Bukka hid himself away with Shamshed and Karthikeya, and planned every last detail for their spies chosen to go to the Koli kingdom: organizing horses for the men, the front they would put on, determining how the three groups of scouts would communicate with each other, and making sure they had sufficient money to go unnoticed.

Fortunately, all the men were not in the camp but had been dispersed around Daulatabad, so the absent spies would not be missed. For a while, Bukka considered sending Karthikeya too, but his absence would be quickly noticed.

He feared he was sending them on a very difficult mission. What had troubled Bukka, Shamshed and Karthikeya was the men's cover story. The only plausible front would be for them to act as traders who procured supplies from the dhows and were trading all the way down the coast to Malabar. Somehow this was just not coming together and he did not want them to improvise. Bukka was willing to delay instead of putting his men in a dangerous situation without the necessary resources.

Late the next evening, Kazi Rahim Rahmatullah appeared out of nowhere. He had a message from Pattu. The Kolis were aware of an impending attack and suspected the 'prisoner generals' would lead the charge. Moreover, the rumour within the military and the court at the Koli kingdom was that if the two of them led the campaign, anything was possible. They were already preparing for battle. The capital city was on a war footing and the main fort at Sinhagad had safely stored provisions and supplies in anticipation of a long siege in order to avoid a situation like Anegundi where the Kampili soldiers were caught by surprise. While it was not a large fort like Daulatabad, it was impenetrable. Sinhagad was located on a hill and the walls were high. The Kolis were buying more horses for the anticipated battle, and iron for their forges to manufacture arrowheads and other weapons.

Hakka enjoyed the compliment of 'prisoner generals' but thought it might be misplaced. This campaign was going to be a challenge like no other, with the enemy forewarned and one's own side not to be trusted while they had enemies in the court.

Hakka and Bukka asked Kazi Rahim Rahmatullah how they might create a front for the spies they were dispatching to the Koli kingdom. The answer was straightforward: he was putting together a supply train carrying a cargo of iron and a hundred horses, which were scheduled to leave in the next few days. The men could join the entourage. Kazi Rahim Rahmatullah refused to accept anything by way of payment from the brothers. His only comment was: 'I will only be fulfilling my debts to Pattu.' Before he left, they enquired about some maps of the kingdom. True to form, he did deliver them in a few days.

While the brothers had solved one major problem, they were confronted with a puzzle.

'Hakka, do you wonder about how big Pattu's trading operations might be? And do we know what he trades?' queried Bukka.

'I know just a little more than you, Bukka. I'd given him help a long time ago by serving as a reference so he could provide military supplies to the Kampili military. Then there was a question about whether his credit was good and I vouched for him. He did exceptionally well and earned the trust of the maharaja of Kampili—trust enough that the maharaja had placed gold deposits with him. I remember hearing later that he became a very influential banker in the kingdom and beyond. I think in the years that we were absent he built a military supply business in addition to a metals trading business. It may well be that our Pattu has conquered more territory than we were aware of!' Hakka said.

'While I consider him to be my sixth brother, he has put our interests above all else,' Bukka acknowledged.

'Don't forget that Sangama was the mother he never had— he has never forgotten that she took him in when he could easily have become destitute. When Pattu lost his wife, it was Sangama who raised his daughter, our niece, Valli. He was always the favourite son, Bukka. Not you, not I. It should come as no surprise that he treats both of us as his dearest family.'

'But, Hakka, to give us the kind of support he has, he needs to have significant means at his disposal. And that brings me back to the question: how large has his trading empire become?'

'If I were to guess, it's very large,' Hakka replied. 'Remember, Bukka, while Pattu was always a very modest person, he was also the shrewdest one. Whenever Sangama needed something, he'd get it. Perhaps, like us, he has become a general but in the world of business and trading.'

'At this distance, he still has us covered,' Bukka chuckled. 'And he knows unusual people like Kazi Rahim Rahmatullah, or employs them. They seem to shadow us and make sure every need is taken care of. How do I thank him on behalf of us and of Kampili?'

'You don't, Bukka, because Pattu does what a brother would do. Should you think otherwise, he would find it deeply hurtful.' Hakka paused. 'Why are you smiling?'

'It's just that Pattu was older than you by quite a few years, yet always treated you like you were the oldest brother.'

'It's because of my regal bearing,' grinned Hakka, which prompted the two men to laugh.

'He is a study in modesty, so it's easy to underestimate how intelligent and savvy he is,' Bukka said.

Later the next day at the training ground, Qutlugh Khan came by unannounced. There was no specific issue to be discussed or plans to be made. Hakka and Bukka just chalked it up to his need to keep track of what was going on and see if there was anything that needed his attention. He watched for a while, seeing how the men were being trained and as he left, he remarked, 'Be prepared to meet the emperor sometime soon.' With that, he was gone.

'What he means is the plan has been set. We'd better be ready to move soon. I just wish we had a plan to overwhelm Sinhagad Fort,' Bukka said.

What do you have for me?

They arrived in the Daulatabad fort in time for their appointment. Barely a few minutes away from where the Diwan-i-Khaas congregated, they saw Malik Zada ride towards them. Once greetings were exchanged, they made their way into the inner sanctum where the Privy Council was seated. Three divans were positioned at the side for Malik Zada and the brothers. The master of ceremonies announced the arrival of the emperor.

He took his seat at the head of the group, saying a perfunctory 'Subhanallah' before pausing for a moment to look at the brothers. To their surprise, he gave them an adaab. They reciprocated with a namaskaram.

'What is the order of business today?' the emperor asked Vazir Khwaja Jahan.

'My Sultan, today we give you a summary of the progress in training the troops and plans for the next campaign.'

'Proceed,' he said.

He then stopped for a moment, spoke to his musaeid (aide-de-camp), and asked the vazir to wait a minute. Returning with a long box, the musaeid held it out before the sultan, who swivelled in his diwan and looked at Bukka.

'I have been remiss in not giving you the honour of returning your sword that you surrendered to Malik Zada. I wish you many victories with it, Malik Bukka,' he said. The musaeid brought it over to Bukka, who accepted it with a bow towards the sultan.

'Proceed,' the sultan said, indicating to the vazir to start proceedings.

'It would appear, my sultan, that the plan to attack the Koli kingdom is to be presented by the two Kampili maliks,' said the vazir, not trying to hide the sneer in his voice. The emperor rubbed his brow, seemingly irritated by the tone of the announcement, but held off from commenting.

Glancing imperiously at the brothers, Vazir Khwaja Jahan called them forward. Hakka stood to the front, facing the emperor, but in the line of sight of the others.

'The Koli kingdom is ready for this attack from your army, my sultan. This campaign will require careful planning; many different groups will have to manoeuvre cautiously to overwhelm the fort. My plan is to use ten thousand men, whom we have trained.'

'That's all?' the vazir interrupted.

The emperor frowned. In a voice that was louder than usual, he said:

'Give this general, who has fought more wars than you have, the courtesy of laying out his plan. Should I feel I need your military insights, I will ask for them, vazir.' He turned to Hakka.

'Continue,' he said. Hakka bowed.

'However, as a ruse, we plan to also use the army that subjugated the Hoysalas—there are still about nine or ten thousand men making their way back to Daulatabad. We recommend they be used to draw away troops from Sinhagad Fort with a feint. They will approach closely and when it looks like they will engage the Kolis, the men will suddenly retreat. By repeating this action a few times, we hope to draw the enemy away from the fort. Consequently, we will employ a flanking action where our troops will come from behind and encircle the enemy.

'The next part of the plan is to use a battering ram we have fashioned with an iron head that should be able to break through the wooden doors of the fort, even though they are thick. We aim to have this campaign completed in three weeks, at the most. Two questions require the attention of the emperor and perhaps the Council. Firstly, is the objective total defeat of the Kolis or just their subjugation? Secondly, what will the command structure be?'

The emperor looked at Hakka pensively. He glanced at Qutlugh Khan and Malik Zada, prompting them to answer the question. Malik Zada went first.

'Why should it not be complete defeat?'

'Because a territory you have not ravaged and decimated is more likely to be a productive and loyal subject,' Bukka responded. 'Subjugation without festering animosity should be the ultimate goal. Besides, a complete defeat will mean we take very heavy losses as well, which is never a good plan.'

Malik Zada appeared surprised. No one ever spoke to him with such clarity and forcefulness. His eyes widened. Turning to the emperor, who nodded at him, he enquired:

'Why are you not using more men, and what is your chance of success?'

'The campaign will succeed if we are quick,' Bukka replied, 'and that is why we advise using the number of men stipulated initially. As for the second question, I will let Hakka answer it.'

Hakka stayed quiet for a moment. 'Three to one in favour of victory,' he announced.

A hushed silence descended on the room. The emperor tilted his head.

'What gives you so much confidence, Malik Hakka?'

'Several reasons, my sultan. For six months we have trained these soldiers. They are capable of waging war with devastating effect and know how to manoeuvre very well. We also need to remember that all of them are battle-hardened soldiers from the north, not fresh recruits that shit in their pants at the sound of the horns announcing the attack. If we move with speed, we will be able to overwhelm the Kolis, who have a very traditional approach to fending off attackers. While they are fearless fighters, they can be surprised with an unconventional approach. Finally, your army is better equipped than theirs, which makes a big difference.'

Nodding his head in agreement, the emperor prompted Qutlugh Khan to speak. He graciously stood up and walked over to the foot of the dais where the emperor sat and said to Hakka and Bukka:

'You are in command of this campaign. I will accompany you and if you need any help, I will give you what I can. But this is going to be an endeavour that the two of you will manage, execute and hopefully complete with a successful outcome. Your needs for preparation will be taken care of by me.'

It was obvious that the Privy Council, with the exception, of Qutlugh Khan and Malik Zada, were unaware of this strategy.

Both the brothers went down on one knee before the emperor and responded simultaneously: 'We pray we bring you success.'

The emperor looked at them keenly with a hint of a smile.

'Go forth,' he said. He stood up and signalled the conclusion of the meeting.

And into the fray they went

'Five days?' an incredulous Qutlugh Khan exclaimed. 'How are we going to organize supplies and prepare in five days?'

'Ten thousand well-trained men can work wonders in five days,' Hakka said. 'We will have the advantage of surprise. The moles in court can't get the Kolis forewarned in time.'

Qutlugh Khan responded with a wry smile.

'In five days then,' he said, and added, 'From now on, the only basith we will use is Faraj. He will come soon with gold that you will need for purchasing any additional supplies.'

'Could you arrange to have the soldiers paid before they leave?' requested Hakka.

Qutlugh Khan nodded as he cantered away on his horse.

Frenetic activity seized the camp. Within three days they were ready. Hakka gave the soldiers a day to rest and made sure the whole camp had a feast early in the day. Departing before daybreak, Karthikeya laid out the route for the four brigades of soldiers. The supply train had already left and was travelling south, and would take five days to reach the fort at Sinhagad. The soldiers however, marched west and then south in four different groups.

After the first day, they travelled at night. Scouts went ahead and neutralized the lookout positions of the Kolis. Each route was led by a scout who knew the path, and the travel plans involved keeping the men fresh and rested when they arrived at their destination. On the fourth day they set up camp in a forested area in the lowlands from where the fort was visible. Qutlugh Khan rode with Hakka and Bukka. As they set up camp that night, he made a cryptic comment.

'It seems like you are now fighting a very different kind of war. I will be interested to learn how both of you execute your strategy and handle the vicissitudes of the battlefield.'

Events played out the way the brothers had intended. Or maybe they anticipated every twist and turn that came their way and they had the gods sitting on their shoulders as they pushed forward.

Bukka rode off with an army of four thousand men before daybreak. Horses and men were gone in the blink of an eye. They went south to join up with Malik Zada's troops that had been heading to Daulatabad. Bukka's men would form the tip of the spear and face off against the Kolis. It would be mainly an infantry operation. Large shields that protected them from archers were used by the soldiers at the front end of the column, a few hundred men would orchestrate movement so they attacked and retreated as required, and four elephants with armour plates were positioned in front.

Bukka saw the smoke signal from Hakka's camp telling him to start in half an hour. He moved the drummers and the horn blowers to the front where the sultan's pennants were in clear sight. Just before he got the troops moving, he spoke to them.

Bukka stood up in his stirrups and, as loudly as he could, shouted:

'Today you fight for the glory of Sultan Muhammad-bin-Tughlaq. You fight for the glory of the empire. You also fight to make sure that once victory is in hand, peace will prevail. Make sure you fight with honour.'

The horns gave the signal and the drummers began beating their drums.

The march to the fort was about two miles. Moving forward at a quick pace they cut a fearsome sight. The ranks at the rear were not as closely packed as those in the front, to create the illusion that the army was larger than it actually was. The Koli army came out from the side of the fort in predictable formation. Archers were in the front with the cavalry and infantry behind them. Bukka presumed that the old Parulekar, the aging Koli general, was leading the opposition. It was the only strategy he used for a pitched battle, so he was going to follow the same formula.

Hakka and Bukka had choreographed the next moves and each soldier knew his role. The Koli column came out of the fort and arrayed themselves in the usual manner. They started marching towards their opponents. When they were about half a mile from each other, Bukka had his men increase the pace of the advance.

'*Sawf nufuz, sawf nufuz* [we will win, we will win]!' The chant rose in a war cry, keeping time with the drums and the thunder of stamping feet while the horns screamed accompaniment. The elephants led the charge. The Koli archers responded with volleys of arrows, but most of them hit the elephants whose armour protected them. Taken aback by their opponent's speed, the archers broke ranks, leaving the cavalry exposed. Just before the elephants reached the cavalry, the Koli army regrouped and moved forward again. The sultan's infantry engaged with them for a short period and then, prompted by a signal, Bukka's army started to retreat.

The sultan's soldiers moved backwards, adequately shielded to prevent losses, but making a lot of noise to suggest disarray in the ranks. The Kolis were convinced that they had the upper hand.

Bukka focused on ensuring that the speed of the retreat was deliberate and exactly as planned. If they gave ground too fast, they risked being overwhelmed. The drummers provided the beat to set the speed at which they retreated. So far, the losses had been minimal and Bukka hoped to keep it that way. He wondered if his timing was wrong.

Finally, he heard the horns.

Sunlight flashing off shields, spears and swords, a massed army came racing like a low dark thundercloud over a slight rise in the ground. The Koli army turned and stared, stunned. Hakka had come, leading his cavalry and infantry. The cavalry raced forward to attack the exposed flank of the Koli army and the infantry the rear. Bukka's army stopped retreating. It turned and attacked from the front and hit the other Koli flank. The two armies led by Hakka and Bukka had encircled the Kolis. Then they let the elephants loose. Once pandemonium had broken out in the Koli ranks, Bukka called the elephants back.

Parulekar was much too slow in reacting. His six thousand men had been encircled by ten thousand of the sultan's soldiers. The latter started to tighten the noose and the Koli forces were crushed. Parulekar realized there was only one option.

'*Amhi atmasamarpana karato*,' he called, which in Marathi was 'we surrender'. Parulekar's men started to yell it out over the din of the sultan's drummers. The Koli soldiers were ordered to drop their weapons and the cavalry was asked to dismount. Bukka's group formed a new circle for the defeated Koli soldiers to walk into. The clanging of the dropped swords and shields was followed by two hours of collecting these surrendered weapons and searching the men for small arms.

Bukka was amazed it had ended so soon and so easily.

He made his way to Hakka, who was with Parulekar, the Koli general, who had surrendered and was now being examined for wounds. They greeted each other. In a bitter tone, Parulekar said:

'I was warned that if the brothers were leading the campaign, the unexpected would happen and there was going to be no easy way out.'

After making sure that Karthikeya and Shamshed had matters in hand, Hakka asked for three horses and they took Parulekar to see Qutlugh Khan.

Qutlugh Khan was a man whose expression was normally severe and difficult to read. This time, however, he was wide-eyed when he met Hakka and Bukka.

Speaking to Parulekar through the translator he said:

'On behalf of Sultan Muhammad-bin-Tughlaq, my emperor, I suggest that you ask your king to surrender as well. If not, we will use your men to build an approach to the fort. Even if we do not, we can wait a few months.'

Hakka was more emphatic.

'Go to the front of the fort and speak to the king. Convey Qutlugh Khan's message. The king will have one day to respond. If he does not surrender, we will begin hostilities again.'

Though losses on the Koli side were low, they were even lower for the sultan's troops. It was remarkable in the context of a pitched battle. The tactic, executed with speed and skill by the men, had resulted in a swift outcome. However, there were two problems that the brothers had to confront. First, managing the prisoners of war; second, finding a way to get the king of the Koli kingdom to surrender and end the affair. It was still a fluid situation, and Hakka and Bukka were on the alert for anything that might go wrong.

Shamshed was given the responsibility of guarding the prisoners. There was always the possibility that they might attempt an escape. The army of Malik Zada's returning troops was designated with logistical duties and the sultan's men set about organizing themselves to ensure the Kolis were prevented from causing trouble. A perimeter manned by a few thousand soldiers was set up. Securing the victory was now as important as the planning that went into the battle.

Bukka left Hakka and Qutlugh Khan to manage Parulekar and the delivery of the message to the king. He had a bigger problem to deal with: how were they going to either get into the fort or subdue it?

The gradient leading up to the fort was treacherous. Bukka, Karthikeya and forty men slowly circled the fort. They were unable to get too close as archers lurked behind the defences. By late afternoon, they were nearly two-thirds of the way around the fort. Karthikeya heard one of his men shout: 'I hear water flowing and it's not clean. In fact, it smells really bad!' As they got closer, they realized that it was flowing out of a concealed earthen pipe.

'What do you think this is, Karthikeya?' Bukka asked.

'Well … it's not a sporadic flow; it's continuous.' Karthikeya paused. 'If that's the case, then there must be a continuous flow of water into the fort. It must be from somewhere that is higher than the fort.' They knew they were on to something promising.

They stood back and examined the fort. Behind the fort were two more hills. Once they had carefully scrutinized the fortifications and the contours of the area, Karthikeya spoke:

'Semenya, it is possible that there is a stream flowing down which has been diverted to the fort.'

'Let's find it!' Bukka smiled.

After an hour of climbing, they located the stream. As they decided to take a rest after the climb, one of Karthikeya's men called excitedly: a part of the water flow seemed like its course had been altered to form a small pond into which water from the stream flowed in and the excess flowed back out into the stream, 'Perhaps they divert water from the pond through clay pipes to take water to the fort,' said Karthikeya. Three men jumped in; the water level was only waist high. One of the men tripped as he walked across the pond and fell into the water.

He dove down and investigated what had tripped him. He came up and hissed out:

'Meladhikari, semenya, it's a pipe that sticks into the side of the bank!' He showed them the diameter of the pipe by making as large a circle as possible using the fingers of both hands.

'That is a large pipe and a lot of water flowing into the fort, if that is where it's going,' Bukka noted. 'That might explain all the water flowing out.'

Never one to leave something unverified, Karthikeya removed his sword and shirt and jumped into the water. He stayed underwater for what seemed like an age. When he resurfaced, he had a huge smile on his face.

'Semenya, it is a very clever arrangement. The only mistake the Kolis made was that they did not cover their tracks at the other end where the water flows out. They were hoping nobody would come close enough to see it. All we have to do is get a few buffalo skins and rope to cover the mouth of the pipe. Then it is only a matter of time before the king of the Kolis gets very thirsty. When should we do that, semenya?'

'Tomorrow morning, Karthikeya. Let's get back to camp, as I am sure there is enough to deal with over there.'

Closing the spigot

Bukka rode back and found all the tents set up, the guards posted and the place functioning like a well-managed camp. He was glad to see that the training had paid off every step of the way, from the time that they left Daulatabad.

Outside a big tent, he noticed Hakka's horse Kappu ('black' in Kannada) and Qutlugh Khan's horse, which was a beautiful grey. He dismounted and handed Chetana's reins to one of the soldiers. He took off her bridle and saddle, and spent some time rubbing her down and brushing her. Despite the days spent at a gruelling pace, she managed it impressively. Bukka thought to himself, 'When all this is over, I will run a horse farm, have many dogs and live on the land.' He stopped himself daydreaming and went to bring Hakka and Qutlugh Khan up to speed with the latest developments.

He walked into the tent to see the two men deep in conversation.

'We were talking about reasonable terms of surrender and the conditions to set for a vassal of the sultan,' Hakka said.

There was a pause before Qutlugh Khan spoke.

'Yet, that might not be immediately relevant as it's possible that the king will try and hold out in the fort. He still does have that option.'

'Not for long,' Bukka asserted confidently. Both Qutlugh Khan and Hakka were startled.

'What do you mean?' quizzed Hakka. Bukka told them about the discovery of the water supply to the fort.

'If it were shut off tomorrow, the fort would be unable to continue for much longer. Thus, a siege would be short-lived.'

The brothers had never seen Qutlugh Khan smile so widely.

Since the meeting was to take place at the door of the fort at ten in the morning, they decided to cut off the water supply at daybreak. As Qutlugh Khan stated, 'We will be instructing the king, and not negotiating.'

Sewer rat

'I will take the responsibility of speaking to the king,' Qutlugh Khan told Hakka, Bukka, Karthikeya, Shamshed, Faraj and Abdul Ghaffar, who were all in the tent. Karthikeya had just returned to let them know that the water supply was shut off and would stay that way. Qutlugh Khan continued, 'It's not that you both do not have my trust.' I want the king to see a face that is more representative of the sultan. Besides, the two of you are much too young for something like this.' He laughed. When they suggested that a contingent of armed guards accompany him to the meeting point with the king, Qutlugh Khan refused.

'Then I will go with you,' said Hakka.

'No, I'll go alone and get this done. Besides, there is little to negotiate. If he does not want to be thirsty, he will come to his senses, Inshallah.'

About fifteen minutes before the meeting, Bukka positioned a thousand soldiers in front of the gates of the fort. Qutlugh Khan prepared to walk up the steep approach to the gates, accompanied by his interpreter. Bukka broached the topic with Qutlugh Khan again:

'Perhaps both of us could accompany you.'

Qutlugh Khan put a hand on Bukka's shoulder and said with a smile:

'Shaqiq, it is not as dangerous as you may fear. This old horse can still carry a load.'

Suddenly they heard a noise at the fort's gates. Bukka warned the soldiers. If the enemy swarmed out, his men were to come up to the front in formation and someone would scoop up Qutlugh Khan and take him to safety. Then they would get ready for an attack. He also had a thousand soldiers out of sight in reserve, which surprised Hakka when he was told.

'After all we have managed with this campaign, Hakka,' his brother stated, 'I do not want to let it slip away. This bird is in a cage and I would like to keep that cage in another cage.' Hakka just snorted at his younger brother's caution, though he knew well enough not to countermand him.

The wicket gate set in the vast gates opened and a few guards came out. It was reassuring that it was a small door that opened and not the large one. Colourfully dressed, they appeared to be bodyguards, and were leading a few horses. The men moved aside as the king and a few others appeared. Bukka and Karthikeya remained on high alert. There were fifteen men placed in different locations monitoring the fort to ensure there was no unusual activity. Halfway up the steep road leading to the fort, Qutlugh Khan met the king along with their interpreters. The conversation began, with the king seemingly objecting to Qutlugh Khan, judging from the rapid movement of his hands. As they continued talking for a few minutes, Bukka's eye caught a glint of light from the ramparts, close to the gate. Two figures stood up and, in a flash, he realized what was going on.

'Qutlugh Khan, *oopar dekhiye* [look up]!' he screamed. Two archers took aim, but Qutlugh Khan had spotted them. He jumped to his right just in time but was hit by the second arrow, which appeared to strike him in the chest. Bukka was already galloping towards him with the reins of Qutlugh Khan's horse in his hand, Karthikeya in swift pursuit. Bukka, crouching down on his horse, screamed the Kampili battle cry, '*Hanuman nannage sakti nidali!*' In an instant he was beside Qutlugh Khan, who had been hit again in his left thigh. Bukka brought the horses around to give cover to Qutlugh Khan and tried to lift him but he was too heavy. The grey mare screamed as an arrow hit it in the rump. Bukka leapt off Chetana and Karthikeya assisted him in getting Qutlugh Khan onto Chetana.

'Get moving,' Bukka shouted at Karthikeya, who obeyed. Bukka mounted the injured grey mare and set off. The archer took another shot. Bukka attempted to dodge it but was hit in the thigh. With an arrow in his thigh and an injured horse, Bukka was in trouble. He urged the horse on, slapping the reins against its side and shouting at it to move. As soon as they were out of arrowshot, he jumped off the horse and handed the reins to one of his soldiers. 'Have its wound taken care of,' he ordered. Then he limped back a little to stand before the fort. He drew his sword and screamed loud enough for the Kolis to hear:

'The king of the Kolis is a sewer rat and I will make sure he meets the fate deserving of one.' The pain in his leg was blinding. He heard, as if from a vast spinning distance, Hakka's voice: 'We need to make sure that the arrows are not poisoned.'

Darkness descended.

The soldiers threw Bukka onto a horse and carried him off to the hakeem's tent.

Qutlugh Khan was losing blood heavily when the soldiers laid him on the ground. The main concern was how deep the arrow head had gone and whether it was poisoned. The hakeem gave him a dose of opium and once Qutlugh Khan became drowsy, eight men held him down so the hakeem could cut open the wound near the collarbone. The arrowhead had broken the collarbone and pierced through another two inches. He carefully put his hand in and eased the arrowhead out. He walked out so he could inspect it in better light. 'This one is not poisoned but it does not mean the others are not.' He set the bone, cleaned the wound and made sure there was no more damage. The wound was closed with a few stitches.

He moved to the left thigh and extracted the arrow.

'This one is from a different archer,' he mumbled. He examined it and exclaimed, '*Hai Allah!*' convinced that the arrowhead was poisoned. He cleaned the wound, and mixed and applied an antidote salve before bandaging the wound. He left Qutlugh Khan to sleep.

Bukka was also losing blood. The hakeem pulled the arrowhead out and confirmed it was poisoned as well. He treated the wound and ordered those in attendance to evacuate the tent with the exception of his attendant. He told Hakka that the patients would sleep for the next day or two. They must continue receiving opium, especially Qutlugh Khan, so the healing would have begun before they woke up.

'Expect both men to have a high fever for a day or two. With Allah's grace it will recede. If the fever breaks, they will have beaten the poison.'

The second day came around and the two men were still running a high fever. That night the hakeem disconsolately said: 'The fever should have eased at midday. I am very worried.' Both men were delirious. Qutlugh Khan was frothing at the mouth. A distraught Hakka sat outside the tent, resting his back against one of the bamboo shafts. Drained by anxiety, he fell asleep.

Hakka was interrupted in his sleep by a sudden jolt. As he opened his eyes, he saw the hakeem's face close to his. Hakka feared the worst. Then the hakeem's face broke into a smile.

'Alhamdulillah! The fever has broken for both of them! They are awake and can talk to you.'

Grim realization

Hakka spent most of his time waiting around the tent and checking in to see how the two patients were faring. While his mind wandered, it also became clear to him that his brother was the one who made the army tick. Bukka's abilities, Hakka realized, were unrivalled. His brother was responsible for training excellent men such as Karthikeya and Shamshed and their subordinates. The army did not work quite as seamlessly with just Hakka in charge.

Meanwhile, Qutlugh Khan and Bukka were recovering slowly but their legs turned blue and they were in incredible pain. Hakka's anxieties were made worse as they reported a terrible burning sensation which felt like their legs were on fire. The hakeem was at the end of his resources.

Strange things happen. The next morning Karthikeya barged into Hakka's tent—something he never did when Bukka was well.

'Kazi Rahim Rahmatullah is here and he wants to see you immediately,' Karthikeya blurted.

'What?' Hakka exclaimed before composing himself and ordering Karthikeya to bring him.

Hakka walked out of the tent and saw that Kazi Rahim Rahmatullah was accompanied by a very small man.

'Subhanallah, Hakka,' Kazi Rahim Rahmatullah said.

'What in God's name brings you here?' Hakka asked.

'Pattu instructed me to bring a vaidyan to you. He heard that the Kolis used poison in their arrows and was worried that one of you or your soldiers would pay the price.'

Hakka shook his head in amazement. 'So, what about it?'

'This vaidyan is one of the few who might be able to make an antidote for the poison.' Kazi Rahim Rahmatullah indicated his companion.

'What's your name?' Hakka asked.

'Pratapa Sharman,' the little man replied.

'Let him speak to the hakeem, and then they can tell us what they want to do.' Hakka turned to Karthikeya, who was hovering nearby. 'Please take him there.'

Once they were gone, Hakka, in a state of utter disbelief, asked Kazi Rahim Rahmatullah how he knew they needed a vaidyan.

'Pattu simply told us to go to the scene of the battle, which we knew was the fort at Sinhagad. He was concerned that you or Bukka might get wounded. As he put it, "The two of them lead from the front," which is always dangerous. When an informer said the Kolis were using poison, he sent us here as quickly as possible.'

'How long did it take you?' asked Hakka.

'We've been riding for three days, semenya. We would have arrived sooner but Pratapa Sharman has never been on a horse before and kept falling off. I was worried I might need a vaidyan for the vaidyan!'

Pratapa Sharman could speak Kannada, so for once, communication was easy.

'The hakeem has been very effective in treating the wounds but his ointment has not neutralized the poison. With your permission, I would like to open their wounds to put a salve on them.'

'Do you know what this poison is?' quizzed Hakka.

'It is one of two poisons that would have this kind of an effect. So, yes.'

'Can you heal their wounds?'

'If Eeswara wills it, the antidote will work,' Pratapa Sharman replied. 'I must get to work immediately but I need a few things as quickly as possible.' He rattled off a list of items and ended with a request for some gold. Hakka grew furious and Kazi Rahim Rahmatullah was dumbstruck.

'If you heal them, you can have all the gold you want,' an irate Hakka replied, upset that someone would ask for payment in a situation like this.

The little man smiled.

'I need it to make the antidote, semenya. I do not need any payment. My work is for Pattu who saved my life. All I want to do is return the favour.'

Hakka was moved by the reply. He took off the gold chain from around his neck, which his mother had given him, and handed it over.

'I may need to use it all up as that big man has more poison in his system,' the vaidyan said. 'Find me fresh neem leaves and flowers, and tulsi leaves. I need a good cook too. Bring me a lot of hot water, some sandalwood and someone to make it into sandalwood paste,' Pratapa Sharman said and went on to repeat the rest of the list. 'Finally, I require some incense.'

Men were sent scurrying around to find the herbs and ingredients. Hakka was struck by a thought.

'Make sure to find out if any of our men who were wounded in the battle are suffering from symptoms of poisoning. If they are, tell them they will all get the same treatment.'

Over the next two days they realized what a little tyrant Pratapa Sharman was. He established a small hospital where he was treating Bukka, Qutlugh Khan and eighteen soldiers suffering from the effects of poison. After three days, Hakka's guard informed him that the vaidyan in the tent next door wanted to see him immediately. Hakka's stomach knotted up. He quickly changed and walked over to see both Qutlugh Khan and Bukka sitting up.

The room was filled with an array of scents: tulsi, neem, sandalwood and, of course, incense.

Though they were both able to talk, both men seemed weak.

'In one week's time the effect of the poison will have worn off completely and their recovery will be swift,' Pratapa Sharman said.

Bukka noted how the burning feeling in his legs had disappeared and that he felt stronger. When Hakka inspected their wounds, he could see they was healing well. Qutlugh Khan appeared much stronger, too. He asked everyone but Hakka to leave.

'You saved my life,' he said, staring at Bukka before turning to Hakka, 'and then you saved my life as well! Allah has graced me with two young men who are even more talented than the first two that I taught. I will forever be grateful for your loyalty.' There was little else to say after that.

Hakka left the tent to see Pratapa Sharman standing outside and smiling.

'Would you like to see your soldiers, semenya?'

Walking towards the other tents, Hakka was tempted to ask the vaidyan about his association with Pattu but thought the better of it. Remarkably, the eighteen men in Pratapa Sharman's care were doing as well as his brother and Qutlugh Khan.

Out of curiosity, Hakka asked: 'How much gold did you use for the treatment?'

'All of your chain, my ring, and seven gold mohurs that Meladhikari Karthikeya gave me.' He paused, feeling the need to explain, 'The karshayam [potion] that I make needs gold powder to counteract the poison by absorbing its chemicals. I fed each patient the karshayam six times a day. That took a lot of gold. In fact, I will need some more tomorrow if you can organize it.' Hakka, deeply impressed by this small man with an outsized presence, smiled and nodded his head.

Will this work?

A week had passed. Hakka went to visit the patients as usual. His noisy entrance woke them up. Sitting by their side was the inimitable Pratapa Sharman. Thanks to the vaidyan and the efforts of the hakeem, Bukka and Qutlugh Khan could stand up and walk without help.

'They should go back to a normal diet but continue to consume the karshayam for a few more months, but at a lower dosage,' the little man said. 'And the sultan,' he added, pointing to Qutlugh Khan, 'has had his bone set by the hakeem. I recommend he gets a massage with a thailam [herbal oil] every day. If Eeswara wills it, those injured will make a full recovery in a week.'

Hakka was going to have to find a way to thank him appropriately.

It had been ten days since the Kolis surrendered on the battlefield. Hakka was exhausted trying to keep up with everything that required attention. It was not just that he missed Bukka taking up so much of the workload; he missed having his brother around as his sounding board. 'Get well soon, Bukka,' he kept muttering to himself. Calling for Karthikeya, he asked for his thoughts as to why there had been no sign of surrender at the fort.

'If they have no water, they should be dying of thirst by now. If they have not capitulated, Karthikeya, either the block you put in place is not working or they have another water source. Maybe they have wells in the fort which might be enough.' Hakka stared at Karthikeya searchingly.

Karthikeya was accustomed to dealing with Bukka, but now here he was dealing with Hakka, whose style was completely different. Bukka was deliberate and patient. Hakka, on the other hand, was impatient and would think about many things at the same time and talk about them at once. Karthikeya decided his best approach was to present all the information to him, as he would to Bukka, and not lose confidence.

'Well, semenya, there is no water flowing out from the fort. The likely scenario is they have a large tank where the water from the stream flowed in. Only when it was full did it overflow and carry away the sewage. Even if they had a well, there would still be some water flowing out. But there is nothing, semenya. I'd be surprised if they didn't surrender in a few days.'

Hakka was impressed by Karthikeya's response. The officer compiled his facts like Bukka. Hakka smiled and thought to himself that there were no officers he could claim to have moulded the way Bukka had.

'Let's give it another day and re-evaluate, Karthikeya. In the meanwhile, send out a party of your best scouts and have them investigate the fort again. Tell them to ride around it and perhaps they might pick up something new.'

Hakka had his lunch and checked in on the two patients. They were missing and so was the vaidyan. Curious, he asked the guard about their whereabouts. The guard smiled and pointed. To his surprise, Hakka saw the two men confidently walking outside and laughing.

'I wonder what these two poor souls are so happy about,' he thought. He picked up his pace and caught up with them.

'Hakka, look at the fort,' Bukka said pointing towards it. There were three white flags fluttering on the ramparts. Qutlugh Khan raised his open palms upwards toward the sky and, smiling, said, 'Alhamdulillah.' They could hear, in the distance, the roar of celebration coming from their soldiers who were posted all around the fort.

Hakka unsheathed his sword, raised it to the sky and bellowed, '*Sampurna geluvu*, Bukka [Complete victory, Bukka]!'

What next?

Grizzled, tired and defeated, the king of the Kolis stood in front of Hakka, Bukka and Qutlugh Khan. He did a namaskaram and then conceded:

'I am you prisoner, so tell me what my fate is.'

'I respect the Koli people and I respect the king of the Kolis,' Hakka replied. 'I do not respect what you did during the surrender negotiation, but my view is that you still deserve the respect due to a king. That would be the honourable way. The final determination will be made on the recommendation of the advisor to the sultan, Qutlugh Khan. You will ride with us as king of the Kolis until we present you to the sultan.'

Karthikeya and Shamshed were to be in joint command of the fort and the kingdom. Hakka was riding back with Qutlugh Khan and Bukka, who were still recovering. Despite their objections, Hakka asked Pratapa Sharman and the hakeem to ride back with them to Daulatabad. They rode out with a guard of honour to see them off in a victory parade. Since Bukka was riding behind his brother, with Shamshed and Karthikeya flanking him, Hakka could hear his brother going through a list of directions and instructions. He finished by saying: 'Remember that the two of you are in command here. This is a large army and you have a fort full of women and children who will be captive there for a month. Be fair, be firm and make sure that your decisions are taken jointly. You are ruling now in the name of the sultan.'

Meanwhile Qutlugh Khan, wincing, was trying to remove his sword belt. Faraj assisted him. Then he pointed to his dagger, and Faraj got that off as well. Qutlugh Khan called to Shamshed and Karthikeya. When the two officers approached him, he asked them to dismount, and he handed his sword and the dagger to them.

'These are the weapons of the emperor, Sultan Muhammad-bin-Tughlaq. By giving you these, I am giving you the authority to rule in his name for the period you are both in command. Be just and be brave in handling this responsibility.' With that, he turned his horse around and shouted in his booming voice the command:

'*Falnarkab* [Let's ride]!'

The other side

It was the end of October and the weather was pleasant, the air was dry, and a gentle breeze blew all day. Riding in these conditions was enjoyable. Since Malik Zada's convoy was still making its way back to Daulatabad, messengers were sent to make sure that camps were ready to receive them as well. Bukka gave his couriers a constant stream of directions while simultaneously receiving information on the state of affairs at Sinhagad. It felt strange doing this with the king of the Kolis riding in front of them.

On the ride north, the king told Qutlugh Khan that the archers were the work of renegade generals and it was not something that he had ordered. Qutlugh Khan's droll response was, 'Let me see if that's what I find out.' Hearing this, Hakka wondered how this campaign would impact Bukka and him, and whether managing the Koli kingdom would be another assignment for them. He hoped not.

They kept an easy pace, which rose with every passing day. Bukka and Qutlugh Khan were improving in health and their wounds were healing rapidly. The hakeem and vaidyan were convinced the poison was neutralized.

'If the poison was still in their system, they would not be healing as well as they are,' said the hakeem. Pratapa Sharman, hearing the translation, agreed and nodded his head vigorously. Yet, it was a painful effort riding in a debilitated state for both Qutlugh Khan and Bukka. Whenever Hakka asked his brother if he was feeling strong enough to ride, he'd look at Qutlugh Khan and say, 'The grand old man is managing, so why should I complain. He suffered greater injuries.'

Twelve days later, they finally made their way to the outskirts of Daulatabad. The effort Qutlugh Khan made to ride back was driven by sheer grit. Moreover, Faraj attended to him with a devotion that was heart-warming to see; a son could not have done more.

As the road turned past a copse of trees, they could see Daulatabad Fort. Turning further left to complete the bend in the road, they saw a company of cavalry, with the emperor's pennant fluttering over it, advancing towards them rapidly at a full gallop. At the head of the company was the emperor, riding hard, flanked by two bodyguards. He seemed hellbent on covering the distance between him and the returning soldiers as quickly as he could. It was difficult to miss the ease with which he sat in his saddle.

As he got closer to the returning army, he yelled out, 'Mudaris [my teacher]!'

Qutlugh Khan raised his hand and answered, 'Sultaana [my sultan]!'

The emperor leaped off his horse, walked up, took Qutlugh Khan's hand and kissed it.

'I feared that your injuries might incapacitate you to a greater extent. Allah has been kind. Now let us make sure that you heal your wounds, and get well soon.'

Turning to the brothers, the emperor smiled warmly.

'Malik Hakka and Malik Bukka, my mudaris has communicated to me his admiration for your great skill as maliks. And he has told of your great loyalty of which he is a beneficiary. *Niemat Allah*: may Allah's blessings be with the two of you.'

Book 2

Rajya: Kingdom

4

Going home

Later in 1331, on their way back from Dilli to Anegundi in Kampili via Daulatabad

The northward caravan

Prostitutes and policemen, cobblers and dhobis, the vazir and the Privy Council, as well as the sultan, made their way back to Dilli. The entourage appeared to be never-ending. It was a transplantation of the occupants of Daulatabad back to Dilli. Informed of the rebellion in Multan, the sultan saw the need to attend to it personally for fear it would spread. To the 'true believers' their return to Dilli was a victory. They felt the sultan gave up on Daulatabad as a capital city as it was not capable of managing the needs of an empire, much less the demands of an expanding and powerful one. Tongues were wagging, not least because it gave that faction the upper hand. Another rumour circulating was that the sultan disliked the warm, dry weather. For these reasons, the sultan was moving to Dilli.

Qutlugh Khan took a more balanced perspective.

'To begin with,' he explained, 'it's most likely that there will be a capital with a subsidiary city to manage the demands of the empire. Second, the sultan needed to be in Daulatabad to understand the southern part of his empire and work on consolidating the area. It's quite likely that he will go back and forth, much to the dismay of the "true believers" who prefer their lazy lives in Dilli. But for now, they might have overplayed their hand.'

The journey north took them the better part of four months and to Bukka it seemed a poorly organized and wasteful exercise.

What did the sultan have in mind for them? For a year and a half in Daulatabad, including the Koli campaign, they had been under Qutlugh Khan's wing but were still not sure what fate awaited them. A powerful emperor could play a cat-and-mouse game with his subjects. Here they were, parted from their men, being taken along to a place very far from familiar lands.

'Could he not have just sent orders from Daulatabad and saved the effort of going north,' Hakka, half joking, remarked to Bukka, as they rode in the long, winding procession. 'Emperors think differently and that is why you sometimes have difficulty understanding my reasoning,' and broke into a loud laugh. Hakka liked his own sense of humour.

Meanwhile, Bukka realized that a decision was being made, which was part of a broader reconfiguration of the chaturanga board. The sultan simply needed more time and, perhaps, more information. This was proven to be true when the next day the basith sought out the brothers to join Qutlugh Khan. They rode through a cordon of bodyguards to where Qutlugh Khan was riding by the sultan's side.

The emperor spoke clearly and concisely.

'I want your views on the southern part of the empire. Tell me your opinions on what we can do to make our army more effective. You have shown how efficient an army can be with good leadership. For the next few days, join me and my mudaris so we can discuss these issues.'

In the ensuing weeks, after the sultan said his noon prayers, the brothers joined him and Qutlugh Khan in the onward journey. His clarity of thought and the precision of his questions were evident. The conversations or the questions were varied, including topics such as the crops raised in various areas, taxation systems, marriage rituals and recruiting sipahis for the army. Yet his most common question was, 'What should a good emperor do?' The sultan had an encyclopaedic knowledge, with a memory good enough to rival Bukka's. It was obvious that the sultan was not only eager to learn but also wanted to hear their thoughts.

He was a gifted raconteur with vast experience. He talked about his experiences managing the royal stables for the Khilji dynasty, and how he made a break for his father's iqta, Dipalpur, riding six days non-stop from Dilli.

'That was only possible because I fully understood animals. If you cannot care well for your animals, you do not deserve to have them,' he said. He recalled how his mudaris refused to start a riding lesson until the horses were brushed, their tackle and hooves cleaned, and their bridles and saddles comfortably in place. Since the day Jauna and Malik Zada started to learn riding, their teacher made it their responsibility to feed and water the animals every day.

One day the sultan said, 'The four of us should go out for a morning ride on a few horses that I've just acquired. You will appreciate how graceful these fine beasts are.' And so, they started their morning rides. At the end of their ride, he removed the saddle himself and spent time stroking the horse's face and ears, and talking to her. If only the horse knew who was lavishing all this affection on her. Though an emperor, this was a man who cared deeply. That only made the conundrum of deciphering his personality more difficult because of all of the contradictions.

He wanted to know what was so unique about urukku steel that made the blades of their swords so pliable and strong. He would ask, 'Did you have a talented mudaris who taught you military craft and your religion?' He would ask them about the food they ate growing up, and how it compared to the food they were now eating. It usually prompted more questions: did they drink? What kind of women did they consider beautiful? And did they have an appreciation for art? The men conversed for two or three hours every day. It was exhausting. One afternoon, Qutlugh Khan stayed with the brothers after one such session. He was amused, knowing full well what they were feeling.

'Ever since he was left in my care as a seven-year-old, he has always been like this. To this day, he can recall the answer I gave to a question he asked then. It never fails to amaze me. The part that you do not see is his devotion to his Hindu mother; he is a loyal friend and confidant, and an incredibly funny person when he's with people he knows. He has shortcomings too— he possesses a fierce temper and is impatient. But Allah must have intended to make him that way for a reason. I believe this because I could never beat these bad qualities out of him.'

A question had been forming in the back of Hakka's mind. As he rode alone with Bukka one morning, he blurted it out:

'It keeps nagging at me why the ulema and the mashaiks do not like him. From what I see, they are looked after. And if they create too much trouble, why not just have them put to the sword? That should teach others to behave and stay in line.'

Bukka was silent for a few moments. Finally, he offered his explanation.

'The ulema and the mashaiks are politicians; they speak to a large following and have an audience that is much larger than what the sultan has. So, executing them would create a backlash of public opinion.

'As to why they dislike him—the sultan knows as much about Islam as they do, if not more. No holy man likes to have to debate. They want to make pronouncements rather than answer questions. When the sultan leads Friday prayers, with greater authority and depth of understanding, it creates insecurity.

'Moreover, insecure people tend to gossip. That, I think, is what might be happening,' Bukka concluded.

'I agree with all of that,' Hakka said, 'but there's one thing you are missing in your analysis. There is history at work here. When Ghias-ud-din Tughlaq ascended to the throne in Dilli, he made sure that associates of the usurper Khusrau Khan disgorged all the gold and treasure that was given to buy their loyalty. Khusrau Khan had thrown open the treasury to them. One person whom Khusrau Khan gave gold for loyalty was the saint of Dilli, Shaikh Nizam-ud-din Auliya. Ghias-ud-din-Tughlaq ordered him to return it as a gift back to the treasury. The saint did not heed the command of the newly installed emperor and that started the strained relations with the ulema. But Ghias-ud-din Tughlaq was clever and in his early years as emperor he successfully neutralized the ulema.

'But his successor Muhammad-bin-Tughlaq was very different. As you said, he knew the whole theological library, chapter and verse. The ulema was outclassed. But, unlike his father, he is not a canny politician. He was not dependent on them, and let them know it. Traditionally, a sultan, due to his own ignorance, would give them a wide berth. With him looking over their shoulders, they discovered that they were checked and constrained.

'Making matters worse, this sultan, like his father, is tolerant of other religions. In fact, the dowager empress is a Hindu. So, the ulema uses surreptitious ways to get back at the sultan: whisper campaigns and compliant proxies in the Privy Council. The lesson I learn from all of this is that while the sultan's word is final, do not be surprised if you get bitten by the scorpions in his shadow as you carry out his commands,' Hakka finished. He looked at Bukka.

'Why are you smiling at me, Bukka?' Hakka demanded.

'I was not aware of your deep understanding of the history of the House of Tughlaq,' Bukka replied, still smiling.

'I am deeply aware of the history of my immediate surroundings,' Hakka retorted.

'That still does not explain your deep understanding of such fine points of history,' Bukka observed, as he looked quizzically at Hakka.

'I learned about all of this from the hakeem, Behrooz Behrooz, who treated you at Sinhagad when you were injured. He is personal physician to the dowager empress and steeped in the history of the family,' Hakka admitted, and burst out laughing.

Encountering a marvellous aesthetic

Qutlugh Khan personally escorted the brothers, accompanied by Faraj, to their new home when they got to Dilli. It was in the neighbourhood of the imperial palaces. A small house, surrounded by an exquisite garden, it gave them their first impression of Dilli. Enormous doors led into a courtyard where a beautiful fountain flowed in a soothing whisper. At that moment, both brothers realized they had encountered another civilization with all its exotic accoutrements. How could humans create such an astonishing effect? The bold geometry of the stone, the complementing gardens and plants that softened the visual impact, and the background of the calming fountain left Hakka and Bukka in a trance. The simple elegance was enchanting.

'Faraj will stay and help until you get settled,' Qutlugh Khan said, and quickly left.

A dignified old man in a green tunic made his adaab and welcomed them in Urdu. He introduced himself as Mansoor Ali, their khidmatgar (butler) and showed them around the house. From every room in the quadrangle surrounding the courtyard it was possible to see the trees in the garden outside and hear the seductive whispering of the fountain in the courtyard.

The imperial palaces were located in the township of Jahanpanah, which was arranged in concentric circles. In the centre was the imperial complex of three palaces set in a gorgeous round garden, like three gems in a beautiful necklace.

They were built of red sandstone, offering a pleasing contrast to
the green of the grass and plants. The circle around the imperial
complex housed members of the Privy Council, distant relatives
of the royal family, and guests of the empire. Though serene and
peaceful, it was very well guarded.

Faraj told the brothers that Dilli was in fact a collection
of four cities: the old Dilli where most of the Hindus lived,
Siri where Sultans Ala-ud-din and Qutb-ud-din had resided,
Tughlaqabad which was named after the current sultan, and
Jahanpanah, the town in which they were situated. Just as Faraj
launched into a description of Dilli and its various features,
they heard the muffled beat of the drum announcing evening
prayers. He would continue 'after prayers, perhaps,' Faraj said
and rushed off. The house suddenly went silent. The mosque
must have been fairly close, as they could hear the muezzin.

'Well, at least we know that we don't have to worry about
losing our heads. However, we are not sure what the emperor is
thinking,' Hakka said in an exasperated tone. 'If only he made
up his mind and sent us on our way.'

'Hakka, the only thing we do not know is the nature of the
assignment. He is not planning to take us on the campaign
to Multan. He will put down the rebellion on his own. Malik
Zada is riding ahead to get ready for the military campaign.
The task cannot be in Dilli as he has courtiers crawling out of
every nook and cranny and generals that could populate any
town. Perhaps, then, we are intended to go to the Koli kingdom
or farther south.' Bukka thought before adding, 'Whatever the
decision, it's not a choice that we make.'

For the next month, the two brothers lived a life they had
never imagined. They rode to different parts of the city with
Faraj. They visited several mosques and ate halwas in the

markets. They spent hours at the sprawling market next to the great reservoir Hauz-i-Khas. It was fascinating: a place where one could buy anything from camels to carpets. Faraj told them that at one point, soon after the conquests of the early sultans, male and female slaves were sold in this market. In the evenings, they heard singers who rivalled the ones at the feast Malik Zada had organized in Daulatabad.

Frequently, Qutlugh Khan accompanied them to observe the army's preparations for the Multan campaign. The rebellion had caused the emperor a good deal of grief. It was led by Malik Bahram Aiba, a compatriot of his father, whose son was a close friend of the sultan. Nobody had foreseen it. To the sultan, it was an act of treachery and his infamous temper had gotten the better of him. Only the blood of the treasonous Aiba would restore the sultan's composure.

Qutlugh Khan showed the brothers maps and plans for logistics and battle tactics. He wanted their opinion of the final training. There were intense conversations and debates between the three men. Hakka and Bukka repeatedly asked Qutlugh Khan to make sure the battle plans were more than a numbers game. Throwing fifty thousand horsemen at the enemy and expecting a favourable outcome would not work. Qutlugh Khan smiled. Finally, he stopped them in their tracks:

'I wish you could build all the plans for this battle but unfortunately you have other tasks to attend to.' He said no more on the matter.

Alongside the discussion of the planning of the campaign to suppress the rebellion, Hakka and Bukka learnt Arabic from Qutlugh Khan. There never seemed enough time to master the language, but over the next year, they managed to master the basics. On Qutlugh Khan's suggestion, they converted to Islam.

In his sage voice he said, 'Learn the rudiments of the religion. It will help you understand us even better, and will help the sultan with his plans.'

The imperial 'I'

Muhammad-bin-Tughlaq decided to stop in Dilli to review the army's state of preparedness before launching the expedition to suppress the uprising in Multan. He also examined the machinery of the empire to ensure it would function smoothly while he was away. Preparations progressed at pace and in the last few days before his departure, the planning and the preparations became more intense and frenetic.

All the activity came into focus at the last Privy Council meeting. Qutlugh Khan sent word to Hakka and Bukka to go to the Diwan-i-Khaas palace just after noon prayers. They waited two hours to be summoned.

The sultan had his sights trained on two people: the vazir and the minister of defence. Qutlugh Khan was worried because the sultan's temper was already simmering. When it rose, its effect was ferocious. Thumbing his prayer beads, he prayed for Jauna to be calm and hoped they would conclude this meeting with no loss of blood.

The sultan commanded the minister to approach the platform in front of the throne. In Dilli, the throne was a huge divan made of solid gold, encrusted with emeralds, and topped by a large silk awning.

The sultan stared at the minister of defence before revealing that he would, from this moment, be the zabitah of a small territory near Jajnagar. The minister began to feel dizzy. He knew where Jajnagar was and realized he was being consigned to the dustbin of the empire. The minister wondered if he should risk protesting. He stood up, but before he could speak, the emperor in his clear voice ordered the minister to leave for his new post immediately.

'You should be out of Dilli by nightfall. Subhanallah.'

The emperor nodded to his bodyguard, who walked over with three others to escort the minister out. Qutlugh Khan was the only member of the Privy Council who was not surprised. Everyone was now on edge.

Next, the vazir was asked to come to the platform. The emperor spoke to seven of the seated members before doing so, not including Qutlugh Khan in this speech.

'My sources tell me,' the emperor barked, 'that at Friday prayers the ulema view the emperor's return to Dilli as a defeat. According to one of them, Allah has chastised me for having moved everyone from this God-chosen and sacred location on the banks of the Jamuna. Another says that it is clear that I am lenient in my dealings with the idol-worshippers. Some mashaiks have referred to me as a half-breed since my mother was born a Jat Hindu from the Punjab. Frequently, I have asked that you attend prayers on Friday at the mosques, and speak to these religious leaders to stay away from making wild and baseless claims. Yet you seem unable to do this. I will make this request to all of you on the Privy Council for the last time. Make sure to address this problem before my return from Multan. Perhaps I need to think of reconstituting the Privy Council with those who will adhere to my demands and serve the needs of the empire.' He continued:

'Additionally, I will make a few changes before I suppress the rebellion. The first is the appointment of the vakildar [master of ceremonies] for the empire.' Two members of the Privy Council

perked up in their seats, anticipating their names to be called.
'My mudaris Qutlugh Khan will take this position, and he, as
well as my cousin Firoz Shah, will conduct the Privy Council
in my absence. Vazir Khwaja Jahan will take his orders from
the two of them. My new zahir-ul-juyush [commander of the
imperial armies] will be Malik Zada, who is now on his way to
Multan.'

Turning his head, the emperor nodded at Qutlugh Khan.
The bodyguards, taking their cue from Qutlugh Khan, ushered
in Hakka and Bukka. Qutlugh Khan brought them both to the
dais of the throne.

'My sultan, I present to you and the Privy Council, Maliks
Hakka and Bukka.'

'Malik Hakka, I appoint you my zabitah for the province of
Kampili and the surrounding territories. You will carry out all
the functions of the empire in this province on my behalf with
my unconditional authority. You will maintain the sovereignty
of the province, collect taxes, build an army from people you
recruit in the kingdom of Kampili, and administer justice.
One-twentieth of the tax revenues collected will be for yourself
and your family.

The emperor looked to Qutlugh Khan again, who handed
over a small silver casket to Hakka.

'This casket contains all the emblems for assuming the
charge of a zabitah,' the emperor announced. 'Most importantly,
it contains my seal conferring authority on you. Rule with
wisdom, rule firmly, and rule so the people of the region will
have a better life.' Pausing for a moment, he added, 'Malik
Bukka will be your alnnayib [deputy]. Should any misfortune
befall you, he is obliged to assume your duties. Besides, the two

of you have performed well together in the past and will do so in the future.'

Beckoned to the throne, they kissed the sultan's ring and performed the konish, an elaborate form of salutation. For the first time, they saw him smile. They made an adaab, as he said: 'Go forth and prosper.'

Life had dramatically changed. As they left the Diwan-i-Khaas, they had guards assigned to them. Faraj, who was waiting for them, was exultant on hearing the news and informed them that Qutlugh Khan would like to ride with them to the outskirts of the city when they left for Daulatabad. When Hakka asked if they might take the cooks Idriss and Fathlullah with them, Faraj smiled and said they'd be instructed to follow in a day or two. Bukka, hearing Hakka, burst out laughing.

'What use is a high station in life if you cannot eat fine food?' Hakka said defensively. Bukka laughed so hard he nearly slipped off his saddle and Faraj had to help him back up.

It's never too long

'My arse hurts,' Hakka declared as they cantered along on horseback into the third week of the journey from Dilli back to Daulatabad, after which they would travel onward to Anegundi, their home. Bukka and the riders near them had a good laugh as he might well have spoken for them. Over the three weeks, optimism had returned. After all the highs and lows, they were now on their way home and on to something new.

Hakka was going home as governor but his promotion meant he would be ruling over the kingdom where he once served its king. As zabitah (governor) he would be responsible for an area that mainly encompassed Kampili. The announcement in the imperial gazette stated that he would be replacing Malik Mohammed, the current zabitah.

Qutlugh Khan privately told them that Malik Muhammad was not up to the task. He seemed incapable of understanding the local conditions to rule effectively in the name of the emperor. The Hoysalas to the south were a constant threat to his army and he was unable to assert his authority on the territory.

It was not lost on Qutlugh Khan that once, another fearless and resolute malik had also been a zabitah. In time, he had become emperor of Dilli: Ghias-ud-din Tughlaq, the current emperor's father. Reading the announcement in the gazette with a wry smile, Qutlugh Khan wondered how the future would unfold. Spending time with the brothers over the last three years had been deeply satisfying, similar to when Jauna and Malik Zada were his students. Their departure would leave a void.

Qutlugh Khan had come to bid them farewell when they left Dilli for Daulatabad and Anegundi, and had ridden with them up to the boundary of the re-established capital—a desolate area with the Qutb Minar the only noteworthy landmark there. He looked at the two brothers with respect and affection.

'Yaraan-e-miafaq [sincere friends],' he said, 'strengthen and uphold the sultan's standard. May the lands you govern prosper.' He glanced at an assistant, who came forward with two brocade bags.

'Open them after you have been riding a few days,' he said as he gave them to Hakka and Bukka. Keeping their word, they opened their bags when they stopped for a rest several days later. Bukka pulled out a beautiful silver dagger with an ivory handle, in a scabbard set with three large gems and with a long well-cured leather shoulder strap. Etched into the hilt was Qutlugh Khan's parting statement: 'Yaraan-e-miafaq'. Also in the bag was a thick gold chain with gems for prayer beads. It had a gold coin attached to it with the inscription: 'In you, the sultan places his faith. *Allahu akbar.*' Hakka found the same in his bag too.

From Dilli, their small contingent of twenty riders had travelled to Agra, onwards to Gwalior, due south to Nagpur, and was now heading west towards Daulatabad. They were skirting the Rajput kingdoms; they had no intention of disturbing them—'Doughty little fellows,' Qutlugh Khan had called the Rajputs. A sense of anticipation kept them pushing forward to get home quickly. It had been nearly three years since they left Anegundi as prisoners.

Bukka sent ahead official orders to Sinhagad and to Daulatabad via the sultan's courier. Shamshed and Karthikeya were to leave their posts at the Sinhagad Fort in the Koli kingdom and meet them at Daulatabad.

'This trip will be quite different from our first one together,' Bukka teased Faraj, who was riding by his side. Faraj smiled sheepishly. He had asked to be assigned to Hakka and Bukka so he could continue his apprenticeship with them. Qutlugh Khan consented to his serving the brothers for the next two years.

God is also a tailor

They were now just two days away from Daulatabad. Hakka, Bukka, Faraj and two young officers from the Kampili army were accompanied by fifteen members of the sultan's bodyguards. Bukka teased Hakka along the way about his new pomp and circumstance. At every way station, they were accorded respect from the officials. While they changed horses each day at the way stations, Bukka ensured that Chetana came along with them. He regularly changed horses to give her a chance to rest.

On their approach to Daulatabad, there was a noticeable change in the tone of conversation. Looming responsibilities began to grow heavy as the brothers engaged in discussions through the day. On the day before they reached the city, they took a break at a small lake surrounded by trees to give the horses a rest and eat their midday meal.

Acknowledging the unsaid issue, Bukka asked:

'Would they have given you the position of zabitah if we had not converted to Islam?' He followed this up with another question: 'Were our actions driven by convenience that put aside principle?'

Hakka was quiet for a few minutes, mulling over the questions. They had spoken about this a few times and he was thinking of a way to be as transparent as he could. If Bukka raised a question more than once, it was not because he failed to understand; he was questioning the underpinnings and the assumptions that led to a decision. Bukka, to Hakka's mind, could foresee outcomes and possessed a foundation of integrity that was unshakeable. In instances like this, when he raised a question again, he was looking for an answer rooted in truth.

With a deep breath, Hakka bared himself:

'Bukka, while I believe in God, I am not devoutly religious. Religions have rules and some people become very powerful by enforcing or implementing them. Where we grew up, I was glad to go to a temple. Celebrations of religious holidays like Deepavali meant a lot because of the elegant symbolism. Yet, when an officious priest would tell our mother, Sangama, what had to be done and what she was not allowed to do as a widow, it made me angry.

'What I am trying to tell you, I guess, is what God means to me. When I see the seasons changing and the variety in nature, I am in a state of awe. The beauty of life and the kindness that people can muster shows me that there is a power that is larger than anything in the world we know. I also appreciate that the power enables individuals to seek the truth.

'Yogis tell us that we can find it through devotion or love, or bhakti. We could perhaps find it in our work, or karma yoga, or through deep learning of what is spiritual, or gnyana yoga. These are ways people find moksha or realization. I am not capable of bhakti or gnyana. The path open to me is karma yoga. But that is no more than doing what is right, and doing it well, in God's name.

'Bukka, this is very hard for me. I'm not the deep-thinking person you are. I reason in straightforward terms. So, when I reflect on what we did by converting to Islam, I do not believe we did anything wrong or made any compromises.' He stopped to collect his thoughts. 'Bukka, I appreciate all the glorious things God represents, and among His many attributes I also consider Him to be a tailor.'

Bukka smiled. He knew full well that Hakka analysed situations and circumstances using simple and powerful metaphors. That was what gave him clarity, which, in turn, made him a persuasive communicator. He waited to hear his brother's thoughts.

'He is a tailor because he sees what fits people's needs in different parts of the world and he stitches them a suit called religion. Those suits shield people from the harsh winds of ignorance and intemperance: the Yahoodi (Jewish) in Quilon or Calicut, the followers of the man on the cross in some parts of our world, or those following Allah—they are just different suits that people wear. When they wander away from their worlds and their clothes look different from everyone else, we think it's unusual. Yet they are merely wearing a suit tailored for the needs of a different place.'

Hakka stood up and began pacing, as was typical when he encountered a problem or was trying to explain a complicated matter.

'That leaves me thinking that my God is the same God, regardless of the suit I wear. I speak the truth, I honour what is honourable, and treat everyone the same way I hope they will treat me. And whether I wear a Yahoodi suit today, or an Islamic suit tomorrow, I will be communicating to the same God, my God. I will just be wearing a different suit when speaking to Him. Therefore, my brother Bukka, if you feel more at ease if I wore one suit instead of another, I will do so: what matters to me is that my love for you does not change.'

Hakka was perspiring, which was brought on by the deep self-reflection. He paced for a while before concluding, 'I realize that people may say I should not have converted but what does it matter? I never betrayed myself, or the way in which I honour God, or my commitment to God.'

He sat down, seemingly at peace with himself.

'I love my family. I adore my God and hope to obtain guidance because of my devotion to work and quest for the truth. To me praying to Muhammad or to Muruga are just different suits. If you think about it, the sultan is really not that different. Neither is Qutlugh Khan, for that matter. It's just they prefer not to change religions. They are content with their beliefs. In this instance, when Qutlugh Khan suggested we convert, it was a suggestion that was prompted to make silly people more comfortable. Thus, if it meant I could return home to do good deeds and protect the well-being of people, I was willing to alter my religion upon the requests of my superiors.'

Hakka continued with his thoughts.

'Would they have given me the zabitah or, more appropriately, given us the zabitah, if we had not converted? I think they might have because it's what they needed. In truth, there was no compromise of principle in my mind. Maybe others are unconvinced, but I am content with myself. As an example, should Kampili want me to convert and join the 'saviour people', and worship the man on the cross, I would happily do so to put their mind at ease.' He walked back to where he had been sitting, rested his back against a tree trunk, and went to sleep.

They could see the fort

The moment the brothers saw the silhouette of Daulatabad Fort rising on the horizon, they broke into a swift canter. Just as the contingent of twenty horsemen started to move faster, Bukka heard the distant sound of dogs barking. The bodyguards took out their lances to prepare for the unexpected. Faraj told them to put their weapons down and move to the side.

Six dogs came running as fast as they could, well ahead of a galloping mass of two thousand soldiers in livery. Bukka dismounted and stood with his arms outstretched to greet the dogs. They were on him in an instant, biting his uniform with excitement. He was licked, pushed over, and overwhelmed by a pack of dogs that had sorely missed him.

The sight in front of them was truly remarkable: a whole division led by Shamshed and Karthikeya, wearing the sultan's uniform, mounted on magnificent horses. Shamshed greeted the brothers.

'Semenya Hakka, zabitah of Kampili, we pledge our allegiance to you as our leader yet again. May all the gods give you and Semenya Bukka their blessings as you take on your new command. We are in your service, as always.'

Hakka dismounted, walked over to Shamshed and Karthikeya, and hugged them. Bukka was surprised—Hakka was not known for public demonstrations of affection. He walked into the formation of troops, exchanging greetings, touching them, slapping their cheeks, and even giving them a bear hug.

They were the ones who helped to achieve this outcome and he openly acknowledged his debt to them. More than an hour passed before they moved again. The spirits of the men were soaring.

When they arrived at the camp they had left behind nearly a year and a half ago, Hakka and Bukka found that Shamshed and Karthikeya had organized an enormous feast for that evening. The kallu was in plentiful supply, lamb and venison were being roasted on spits at great fires, and there was merriment in the air. The men who had travelled to Dilli were telling their compatriots stories of the wonders they had seen and experienced. Bukka and Hakka walked about, speaking to the men. They were plied with questions ranging from the mandate they had from the emperor to the availability of kallu in Dilli. The men had not spent time with the brothers since the battle of Sinhagad Fort. They basked in their heroes' accomplishments.

Standing off to the side, watching the joyous exchanges were Kazi Rahim Rahmatullah, and Pratapa Sharman the vaidyan.

The brothers thanked the men and urged them to eat and drink. Kazi Rahim Rahmatullah took the opportunity to draw Hakka and Bukka aside. He requested meeting them privately and added he had a letter from Pattu. Hakka suggested the next day as they were set to move on the day after.

A little later, Hakka stood on a large rock to speak to the men before too much drink was consumed.

'We will soon start our march home. We have been away for nearly three years. I hope all your families are well, though we know they have been taken care of. I am glad the emperor appointed me his zabitah and Semenya Bukka my alnnayib [deputy], but there is something more important to which I wish to dedicate tonight: our fallen brethren at the battlefield in Anegundi. Without them this outcome would not have come to pass. Taking care of their loved ones will be our lifelong responsibility. To all of you I say: the teamwork and dedication each one of you has shown has been exemplary. When we get back to the kingdom of Kampili, we will reward each of you with wages for three years, a new home, a bigha of land, and five heads of cattle.'

The men cheered with shouts of joy. Hakka raised a hand and the noise died down; he continued.

'There are two others who must be mentioned as well. The fearless drive shown by Shamshed and Karthikeya has been our shield. Today, as zabitah, I promote both of them to the rank of full semenyas in the Kampili army.' The roaring began again as the two men were hoisted up and carried to where Hakka was standing. Karthikeya performed a namaskaram in the direction of Hakka and Bukka, and Shamshed offered an adaab, after which they held their clenched hands to their hearts. The crowd cheered them and now took up a new chant:

'Semenya Bukka, Semenya Bukka, Semenya Bukka!'

Hakka grinned and offered his brother a hand to haul him up to stand on the rock next to him. Bukka greeted the men and spoke:

'The zabitah has given us exceptional leadership through all of our trials, and for that I thank the gods. Yet, every single one of you is part of this accomplishment. Now let us march with speed and get home to our people as quickly as we can. *Nanna alavada dhanyavadagalu* [my deepest thanks].'

There was every reason to celebrate: many of the Kampili army had survived and were going home with a sizeable reward. None of them needed to work for another person for another day in his life, should he choose.

Kazi Rahim Rahmatullah appeared the next day, accompanied by Pratapa Sharman. He brought a hundred thousand silver tankas on the instructions of Pattu, as they would need to pay for supplies along the way. There was also a sealed letter. The brothers read the contents of the parchment.

My dear brothers Hakkappa and Bukkappa,

We have heard news of Hakka returning to Kampili as the zabitah and Bukka as his alnnayib. Through all your trials, the two of you have triumphed in ways that leave us amazed. I have offered an archanai [offering] at the temple of the Long-tailed One. We express our thanks to him for your safety and your victories. Kazi Rahim Rahmatullah has been my source of news, though we heard about this great appointment from the local administration.

The family is well. Sangama just came back from the pepper plantation a month ago. She says that she will go back and spend her last days there because she liked it so much.

Please pardon me, but I have put a few plans in place to make sure that you can address your responsibilities soon after you arrive. First, I have bought a large house for Sangama and the rest of the family. The zabitah's family must have a respectable home to live in, while the two of you will be located in the official palace close by.

The finances of the kingdom will preoccupy you immediately. I have some of my kannakupillais [accountants] doing an estimate of all of the revenue available to you. You must remember that the king of Kampili had left me with a deposit of eight thousand eight hundred mohurs of gold. I have at hand half of that for your immediate use. The rest that was lent has been recalled so it will soon be available to you. I understand that you are aware of the location of the treasury at Anegundi. Still, you should also know that there is a separate treasury in the fort at Hosadurg, for which I have the keys. The contents are similar to the treasury that was looted by Malik Zada. No one else is aware that it exists.

There will be new staff for your household and they have been trained. The state of law and order will require immediate attention; the farmers have been in a state of revolt for about six months so no tax collections have taken place. The maps of all the holdings in the kingdom and the records of tax collections have been sent to your residence. My kannakupillai will give you a complete overview of accounts. Should you need to retain their services, I will employ new men for my businesses.

As a final issue, the Hoysalas to the south have taken much territory and they continue to raid the kingdom. The current administration is corrupt and the judicial system has failed. The challenges you both will face are considerable.

I look forward to having both of you back home. In the meantime, please send your orders via Kazi Rahim Rahmatullah and they will get to me before you are back. I offer my prayers to the Long-tailed One that you have a safe journey back.

Forever in your debt,
பட்டு [Pattu]

Bukka quickly wrote out a response to Pattu, sealed it, and handed it to Kazi Rahim Rahmatullah, who handed over two large bags of gold mohurs to the brothers.

'What's that for? Whose is it?' enquired Bukka.

'You gave this gold to me when you arrived in Daulatabad,' replied Kazi Rahim Rahmatullah.

'Why are you returning what we have given you? We must repay you for your services and loyalty,' Bukka protested.

'I have been paid and all my accounts are settled by Ramaswamy Mudaliar [Pattu],' Kazi Rahmatullah stated.

'So, how much did you spend?' Bukka pushed on.

'Ramaswamy Mudaliar will give you an overview because I am not at liberty to give you that information, semenya.'

Bukka cast aside his caution for a moment and presented a question that had puzzled him for a while.

'Do you work for him, Kazi Rahim Rahmatullah?'

'I do, semenya, along with a small organization, who are his representatives in this part of the country.'

'So, what do you do?'

'Semenya, Ramaswamy Mudaliar is one of the largest traders in the southern peninsula. The only thing he does not trade is grains and pulses, as a matter of principle. Anything you touch has most likely gone through his organization. As his representative, I manage the supply of goods for a few kingdoms. Many, like me, who work for Ramaswamy Mudaliar must be aware of what is going on in each kingdom. We lend money to noblemen and people at court, we trade in most commodities, as well as horses and cows in the peninsula. Ramaswamy Mudaliar is possibly richer than most kings in the peninsula put together. I was asked to make sure you had everything you needed, including information that could be useful to you. Those were Ramaswamy Mudaliar's instructions.' Bukka thanked him for all he had done for them and Kazi Rahim Rahmatullah departed.

'Recalling our chats from a long time ago, we now know what Pattu does,' Hakka remarked with a smile. 'I think he is one of the most enterprising and intelligent persons I know but I would never have guessed that he had built a business empire right under our noses.'

'Bukka, you know, prosperity is like a thailam [balm],' Hakka said.

'Here he goes again with one of his similes,' Bukka thought to himself and hid a smile. He prodded his brother on.

'What do you mean, Hakka?'

'Let me put it this way. When we were away from home, we knew that Pattu took care of any expense or outlay that the family needed. He did this regardless of whether we sent money home. Not once did we have to worry that our family might need something we could not provide. What I am saying is, his prosperity and success helped the family rid itself of concerns while it soothed any anxieties we had.'

'I agree with that, Hakka. However, I sense you are trying to make a larger point. What is it?' quizzed Bukka.

'We need someone to teach us how to make the kingdom more prosperous and tell us how all might benefit. It will be in the interest of everyone to have a man with Pattu's abilities help us develop more prosperity and wealth. When people are prosperous, they tend to be good citizens by helping each other because they are invested in the well-being of the kingdom. Citizens then pay less attention to those who sow seeds of doubt. We need to have Pattu on the council assisting in the administration of the kingdom, Bukka.'

'Anna [older brother], please do not do that,' Bukka pleaded. 'Pattu is best left doing what he does. His view of the business world he operates in will be ruined if we take him away from what he does. Besides, how happy do you think he will be if you did that? It would be like tying up his hands. I agree he knows a lot and he can teach us, and there is no doubting that he is very capable. I think he would give us his advice if and when we asked for it. But let him be a free person and manage his own business. We will get more from him that way, Hakka. As a gesture, you may want to offer him the position of diwan of the kingdom, but make sure that you give him the opportunity to decline. If you do not handle it carefully, all of us are going to be worse off if he feels duty-bound to accept your request. So please, let him continue the way he is. It will be in the greater interest of your new kingdom.'

'So be it,' Hakka consented. Bukka was amused.

'Why are you laughing?' Hakka enquired.

'You sounded just like a zabitah,' Bukka replied with a grin.

'The zabitah was only repeating what his very intelligent alnnayib suggested,' retorted Hakka, smiling back at his brother. Then he looked sober.

'Bukka, I can't function effectively without you by my side. It has always been that way. I confess that when you were wounded in Sinhagad after rescuing Qutlugh Khan, I prayed to the Long-tailed One. I told him that my life would be worthless without you. My request was to heal you or take both of us from this world. I promised to stay true to Bajrangpalli and build a temple to consecrate his birthplace on the top of the hill near Anegundi. Just this one time I will say to you, Bukka, you are my conscience, my best friend, my favourite general and my beloved younger brother. Life is rich and wonderful and worthwhile with you by my side.'

'How does a Muslim build a Hanuman temple, Hakka?' Bukka asked.

'Well …' he said, and pondered the question. Then he said with a glint in his eye: 'We'll have Pattu build it.' Hakka broke into a smile and added: 'Let's get ready for the trip home, Bukka.'

To the Tungabhadra!

Watching a well-trained contingent of soldiers riding was an awe-inspiring sight. There were two thousand men on horses, with six dogs running beside Chetana, trotting along in formation. By the time the sun rose they were well on their way to Anegundi, the capital city of the Kampili kingdom.

Karthikeya had won the draw and was given command of the regiment for the trip home. He was in his element. At the head of the troop were bannermen with the sultan's standard alongside that of Kampili. Behind two rows of the zabitah's new bodyguards were Hakka, Bukka, Faraj, Shamshed and the dogs. As they left town, Karthikeya had a soldier blow his silver kombu to signal the troop to pick up pace. He roared:

'To the Tungabhadra. Let's make haste!'

'To Kampili. To Kampili. To Kampili!' The roar erupted from every throat in the vast column of men.

As they travelled, Hakka's mood began to shift from unfettered optimism to practical matters.

'Training an army, dealing with logistics and fighting wars, Bukka, are very different from running a kingdom. I have no experience of it, though I imagine that you would be a lot more pragmatic with the task. However, not even you have done it. Yet here we are, on our way to Kampili and a vast territory that requires capable and intelligent leadership. The more I dwell on this the more I consider how unsuited I am to the task. Isn't it strange that men who succeed at military pursuits go on to rule kingdoms? Few of them are trained for the job. When I joined the army there was a clear training process for that career. But here we are, the two sons of Sangama, starting on a venture for which we have no experience.'

'Small steps, Hakka,' came the reassuring words of his brother, 'and common sense. Appointing good people will be key. Living within the revenues of the state and taking advice from those who have useful insights. All of that put together will make it easier.

'First, let's make sure we know the military situation and the seriousness of the Hoysala threat. I guess that bastard Balalla will test us soon. We'll soon know the state of the finances. I understand that we have some flexibility with about six months of expenses taken care of. We can seek Pattu's advice on raising and managing revenues. He will also know good people that we can trust to help run the kingdom.

'At the same, time we ought to start building the army. Let's dismiss the idea of raising an army simply to fight wars. We should have a standing army at all times as well as reserves we can draw on if the need arises. But we need to know how large a force we can afford. As we establish ourselves in the first few weeks, let us assert our influence slowly and not try too much too soon. Take small steps that are driven by logic and with the interest of the kingdom in mind. That is the way to proceed, Hakka.'

'I knew you would be two steps ahead of me,' Hakka remarked. 'I feel better that you have a plan, which we can start implementing. Before we go any further with this, let's make a promise to each other. We will not make decisions without consulting each other. No matter how urgent it may seem, the two of us have to agree before we proceed with a plan.'

'Hakka, you are the zabitah, the head of the kingdom. You do not need to consult me. But I must consult with you. It is your prerogative, and I respect your view but there is no obligation to make that commitment to me,' Bukka said. 'I will continue to operate the way I always have until you tell me otherwise.'

They were quiet for a while, lost in their thoughts as they rode on. Bukka remained puzzled that Hakka, the second-oldest of his four brothers—five, if one counted Pattu—took so much time and effort with him, since he was the youngest. For as long as he could remember, he had struggled to keep up with Hakka and found it frustrating that he always lagged behind. Bukka the child never took into account the difference in years separating them. Sangama would laugh and say, 'Bukka can never understand that he is seven years younger than Hakka.' It became a standing joke in the family after young Bukka once asked what was wrong with him because he was so short while all his brothers were tall. 'Please, Sangama, tell me, am I going to be a dwarf, like Kantha?' Kantha was a friend of Hakka's in the village, who suffered from dwarfism. Bukka was never permitted to forget that.

Bukka's throat swelled with emotion as he thought about his family, whom he had not seen in a long time. He recalled how his father—also a military man—died in battle when Bukka was five years old. After all they endured over the years, Sangama was going to be intensely proud to see Hakka return to his country as the head of state. She was a woman with fantastic drive, raising all six boys (including Pattu) by working to the point of exhaustion every day. They scraped along the edge of poverty and would have fallen prey to it had it not been for her fortitude and resourcefulness. She learned how to weave, fed them from the small plot of land she received from the king as compensation for her husband's death, yet still raised them with a great deal of pride.

Pattu was the only son of Sangama's friend, a woman of no means, who died during an outbreak of cholera. Sangama had promised to take care of Pattu. He proved to be her favourite among the six boys.

Their fortunes changed when Pattu began his small business. He traded livestock, then horses, which earned him enough money to set up a business that constructed bullock carts, the most sought-after in the kingdom. Once his businesses began to flourish, everything changed for the better. It was not as if Sangama worked less around the house, but at least she was not constantly toiling at the loom, trying to finish another dhoti, saree or batch of towels to sell in the market. Pattu left for work early and returned late, and even when he was at home, he was busy helping Sangama.

Two of Bukka's older brothers left home when they turned eighteen. Marappa was a trader and lived in the Tamil kingdom on the east coast. Madappa, the third brother, also entered a trading house and moved to Quilon in the Malayalam-speaking country to the south. By that time, Hakka had joined the army but lived at home.

They moved to a comfortable house that Pattu bought in Anegundi. It was always called Sangama's home—a little ironic because she had left her own house and land on the outskirts of Anegundi where they had originally lived.

When Bukka was ten, Pattu got married and brought his wife home. The whole house lit up when his wife Kanthi came to live with them. He had not seen Sangama happier. The two had similar interests and it was comforting for Sangama to have another woman in the house. However, Kanthi died during childbirth and it marked a dark period in Pattu's life. Sangama was not one to stay downcast for long, though. She now had a grandchild called Valli and she was determined to make the most of it. Valli absorbed all their attention and grew into a smaller version of Kanthi. It was also because of Pattu that Bukka was able to go to school, so when he was ready to join the army, he did so as an officer and not an enlisted man like Hakka.

Thinking about Hakka in those days, he remembered how through grit and hard work Hakka made it to the officer class. He never forgot where he started his career, and it showed in the way he mingled with his soldiers. He was able to teach Bukka the ropes, which helped him learn fast, and it was not long before they both moved out to work for the army of another kingdom.

For the last nine years, Bukka and Hakka had been away from home. It brought a wry smile to his face thinking about being home again under very different circumstances. He wondered if he would ever hear anyone other than Hakka tease him with the line, 'Please, Sangama, tell me, am I going to be a dwarf like Kantha?' If he were to hazard a guess, the answer was no. Circumstances in life had changed, but the question was whether it would be for the better.

∿∿∿

'Coluuuuumn! Stoooooop!' Karthikeya bellowed. They were at the campsite for their last night before they got to Anegundi. It struck him that there had been no communication from the incumbent Malik Muhammad about managing the change of command. 'Curious,' he thought. Just then the scouts noticed two riders approaching them. They appeared to be civilians, probably with a message from Pattu. Sure enough, it was. The messengers reported:

'Malik Muhammad left Anegundi two days ago. He left instructions regarding the change of command. One of his deputies will provide the necessary information when you arrive.'

Hakka was furious upon hearing this, calling Malik Muhammad a baboon's arse.

'He did not have the honour to see it through to the end but slithered away before we arrived,' Hakka growled at the messengers. 'How many men are in Anegundi, and at the fort?'

'Semenya, there are about twenty men at the fort and another thirty in Anegundi. They are wandering around town, drunk, forcing traders to pay them protection money, as well as harassing the women.'

Weighing the alternatives, Hakka told the messengers that the contingent would enter the township of Anegundi an hour before noon. Sending troops now in the evening would not solve anything. From a political standpoint, it was a black mark against Malik Muhammad because he had not followed procedure. It was a four-hour journey, so the men would start early to make sure they arrived on time. Hakka informed the messengers that they would first go to the palace and then see Sangama. The messengers were to let Sangama know they were coming for dinner with a guest. The messengers left with their instructions.

Hakka marvelled at how well-organized Pattu was. There was much to learn from his older brother. It gave him a sense of comfort knowing he had both his younger and older brothers to help him. Both were wise and astute men.

Karthikeya followed his orders to the last little detail. There was a Hindu priest and a mullah present as the division prepared to ride out early in the morning. The priest, a small man with a surprisingly loud voice, came to the head of the column. He asked for silence from the troops. Catching Bukka's eye, he immediately changed his tone:

'Semenya, pardon me for being rude.'

'You were not, shastri; you were only getting a group of boisterous soldiers to listen, so please proceed. Just make the incantation short.'

The Hindu priest was none too happy sharing the stage with the Muslim priest who was there as well. Bukka asked them to invoke blessings from all of the gods that looked over them.

The priest quickly said a prayer to Ganapathi, the elephant god and remover of obstacles: '*Vakrathunda mahakaya ...*' and ended with '*Eeswaro rakshatoo*'.

He broke a coconut, and placed a vermilion mark on Bukka, Hakka, Shamshed and Faraj. Bukka winked at Faraj.

Hakka thanked the priest, after which he indicated to the mullah to come forward and give the men his blessings. Kadar, a handsome young man who was the muezzin, read out his prayer: '*Bismillahir rahmanir raheem ...*' and concluded with '*Alhamdulillah*'.

The men were ready. Since this was not going to be a long ride, Bukka let the dogs off the leash. As soon as they heard Karthikeya give the orders for the division to begin its march, they started barking and dashed ahead of the horses. Chetana was now used to them but a lot of the sultan's horses remained wary when they were around. The men settled into a graceful canter, keeping their places, and followed the well-trodden pathway for the last part of the journey. After reaching the crest of a long and steep incline they were able to see the Tungabhadra in the valley below them, with dwellings and buildings clustered along its banks. It was as if nothing had changed. The river was flowing at its fullest, common for this time of the year, nourishing the plains and the lives of people as it had through millennia.

As the ground became less steep, Karthikeya, on Hakka's instruction, delivered the order for the division to get into meticulous formation. Hakka had decided they would arrive at Anegundi in a show of orderly force. As they passed through the market place, people emerged from the shops and houses to behold the sight; the rumours were right, after all: Sangama's sons had indeed returned to rule the kingdom. The crowds began cheering

'Jai Kampili! Jai Hakka! Jai Bukka!' they shouted. Children scampered about almost under the hooves of the horses, young women looked interestedly at the passing soldiers and young men decided they would enlist, too. Older citizens simply felt relieved and hopeful.

The soldiers retained their formation as they marched through the market. Then, turning right, they approached what used to be the palace of the king of Kampili. Karthikeya commanded the column to stop. He dismounted from his horse and walked over to Hakka for further instructions. A mid-level officer hurriedly came out of an unguarded palace and spoke. Faraj translated.

'My name is Aslam Iftikhar and my directives are to hand over command to you.'

Hakka ignored him.

'Faraj, have some junior officer in your battalion see what this man has to say and take notes. Tell this man that he and his men are to leave Anegundi by nightfall.' No sooner had Faraj translated Hakka's message than the officer started to protest. Hakka looked at Faraj and said, 'Let him know that it is on the order of the zabitah, Malik Hakka, and that's final.'

Hakka entered the palace, accompanied by Bukka, Shamshed, Karthikeya and Faraj.

It had been poorly maintained in the years after the war; nothing that some repair and paint wouldn't fix. But then, he thought to himself, there was going to be much repairing, cleaning and painting needed for the whole town over the coming weeks and months ahead.

'Karthikeya, dismiss the men except for a hundred of your scouts to keep guard for the night. The others will be asked to assemble here tomorrow evening for further instructions. They will each be given a bag of fifty tankas of silver but please make sure with Pattu's men that our currency will be good in the market, especially in the kallu kadai [the beer shop]. Ensure that the whorehouses close down for the day, so the men do not get out of control. All of us are going to have to learn to live in ways we have forgotten. Make sure to disperse some of our guards in mufti [plainclothes] around town in case some go overboard.'

He then changed his mind.

'Karthikeya, have the kallu kadais come to the camp and serve the men. Everyone will stay there, drink, eat well and rest. Tired men and alcohol do not mix—they might cause trouble in town. We will pay for all the kallu they drink. Only men from the town will be permitted to go to their families. Is there anything else we need to consider, Bukka?' Bukka shook his head.

The men were given orders to disperse to their campsite, and the cheering outside, 'Jai Hakka, jai Bukka' continued for a few minutes. Hakka was overwhelmed at just how suddenly life had changed and the enormity of it all seemed daunting. Bukka and Faraj read his face and smiled.

Bukka instructed Shamshed to prepare the camp and to spare no expense in attending to the men's needs. Just as they were getting ready to leave for Sangama's house, they suddenly realized they did not know where her new house was.

'We do not know where our mother lives,' a bemused Hakka said and laughed sheepishly.

There was a knock on the door. A guard came in and told them that a man from Ramaswamy Mudaliar requested to see them. He was there to accompany the brothers to Pattu's residence. Hakka greeted the news with joy.

'Now we can find out where our mother lives!'

That's a big house

There was a new sense of order. Hakka, Bukka and Faraj walked out to find guards waiting, holding their horses' reins. As they began moving out, the guards formed a cordon around them. In just a few minutes the messenger halted. They had reached their destination.

'Which house?' Bukka asked. The man pointed to the big white building in front of them.

'That's a big house,' exclaimed Hakka, surprised.

'Bukka!' They heard a young voice. Valli came running out with Sangama and Pattu in train. They embraced Valli before Hakka walked to his mother, bent down and touched her feet. They hugged and she stood back with her palms clasped in front of her face, tears streaming down. She reached out to Bukka to embrace him as well. She had thought about their homecoming countless times but now she was speechless. As Hakka went to touch his older brother's feet, Pattu drew him up.

'An older brother is a friend; so that's not warranted, Hakka.' They hugged for a long time and then pulled Bukka into their embrace.

'I thank the Long-tailed One for your safe return home, my brothers,' Pattu declared. Never an emotional person, this occasion brought tears to his eyes.

Sangama returned to the house, to welcome them at the doorstep. She held a large silver plate with a little lamp burning in the middle. Valli helped her make a mixture of water, turmeric and vermilion kumkum in the plate. Sangama held it up as she mouthed a prayer invoking blessings for those who were about to cross the threshold of their house for the first time. Her face glowing with love, she softly whispered: 'May you never leave home for so long again.' She put her thumb in the kumkum and marked their foreheads with a bright red mark.

After handing the tray to Valli, Sangama turned back to her two sons.

'Welcome to your new home, Hakka and Bukka. It augurs well that when we moved in, we heard news of your return home. Our humble abode might not be as comfortable as your new palace, but it's certainly nicer than the little house we lived in all those years ago.'

5

How do you build a kingdom?

1331–1336: Kampili

They get answers

Comparing the palace of the king of Kampili to the grandeur of the palaces in Dilli would have been ludicrous, but still, it was the finest building in the city of Anegundi. In little more than a few weeks it had been cleaned and restored so it was usable. Hakka insisted Bukka live with him. His argument was he needed competition in learning how to cook Pharsi and Kabuli food once Fathlullah and Idriss, the cooks from Dilli, arrived. Bukka was confused about how the new protocol would work but ultimately relented. Sangama and the family refused to move.

'You still need a place to call home, Hakka,' Sangama said. 'Besides, it's time you found a wife. All the rumours about you are good, except the ones about the parade of women marching through your life,' she added.

The palace was on two levels, situated in a large compound and enclosed by high walls. It had once had a well-tended garden but neglect over the last three years had left it a scrubby wilderness of weeds and shrubs.

The weeks following their arrival were frenetic. Pattu attended to all their needs. He arranged for gardeners, painters, cooks and servants for the house—everything to make the place comfortable and homely. Bukka nearly choked in amazement one evening as he looked around.

'This is looking like a palace but I am not sure that Hakka can afford it,' he informed Pattu.

'The zabitah and his deputy can afford this and more,' Pattu replied in his quiet manner. 'Besides, Bukka, from now on you need to convey an aura of credibility. Appearances count for a lot, so get yourself ready to live in comfort.

'Tam'ma [younger brother], keep your values, but do not confuse them with the circumstances,' Pattu said. Bukka could only think how unusual these circumstances had become. His foster brother went on:

'Kings live in palaces and their advisors wield power. Their lives are scrutinized and they are expected to lead by example. So be honest, true to your values and remember where you came from. Should the stage require embellishment for a grand drama, do not get in the way.' It was perhaps the first time Pattu had ever given him advice.

Frequently the brothers were informed that Sangama and Valli had visited. There would be evidence of that as something new, elegant or comfortable would have been added to the palace.

Every last little detail of their finances had been covered
by Pattu. The treasury would last them a year but he advised
they should consolidate revenues quickly. They would be able
to afford an army of ten thousand quite easily. Strategies for
revenues were evaluated and taxation was set in place with the
reach of the zabitah extending to the whole territory.

Pattu's competence left the brothers in awe. When Hakka
asked if he would help them run the kingdom, Pattu changed
his tone.

'Without hesitation, I would do anything to take care of
our family but I must decline any part in the administration
of the kingdom. As a trader, people will interpret this as a
way to enrich both myself and us. That will undermine your
authority and reputation for being honest people. To make sure
that our reputations are safeguarded, I will stop trading in the
kingdom of Kampili in one month's time. Then you will never
be challenged by claims that I profit from knowing the king,
excuse me, the zabitah.'

'How are we going to be able to manage this task ourselves,
Pattu, when we are not even aware of these kinds of skills?'
Hakka asked.

'The answer to your question is waiting outside the door,
Tam'ma,' Pattu remarked, gesturing to the visitor outside to
enter. A small man walked in, thin to the point of emaciation,
wearing a panchakaccham, with a cotton shawl draped around
his torso. Hakka could have lifted him with one hand. 'Is *this*
man going to help us run the kingdom?' Bukka thought.

Mani Iyer was the priest at a local temple. He was around
Bukka's age and had the ashen marks on his forehead indicating
he was a Shaivite. His head was tonsured, leaving a small tuft

of hair at the back of his head. Asking him to sit down, Pattu asked:

'Will you help my brothers run the kingdom?'

Mani Iyer sat on the floor, refusing a cushion, and began gently swaying back and forth, considering the question. He replied in a surprisingly deep voice.

'Ramaswamy Mudaliar, I am a priest and that is all I know. I would have been on the street had you not paid for me to go to the patashalai [religious school] to learn the vedas and the other scriptures. It was you who asked me to preside over the Hanuman temple by the tank. It has been an honour taking care of the Long-tailed One.

'While I consider your request seriously, I fear the gods might not be able to help me overcome my lack of skill or understanding of what will be required. Even the great strength of the Bajrangpalli might not be enough. Were that to happen, I would have disappointed you. At least at the temple, my decisions do not harm anyone. Whether the Lord is adorned one way or another, according to my whims on any given day, has no consequences. Yet this is not the same situation. Great matters of state are to be decided—matters I know nothing about.'

Having spoken, he returned to swaying gently back and forth. They were all facing Mani Iyer. Pattu looked serious, weighing how to proceed.

'Managing the affairs of state will be no different from managing the temple, Mani Iyer. I am sure if you are persuasive enough, you could convince the brothers how you would like to adorn the Lord on any given day. Come to the palace tomorrow morning and we will find you a place to work, and if Eeswara is amenable to this plan, it will work.'

Mani Iyer rose to his feet. He offered a namaskaram to those in attendance, looked at Hakka and Bukka, and said:

'I will stop at my temple in the morning and say a Hanuman Chaleesa for the three of us and bring you some prasaadam. This is a task that will require great strength and I will request assistance from the Long-tailed One to make this kingdom like a temple. *Eeswaro rakshatoo* [may God take care of us],' he declared, and was gone.

Hakka and Bukka felt dazed. They were swimming in unfamiliar waters. It was getting dark and Pattu asked a servant to bring them some kallu. Hakka started to chuckle.

'Anna [older brother], this is truly a very strange day but the kallu should help us consider the issues at hand.'

Bukka roared with laughter.

'That is as diplomatic as I have ever heard you be, Hakka!'

Fresh and tasty, the kallu washed away their tiredness and stress. After some light banter, Pattu returned to his earlier thoughts.

'Tammagalu [younger brothers], my recommendations are those of a trader who has travelled a great deal and witnessed the strengths and the weaknesses of nobles and kings. The two of you have many military accomplishments but it does not necessarily translate to the political sphere. They are not one and the same thing. I request you to be patient as I share some of my observations with you.

'What you are embarking on is a challenge you have never encountered before. I know you both like to play chaturanga. A good way to visualize this is to think of playing many chaturanga mats at the same time: what happens on one mat might influence the outcome of another. You will not be able to play each of these games by yourselves, as you have for many years. You will have to manage them through the eyes and minds of others.

'Ruling Kampili will require a group of people who are your eyes and ears. People who are hardworking, possess integrity and intelligence, and speak their mind. You may not agree with them or take the same view. Reward them in ways that are beyond their expectation so outside sources cannot corrupt them. You must be prepared to trust them as much as you trust each other.

'Let me say two more things: first, I identified Mani Iyer because he has all of these qualities. He also has a deeply scholarly inclination and a practical way of approaching problems. Within a month he will know more about Kampili than the two of you. His memory will rival yours, Bukka,' Pattu chuckled.

'My second observation is that both of you are going to be doing things that are greater than just ruling Kampili. See the bigger picture and do not get swamped by detail, because Mani Iyer and his little army will deal with that. If I were an astrologer, I would say your stars are aligned and have destined you for big challenges in the course of your lifetime.' Pattu smiled and, after a sip of his kallu, added: 'Henceforth, I will avoid giving you advice unless you ask for it.'

'Anna,' Bukka responded, 'my request is that you shouldn't ever hold back. Even if we disagree, I solemnly swear that I will be agreeable in my approach.'

The three men grinned affectionately at each other and raised their cups of kallu in salute.

'I will add to what Bukka said by suggesting you be an unofficial member of the Privy Council, as an elder or advisor,' Hakka said. 'Come when you can, and there will always be a seat for you. While I respect your need for discretion, I hope you will respect our desire for your involvement, even if it's not in an official capacity.'

Pattu stood up and pulled the two brothers into an embrace before looking very seriously at the two of them. He said: 'Keep looking for what lies beyond the horizon.'

He left, escorted by three of his bodyguards.

Once Pattu had gone, Hakka drained the last of the kallu, glanced over at Bukka with wide-open eyes and whispered:

'How is this small man going to help up manage so many problems?' Scratching his head with bewilderment he added, 'I hope he is in the business of performing magic.' He held his hands up in disbelief and started to guffaw at how ridiculous this proposal seemed.

'Hakka,' his brother responded, 'Pattu can seem unconventional, but that's what has made him so successful. Inshallah, this idea works.'

A little tiger

Big and strong soldiers do not have a monopoly on ferocity. Devotion can frequently drive those infused with it to be dedicated in the pursuit of their outcomes. In this instance there was a distinct case of intellectual ferocity at work.

Bukka's dogs started to bark as the sun was rising. One of his servants knocked softly on the door with a message:

'Mani Sastrigal was here, and he left a long letter and two large wooden cases for the two of you, semenya.' Intrigued by this, Bukka asked the servant to bring it to him. It was a thick letter with many pages of parchment, accompanied by the two wooden cases. He first read the letter:

My lords, the zabitah and the alnnayib of Kampili,

My work has begun but I must make sure that it is appropriately conducted. A letter will be the means by which I communicate with you when I am unable to meet with you directly.

You will notice an addendum with four hundred and twelve questions that I would like the two of you to consider. The answers will determine what direction the administration of this kingdom will take. May I request that you both read and consider them carefully. We will meet in one week, four hours after sunrise at the Green Palace, where administrative affairs are discussed and conducted. It would be appropriate for us to meet for two hours so we can begin to address all issues of state.

In the wooden cases you will find two copies of Kautilya's *Artha Shastra*, and if you have not already read it, please do so. Kautilya provides new kings with the wisdom and thought processes needed to govern effectively.

The small bag contains a broken coconut and prasaadam from the Anjaneya temple. The prasaadam is from this morning's prayers when I asked the Long-tailed One for strength to manage this huge undertaking confronting us. I realize that you are both Muslims but I presume that a Hindu offering will not be offensive. We need the help of all of the gods as we set out our objectives.

During the week, I will be in the Green Palace arranging records, hiring administrators and preparing material for the two of you to study. Other appointments

will await your insights and approval. Should you need
to see me, I will be glad to come over to the palace to
serve you in any way I can.

With due respect to your eminences,
Mani Iyer
Priest of the Hanuman temple (by the pond)

Accompanying this brief letter was a thick sheaf of parchment
with his list of four hundred and twelve questions.

'He's two steps ahead of me,' thought Bukka. 'Will I be able
to keep pace with what is coming my way from Mani Iyer?'
After thinking through what they had to work on the previous
day, Bukka had come up with sixty questions and issues. The
idea of all those questions and a huge book to read prompted
a chuckle.

Hakka walked into the room and sat on the edge of Bukka's
bed.

'What's possessed you this early in the morning, Bukka?'
he growled, rubbing the sleep from his eyes. 'Your dogs were
barking so loudly I am sure they woke up all of Anegundi. They
are mostly good animals but this noise must stop.' Bukka was
amused by his brother's irritation. He passed the letter over to
Hakka, who had to take time to absorb the import of it all.

'When you were working yesterday, how many items did
you come up with, Bukka?'

'Sixty!'

'He is seven times more intelligent than you, Bukka. He has
seven times more questions than you do, Tam'ma. And what is
that wooden box?'

'Didn't you read the letter, Hakka? He's set us homework.'

Hakka bent his head over Mani Iyer's epistle again. He was aghast.

'He wants us to have this read by next week and says there is more for us to study. Is Pattu trying to play an elaborate joke on us? Really, Bukka, do you think one of our generals would ever dare give us tasks like this? I'd have them clearing horse dung in an instant. The temerity of that swaying midget.'

'Hakka, think about it for a moment. He is doing your work. But to do it effectively, he needs you to reciprocate. I think we are in a world that we never imagined, but at least we have someone who is ferociously intelligent to help us out. It may well be that he is the best thing that ever happened to us.'

Hakka stood up.

'May all the gods help us.'

Bukka spent considerable time reading through the list of all the issues Mani Iyer raised. How was a simple priest with no experience in statecraft asking questions about the military, taxation, hiring practices and salary structures for the administration? And how did he do this in the span of one evening?

A week later, they were at the Green Palace where Mani Iyer greeted them with a namaskaram and led them into a large well-lit room at the back of the building. Nine men were lined up at the entrance: four tonsured Hindu priests and five Muslim men of varying ages. He introduced them, one by one. The priests were hired as scribes while the Muslims were employed as accountants. Hakka looked quizzically at Mani Iyer. Priests were accustomed to writing a great deal and the Muslims were merchants, but he still did not understand the reasoning.

'Zabitah, merchants need to be very good at accounting. Two of them have great experience in recovering loans. In the

case of Kampili, there are a great number of landowners who
have not paid taxes in more than a year, some even longer. We
need their skills to get those revenues for the treasury. Without
money you are powerless and there is no one who will lend you
money. Besides, asking the sultan for funds at this stage might
not be in your interest and could take long.'

Hakka and Bukka sat on two divans in the room with Mani
Iyer, a scribe and an accountant in attendance. In the span of
two hours, he had given them an overview of everything that
needed attention, the revenue they had at their disposal, and
plans for the future. He asked the two men to bring over a large
bamboo mat. Laying it out at their feet, Mani Iyer sat down
between the two brothers. On the mat were arranged about a
hundred pieces of parchment, mapping an elaborate plan for
what they could accomplish over the next year, with monthly
targets. No stone was left unturned. It addressed the military
and the progress in recruitment, ideas on raising tax revenues,
consolidating the territory, and hiring administrators for the
well-being of the kingdom.

After inspecting the map, Hakka asked:

'How many wells can we provide during the first year for
the people?'

'Eighty-five, with twenty in the first six months and then
sixty-five in the next six months,' Mani Iyer responded.

'Why more than double the number in the last six months?'
Hakka asked, puzzled.

'Hiring people to dig wells is not easy, and we would have
to determine which areas needed them. In six months, we will
have a clearer plan in terms of locating the wells, with a small
army of people to dig the wells.'

At the end of the two hours, Mani Iyer had covered all the issues he had in mind and obtained approval for his plans. Getting up to leave, he handed over another wooden document case containing letters and plans for them to examine, which included an accounting of their personal balances and funds. Walking the brothers out, he reminded them of their next appointment at the same time the following day.

'Again?' Hakka asked.

'Yes, building a kingdom takes a lot of time and effort, zabitah. And I am sure that you want to build a good one,' Mani Iyer said.

Riding back to the palace, Hakka appeared to be in shock.

'I cannot imagine what is left to talk about tomorrow, Bukka,' he said in an exasperated tone. 'This is a cruel joke that Pattu is playing on us. He's unleashed this little tiger on us and I feel like we are getting scratched, mauled and bitten. He will be the end of me, Bukka. All I wanted was someone like you that I could handle. I cannot deal with ten Bukkas rolled into one!'

Smiling, Bukka assured his brother, 'You'll get used to it.'

'Hah!' snorted Hakka.

A sylph in the soup

Respite came in the form of having dinner at the family home that evening with Sangama, Pattu and Valli. Sangama liked the new house but complained about missing her friends and how people were staring at her in the market and pointing in her direction. Before Hakka voiced his thoughts, Pattu interjected: 'She is there with protection, Hakka.' Sangama was none too happy on hearing that she was being accompanied without her knowledge.

'Ajji [grandmother], I told you we were being followed,' Valli remarked.

'Relatives have been showing up asking for jobs, friends who I'd lost touch with want favours, and everyone is so pleasant, including Kamala, my grumpy cousin,' Sangama observed. 'Honesty and forthrightness seem to have vanished after the two of you took your positions, putraru [sons].' Sangama laughed.

The brothers were aware that Valli had changed. She was a beautiful young woman. Sangama was of the opinion that it was time to find her a good husband.

'Do that and I will leave for an ashram and dedicate myself to it for life,' Valli mumbled in the background. She was tall, like Pattu, fun-loving like her mother and hard-working like her grandmother. True to form, she administered the hiring of staff in the palace and had taken responsibility for making it habitable.

'All sweet talk from Ajji, who just wants to send me off to some fat trader's home for good,' Valli added.

'I would have you here all my life my dear, but you have to get on with your own life,' Sangama replied.

'My life here is just fine and there is no need for you to arrange my life. By all means let me know if I need to mend my ways, but don't punish me by sending me away.'

Sangama had that sad look of a parent of a young daughter, who had seen and heard this before. 'Oh, how will this all end?' she thought, 'At least for now all are safe and happy, and there is little more one could ask.' She put her thoughts aside.

'Dinner,' she announced, and they gathered to sit in a circle on the floor.

Hakka recognized that life had changed. Normally Sangama would have served them but instead there were two women assisting her. Valli was helping them out too. The banter was all about the infamous Mani Iyer, the scribes, the ways in which Faraj was adjusting to his new environment, and Hakka complaining about the dogs barking too much.

'I would send them away but I know if I did, Bukka would leave because he loves them more than me.' Then he proceeded to complain that Mani Iyer was overwhelming them with official matters to read.

With that, Hakka revealed he had a brilliant idea:

'I will make Mani Iyer work just two days of the week and that way I will be able to tame the little tiger.'

Pattu burst out laughing until he nearly choked on his food. 'That is an uncanny description of the man!' Still, he was glad that the little tiger was surpassing even his high expectations of him. They talked for a while about where Hakka and Bukka needed to travel. Pattu gave them an update on the upcoming harvest and what was happening in the neighbouring Hoysala kingdom, which was always a topic of interest.

Amid all the banter, Bukka remained conspicuously quiet. Though never loquacious like Hakka, he was not a reticent person, either. A hint of a smile occasionally appeared. He was nevertheless enjoying the food and the attention he was getting from Valli. Contented certainly, but Bukka was unusually distracted.

'Bukka was looking at the accounts that Mani Iyer gave us and it seems we have a few tankas to spare,' Hakka announced. 'Amma, what do you need for the house? Do you think we should get some jewellery made for the wives of our three brothers and for Valli?'

'I hate jewellery,' a voice called from the kitchen.

'Give her a plant, give her an animal, give her a homespun saree or a piece of artwork, and her eyes will light up. Give her jewellery and she will smile because she wants to make you happy, but that is not something that makes her heart sing,' Sangama said.

'You can get me a puppy,' Valli mischievously remarked as she walked into the room where they were eating.

'There she goes again,' Pattu said indulgently.

'If we had a puppy, you and Ajji would be beside yourselves,' Valli said.

'Vallima, if you were to get married who would take care of the animal?' Pattu enquired.

'Since I am neither getting married nor going away, it's not an issue. So, when can we get a puppy?'

It was a normal enjoyable evening with their mother and brother. Hakka and Bukka decided to walk back to the palace, yet oddly they did not converse with each other and the evening ended with each of the brothers heading off to sleep. Hakka was far too alert to contemplate sleeping. He quietly sent a note to Pattu, informing him he would come over early in the morning to go for a ride.

'Pattu, how did you know when you met your wife that she was the one you would marry?' Hakka asked the next morning as they rode out.

'Hakka, she was a beautiful woman and a kind person. She also seemed to be brimming with goodwill and energy, easy to talk to and surprisingly open for someone who grew up in a very different setting.'

Riding on for a while longer Hakka decided to push the matter further.

'Pattu, do you know what my next question is?'

'Yes, Hakka. There is little in life that can truly surprise if you are observant. Since both of you came home to Anegundi, I've noticed how Bukka's face lights up whenever he sees Valli. Let us also think about the circumstances we are talking about. First, in our families, there is nothing unusual for a man to marry his niece. If that seems objectionable, in this case, I am not a brother by birth but rather by adoption. So that clears the way. If Valli finds this acceptable and, quite obviously Bukka does, it would be a blessing. Personally, I would never have raised the possibility. Yet I will be honest and tell you this is something I had hoped might happen. How often do you come across someone as steadfast, kind and capable as Bukka? One advantage is I will not have to get her a puppy!'

Pattu continued with his thoughts about the situation.

'Joking aside, they complement each other very well, while at the same time they have very many similar interests. However, it leaves me with a problem, tam'ma. It will require me to distance myself even more from the family to ensure there are no gossipers claiming that I have an undue influence on you and Bukka.

'If this works out, and I think it will, there are a few things you need to be aware of regarding my work. I have businesses in the Kakatiya kingdom, the Hoysala kingdom, the sultanate of Madurai and the Kerala kingdom, as well as with your sultan. In short, I deal with markets all across the peninsula. These are kingdoms that are, or will be, enemies of yours—that is inevitable.

'That raises the following question: should I move out of Kampili to avoid complications? If I do stay in Kampili, it will be necessary to keep a very low profile when I am in town. While you are my tam'ma, you are also my zabitah and I do not want to compromise you. Before you respond, let me add something more. Should this betrothal work out, I give you my solemn oath that I will not send a single gold mohur to help Bukka and Valli. They will reside where he lives using whatever means he has.'

Riding across the plain fields away from Anegundi, with twenty bodyguards in tow, Hakka expressed his thoughts out loud.

'Pattu, money is not something Bukka needs to worry about. There are no claimants to the treasure that Kampiladeva left behind, which is significant.

'However, there were also two other secret hoards that Kampiladeva seized when he attacked the Hoysalas and Kakatiyas. He took a large amount of tax revenues that were being transported and they were not aware of the identity of the attackers. While I intend to use a large part of it for the care of soldiers and families of the noblemen, some is also due to us. It is enough to last our family several lifetimes. Then there is the share of revenues that I get for my maintenance. I want to reassure you that Valli will live very comfortably, so you should stay true to what you want to do. I will not ask you to make a single compromise.'

'Very well. You speak to Bukka. I will speak to Sangama and Valli,' Pattu suggested.

'And then?' Hakka enquired.

'Let's discuss the details again. If all is settled at your end, we will meet in the evening, maybe even for a family celebration.' Pattu tried to brush off a tear as discreetly as he could.

When Hakka rode back to the palace, Bukka had finished the daily exercises with the troops. He noticed something unusual in his brother's demeanour.

'Hakka, are you okay?'

'Yes. I am simply overcome with happiness fit for a king, and I find it difficult to contain myself. Anyway, let's cancel dinner with Faraj. I would like to spend the evening to discuss how you will get paid and our finances. I have not given you a clear idea of what we have and what we should do about our money.'

Bukka nodded in agreement. If Hakka thought this was important then he would change their plans for the evening.

The day had been busy: recruiting for the military and judiciary, evaluating tax plans, deciding on buildings to be renovated, rewarding loyal men, and reviewing intelligence with Karthikeya and Shamshed. It was a warm evening and after returning to the palace, they settled into the newly designed garden under a huge mango tree. A glass in hand, Hakka contemplated how he would raise such a delicate issue. Discussing money was a good start.

'Bukka, you know that one part in twenty of taxes is what we get from the sultan for our maintenance. Mani Iyer calculates that it equates to four manns of gold, so half of that is yours. Let's share expenses. What remains is divvied between the two of us.'

Bukka stayed quiet. He looked down, smiled and collected his thoughts and took a quick quaff of some sharayam.

'To this day, Hakka, neither of us had much to live on, mostly because we sent what we had to Sangama and the sultan never paid us in the last three years. You overwhelm me by wanting to share what you have. Are you not being too generous?'

'That's not all, Bukka,' Hakka said. 'There is the treasure that belongs to the two of us. It is worth about a hundred and twelve manns of gold.'

Bukka decided to interrupt his brother.

'Hakka, your accounting is incomplete. It actually is about one hundred and ninety-six,' and he outlined where the defunct Kampili kingdom had stockpiled its treasures. 'Yet the chief problem is, how we are going to store all of it in one or two locations? Should we ask Pattu for help? Otherwise, having our names attached to so much wealth will only create more problems.'

Thinking about the ramifications of the money, Hakka remarked:

'Neither of us is a poor man, Bukka, and that is even after we spend it on friends, family and pensions for old soldiers, not to mention assisting old noble families who have fallen on hard times, and building schools.'

Pragmatic as ever, Bukka advised they speak to Pattu. Hakka agreed. He collected his thoughts. 'Bukka, I'm incapable of being diplomatic like you. I never keep anything from you, at least not for long. My question for you quite directly is: what does Valli mean to you? Do you love her?'

'She means a great deal to me. I do love her,' Bukka answered, looking straight at Hakka. 'It puts me in a difficult situation. I have wondered what you thought of it. What would Sangama's and Pattu's reaction be? Above all, would Valli even consider marriage? This is why I have remained quiet, trying to think of a way to solve this problem.' He smiled ruefully.

Hakka made a comical face before reassuring his brother.

'All of your questions have been solved.'

'How would that be?' quizzed Bukka.

'I think it is a wonderful idea and Pattu would be ecstatic if this were to come to pass. If I were to predict Sangama's thoughts, I'd say she's likely to be very happy. So that leaves

Valli, and I wager you, she will say yes! Actually, I think she will burst into a smile and say yes. For my part, I'll say how happy it would make me to see you settle with someone as wonderful as Valli.' Hakka laughed joyously.

'I have some very selfish motives as well. Valli will likely teach us how to behave like kings. Without her we will be two clueless soldiers all our lives and suffer the results!' Hakka noted with a chuckle. 'There are many ways in which we have to grow and the woman you hope to marry may be the one to help us do it. So, what do you think?'

Bukka looked bemused.

'How did all this become so easy, Hakka? I had myself going through unending loops of stupid logic about how I was going to solve this problem, and was on the verge of asking you about it.'

Meanwhile ...

When Pattu came home later that morning, he took Sangama aside to speak to her.

'I think I have a suitable groom for Valli.' He listed out admirable characteristics as Sangama nodded in approval. She smiled.

'Pattu you are either talking about one of the gods in the firmament or one of my sons.' They burst into laughter.

'Sangama, you are too clever for me. You've read my mind.'

Pattu sat by her side on the large balcony of the new house. She put her hand on his shoulder and addressed him, using the affectionate form of his name:

'Pattuma, as my grandchild and someone I have been with every day since she was born, Valli is the girl I never had. Like any mother or grandmother, I have wondered who would be good enough for her. The possible candidates were usually inadequate. Of late, I have thought of Bukka as the one who might suit her best. While she might be considered his niece, it's not true in blood. Suppose you had not been raised by me, and if you and Kanthi suggested Valli for Bukka, I would have said my prayers had been answered.

'In this case, I know the child like my own and I am even more sure that this will be good for them. Let us see if she finds this acceptable, because I'll not force her into it. Over the years I've learned to convince her but never force her. That's another reason why Bukka would be so well suited. Unlike Hakka, he is thoughtful and takes the path of reason. Hakka is a like a good-natured bull: if he sees something in his way, he will charge and knock it down. I am delighted with the idea. Let's call Valli and ask her.'

A servant went to fetch Valli from a far corner of the house. They could hear her anklets tinkling as she approached. She walked up the long verandah, her gait confident with a hint of the sensual, her long hair tied in a rough knot—usually it hung loose down to below her knees, and was perpetually getting tangled. A hint of a smile appeared when she neared them.

'This must be important if I was sent for while supervising the birth of a calf.' There was a divan in front of Sangama and Pattu. She sat down, putting a hand on each of their knees. 'What is it you wanted to talk about?'

Neither Sangama nor Pattu knew how to proceed, but Sangama took the lead.

'Valli, what I am going to say is important, so hear me out in full and I will answer any questions you have. We have an exceptional varan [marriage proposal] for you and think it would suit you both well. More to the point, you know this person well.' Valli's brow furrowed as she listened. 'As I have promised you from the start we will not take another step unless you are comfortable with what we are suggesting.' Sangama paused before mustering up the courage to ask, 'What would you think of Bukka for a husband?'

Valli remained calm, but her surprise and then her delight got the better of her and her face brightened. Sangama was impressed how she managed her emotions like her father.

'Ajji, if I may be permitted to think about it, I will give you my answer after dinner.'

'Why after dinner?' Pattu was perplexed.

'Because, Appa, I'm cooking today with Fathlullah and Idriss, the new cooks from Dilli who've come to work at the zabitah's house. They are coming to teach me today. Once that's done, I will be able to talk with the two of you. I must return to the cow and her calf. May I leave if you have nothing else to add?'

They watched her walk away. Sangama recalled how little effort it had taken to raise her. She'd become her companion, the daughter she never had, and a confidante. But most of all, Valli was shrewd and intelligent like Pattu.

'She is so much like you, Pattu,' Sangama smiled.

'I hope that is a good thing,' he said in jest.

Returning to his work, Pattu had a stream of people waiting to meet him. There was a large room at the side of the house where he attended to his business. Sangama noticed that Valli was conspicuously busier than usual, pushing herself as if to avoid having to deal with such a weighty question.

At dinnertime Valli introduced the Dilli cooks to Pattu and Sangama. Dinner started with a rose sherbet, followed by a fragrant pilaf and roast chicken. Then she served some plain rice with a meat stew delicately flavoured with spices. For the final course they were given a stuffed naan with a lentil soup to dip it in, along with a vegetable sautéed in onions and garlic. Dessert was Hakka's favourite, almond barfi.

Sangama was overwhelmed by the experience. The array of flavours was like nothing she had experienced. It felt like listening to a wonderful singer who presented a series of raagas she had never before heard. They were executed artfully, and left them feeling greatly satisfied.

Valli joined them at the verandah after dinner. This time she pushed the divan aside and sat on the ground by their feet. Looking at Pattu and Sangama, she said she had just one question: 'Do I have to become a Muslim since Hakka and Bukka converted to Islam?'

Sangama responded in an authoritative tone.

'No. It was their decision. You should have the ability to make your own choice.'

Valli looked down, and seemed to be searching for the right way to reply.

'If that is the case, Ajji and Appa, it would make me very happy to marry Bukka.'

Sangama pulled Valli up, took her by the hand, and walked her over to the little altar by her room. She brought out a bowl of vermilion and made a mark on Valli's forehead. Holding her head with both hands she whispered: 'May you be blessed and forever be a sumangali.' Sangama began to cry. As Valli embraced Sangama, they went out to Pattu. He felt a deep sense of joy mixed with an impending sense of loss. For so long, Valli had been the one who lit up the house.

'Must I live in that musty old house with those two crazy brothers?' Valli joked. 'If so, I have two conditions. First, my new husband better get me a puppy. Second, I do not want a big wedding.'

'Vallima, that crazy man already has six dogs—you don't need another one!' Sangama smiled.

'Seven is a good number, Ajji. Besides, the other six will look after the puppy. I should clear up now and thank the cooks,' Valli declared and walked away. It took Sangama a few minutes to regain her composure.

'I had hoped her wedding would be the biggest in the southern peninsula this year,' Pattu remarked ruefully.

'You may have wished that, but did you really believe she would agree to it?' Sangama said. 'Pattu, her perspective on life is to live it to the fullest and to be a good person. Grandeur, pomp and appearances have no place in her world. Yet she has an eye for beauty and elegance and grace. That is what she will bring to the Kampili kingdom.'

Pattu nodded and absentmindedly added: 'At least she will be living close by.'

———•———

Hakka and Bukka had finished dinner. A guard rushed in to seek permission to let Ramaswamy Mudaliar in. It was late but Pattu was accompanied by a retinue of servants. They brought with them trays of gifts, clothing and sweets. Greeting Bukka, he said formally:

'It would be a great honour, Bukka, alnnayib of Kampili, if you would accept the hand of my daughter in marriage.' He then gave him a stream of gifts.

'With pleasure, Ramaswamy Mudaliar,' Bukka replied. 'Does the bride have any conditions?'

'Yes, she does, Bukka,' a surprised Pattu replied. 'She wants a very small wedding, and ...' He stopped.

'What is it?' Bukka asked.

'She is not willing to convert to Islam.'

'That was never a condition,' Bukka replied.

'Then there is one final request, Bukka Raya, which is she wants a puppy as a wedding gift!' Pattu said, shaking his head in disbelief at what he just said.

'I'll be back in a minute, Pattu,' Bukka said and walked away, leaving Pattu and Hakka celebrating the good news. Bukka returned with a cloth bundle in his hand for Pattu.

'My wedding gift is ready, Pattu. I just got this kombai puppy delivered today. Let's make sure the wedding takes place while she is still a puppy.' Bukka touched Pattu's feet and then, for the first time, touched Hakka's feet to ask for his blessing.'

Mani Iyer was delighted he was asked to officiate at the wedding, but requested to see the horoscopes of the bride and the groom before he accepted. The next day Mani Iyer jubilantly informed Pattu:

'I foretell this marriage will raise the stature of this family to a level seen once in a millennium.' Pattu rolled his eyes upon hearing such a declaration but obliged him nonetheless with a smile.

Just as she wanted it

Valli married Bukka on a clear December morning at Pattu's house with about seventy people in attendance. Mani Iyer was in his element as he presided over the ceremony. The final act to bind them together was to have the bride and groom walk around the fire with his angavastaram tied to her saree. And with that, they were declared husband and wife.

Faraj watched the ceremony intently, with Karthikeya and Shamshed offering conflicting commentaries. Some generals were present, as well as a few of Pattu's close associates and friends from the early days when the family lived in a different neighbourhood.

After a delightful midday meal, Valli handed out gifts to their guests as they left: sweets they had made in their kitchen, along with pieces of clothing she had commissioned from weavers in Anegundi.

Not long after, the family and their servants accompanied Valli to her new home, 'the musty palace', as she called it. Karthikeya's wife, Sharada welcomed the new bride with an aarti, and the retinue left her at the doorstep. Despite being blissfully happy, it hit Sangama and Pattu hard, knowing Valli was no longer going to live with them. As they left, Valli shouted:

'Come for dinner tomorrow!'

Pattu just smiled and looked at Sangama as they walked back and said, 'I just hope she does not change.'

Within a month Valli had completely transformed the palace into a home. Nothing went untouched. A smooth and delightful order descended, with every hint of mustiness exorcised. One evening, as she sat by Hakka's side, she suggested:

'Hakkanna, it's time you and Bukka invited people for dinner. You cannot remain aloof, sitting alone over here every evening, drinking and eating before heading off to sleep.'

'Whom would we invite, Vallima?'

'Well, there are generals, some of whom are your friends. You should get to know your administrators too. It doesn't have to be very often but you should have people come to your palace with some frequency, Hakkanna. Moreover, we have musicians who can entertain our guests.'

'And you will arrange all of this and do all of the work, I presume, Vallima?' Hakka replied, laughing.

'Of course. Let's make sure that your kingdom knows that you are a man who has other characteristics than just being a semanya. Besides, you need to know individuals outside of your regular interactions. Imagine what you will discover after a few tumblers of kallu.' Valli was enthused with the idea.

Just then, Bukka walked in after having spent a few painful hours reviewing accounts with Mani Iyer at the Green Palace.

'Bukka, I've asked your bride to reform the tax system for Kampili,' Hakka announced as he roared with laughter. Valli put on a serious look, however, and announced:

'The two of you need to change the way you live your lives. You are not just in the military any more. After dinner, let me make a few suggestions of people you can invite to your first gathering.' Bukka rolled his eyes, staring at Hakka as if to ask, 'What is this all about?'

'Vallima thinks we behave as if we are recluses. She thinks we need to welcome more people into our home and entertain them. Otherwise, she believes, we are going be considered mad kings.'

'That's a good summary, Hakkanna,' a smiling Valli exclaimed, then welcomed Bukka home and left him to his drink.

Soon after dinner, she sat with the two of them and listed out the names of individuals she wanted to bring to the first gathering. They included two musicians for entertainment, a group of friends and recently recruited senior officials. They nodded meekly and she was off to organize it all.

Hakka increasingly complimented her about the palace which began to look elegant, yet simple. He was not just flattering her—the brothers agreed they now lived a more dignified lifestyle.

A parade of scorpions

Working at a relentless pace with Mani Iyer was exhausting, but the administrative structure for the kingdom needed to be set up. Hours were spent on making sure that capable people with unimpeachable integrity were hired. Recruitment for a standing army proceeded with little trouble because of the brothers' reputation as generals who took care of their men. While efforts to care for families of fallen soldiers were managed discreetly, it ironically made the rumour mill more credible and recruitment easy.

Mani Iyer had complete command over developments in each of the kingdom's districts and gradually the treasury saw an influx of revenues from landowners who previously fell behind on payments. Terms of repayment for large landowners were harsh but a milder tone was taken with smaller farmers. Occasionally the latter had their dues waived. Hakka grew increasingly satisfied knowing that the little tiger was constantly working on ways to solve every single problem of state that he encountered.

With an intelligence service in place, and a basic judicial structure set up, the brothers now heard about the seamier side of issues affecting the kingdom. There were vendettas among large landowning families, tribal animosities, and a palpable religious divide. The rumour mill was rife with gossip about the brothers. After the Muslims claimed them as their own, Hakka and Bukka were regarded as opportunists by the Hindu community. It did not help that they needed to adjudicate criminal and civil issues where they acted as the final arbiters.

The first case that came to them had huge ramifications. A young Muslim woman from a small village of tanners had been beaten and raped. She received attention from a kindly old vaidyan from the next village where she recuperated. It was a case nobody wanted to deal with.

Hearing about this got Hakka furious. They immediately summoned the young woman and her father, as well as the accused, who was a large landowner. The latter was invited to explain the course of events as he saw it. The arrogant man, who had never done a day's work in his life, had the temerity to state:

'The woman is a known whore, a conniving slut who has brought a false accusation against me.'

'How has the girl suffered such serious injuries?' Bukka interjected.

'These low-class people have devious ploys to extract money from god-fearing Hindus like us.' He paused for a moment, then pointed his finger at Bukka and declared:

'If you know what is good for you, son, do not make accusations.' Bukka held Hakka back, coaxing him to sit still.

The young woman appeared with her father. She still had a bandage on her head and had a severe limp, and was still obviously in pain.

'She was walking home from the village well in the evening, my lord, when she was accosted by the gentleman who wanted to take her to his house. She refused and started to walk faster.

But he caught up with her, pushed the pot off her head and threw her to the ground. As she screamed he kicked her in the head and other parts of her body as she lay on the ground. She was partly unconscious when he ripped her clothes off and raped her.'

'*Keḷamaṭṭada jeevana* [low life]!' the landowner retorted, and claimed that their account was untrue. He then made the mistake of walking up to where Bukka, Hakka and Mani Iyer were seated behind a table, slapping his hand on it.

'If you know what is good for you and your kingdom,' he advised in a harsh tone, 'you will eliminate barefaced lying by not giving it any audience. They are vermin and not respectable people like myself.'

Hakka's self-control gave way. He called the guards to bind the man's hands and to remove him from the room, and to have his mouth gagged. Only then did they bring him back.

When he returned, he looked dishevelled. Hakka turned to the young woman and asked what an appropriate punishment should be.

'Zabitah, he should make amends to all the women he has done this to.'

Hakka was in shock.

'How many are there that you know of?'

'At least seven in the last two years, zabitah.'

Showing masterful self-control, Hakka leaned over and consulted Bukka and Mani Iyer.

'Life in servitude to these families by doing menial work to repay them,' he suggested. They agreed and Mani Iyer rendered the judgment. The landowner would have screamed had he not been gagged. Then looking at the guards Hakka ordered:

'Take him back to his village with an armed guard, have him shaved bald, stripped naked, tarred and tied, and paraded around sitting backward on a donkey.' He stood up and walked out.

Two days later matters worsened. Reports came that the landowner's kinsmen from the neighbouring village had risen up against the tanners, not only killing many of them but also burning all their houses to the ground. Twenty-seven people were dead, including women and children. Hakka dropped to his knees, weeping and heaving with grief.

'Where does this poison come from?' he kept repeating.

Later that morning, instructions were given to find the ringleaders of the landowner's village, who had massacred the tanners. Bukka rode out from Anegundi with a contingent of five hundred soldiers in a show of force. The landlord's allies had built barricades on the road leading to the Hindu village, with about fifty men armed with scythes, clubs and knives waiting behind the defences they had built.

'Tell them to put their weapons down and ask the headman to come out and talk to us.'

As Karthikeya delivered the message a rock came flying, narrowly missing him. A man approached the barricade and screamed:

'We do not recognize your authority, Muslim zabitah. You decided to take vengeance against your own fellow people by believing the godforsaken Muslims and inflicting a grievous punishment against one of ours. Be gone, you two-timing bastard.'

'That sounds like a declaration of war to me,' Bukka announced. Karthikeya nodded in agreement.

'Charge!' Karthikeya bellowed. They moved forward. Unknown to the rebels, another company of soldiers had come from behind and surrounded them. The skirmish was over before it even started. The men were disarmed and had their hands tied.

As they disarmed the men, Bukka ordered:

'Have them shaved, stripped and tarred. Then parade them back through as many villages as possible all the way to Anegundi. The women and children can stay here but will not be permitted to go to their homes.'

Two days later, the naked men arrived at the capital. Hakka delivered their sentence in front of the Green Palace.

'Your sentence will be an example for the rest of Kampili. One faith will not raise its hand, individually or collectively, against another; and definitely not against women and children. Your properties will be used to compensate those whose lives you have taken or ruined. You will never again set foot in Kampili. You will do hard labour at the border of the kingdom with no possibility of redemption.'

A huge crowd gathered to watch the proceedings and hear Hakka's judgment. As the prisoners shuffled away, there was a sudden outbreak of chants.

'Jai Hakka! Jai Kampili! Jai Hakka! Jai Kampili!' This went on until Hakka and Bukka rode back to the palace.

Later that evening the brothers sat below their favourite mango tree and began an evening of hard drinking. Valli left them alone, with explicit instructions to the servants to make sure they ate. She went to bed realizing that problems would only get bigger with time. Yet there was solace in the fact that the crowd at the Green Palace had showed their support for Hakka's leadership.

Thuriferous

Numerous fragrances filled the palace at different times of the day. In the mornings she had jasmine in her hair with a faint hint of incense. During the day it changed to a barely detectable smell of sandalwood oil. By the evening it was just jasmine, though there were times when she wore different flowers depending on the season.

Bukka could smell the jasmine and incense when he woke up. As he opened his eyes Valli was there, smiling, but clearly she had something on her mind. She handed him a tumbler of hot brew.

'Drink it, Bukka, and your headache from last night should go away.' With a sheepish smile he drank it.

'The problems of state are only going to grow larger and more complicated with time. Kallu and sharayam will not ease your problems. Please enjoy it but it is no solution to the wider issues at hand. Find a different way to release your energy. For example, you may want to learn to cook Pharsi and Kabuli food from Idriss and Fathlullah who came all this way for you and Hakka, ostensibly to teach the two of you to cook. You could also take some time to teach me how to ride a horse.'

Bukka nearly spilt his brew.

'Since when have you wanted to ride?'

'Ever since I married you, Bukka. I want to see different places, and at a fast pace too. Not in a palki. I want to travel with you. I want to be able to teach our children to ride. If their mother can ride, they will be good horsemen. Besides, I love horses.'

Bukka was unable to contain himself and laughed till it gave him a bellyache.

'Ok, so get the tailor to make you some pajamas and you can wear my kurta from Dilli. We start tomorrow but don't complain that your body hurts after your first lesson.'

Valli jumped up with a huge smile on her face.

'Beware of what she comes up with next,' Bukka told himself, and went into another fit of laughter.

As they rode to the Green Palace later, Hakka was curious why his brother was so amused in the morning.

'You never laugh, Bukka,' Hakka prodded, hoping for a response. Bukka obliged. He told him about Valli wanting to learn to ride.

'All good queens know how to ride, Bukka.'

'Hakka, for that, either you would have to steal my wife or I would have to be out of the picture for her to be a queen,' Bukka said incredulously.

'She will be your queen and will know how to ride. It will be a great example to set,' Hakka said tranquilly. Then, with a mischievous smile, he added:

'May I come and watch her learn from you?'

At the Green Palace they had settled down to dealing with the issues of the day. Mani Iyer revealed an issue with revenue which needed resolving. Twelve families controlled nearly a third of the kingdom's land and all of them were delaying payment of their taxes. He advised Hakka and Bukka to pay them a visit and inform them of their obligations.

'I have an idea!' Bukka proclaimed. 'What if we invite one family every month to Anegundi, put the strength of the military on display and demonstrate the efficiency of the kingdom's new administration. After the display, invite them to one of the celebrations that Valli was planning. That way we mix a social occasion with a matter of state.'

Hakka was delighted.

'Show these bastards how big the military is, have Valli charm them after they have drunk sharayam, and their wives will be impressed by the pomp and circumstance. It would be an effective way to tickle these buggers into coughing up what is due and bring them into line.'

'Let's make it two at a time,' Mani Iyer interjected, nodding in agreement. 'That way they can begin competing with one another when they are here. It also means we will get the job done in less time.'

'Some people have a gravitational pull towards animals, and animals know kindness when it is shown to them,' Karthikeya said to Hakka at the paddock as they watched Valli go through her training routine. Bukka rode by her side. The cavalry was under Karthikeya's command and he was always on hand to make sure all was well at these evening sessions. Today Hakka was present as well. He had come to watch the progress Valli was making.

Valli had been taking her riding lessons for a few months now, and was now riding Chetana with a confidence that only came to someone who was fearless, athletic and appreciated animals. Not once had she complained about bruising the insides of her knees when learning to trot.

'I will suggest to Bukka that he should take her out on long rides in a quiet setting, so she really enjoys it and gets more confidence. Karthikeya, it's a pleasure to see someone take to a horse so naturally. Much of what they do comes instinctively. Qutlugh Khan used to tell us stories about how the Rajput noblewomen were taught how to ride. I think more women should learn to ride and more women should be involved in the service of the kingdom.' To himself, Hakka thought, 'I am amazed at the ideas that she comes up with.'

'We seem to spend more time with you in the Green Palace than my brother and I do elsewhere,' Hakka declared as he looked over at Mani Iyer, who was sitting cross-legged under a shady tree.

'As it should be, zabitah, as it should be, for you are building a kingdom from virtually nothing. The good news is that you have now built a solid foundation—but you still have a lot of work before it is perfect.'

'Perhaps not in my lifetime,' Hakka groaned.

Back in the Green Palace, once the key issues were debated, Shamshed informed the ministers that the intelligence services detected a few visitors from Daulatabad who were visiting the local mosques.

Information had it that they were circulating large amounts of money along with misinformation. The local mullahs and the ulema, of whom there were not many in a small kingdom, were being fed a diet of lies about Hakka and Bukka. Through trickery and deceit, it was claimed Hakka, Bukka and Qutlugh Khan had fooled the emperor into promoting the brothers. They further asserted the brothers had no moral authority and even the ulema and mashaiks in Dilli were opposed to the appointments. Consequently, there was no reason to pay heed to their rule or observe any directives from them, especially those that concerned matters relating to religion.

'Who reported this?' Bukka enquired.

'It was a young mullah from the same town that the riots took place a few months ago,' Shamshed replied. 'He was of the opinion that the rebels were treated justly and the visitors were intent on creating trouble.'

'You should have a conversation with him. Do you suggest these visitors be guests of the state?' Hakka asked.

Mani Iyer swayed back and forth.

'Yes. Imprison them for now and when we send the next courier to Daulatabad they should be returned with charges of undermining the emperor's command. I will draft the letter for you to affix your seal, zabitah.'

Pattu was present. Conscious of the seriousness of the affair, he mildly added,

'If the mullahs are so easy to prey on, take the initiative by bringing them into the fold. Make them feel that their flocks are being tended to. A bit of attention can pre-empt problems later on, like the way you found out about this from the young mullah.'

'Evil little scorpions creep up on you and sting you if you are not careful. Pain comes first, but if you are not mindful, their stings will kill you,' Hakka declared, noting how the problems of state compared so easily to those nasty creatures. 'And they never seem to stop causing mischief,' he mumbled.

'Zabitah, be prepared for bigger and more poisonous creatures coming at you in the future. This is what happens when you rule a kingdom, but it's our job to neutralize its impact before it does harm,' Mani Iyer said reassuringly.

Sitting on the side, Pattu had a wry smile on his face. In such a short time, the brothers had settled into managing the affairs of state exceptionally well. He remarked to himself that intelligence and drive had a way of overcoming most problems and it was obvious with the progress these three men were making.

Lured in

Ostensibly, the main reason for inviting the two important zamindars (large landowners) to Anegundi was to solicit their opinions on how the new administration should be arranged. With their experience and significant land holdings, they were well suited to provide counsel, they were told. A contingent of guards personally delivered the invitation to join the zabitah for consultations and celebration followed by dinner at the palace.

Kempayya and his family were landholders in the southern part of the Kampili kingdom. His family had held the fiefdom for two centuries, which adjoined the border of the Hoysala kingdom to the south. Devaraja, one of the other lords of a fiefdom, had holdings located to the east and close to the Kakatiya kingdom. The invitation was couched in a way to appeal to their egos. A day was set and the guards would accompany them to the capital city. The stage was set.

Arriving in the city, the zamindars were feted with sumptuous accommodation and an impressive itinerary. The day after they arrived, Bukka arranged for the military to provide a demonstration and a parade. With recruitment now standing at nearly eight thousand, it also provided Hakka and Bukka a chance to see how well the new men were shaping up. Horses thundered by, lancers galloped to ear-shattering war cries, and a parade of the whole army shook the ground as they marched past their guests.

Mani Iyer softened them up later in the day by discussing their suggestions about how the structure of the iqta might be improved. Every recommendation he heard was driven by self-interest but phrased as an initiative of national importance. They even brazenly suggested reducing land taxes and disciplining Muslims. Mani Iyer patiently heard them out.

Celebrations followed that evening as Valli had proposed. A grand concert by local Muslim and Hindu artists was followed by a spectacular meal. Valli further impressed the guests by introducing Idriss and Fathlullah to the guests. Mani Iyer stood by marvelling at the simple but elegant manner in which Valli choreographed the event. After dinner the crowd continued to mingle. Bukka introduced Pattu to the special guests. When he presented Pattu to Kempayya as his father-in-law and Hakka's brother, the man was nearly speechless.

'Ramaswamy Mudaliar, I was unaware you were related to the brothers,' he muttered. Within a few minutes the man left the party.

'He looked like he saw a demon, Pattu. What did you say or do?'

'It's my dealings with him in the past that are of interest.'

'Tell us, Pattu,' Hakka said.

'In this case I will put aside my business discretion as this man doesn't deserve it. It all started when Kampili was defeated, and Kempayya requested a large loan. He never paid his interest on the loan and when it was due a year ago, he refused to pay it. My representatives went to negotiate the collection but he directed Hoysala soldiers to harass them. Mind you, this was taking place within the borders of Kampili. It must have surprised him to see me here today. Anyway, why is he here?' Pattu said.

Mani Iyer had joined the group and bluntly replied: 'To force our two guests to cough up their overdue land taxes, which are quite substantial.'

Pattu rubbed his chin doubtfully.

'The man is not honourable and he perpetually plays both sides. I just hope that his double-crossing will come to an end. Am I to presume that this lemon will be squeezed by you, Mani Iyer?' Pattu asked.

'Of course. It will be the first major test of my persuasive skills.'

Mani Iyer's idea of persuasion was demonstrated the next day. The two zamindars were roused early in the morning with an 'invitation' that brooked no delay and were escorted to the Green Palace. He courteously presented the two men with the state's formal demand of overdue taxes. When the zamindars protested, Mani Iyer informed them that if the dues were not paid, he would be obliged to use the army and take control of their lands in compensation.

Kempayya blustered and threatened, claiming he had friends to the south, the Hoysalas. Mani Iyer lost his patience. The velvet glove came off to reveal the iron fist. He told Kempayya that if he tried that he would not only lose all of his lands, but also be branded a traitor of the state. He laid down the law.

'If you cooperate, for the next two years you will both forfeit control of your lands to the kingdom. Once you have paid your dues in full, they will be returned to your control. During this period, a contingent of the zabitah's soldiers will be stationed on your lands, along with an accountant who will have access to your books. They will post signs that the land is temporarily seized by the Kampili kingdom as a result of delayed taxes.'

Disconcerted, the other landowner Devaraja sputtered and said they would appeal to the sultan and lodge a complaint about their treatment. Mani Iyer sat swaying back and forth.

'The zabitah *is* the sultan's voice—you don't want to draw his majesty's attention to yourselves. The zabitah is going to be here shortly. I would suggest you both acknowledge his kindness since he has not yet pursued any harsh measures with either of you. I would also advise you express your lifelong fealty to him. It would be a wise gesture on your part.'

Hakka and Bukka walked in shortly afterwards and suddenly found the two men thanking them profusely before going down on their knees promising perpetual loyalty. Hakka stifled the laughter bubbling up within.

News quickly circulated about the fate of the zamindars. Six months later, the Privy Council was informed that all major landowners had paid their taxes.

'The treasury has more than enough resources for expenditures for the remainder of the year,' Mani Iyer declared.

Pattu, who was attending this session, added:

'Quite surprisingly, all my loans have been repaid with interest, as well.'

'Valli ought to be thanked for her idea about hosting these celebrations,' Hakka declared, 'and Mani Iyer should be commended. To see the two wretches on their knees was satisfying. I'm amazed just how persuasive Mani Iyer can be.'

Drip, drip, drip

Before they had left Dilli, Qutlugh Khan had informed the brothers that he would occasionally inform them about significant developments at the capital. A courier would meet Faraj, deliver a letter and supply him with other information that was not safe to be recorded in a letter.

Faraj walked into the palace, covered in dust from a long ride. He and Karthikeya had been out on a tour of inspection of the forts to the north and east of Kampili. Bukka met him in the courtyard as he handed his horse to a groom.

'I met a courier from Qutlugh Khan when we were out north. He brought a letter. It is not what's in the letter that is worrying. The courier, who is someone that Qutlugh Khan trusts, brings worrying news. There is much to discuss, so let

me know when I can give you and the zabitah the full picture,'
said Faraj.

'If there is no need to reply right away, then let's meet this
evening and you can have dinner with us,' Bukka replied.

Neither Hakka nor Bukka got a word in edgewise at dinner
as Valli kept Faraj busy with questions about his trip, the
condition of the forts, how the horses handled the ride, his
observations of the countryside, and whether he felt the people
he saw were content. Bukka teased her after dinner.

'It's time we appointed you minister of happiness.'

'Bukka, how do you know what conditions are like out there?
You need to find out. A hungry child today is a blemish on the
kingdom, and may be the cause of an uprising tomorrow,' Valli
astutely responded.

'Excuse me, I meant to say minister of well-being,' Bukka
replied, continuing to tease her.

'I have that position already, Bukka,' she retorted with
twinkling eyes.

The men then gathered under their beloved mango tree in
the garden, and Faraj began to summarize the letter.

'Qutlugh Mian sends his greetings and the messenger has a
gift from him to celebrate Bukka's marriage. I am not surprised
Bukka was married first because no woman in her right mind
would want to marry Hakka. He wishes Bukka and his bride
good health, much happiness and many beautiful children. He
says he misses your company at Dilli. He notes near the end, "I
deeply miss your honesty and friendship."'

Faraj paused to remember the verbal message.

'Qutlugh Mian commends the zabitah on the exemplary job
he has done, as well as the alnnayib of Kampili. He says you have
given no quarter for any criticism and even the conservatives,

and you know who I mean, have not been able to cast doubt on the management of the kingdom. He understands it is a model from which other zabitahs can learn. Wishing the two of you continued success with this endeavour, he concludes by saying, "I hope your work will continue to shower blessings on the people of Kampili, Inshallah."'

Before proceeding with the rest of the message Faraj was forced to collect himself.

'The final part of the message is troubling,' Faraj revealed. 'Events in the empire have taken a turn for the worse. Though the campaign to Multan was a military success, the Sunni population suffered many massacres after the war—it was said to be retribution for the uprising. The uprising was helped by a rogue Khorasan army that greatly exacerbated the uprising. Forces opposed to the sultan are using the disturbance to discredit him and his reputation.'

He continued.

'There have also been uprisings in the Doab, where the taxation of the landed peasants has been misrepresented. These administrative failures have not been helped by the fact that the rains have been poor.

'To make matters worse,' Faraj said, 'the ulema and mashaiks feel they are not given the privileges they were once granted and they find the sultan's interpretation of Islam to be offensive. Unfortunately, it may well be a case that they do not have as deep an understanding of the holy book as he does and a campaign of false rumours is all they can muster. It does not help that the sultan's introduction of a new currency went horribly wrong. And having kept a large number of the maliks in Dilli while their families remain in Daulatabad has led to a great deal of dissension and plotting. This has created strife and an inability to conduct the business of the empire.'

With a deep breath, Faraj relayed the last of the bad news.

'Qutlugh Khan's deep concern for the future is that uprisings in Multan and the Doab will encourage more fractious behaviour. And the sultan's temper and lack of diplomacy has made situations worse than they needed to be.'

Faraj concluded Qutlugh Khan's message:

'He says, "Finally, Hakka and Bukka, Yaraan-e-Miafaq, continue with your good work. Please be wary of any malign influences in your part of the world, though I presume that the artists of chaos have much to busy themselves with in the north. May Allah's blessings be with you."'

Faraj stood up as he prepared to leave. But he clearly had something more to say.

'What is it?' Bukka asked.

'Zabitah and alnnayib, my apprenticeship with the two of you ended three months ago. I had asked for it to be extended. As that extension is now ending, if Qutlugh Khan is agreeable, may I be employed by you? I would like to make the Kampili kingdom my home and, if I am worthy, be a member of your army.'

Hakka stood up and walked over to Faraj.

'The two of us would certainly welcome you. In your years of service to us, you have proven to be more than worthy. Let us discuss an assignment that would suit you.'

With that, Faraj departed.

'What do you think of the news, Bukka?' For a moment, his brother simply rubbed his forehead to gather his thoughts and process information he just heard.

'Hakka, we are facing very dangerous times. For as long as the sultan was a credible threat, the Hoysalas to the south left us alone and the Kakatiyas to the east were quiescent. That will rapidly change now. We have always been an irritant to the Hoysalas. It won't be long before they start to test the perimeters of our territory or, worse still, launch a full-scale invasion. I would suggest that we use an opportune moment—and pre-empt them. Remember, our scouts report Balalla is presently obsessed with seizing territory on his southern borders. When he next goes to war there, it will divert their attention and resources. Then we launch an assault into their territory from the north and push into it as far as we can. If nothing else, it will give us a useful tool to bargain with. The army is primed and ready.'

'Let's do it, alnnayib,' Hakka responded with determination. The two brothers set to work.

6

Apostasy

1337: Kampili—Waking up to possibilities

'Zabitah, if I've been too forceful in promoting an agenda of building the administration and it's been to the detriment of the kingdom, you must tell me. I'll remove myself and return to the temple,' Mani Iyer said with a deep namaskaram that underlined his affronted feelings. The brothers were alone in the Green Palace with him. Mani Iyer had been giving them an update on important developments and future plans. Hakka had balked at the volume of work being asked of them.

Bukka immediately sought to address the matter.

'What makes you say this, Mani Iyer?'

'It's my opinion that the zabitah feels I'm getting the two of you bogged down with the administration of the state. If you recall, I laid out a plan for the kingdom and I've been following it closely. Unless that work is completed, the rest will not come together,' Mani Iyer replied.

'What do you mean by the rest not coming together?' Hakka interjected gruffly.

'While you've secured the borders of the kingdom, it is clear that the upheaval in the surrounding kingdoms will have consequences for Kampili. Should you want to invade others and seize territory or wage war against invaders seeking to seize your territory, Kampili will need to rely on its resources, zabitah. The sultan and his vast treasury and army will be of little help.

'When that happens, the administration of this kingdom will come under severe pressure, and all your initiatives will come to nothing if your structure is not strong enough to withstand the challenges it will indubitably face. My job is to make sure you complete the work before events beyond your control begin to unfold. If you're willing to persevere with the plan you accepted at the beginning, I'll continue working on it. Otherwise, I'll return to the temple.' Mani Iyer's ultimatum to Hakka was blunt.

Unaccustomed to such demands, Hakka was initially upset to the point of wanting to dismiss the petulant priest. But as he took a deep breath, he realized that the kingdom's progress was due to the little man. His brilliance was incomparable, his integrity was unquestionable, and his loyalty total. Hakka stared at his brother and noticed the telltale sign: Bukka was sitting with his hands cradling his chin, gazing intently, which meant he was concerned and this was looking like a major problem.

'What initiatives do you think I, or Bukka and I, have in mind, Mani Iyer?' Hakka enquired in a tone of voice that was respectful and soft.

'Zabitah,' he began when Hakka cut him off.

'When it's just the three of us together, please do not use the honorific, Mani Iyer. You have the liberty to call us by our names. You have earned that privilege.'

Mani Iyer smiled, something they'd rarely seen.

'Hakka and Bukka,' he started again, 'the Kampili kingdom is not where your enterprise and efforts will end. Both of you are too large for a kingdom so small, not that it is a small kingdom. You will accomplish more, consolidate territory and definitely make your mark. And events as they are now playing out are ones that you can and should grasp. But you must build a structure that will support your plans. Great kings, Hakka and Bukka, are exceptional generals and superb administrators. Without both, there's no room for greatness. So, should I return to the temple tomorrow morning for the first prayer?'

Hakka was stunned. Bukka chuckled to himself. The 'little tiger' had expertly mauled Hakka.

'Wonder how Hakka deals with this?' Bukka thought, realizing he had never witnessed anyone pull up his brother before, much less take him to task for a lack of effort.

'Mani, my problem is trying to keep up with you. Please forgive me if I have appeared impatient, especially when the blame lies with me,' Hakka apologized. Bukka found it difficult to hide his smile.

'No need to apologize, Hakka. It's your kingdom and you need to make sure you build it well,' Mani Iyer said as he got to his feet. Before he left, he stopped in his tracks and turned around:

'There is an issue that the two of you need to give some thought. I hear rumblings in the kingdom about the two of you being Muslims. Not that anyone feels you are partial, but looking at the broader picture, it may become a major obstacle to your plans.'

Mani Iyer wished them well and left. Hakka glanced at his brother.

'Do not laugh! I am still feeling the effect of the scolding I just got from the little tiger. He is fearless and his honesty is his most effective weapon. Not even Sangama has scolded me like this.'

Back at the palace, Hakka paced the long verandah.

'What do we do about our faith, Bukka?'

'It's becoming a problem and it impacts a large number of other issues. Let's speak to Mani Iyer about it and perhaps get some advice,' Bukka suggested.

They heard Valli laughing at the entrance of the palace. She walked on to the verandah announcing:

'A loyal subject would like an audience with the rajas.'

'Who?' Bukka asked.

'Your father-in-law,' she said. The two of them sat up in an instant. 'There is not one other person in the world who commands that kind of respect from the two of you,' Valli observed, amused.

'That, Vallima, is because emperors must be given the respect due to them from petty kings like us,' Hakka replied, laughing at the reference to themselves as petty kings. They walked over to greet Pattu, who had been travelling for a month.

'He's staying for dinner, and I've asked Sangama to come as well,' Valli informed the brothers.

Settling down under their favourite mango tree in the garden, with all seven dogs nestling next to them, it felt like an evening when they could just relax and enjoy themselves. A servant poured fresh kallu and Pattu looked at Valli.

'I have things to look after,' she announced as she took the unsubtle hint. Sangama got up too and left with her. It was Hakka who spoke up:

'Pattu, she knows more state secrets than you do.'

Pattu smiled and then grew pensive.

'Tammagalu, what I am about to say puts me in a very awkward situation. A few important nobles in the Hoysala nation are deeply concerned the king is on his last legs and the heir will be unable to manage on succession. They are aware that I'm related to the two of you and want to know if you'll meet them.'

'Traitors! If they are scheming now, they'll do it again,' Bukka burst out. 'While I'm not sure what Hakka's view is, I find it repulsive. Accepting their offer will bring us down to their level.' He angrily shook his head.

Hakka turned to Pattu.

'I'm in agreement with Bukka. Let's not entertain this. It's useful to know what other leaders are thinking, but if we address the Hoysalas, let's do it with a sword and not deceit.'

Pattu took a long, satisfying swig of his kallu.

'I anticipated your answer so that's what I conveyed to the individuals. They seemed sceptical that a small kingdom like Kampili would not be inclined to consider such a proposal.'

'Bukka would agree with me that once you act dishonourably, you'll never restore your reputation,' Hakka responded. 'All that remains then is to swim in a swamp with poisonous creatures.'

After Pattu and Sangama left, the brothers discussed the matter some more.

It was Bukka who had taken the measure of the situation.

'All the challenges we are facing are connected, Hakka. Changing our religion will mean a break from the sultan.

Meanwhile the sultan's world is increasingly more fragile and may begin to collapse. This might require protecting ourselves and our own interests by declaring independence. That would be more manageable if we were to change faith, yet again. Using your metaphor, we may have to ask the Great Tailor for another suit. Then we'd be able to examine the three major threats: the Hoysalas to the south, the Kakatiyas to the east, and then Ma'bar, the Madura Sultanate and the Pandyas further south.'

Hakka lay on his side on a long divan with his head propped up by his hand.

'Bukka, how will we reconcile ourselves to an act of betrayal, given the oath we took?'

He looked deeply troubled.

Imperatives

Bukka was riding behind Valli as they made their way down to the valley that cradled the Tungabhadra river. Riding down the steep incline, her head covered in the folds of a light cotton dupatta she wore to avoid the dust, she sat tall in her saddle, in total control of Chetana. Over the last couple of years she'd perfected her riding skills and, like everything else in her repertoire, she did it elegantly. She'd conjured up a riding outfit. She wore a loose kurta in the brightest colours she could find, a well fitted pair of pajamas and a dupatta she invariably used to cover her hair. She'd ordered leather slippers after hearing from Faraj about what the Rajputs wore in the north. And when it was cold, she wore a quilted jacket, like the ones that she'd had made for both Hakka and himself. In fact, even Chetana had the brightest saddle cloth with bells and clearly identified her rider as a woman. He followed, delighted to just watch her.

His mind wandered: she'd grown with time, and she'd forced them to grow along with her. She was still mischievous and fun-loving, but also shrewd like her father. Bukka thought, 'She's the only person in the world who works harder than Mani Iyer, Hakka and myself.'

Karthikeya, one of Valli's favourites, was riding next to her and she talked to him about his wife and children and the village they'd just visited. Bukka caught snippets of the conversation, which he knew was not going to end soon. This gave him a chance to sift through and weigh all of the information that had come their way recently. And it was becoming clear life was soon going to get complicated.

His mind went back to the sultan coming down south last year, on his way to the Ma'bar to quell another rebellion, this time by one of his hand-picked governors: Sayyid Ahsan Shah. This was the fifth rebellion in as many years. The sultan had brought his imperial army of a hundred and forty thousand down south and wanted to finally overwhelm the Kakatiya kingdom at Warangal before going on to extinguish Ahsan Shah's aspirations in the Ma'bar.

The imperial army had been decimated—not by the opposing side, which did not have a chance, but by a mysterious disease. As one of the informants told them 'the stench was in the air for miles around the fort of Warangal. The soldiers suffered from dysentery and then died in short order. The bodies' extremities turned black. The sultan lost half his army and nearly died himself. He was saved by the hakeem who had saved Qutlugh Khan and Bukka at the battle of Sinahagad, Behrooz Behrooz. Limping back to Daulatabad, the sultan barely recovered and then began to make his way back to Dilli. Rumours of a rebellion near Daulatabad forced him to retrace his steps.

'Finally, putting down the rebellion, the sultan had begun his weary trip back to Dilli, only to hear of two more rebellions that had erupted in Lakhnauti (Bengal) and Bihar.'

Bukka was convinced that the emperor was losing his ability to keep the far-flung provinces in check. The powerful, the capable and even the intelligent kings and emperors fall when they tread on the slippery assumption that they can do it all. Yet, that posed an immediate problem for Kampili. The Hoysalas to the south, and the Kakatiyas to the east would certainly begin adding this information to their calculations. Bukka saw that the survival of a small kingdom like Kampili would require quick and decisive action on their part. Yet there were a number of issues that would still have to be resolved.

He could see Valli pulling back on the reins and Chetana slowed down to a trot. As she came up alongside him, she was smiling indulgently.

'What?' he asked.

'I knew you were daydreaming, so I thought I would wake you up since we are a few minutes away from the palace.'

Faith, independence and territory

It was late in the afternoon and Hakka was in the Green Palace working with Mani Iyer on the administrative and military command structure, debating how supplies could be stored in forts and other parts of the kingdom. He had taken Mani Iyer's admonition seriously and concentrated on getting these issues resolved. They deferred the military command structure until Bukka returned from his trip to a troubled southern border town.

As they were bringing their discussions to a close, Bukka and Karthikeya walked in. They were covered with dust and dirt from the ride through the countryside.

'It might be best if we finished this conversation at the palace once you have cleaned up,' Hakka suggested, before teasing his brother: 'Besides it's going to be fun to see how Valli deals with someone who looks like he has been rolling around in the dirt and playing in the mud like we did when we were kids.'

As they entered the palace, Valli was waiting for them. Hakka could not stop laughing out loud as he saw Valli roll her eyes. She directed Bukka outdoors to the garden to wash up.

Mani Iyer and Hakka relayed to Bukka the news they had heard, after which Mani Iyer returned to the Green Palace.

'I think we should get Mani Iyer a horse-drawn carriage so he can get around faster. He walks everywhere and it is funny to see a little mendicant surrounded by a bevy of guards,' Hakka declared.

'I'll organize it, Hakka,' Bukka replied. 'For now, however, it might be useful for us to think about how the chaturanga mat is changing.'

'Tell me then, how do you see the circumstances changing?' Hakka asked.

'Faith, independence and territory. Those are the three parts to the puzzle. The first is personal, the second is a consequence of the first, and the third is about how we view our prospects once the first two are in place. But each, in its own way, is interconnected to the others.

'If we are to consider conversion, let's have a meaningful conversation with Mani Iyer. He's likely to be best placed to guide us through this predicament. Maybe it is something we should consider quickly. If we convert, the sultan would consider us to be apostates, and it would be interpreted as a declaration of independence.

'The third, while not of immediate importance, is something we had better start planning: battle plans, preparing the soldiers, arranging supplies, setting out attack routes and making sure our flank is protected when we proceed.

'Yet the simple question you, or we, must answer is: do we think the tide has turned against the sultan, and he's implicitly given up on the south? If yes, we start to take the initiative and move on all three matters. That's how I see the chaturanga mat, Hakka.'

Hakka stood up and began pacing.

'You do realize, Bukka, that this is audacious? Are we capable of doing this? Do we have the wherewithal to pull off a manoeuvre like this? Do we have the grit and the determination to get this done? I start to whine when Mani Iyer pushes me to do more. How will we manage such big responsibilities? We were not trained to be kings. In fact, if it had not been for you and the little tiger, I would not have even managed to be a capable zabitah.

'My big concern is: am I up to this huge challenge? Because I know that I cannot do this on my own and I will need you on this journey.'

Hakka kept pacing, waiting for Bukka to respond.

'Hakka, without audacity we wouldn't be alive today. Neither of us shirks hard work or great effort. I'd even say, we have enough "chaturanga sense". Of course, not all great kings, Hakka, are trained for such eventualities. Mostly they are great generals who learn how to lead and govern as they progress, being fully aware they need good counsel and help. I think you can deal with big problems because the resources you have are equally large.

'Then, Hakka, remember that Valli and I will give you our all to make sure you succeed. And on the battlefield, I'll lead the charge for you. To answer your question, I'm ready whenever you are.'

Hakka sat down. He seemed pensive and remained quiet for a while. Valli came into the room to call them to dinner. The moment he saw her, his face lit up. He announced:

'Vallima, it is time to make you a queen because you deserve to be one.'

Valli looked at Bukka, puzzled. He looked at her as if to say, 'I'll explain later.'

Divine tailoring

'I'm not going to drill with the regiment today,' Bukka announced when Valli nudged him awake and stood by his side with a hot drink to wake him up. Sitting up, he took the drink and all he did was drink it. He stayed quiet and still. She looked at him quizzically as she sat down next to him. She'd come to understand just when he was wrestling with inner demons. And this one had him in its grip. For a few days now, it was clear he was on the losing side of this joust.

When it seemed like this altercation with his loyalties and ethical predispositions was not going well, she felt it was time to help him.

'Bukka, if you cannot talk about it, you will not be able to fight off the monsters you're wrestling with,' she declared in a firm tone. That woke him up. He started to speak. From that point it was a deluge. He was struggling with breaking an oath and seemed consumed by guilt for what would seem like opportunism when they changed religions again.

He told her why he converted to Islam, and how they were now considering returning to being Hindu.

'This time I feel it might be seen as outlandishly opportunistic,' Bukka admitted.

'You and Hakka might feel that way, but it would not be misunderstood,' she said bluntly.

'Why?' he asked.

'Where most people are Hindus, your action will be greeted as coming back into the fold. You may even gather some goodwill and support from the people of Kampili, excepting the Muslims. For all the plans that you and Hakka have in mind, you cannot manage them as Muslims.

'Having said that, you need to come to terms with it. Make sure you believe in what you are doing—that it is for the right reason—consult some holy person to guide you through your intentions. If you do go ahead, make the transition with grace and have a wise man walk you through this journey.

'Most of all, Bukka, if you break a promise or an oath, make sure that what comes of it is good, righteous and in the interest of all. Not just for self-aggrandizement. If you do it for the right reasons, you will overcome your apprehension. Appa has often spoken of a pragmatic holy man who lives north of here. He would frequently see him in the years following Amma's death and was always able to find solace after conversations with him. His name, if I recall correctly, is Vidyaranya.'

When Hakka and Bukka raised the question of changing faith and converting back to Hinduism, Mani Iyer told them:

'In religion and religious affairs, I am not even an artisan. At best I could be a housekeeper for the gods and their abode. You must meet someone who understands the realm of the sublime and who can speak clearly to your spiritual state, even if you are unaware that you might be in need.'

Hakka frowned.

'Mani Iyer, is this person pragmatic like you?'

'Yes. Vidyaranya is one of the most pragmatic persons I know.'

The journey to where Vidyaranya lived was a two-day ride. Mani Iyer advised them to take Valli 'because you are the three legs of the stool on which this enterprise rests'. It did not take much convincing to get Valli to join them. Karthikeya, the dogs and bodyguards accompanied them too. They spent a night at one of the resting places built for travellers. Valli was in her element, observing flowers she had never seen before, and making the men pause whenever she saw a beautiful vista. Bukka was grateful she was with them because it distracted them from the bigger issue at hand.

Early in the next day's ride, they were met by one of Karthikeya's scouts. He guided them to a small farm on the outskirts of a tiny village. The stray dogs barked as they noticed the approaching visitors. Valli called on their own dogs to stay back while the men dismounted.

A tall, handsome man, with a sculpted torso, walked out to meet them. Hakka thought that he looked like a king. The man had a broad smile. He did a namaskaram and welcomed them.

'My name is Vidyaranya.' Pointing in the direction of a small house he invited them to meet his wife Andal. The woman was almost an older replica of Valli: tall, gracious, and beautiful. She was a trifle more reserved than her husband but became very animated when she heard that Valli had ridden all the way.

'I think a queen should know how to ride; so should a lot more women,' she exclaimed. Valli, in her inimitable direct style, said:

'Andal, I am not a queen and do not aspire to be one.'

Accompanying them into the house, she replied:

'But aspirations and outcomes in life are not always aligned. When you are a queen, you will serve as an example for all to draw on.'

The interior of their house was simple and graceful, consisting of three large rooms: one for cooking and eating, another for sleeping, and a third to receive guests. Andal asked them to wash at the well outside and then come to eat. Hakka, used to assessing his soldiers, was impressed by Vidyaranya's excellent physique as he pulled on the rope to draw water for them. This was an unusual hermit who led a demanding and active life along with his deeply contemplative practices.

They sat on the floor, and Andal and Vidyaranya served them a simple but tasty meal. After lunch they all went for a walk through the farm. All day the conversation was about the two brothers' travels and the various places they had visited, with their hosts asking many questions about the emperor, the nobles and the ulema.

Hakka tried to steer the conversation to the sensitive issue of conversion. Vidyaranya gave him a level look and said:

'Hakka, there may be a time when it will be appropriate to speak about such issues. For now, let us just enjoy the day, your company and share our experiences. We are delighted that you have come to us, and weighty matters should wait for the right time. I hope they will.' Bukka detected a steely determination in his voice. This man and his wife were not at all what he had expected.

They left early the next morning, and for the first few hours the brothers were silent. Valli chatted about their hosts, their home, garden and livestock, and their gracious hospitality.

As they rode back to Anegundi, Hakka asked out loud, as he frequently did, the question that was preying on his mind.

'Even in the presence of an emperor, Bukka and I were never hesitant to express our views or ask questions. What was it about this man that stopped me from asking the question that was the objective of this trip? Wasn't this a simple yes-or-no answer?'

As Hakka pondered, he noticed Valli smiling.

'What is it that you see and I have missed, Vallima?' Hakka quizzed. Valli paused. She glanced over to Bukka in search of reassurance, to which he instinctively nodded.

'When you both became Muslims, it was to reassure the sultan. There was nothing unusual in that scenario. Many people did that. You were just two more who offered a gesture of fealty to the emperor by converting to Islam. Your situation today is totally different,' she remarked.

Bukka marvelled how, in the years since he had married Valli, she had become a third participant and advisor in most of their deliberations. There were no secrets from her; while she rarely offered her opinion, they frequently asked for her views. The brothers respected her judgment. Very often she would decide the outcome when Hakka and Bukka had a difference of opinion. While Bukka would follow Hakka's decision, it was Hakka who looked to her for an additional voice. Her insights, while simple, cut through the clutter of any debate. Most of all, she could take the measure of a person in an instant. When she found someone wanting, ignoring her opinion usually led to problems later.

'How so?' Hakka asked.

'Hakkanna, Vidyaranya's making a very important decision. He needs to be sure before deciding whether he should ally himself with a king in the making. A mistake of this magnitude could lead to losing a great deal of the authority that he commands today. Yet, the right decision means he could be an even greater force of good.

'And there is more. He spent his time sizing you up, as well as Bukka and myself. The questions he was asking, I think, concerned whether you are a good person. Do you exhibit integrity? How do you express your conviction and what evidence is there to suggest that you follow the just path? Do you listen carefully to others and their opinions? And are you arrogant?'

Hakka was silent. Then she added:

'While I think he will give you his benediction unconditionally, he obviously does not think the time is right. But I think he will send for us.'

'Neither Bukka nor I would have thought that, Vallima.'

'Hakkanna, my only advantage is I can visualize and comprehend matters more effectively, unlike the two of you,' Valli said, making the most of her opportunity to poke fun at them, and mimicking Hakka's sometimes imperious tone.

Caged animals

A month had passed since their visit to Vidyaranya. Hakka's increasing anxieties were clear to see and Bukka was equally consumed by doubt. They would fall back on the familiar framework of raising queries and then finding answers. It usually worked. Bukka knew they'd have to talk their way through it. There was too much at stake. Not to flesh out every single outcome would be foolish.

'Bukka, think about this,' Hakka propounded. 'The emperor has gone north. It's been a year since the rebellion in Ma'bar by Ahsan Khan. Normally the emperor would have given free expression to his wrath, but he's left Qutlugh Khan in Daulatabad with a contingent of just four thousand soldiers and little by way of cavalry. That's barely enough for a defensive force and little else. Besides, Qutlugh Khan is getting old and the injury at Sinhagad set him back significantly. He is in no state to take on an aggressive rebellion.'

Hakka picked up a twig where they sat under the mango tree and started snapping off pieces, one at a time.

'Bukka,' he muttered, 'we will get snapped like this twig if we do not get this right, or take too long to move.'

Bukka looked squarely at Hakka. He said:

'First let's consider all that the sultan has endured and achieved over the last two years. Problems started when he had to deal with the rebellion in Multan after Bahram Aiba Kishlu Khan refused to move to Daulatabad. Whatever was said in the orders to him by the sultan, or however it was relayed, he refused outright. That is not acceptable to a sultan, especially when everyone knew they were childhood friends. He defeated Kishlu Khan's rebellion and then moved back to Dilli, after all.

'Then he disbanded the army of four hundred thousand he had assembled for his expedition to Khurasan, which was to be a crowning accomplishment. Two things happened: first, the soldiers were let loose after he called off the plan. Bear in mind, the cost of it meant he had also run his treasury dry. Second, he pressured his tax collectors, the ummals, to generate more revenue.

'This is where things went wrong. I think that the plan was a bungled mess. It was also the malign hand of the ulema and mashaiks, who used the increased taxation to sow discontent. There may have been grave mistakes in the way the tax increases were carried out because all the sultan did was raise the taxes from about 10 to 20 per cent.'

Hakka became increasingly impatient.

'Bukka, are you telling me the story of the Ramayana? Is there no end in sight?' he growled, throwing up his hands in frustration.

Bukka calmly responded, pointing to the need to appreciate the wider context. Hakka calmed down and prompted him to continue.

'So, the discontent with the taxation, together with the footloose soldiers, leads to the next rebellion in the Doab, the triangle between the Ganga and Jamuna Rivers. The sultan rushes off to quash the insurgents. The rebellions began for multiple reasons: a large part of the north was struggling as a result of a drought and a terrible famine. Add the rebellion in the Ma'bar led by Jalal-ud-din Ahsan Khan into the equation and the problems mount for the sultan. On his way to Ma'bar, he loses about half his army to disease at Warangal and nearly dies himself. Limping back to Daulatabad to recuperate, he has to quell another rebellion before finally heading back to Dilli.

'Implicitly he was conceding that his experiment of moving the capital to Daulatabad was unsuccessful. And then there was the rebellion in Lakhnauti, followed by the rebellion in Bihar.'

'Stop the recitation of the epic,' Hakka interrupted. 'What does this mean for us?'

'I'm at the most interesting part!' Bukka protested, amused by Hakka's need to rush through any discussion.

'Three useful observations come out of all of this. First, the sultan has sidelined Qutlugh Khan, his most trusted advisor, and he lost Malik Zada, his trusted military leader, in the battle of the Doab. Second, he has little support. In fact, much of his malicious opposition is in his Privy Council. They are working at cross-purposes. Finally, the critical mistake he made was to address all his problems on his own. With no support within, and racked by rebellions around the northern periphery of the empire, he's given up on the southern campaign which was part of his grand plan.'

To Hakka, it seemed like the clouds had parted and he could see with clarity.

'Three, Bukka, three,' Hakka declared. 'The chaturanga mat has three players to contend with, so we must contend with them. First, the Hoysalas and that two-timing bastard, King Ballala; second, the Kakatiyas or what's left of them; and finally, we need to challenge the new Madura Sultanate and the Calicut kingdoms. The key question will be how and when we deal with these challenges.'

Bukka answered confidently.

'First, we take on Ballala but we need to make sure the Kakatiyas are mollified beforehand. At least with the Hoysalas, it will be a process of cutting off parts of their territory over a period of time, like pulling meat off a roasted lamb. There will come a point in time when they will realize they will have to confront us directly. Then we will serve up an appropriate response.'

The pacing had slowed. Hakka was absorbing Bukka's assessment as he formulated another round of questions. Just then Valli came into the garden to say Mani Iyer had come to see them. She ushered him in but when she was about to leave, he requested her to stay, as the news concerned her too.

'I just received a message from Vidyaranya. He would like to meet the king of Kampili to discuss the question he had on his recent visit. He welcomes his brother and sister-in-law as well to visit him at the Hanuman temple.'

Bukka saw that Hakka was shaken.

'Why did he refer to me as the king of Kampili, Mani Iyer?' Hakka asked.

'I think you know the answer, zabitah,' replied Mani Iyer.

Soliloquy

Vidyaranya knew his decision would change everything in his life. He had always avoided being the focus of attention, which was primarily why he had moved away from the Sringeri Mutt where he had been a teacher. His reputation at Sringeri Mutt was unparalleled: a master of religious texts who had the rare skill of making the sublime comprehensible—with a brilliant intellect, he was never dogmatic and was a man of deep faith and conviction. He was considered a luminary while still young. It was there that he met Mani Iyer—his student for two years studying the Vedas.

It would take Vidyaranya six days to walk to Anegundi if there was no rain. Mani Iyer wanted to send him a carriage for his journey, but he flatly declined it.

'For now, I am no more than a mendicant and that is the way I would like it to be,' read the message the carriage driver brought back.

Andal wanted to accompany him but it was a trip best made on his own. However, he spent many days talking about his decision with her. It would pry them out of the quiet, pleasant, contemplative life they had come to enjoy. While they lived the lives of farmers and worked hard, it afforded time for thought and meditation. While they knew they would be able to continue with a routine that was important to them, everything else would change in the world that was rushing towards them. Vidyaranya was interested in what Andal concluded about the family that visited them.

'They were born to be royalty. What makes the three so endearing is they have not forgotten who they are and where they came from. Hakka is forceful but a very kind person. He masks that well. Bukka is extremely thoughtful and is unshakably loyal to his brother. I also think they possess a deep sense of integrity. Valli is nature herself, the sort of person who brings beauty and harmony everywhere she goes. Her sense of aesthetics extends to every part of her life and she will always be the force that inextricably binds the three of them together. Whoever Hakka marries will find it impossible to break into this implicit circle of trust. She will have to be an exceptional person in her own right, which is highly unlikely,' Andal opined.

It took a little over five days of trekking over steep, hilly terrain to reach the valley and the Tungabhadra. Stopping for the night at way-stations for travellers, he largely depended on the hospitality of temples and families he knew along the way for food. He distracted himself by thinking of the analogy he drew himself: climbing up an incline required muscles he did not frequently use; perhaps he needed to act accordingly if he and Andal were drawn into a new situation. Putting that aside, he focused on the many questions he wanted to consider. He had enough time to wrestle with them and he was glad for that.

There was no doubt that Hakka and Bukka would be kings. The circumstances and horoscopes seemed to have preordained it. Vidyaranya had no disagreement with Andal's assessment. His deeper concern was whether Hakka had the inner resources to follow the path of dharma, or the righteous way.

Kings had near-absolute power and unless they were very closely tethered to the path of righteousness, they could run amok. Once military victories were won and there were few external constraints, would they still listen to the inner voice, or would honour, integrity and the righteous way be cast aside? Maybe it depended on the three individuals acting as a counterbalance to each other. Perhaps, but there also had to be an external force to disentangle intractable ethical conundrums. It might be the role required of him, Vidyaranya.

He felt he was being dragged into the temporal realm and he worried about it. Being the king's conscience and spiritual guide was a concept he was uneasy with. Yet, he reminded himself, a good king could be a powerful force for the good of the people.

Finally, he got to the crest of the last hill and looked down on the Tungabhadra. He remembered Andal's advice: enjoy your long walk and don't get too absorbed in your own thoughts. Thinking of her, he decided to sit for a while and watch the river in the valley below.

After a short rest he headed for the valley. It would be good to see his former pupil after all these years and ask him how he managed his transition to the temporal world. Mani's reputation had grown as he nurtured the kingdom in his charge. Despite that, Mani Iyer remained the priest he always was, and none of the external influences had affected his life. He lived the same simple way he had done when he was at the Hanuman temple. Yes, Mani had been perhaps the most astute of all of his students, but he never had any desire to do anything but tend to a flock.

Which, he imagined, he was doing now as well: a very large one.

Getting closer to the river, he saw a group of horses riding towards him and saw that it was Ramaswamy Mudaliar with a few others accompanying him. Pattu dismounted and offered a heartfelt namaskaram.

'We are honoured that you chose to come all this way to visit us. I thought I would meet you here to ask if I may walk the rest of the way with you to the temple.'

Vidyaranya was delighted at the chance to talk to Pattu.

'You do know that Valli and the brothers came to visit me, Pattu?' Vidyaranya said.

'No. I just got back from a long trip this morning and have not seen her.'

Vidyaranya put his hand on Pattu's shoulder:

'Do you remember me telling you not to worry about Valli getting married?'

Pattu laughed. 'Do you blame the father of a motherless child for worrying?'

'Not for a moment. I bring it up only because she and her husband make a wonderful couple, Pattu. I did tell you that her husband was always right in front of you, even though you were sceptical. In good time you will have the pleasure of having accomplished grandchildren. Do not be impatient.'

'I can only say that my heart is full, and we look to you for your blessings,' Pattu said.

When they got to the Hanuman temple there was a small crowd waiting for him.

Sangama and Valli had come to meet him, as had Mani Iyer. Hakka and Bukka had been down south and were riding back, said Valli, and they would arrive later in the day. Vidyaranya was going to spend his days at the temple and stay with Mani Iyer. As a Brahmin, he would only eat at another Brahmin's home.

As she prepared to leave, Sangama thanked Vidyaranya for bringing her two sons back to the fold. It was the first time she had expressed any concern about what religion they followed. He cocked his head, paused and said:

'They just travelled to other parts of God's realm. I'm just welcoming them home.'

It was a feint

Hakka and Bukka were, in fact, riding back south from a trip north. The report they had gone south was a feint. They had departed Anegundi two weeks earlier and few knew where they were. Bukka made sure the planning was meticulous, while Karthikeya and Shamshed helped with the organization, including visible arrangements for a supposed trip south while discreet preparations were made for the northward journey. Horses were dispatched in advance with necessary supplies. It was going to be a long and fast ride back and forth. This was business that had to be concluded before the meeting with Vidyaranya. Hakka and Bukka had decided the honourable course of action would be to meet with Qutlugh Khan.

Twenty horsemen from the personal guard assigned to Hakka, along with ten scouts from the brigade that Bukka and Karthikeya had trained, formed the elite force. The scouts were prepared for reconnaissance missions: superb horsemen and exceptional soldiers, they cleared the way for every stage of the trip.

Faraj sent a secret message to Qutlugh Khan who was still in Daulatabad, asking if he would meet the brothers somewhere close to Barshi, which was not a long ride for him and would minimize the inconvenience. He consented and a meeting place was agreed. Qutlugh Khan anticipated that a significant move was afoot since they asked him not to disclose his trip to anyone. In fact, he had expected this for some time, with the sultan rapidly losing his grip on the empire. He felt a twinge thinking about it, but admitted he might have done the same under similar circumstances.

Faraj accompanied the brothers on their journey. It was managed by Karthikeya, who felt a keen sense of responsibility for their safety. Knowing that it marked a pivotal moment in their life, he had insisted that Bukka take him along. And so it was, four of them riding abreast with a contingent of soldiers both in front and behind them.

Halfway through the ride each day, all thirty-four of them, scouts included, would change horses and rest for a short period before riding again. They arrived in Barshi a night in advance. Karthikeya, the ever-careful soldier, cleared the site. To him assumptions about security were a luxury that he never permitted himself.

'The sultan's contingent is encamped about three hours away, semenya,' he informed Bukka. 'The rest of the area is safe and I've found a suitable campsite for the night.'

As they settled in for the night, Hakka and Bukka called Faraj to join them. Hakka revealed how he expected events to unfold. He began:

'I am glad that we asked you to bring along newly trained recruits for this mission. Their horsemanship is good and they coordinate well. My only other comment is that they should be more confident when they talk to me or to Bukka. They seem to quake in their shoes and begin stammering.'

Karthikeya responded with a grin:

'Semenya, I still sta-sta-sta-mmer when I speak to you. To them, you are legends and they just get overwhelmed. But I will instil more confidence in them.'

Entertained by this, Hakka shifted attention to the business at hand.

'Tomorrow, both Bukka and I will renounce our connection with the sultan. We are going to tell Qutlugh Khan that we will declare Kampili an independent state. It is a matter of personal honour for Bukka and I to do this face to face with Qutlugh Khan, who has been a father figure to us. We will also be converting back to being Hindus. Once we return to Anegundi, we will have a simple coronation to announce the establishment of a new kingdom. Faraj, I'd like to say that you are free to either join Qutlugh Khan or stay with us and be part of the new kingdom.'

Faraj was taken aback. Looking at the brothers he stated:

'I thought that decision had been made a while ago. But to repeat myself, I will stay with you, Hakka and Bukka. This is now my life. My only question is, will I be asked to change faith as well?'

'Not at all,' Hakka replied in a firm yet reassuring tone. 'You are free to practise your faith in Kampili, like anyone else in the kingdom. That is a promise I make to you today.'

Karthikeya seemed eager to contribute so Bukka urged him to speak out.

'Semenyas, is it reasonable to say that we are now initiating a military campaign that will last for a while?'

Hakka glanced over at his brother and decided to be completely honest with Faraj and Karthikeya.

'Yes, Karthikeya. Soon after we have completed the coronation, we will begin a campaign against the Hoysala kingdom. For now, this is a state secret and you know the consequences of divulging this information. We will consult you on the plans for the campaign. Bukka is of the opinion that we should proceed gradually by seizing small parts of the Hoysala territory until we engage in a full assault.'

As the sultan's soldiers rode towards them the next morning, Qutlugh Khan was easy to spot. He towered over all the other soldiers and rode a beautiful black charger. Hakka and Bukka were already on foot and, in a mark of respect to their mentor, had put aside their swords. They walked towards him, and he dismounted as well. Walking up to them, he reached out and embraced them both.

'Allah had kept you both well.' A soldier handed him a large engraved box that he handed over to Bukka.

'Unfortunately, I was unable to be at your wedding, so this is for you and your wife.'

Bukka bowed and thanked him. Qutlugh Khan said:

'I know this is difficult and what transpires today will always be difficult for us to deal with in our memories. But remember that statecraft is different from military craft or the craft of managing a state. Go ahead and give me the news and let us deal with it quickly. I say quickly because I do not want the sadness to last longer than it needs to.'

Bukka marvelled at how perceptive and shrewd Qutlugh was. Hakka spoke:

'Qutlugh Khan, Naib of Daulatabad, I hereby formally announce to you as the representative of the Sultan Muhammad-bin-Tughlaq, that I, Hakka the son of Sangama, will announce a week from this day, that the kingdom of Kampili is independent and is no longer a dominion of the sultan. I will also give up the religion of Islam and resume my practice of being a Hindu. And with that, I hereby hand over to you the silver box containing the seals of office, which accompanies the assignment of a zabitah.'

Hakka paused for a moment as the silver casket was handed over by Faraj to a soldier standing by. Then Hakka went on:

'On a personal note, this decision is one that has caused Bukka and me much anxiety and concern because of the hurt it will cause you. This initiative on our part is driven by the need of the moment and we do so despite realizing that it will be considered an act of betrayal. We will always remember you and the kindness you showed us. And strange as it may sound, there will always be a place for you in our home as a member of our family.'

Hakka felt compelled to hand back the silver daggers that Qutlugh Khan had given them many years ago when they left Dilli.

'Of course not, Hakka and Bukka. Keep them and remember me,' Qutlugh Khan protested. Next, Hakka reached into a large leather bag and pulled out a shining sword. It was a replica of the one worn by Qutlugh Khan and made of the finest urukku steel. Bold Arabic script inlaid in gold read, 'Allahu akbar'. In smaller script below it said, 'From your Hindu brothers, Hakka and Bukka'. Set into the hilt of the sword was a very large diamond. Hakka presented it to Qutlugh Khan and said:

'We hope you will wear it and remember us.'

Hakka embraced Qutlugh Khan and then reached down to touch his feet. Qutlugh started to try and stop him, but then he gave his blessing. Bukka did the same, and was followed by Faraj.

Qutlugh Khan and his men turned, walked to their horses, and rode away. Bukka noticed Hakka looking away and wiping his eyes.

Leaving and arriving

For the first few days on the ride back, all anyone heard was the thundering noise of the horses' hooves as they galloped along. It was not until they were getting near Anegundi that they started talking again.

'When should I start addressing you as Hakka Raya [King Hakka]?' Bukka jokingly enquired.

'Never!'

'Why? You are shortly going to be the king of Kampili and that would be the right form of address,' Bukka observed.

'Because, Bukka, you are as much the rightful king of Kampili as I am. This endeavour was not mine alone. You have been as much the architect of these developments as me. So, Bukka Raya, once we find an appropriate honorific for it, you will be the junior king.' They were just a day from home when they decided to rest for the night at an encampment. After dinner, Hakka was fiddling inside a pouch trying to find an item. He pulled out a leather wrapper and unfolded it to reveal a huge diamond.

'Do you think this is larger than the one on the sword we gave Qutlugh Khan?' Hakka asked.

'Definitely larger, Hakka. At least by half.'

'You are right. This is the biggest one I found in the treasury and Mani Iyer says it is a lucky stone.'

'I never knew you to be interested in gems. What are you doing with it?' Bukka asked.

'I am having it set in a necklace, Bukka. On my coronation day, I will give it to my sister and my brother's wife. It symbolizes her being the "Gem of the Kingdom".'

Bukka shook his head. 'You should save it for your wife.'

Hakka gruffly responded:

'If I ever have one that is as deserving as the intended recipient, I will go looking for another one of these. But I don't expect to.'

The realignment

It was early in the morning and still dark, but Bukka could hear Valli moving around. As usual she had taken it on herself to make sure that all the preparations for the ceremony at Mani Iyer's small Hanuman temple were complete. The fruit, the camphor, the crystal sugar, kumkum (vermilion powder), sandalwood powder, new clothes for the brothers ... her list went on. She had made an appointment to meet Mani Iyer at the palace in a few minutes and she would walk the three miles to the temple with him.

She left Bukka with the admonition that the two brothers should meet them there in two hours, as they needed to leave the house at an auspicious hour. Bukka groaned as he was tired. They had only arrived late the previous evening and he was still worn out.

'Valli, it's not a wedding, you know,' Bukka said.

'I know; it's just more important, especially with Vidyaranya giving his benediction,' Valli responded. 'Do not be late, Bukka, and roll Hakkanna out of bed if you have to.'

With that she was gone. She met Mani Iyer who was waiting for her and they started walking to the temple. Suddenly she noticed that there was a contingent of guards ahead of her and behind her, with Karthikeya on a horse leading the group.

'Do we really need all these soldiers going with us, Mani Anna?' she asked Mani Iyer.

'Sadly, I think the answer is yes. I cannot move around without bodyguards and it is only getting more stringent. The brothers want me to move closer to the palace, so I do not have to walk the five miles to the Green Palace every day. And in your case, I have had four bodyguards around you whenever you left the house. Your ability to just wander off to the market, or go visit the weaver or walk to the orphanage is a thing of the past. You are now royalty,' Mani Iyer responded.

'Was it Bukka who asked for this, Mani Anna?' she asked, wanting to give Bukka a talking-to.

'No, it was Hakka. And even though Bukka disagreed, Hakka was adamant. There are times, you know, when you cannot change his mind. And you would be well advised not to push the issue. Nothing in the world matters to him more than your and Bukka's well-being and safety. He will not compromise, I fear.'

'*Eeswaro rakshatoo* [may God help us],' Valli exclaimed and started walking faster.

By the time everyone had congregated at the temple, the small place was looking festive. Valli had organized a group of women to help her decorate the place. It was festooned with flowers, incense sticks were burning, and it seemed that she had lit up a thousand oil lamps. Pattu arrived early and hugged her as he had not seen her for a while.

'You've made this place look as if we are going to have a celebration, Valli,' he commented.

'It is a celebration, Appa. This marks the beginning of many of Hakka's and Bukka's plans, and they need to commemorate it.' And she was off somewhere else.

When Vidyaranya was seated before the homa (a small sacred fire), he asked Hakka and Bukka to sit across the fire in front of him and for Valli to sit at Bukka's side. In a soft and mellifluous voice, he recited Sanskrit shlokas for about ten minutes and declared that the two brothers could now practise their faith as Hindus. He asked both Sangama and Pattu to give them their blessings.

It seemed like a bit of an anticlimax for an event that seemed so laden with significance and import. Once the ceremony was over, Vidyaranya took the three of them to a side.

'Hakka, looking at your horoscope, it seems to me that your coronation should take place a month from today. If you want me to, I will preside over the formal investiture ceremony. But to do so, I will have to make sure that Andal is with me. Please give me your answer so I can return to the village and bring her back with me.'

The only point of debate was over the travel arrangements. And even here, Vidyaranya realized that the temporal world was crashing into his. A contingent of soldiers would walk with him to the rise overlooking the Tungabhadra River, after which he would be conveyed to the village in a horse-drawn carriage. He would return with Andal a few days later in the same carriage.

The coronation would take place at the Virupaksha temple, which was on the southern bank of the Tungabhadra. At this time of the year the level of the river was high. Faraj took the responsibility of organizing the crossing and the coronation. As a family, they decided it would be a very modest event. The only concession to this simple affair, on Valli's insistence, was that every child in the kingdom be given a new set of clothes and a box of sweetmeats after the coronation.

Becoming the king

Faraj threw himself into the preparations for the coronation, turning to Valli for advice. He made arrangements for travel across the river. He oversaw the construction of a mandapa that Valli designed for the occasion. It was large enough to hold a hundred Brahmins as well as the family. A small fire pit was built for the homa. Every last detail was covered.

Bukka, Valli and Pattu accompanied Hakka across the river early in the morning on the day of the ceremony. Shamshed, Faraj and Karthikeya were in attendance. Mani Iyer assisted Vidyaranya in conducting the ceremony. At exactly eight o'clock, Hakka was asked to approach. He stood there before the sacred fire; behind him was his mother, Sangama. Vidyaranya began with a question:

'Hakka, son of Sangama, are you ready for this ceremony to begin that will anoint you king of Kampili?'

'Yes.'

'Hakka, son of Sangama, do you hereby promise to pursue the path of dharma as long as you are king of this land?'

'Yes.'

They were asked to sit. The voices of Mani Iyer and a hundred other Brahmins rose in the grandiloquent chanting of shlokas that had formed the basis of investitures of Hindu kings and emperors for centuries. It was a simple ceremony, in the courtyard of the temple, by the banks of the river Tungabhadra where Hakka had grown up. Sangama wept throughout the ceremony.

In a well-practised chorus, the voices came to a halt. Vidyaranya stood up, bowed to his new king and invoked the blessings of all the gods to help him rule justly, before wishing him and his kingdom prosperity. After Vidyaranya gave his blessings, Hakka prostrated himself and asked for his benediction. Hakka would henceforth be called Hakka Raya (king), the first king of Kampili of the Sangama family.

In a surprising development, Hakka asked Vidyaranya to confer the title of Raya on Bukka as well, who would henceforth be called Bukka Raya. To those who knew the brothers intimately, the gesture was understandable. Bukka was an inextricable part of all Hakka had accomplished. A short ceremony was required to consecrate Bukka in keeping with his new title. The person caught completely off guard was Valli. By implication, she was now a queen.

A crumbling edifice

He realized just how much he missed having Qutlugh Khan with him, and his mother missed his visits as well. Life had been dreary. After nearly succumbing to the disease that decimated nearly half his army in Warangal two years ago, he never regained his old stamina again. Perhaps he should climb down from his high horse and summon Qutlugh Khan back to Dilli. Qutlugh Khan's banishment to Daulatabad was nothing more than a bone he had thrown to the conservative faction at court who had been snapping at his heels. Jealous of his old mudaris's

influence, the malign forces continually sought to undermine
Qutlugh Khan and any endeavours touched by him. The sultan
realized that he had conceded too much without a fight.

But there was also a degree of self-loathing that had taken
hold. He had grown weary of Qutlugh Khan's advice. It was
never off the mark but was difficult to deal with. Ah, the
tiresome teacher who wanted his charge to do better. He was
now confronted with a Privy Council absent of talent, unctuous
but incapable of doing anything constructive. They resorted to
twisting religious interpretations for every scenario, and it was
clearly self-serving too. Happiness, that ephemeral but beautiful
state of being, had been sucked out of his life.

There was a knock on the door. A slave walked in with
the distinctive imperial post bag the imperial couriers carried
around the empire. Only members of the Privy Council could
use one of these red leather pouches. As expected, it was from
Qutlugh Khan with an important message. The news did not
improve the sultan's mood. It only made him feel more isolated
and defensive.

The letter was short: Hakka and Bukka had assumed control
of Kampili, and had declared themselves an independent
kingdom. They had given up Islam. Muhammad-bin-Tughlaq
gathered his thoughts for a moment. The shortness of the letter
was ironic. Through the years Qutlugh Khan had urged him to
give the brothers more responsibility.

'Trust them and they will return it tenfold,' he would say.
'But dismiss them to the fringes at your peril. If your courtiers
advise this, they will only use it for their own ambitions. The
brothers are not cut from the same cloth as governors who come
from the north of the empire. Involve them in your plans and
you will be able to consolidate the south.' The words rang in his

ears painfully, because he recalled the number of times Qutlugh Khan had repeated it.

'Apostates!' he hissed as he threw the letter into the fire in the sigri in front of him. Suddenly he felt as if it had turned cold. Very cold.

Book 3

Samrajya: Empire

7

That hyperactive bastard!

1341–43: Kampili, Adenke, Dorasamudra, Reddi kingdoms

Is surprise the child of unpredictability?

Vira Ballala III, emperor of the Hoysalas, was erratic, eccentric and continually scheming about ways to expand his realm. Principles and integrity were inconvenient in his worldview. His frenetic energy and inconsistent policies had created internal strife in his kingdom, and the disruption plainly took its toll on his people. Fortunately, the land was fertile and, with few external threats, the kingdom stayed prosperous despite the king's antics. However, his grip on the court slipped considerably, to the extent that he now shared power with several prominent nobles. Ballala was close to eighty, short, unprepossessing and significantly overweight. He was also perpetually hyperactive. While prancing around the kingdom with multiple projects, it was the more sedate but sinister forces who consolidated power in the capital city of Dorasamudra.

Much of the overseas trade went through the port cities of the sea-facing kingdom of Tulunad that lay across a large chunk of the southwestern flank of the Hoysala kingdom. The ships came from Arabia and even Africa. While the Hoysalas did a good deal of trade in this region, the heavy taxes exacted by Tulunad diminished what could have been a lucrative business. Ballala concluded that marriage would solve the problem and proposed to wed the queen of the Tulus, Cikkayi-tayi. Coming from a large kingdom with military muscle encouraged acceptance of his suit. Thus, it seemed that Ballala's desire to add territory would be achieved and his kingdom would have an uninterrupted western coastline.

The marriage was not without its complications, however. The Tulus were practitioners of a rigid form of matrilocality. Ballala would be one of many husbands living in the queen's palace—that did not sit well with the court at Dorasamudra. He hoped the queen might give up the practice out of respect for him. The prospect of his queen having a bevy of young kings serving her was unpalatable, both for him and for the court. But, for the time being, the prospect of more land and tax revenues won the day.

As Pattu told Hakka, Bukka and Valli about Ballala's quest for territory, the three sat listening wide-eyed with broad smiles on their faces.

'But the story gets spicier,' Pattu said. 'On their wedding night, when they got ready to consummate their conjugal obligations, Ballala appeared in all his natural glory and presented himself to his new queen. Aghast, the bride exclaimed that he reminded her of a bear because he had hair covering all of his body! It was not appreciated by his eminence, the king. He was accustomed to women flattering him. Yet it seems her horror at his highness's hirsute exuberance did not prevent the required conjugal concatenation.'

The four of them roared with laughter as Pattu relayed the story he'd been fed by his sources. Hakka dropped his glass, Bukka stomped his feet, and Valli, who had covered her face with the pallu of her saree, was shrieking. But that was not all. Pattu continued:

'Soon after, the king asked his bride to join him for the evening. She demurred and indicated that she was going to invite one of her more attractive young husbands! Ballala apparently looked like he was going to die from gagging. He could not imagine how he—the emperor of the Hoysalas— could be turned down by his wife in favour of a mere king consort, albeit a younger, more vibrant man. The queen's counsellors were called in and informed Ballala that there was nothing unusual about her behaviour, but they were concerned about *his* instability. To make matters worse, Ballala, by way of revenge, sent for a contingent of his own harem to join him in his newly acquired kingdom. Word was out, and the courtiers in Dorasamudra were resorting to the refrain of "there he goes again".'

Conditions in the Hoysala kingdom had grown critically important, so recent developments were being followed carefully by Hakka and Bukka. The brothers were now in the final stages of building their strategy against the Hoysalas. Once Pattu left, Bukka commented:

'Do we create another distraction for Ballala or wait until he falls prey to some other strange plan of his own making before striking the final blow?'

Pondering the question for a while, Hakka responded:

'I suspect we won't have long to wait. Ballala has always wanted to annex parts of the Cauvery valley and has never completely succeeded. After this Tulunad farce, he's going to salve his ego with another attempt.'

A decision

'I've decided to accept Raja Komati Vema's proposal to marry his daughter,' Hakka declared one afternoon as the brothers were making their way back from surveying the southern and eastern borders.

'Are you sure this is going to suit you? Or is this purely a marriage of convenience?' Bukka quizzed quietly, conscious that their escorts were riding alongside them. Bukka signalled to Karthikeya that they wanted some privacy so the brigade spaced themselves out.

Hakka stayed quiet for a while, pondering Bukka's question. Moving his horse closer to his brother he whispered:

'Bukka, there are times when you know two people are just meant to be together, like you and Valli or Vidyaranya and Andal. Not every marriage is aligned nor, for that matter, do the gods smile as much at every wedding.' He then laughed at his own description. 'In this scenario I know our primary interest is to secure the eastern border. Komati Vema of the Reddi kingdom is a good and honourable man. He is respected among his people. I know little about his daughter, Malaa, her temperament or disposition. But this marriage will not change anything with you or Valli and our bond.'

Bukka shook his head.

'It's not about our relationship. Hakka, you need to think more about this. Your life and happiness are paramount.'

'You do not understand, Bukka. Using you and Valli as a model for my own marriage is a fool's business. You were both ordained to be together and become a great king and queen.'

Bukka continued to shake his head in disagreement.

'Hakka, let me be clear: neither Valli nor I have any ambitions other than serving the kingdom. You keep talking about us becoming king and queen but I find that to be inappropriate. You are Kampili's king and you are our king.'

Bukka paused. He added:

'Please think seriously about whether this marriage will suit your personal needs and wishes. Everything will then fall into place.'

Hakka instinctively reached out and put his hand on Bukka's shoulder.

'What you said only reinforces my argument, Bukka. If we are to be a great kingdom, it will be because I have the two of you by my side. It will unlikely be because of the woman I marry.' Sensing an awkward silence, he quickly changed the subject to ease his brother's concerns.

As was normal after a long trip, Valli had baths, food and drink ready for the two 'savages' as she called the brothers. When they were comfortably settled in, she asked the servants to bring in a large bamboo panel. Stuck on it were sheets of parchment with detailed drawings. She was unveiling the plans for the palace of the king of Kampili in the new capital, Vijayanagara. They had decided a few years earlier to build a new capital on the Tungabhadra's southern banks. Surprisingly, it was Valli who once asked Bukka why the capital should not be positioned on the south bank since it was more secure and easier to defend against attack. Bukka threw up his hands in astonishment and asked how she came up with the idea. In characteristic fashion Valli had simply responded, 'It makes more sense.'

The brothers stared at the drawings before asking a range of questions. Then Hakka stopped and stared at one particular picture.

'Where are your quarters?' he asked, looking at Valli.

'Hakka, I presumed this would be only for you and your future family.'

The mood in the room suddenly changed.

'You are both my family!' he growled. 'Why, aren't we all going to live together until the day we die? My vision of a palace is one with different wings. One for me and the other for you and Bukka. We would be right next to each other. I would want to walk over to see both of you. Why does anything have to change? Unless you have other ideas, I would like to have you by my side, even in difficult times when we disagree on something important. So, if you agree, why not add a nice big wing for Bukka and Valli?' He sat back and smiled at that prospect.

'Okay,' she conceded. Examining the panel once more, she proposed where she would add the new wing.

It was at that point Hakka finally informed Valli of his decision to marry. She smiled but cautioned him:

'Do it only if it makes your heart full, Hakkanna. Nothing else matters.'

I will be the queen!

Late in September, the convoy set out to Addenke, the capital city of the Reddi kingdom. Sangama started first with Valli and Pattu. The women would travel in a slow horse-drawn carriage, as Sangama did not ride—nor could Valli for such an occasion. They would be followed by Hakka and Bukka who would catch up with them at the edge of the Nallamala forest on the border, after which they would travel together to their final destination.

If strategic imperatives were driving this wedding, Bukka thought to himself, then it should be made clear to the Reddis who they were dealing with. Under no circumstances should they think that Hakka was an upstart king of a fledgling kingdom. For his army to accompany him was important: it reinforced the perception that Kampili had a standing army of consequence. For the time being, however, Bukka deemed it best to deter right at the beginning any thoughts the Reddis might have of arrogant misbehaviour.

Bukka accompanied Hakka to the parade ground from where they would begin their trip. The sight was spectacular: two thousand horsemen in battle gear, most of whom were lancers. They formed into twenty companies of a hundred, each flying the new king's standard. Pomp and show had been set aside. Instead, this was a group of soldiers designed to project power and force. Hakka looked surprised. Knowing better than to question Bukka, he remarked:

'It looks like we are going to war.'

Bukka cocked his head, looked him straight in the eye.

'We are going to appear as if we want to prevent a war. Sometimes it's the same thing,' he remarked. Once again, Hakka looked on in admiration. Bukka was always three steps ahead of him. It was an unambiguous statement: theirs was a military tradition not to be trifled with.

The recently appointed general, Chinayya, a protégé of Karthikeya and Bukka, was going to lead the troops. It would be his chance to showcase his skills in front of Hakka. After a nod from Bukka, Chinayya called the brigade to attention.

'To the Reddi kingdom. Make haste and be alert.' The three soldiers in front of the column blew on their silver kombu horns, trumpeting the signal, and they were off. Mani Iyer and Shamshed waved as they rode past the Green Palace. They would manage the kingdom in Hakka's absence. Hakka had gone over his instructions with them several times, ensuring that all arrangements were in place while he was away.

'What have you arranged for communications?' Hakka asked, as they departed.

'You will have a courier coming in every day,' Bukka replied. 'In case you see the need, we are prepared for it to be twice a day. It will take them two-and-a-half days to make the journey riding in a relay arrangement.'

Visibly satisfied, Hakka mentioned that he was going to spend some of his time riding with the men.

'I do not know the new lot well, and it's time I corrected that.' He cantered off and put himself right at the centre of the first contingent of lancers. As he left, Bukka and Karthikeya started to laugh.

'The poor bastards are going to be shitting in their pants by the time he is done making their acquaintance,' Karthikeya blurted.

They travelled through Ballari, Guntakal and Banganapalli. At the end of their third day, a scout who had accompanied Valli rode towards them. He informed them that camp was set up at the edge of the Nallamala forest and he would lead them there. Looking at the scout for a moment, Hakka asked him if he was related to Kitappa. The young man broke into a smile and said he was his son. Content he'd not lost his touch, Hakka chatted with the young man as they rode to their location.

'What is Kitappa doing these days?'

'He runs a dairy farm: he also supplies the palace, Hakka Raya. Rani Valli knows him well and has visited the farm,' the young man replied.

'Ask him to say hello the next time he comes to the palace,' Hakka said as they reached the camp.

Bukka was impressed by the layout of the camp. As Hakka and he were drawn into the affairs of the kingdom, the next generation of military leaders had taken over operations.

Arriving at the outskirts of Addanki, they were met by Raja Komati Vema's messenger who informed them that the king's welcoming delegation was running late. When they arrived three hours later, there was much fanfare with many elephants, but it was a poorly orchestrated reception. They were escorted to an evening of celebration and merriment at the king's palace. Komati Vema was the same age as Sangama but time and wars had taken their toll. He walked with a limp and needed assistance at times. His wife was wider than she was tall. Given to eating paan (betel leaves) incessantly, her mouth was stained blood-red.

When Valli saw the bride, Malaa, for the first time that evening, she was struck by her haughty bearing, even when she was being introduced to Hakka and Bukka. Sure enough, it conformed with Pattu's assessment that she was arrogant, inflexible, never did a day's work and expected to be waited on.

'Interesting,' Valli thought. Even when the bride was introduced to Sangama, there was little show of deference.

No sooner had Valli processed this, than she felt a tap on her shoulder. She turned around to find herself facing the bride and Sangama. The first words out of Malaa's mouth were:

'I hear you like to be referred to as the queen of Kampili.'

Valli was taken aback. She smiled politely and remarked:

'Sometimes people do call me that but I try and correct them.'

'You'll have to do more than try because I will be the queen! There will be nobody else who will use the title.' With that, she turned her back on Sangama and Valli, and went to join her mother.

Sangama suddenly went pale. She asked for a glass of water and requested a seat to sit down. Waving away Pattu and Bukka, she nodded to indicate she was all right. But clearly, she was not impressed. After departing the festivities later that evening, walking with the help of Valli and Pattu on either side, Sangama quietly whispered:

'This does not bode well for Hakka, or for us.'

Pomp and ceremony marked the wedding day. A lot of money had been spent but little thought had been given to the organization of the celebrations. Soon after the wedding, the new couple met the dignitaries who had come to wish them well, while simultaneously taking the measure of the new king. Bukka, Valli and Sangama were part of the receiving line and were introduced as part of the family. Pattu, despite knowing most of the noblemen in the crowd, managed to find a quiet spot away from the crowd.

He started to give more thought to what had happened. Looking around, he couldn't help but think the ceremony and celebrations had been conducted in a tasteless manner. It reminded him of Valli's impact on their sense of aesthetics. She had infused everything around the kingdom with simple, earthy elegance. It showed in the architecture, the uniforms she had designed and the general planning of the new capital. Even the old palace was beyond recognition. Though it was not ostentatious, the old place had a grand presence to it. She made simplicity into an art form that caught everyone's imagination.

He wondered how Hakka's bride would complement the tight-knit group of Hakka, Bukka and Valli, who had become a tour de force in the last few years. For a short while, he agonized as to how this would play out.

After some consideration, Pattu realized this new woman might merely be a nuisance but one they had to deal with for now. What she lacked was an inability to operate at the same level as the others. Even Hakka, for all of his vaunted simplicity, was an exceptional judge of people. Valli would always accommodate to what was necessary. Malaa was going to realize Valli's steely determination if pushed too hard. And Valli certainly knew how to hit back. He laughed aloud as he thought about how Valli spent her childhood playing with much older brothers. They treated her like she was a little boy: she got roughed up, pushed and challenged, while at the same time they all showered her with affection. It put Pattu at ease. Sure enough, Malaa was going to be a nuisance but the three would learn to deal with her. It was she who had the problem.

As Pattu was deep in thought, Malaa looked at Valli standing next to her and asked where she and Bukka would live once she moved into the palace at Anegundi. This time Valli had her rapier response ready.

'Wherever the king asks me to, Malaa, wherever the king wants me to.' Her sharp and abrupt answer ended any more deliberation on the issue.

The tension was still in evidence the next day. On hearing from Hakka that they planned to leave in a day, the new bride began to protest, claiming she and her retinue needed more time to prepare for the journey. Unaccustomed to this kind of response, Hakka resorted to his military-like manner:

'We leave in a day, and you get to bring one person with you. You've had plenty of time to plan for this trip. Get ready as we leave at daybreak.'

King Komati Vema attempted to intercede on behalf of his daughter but Hakka was unmoved.

'Komatigaru, I have a kingdom to rule; if my wife intends to be queen, she must be ready to leave with me, and on time. There is much work to do. Frivolity and fecklessness are not something I will entertain.'

Pushing the matter further, the old king suggested Malaa follow at a later date. Arms akimbo, in palpable displeasure, Hakka declared:

'If she plans to be my wife, she leaves when I do. And if she wants to change plans, she can speak to me. An adult woman does not need her father to intercede on her behalf.' Doing a namaskaram to the old king, Hakka walked out.

Malaa was permitted one large chest. When it came to departing, she barely managed to get to the horse-drawn carriage on time. She heard Chinayya commanding the brigade:

'Back to Kampili, back to Kampili. Make haste and ride smart.' Then came the sound of the three kombus trumpeting the signal and the convoy began their march. With that, there was a roar from the soldiers to celebrate their newly married king: 'Jai Hakka Raya, jai Hakka Raya!'

Malaa joined Sangama in the carriage. There was no appetite for idle chatter. In an attempt to break the silence Malaa cleared her throat and gently enquired about the whereabouts of Valli.

'She's riding with Hakka and Bukka,' Sangama replied. It was only then that the new bride realized she was up against someone different. Sangama managed to inflict a painful silence for the remainder of the trip back to Anegundi.

'Perhaps Bukka and I should move into a few of the rooms that have been built on the site of the new palace, Hakka, while you and Malaa get to know each other,' Valli suggested as they rode towards the banks of the Tungabhadra river. The building was not quite ready yet, but that portion could be made reasonably habitable. She wanted to give Hakka the right to decide on his living arrangements as a newly married man.

'Why, Vallima? We have enough space in the palace. I cannot imagine not having the two of you by my side.' The four of them would live in the palace as a joint family, and Malaa would have to learn to adjust.

Relentless

The floor was covered in a chalk drawing of a map of the subcontinent, spanning more than half a room in the Green Palace. It was drawn so the participants could see it from every perspective. Effectively, it exemplified the ambitions of the brothers, their five senior generals, Mani Iyer and Pattu. At best, the plan being put in place was audacious; at worst, some might have thought it was delusional.

Hakka stared at Pattu, prompting him for an opinion, but all he did was rub his forehead. Even though he was used to risk-taking, what he saw was bordering on insanity. Here were the two brothers redrawing the map of the subcontinent. To be sure, Hakka had the drive, the ability to motivate and the mental stamina to achieve his plans. And he had a near-invincible weapon: his brother. Bukka was meticulous in planning and brilliant at changing the dynamics on the battlefield, and had exceptional foresight. Maybe their vision could succeed. But Pattu's stomach turned.

Should he, as their older brother, counsel caution? Was it his place to warn them against such foolhardiness, or ask them to work slowly and gradually? If he were honest with himself, he had very nearly done the same thing in the course of his business. He could feel Hakka's eyes flashing like a mirror, reflecting the blinding sunlight in his direction.

Pattu collected his thoughts.

'It always helps if you consider every aspect. Your assessment of finances and administration make sense. Mani Iyer has built a solid foundation and it will eliminate much of the stress. However, make sure you know everything: an awareness of spies, your own reliable intelligence and, crucially, what the weather might be like during the campaign. What will you do if disease breaks out in the ranks? If one of you gets hurt, how will the battle plans be managed? How will you manage your couriers? These are military concerns and you know them better than I do. But the biggest risk I see is how to manage success.'

'Pattu, I do not understand what you are saying,' interjected Bukka.

'Bukka Raya and Hakka Raya,' he said, addressing them formally, 'I am used to making wagers and winning, and I am willing to wager that you will succeed, but think of the consequences. It will stretch loyalties, change the way you do business, and hamper your ability to manage. What you are planning is to conquer an area more than fifty times the size of Kampili. Of course, you will become one of the dominant forces in the subcontinent. However, it runs the risk of being overwhelmed by subsequent developments.' As if to reinforce his argument he warned them in no uncertain terms: 'You will sow the seeds of failure if you do not plan for success right now.'

Mani Iyer interjected:

'What Ramaswamy Mudaliar says warrants attention. We run the risk of chaos. I will build his concerns into our plans, and we can discuss it at our next meeting.' Hakka and Bukka recognized how farsighted Pattu could be: military achievements did not equate to being able to successfully manage a much larger kingdom. They not only needed to win battles, they also had to win over the people they conquered.

While Pattu's advice might have been viewed as a setback to the maturing plans, Bukka was nevertheless satisfied with the collaborative effort. They worked from a massive sheaf of parchment documents which Mani had prepared for them. So intense were the preparations that they had the plans committed to memory. Throughout the deliberations, Mani kept up his constant refrain: 'Know what resources you have, know what you must do at every stage of the campaign, and do it effectively.'

A few days later, coming back from their morning workout with the troops, Hakka's mood was one of frustration as they rode back to the old palace. It showed as he grew irritated at the contingent of bodyguards surrounding him and his brother.

'Karthikeya is just paranoid and goes overboard with security,' he grumbled.

'Hakka, it's only going to get worse, much worse,' Bukka replied, amused.

As they dismounted at the palace entrance with Valli and the dogs scampering down the steps, along with Pattu, they noticed Mani Iyer's new horse-drawn carriage racing towards them.

'He's become a speed fiend now,' Pattu said and they all smiled. The mood was not reflected in Mani Iyer's serious demeanour, however. Doing a namaskaram to Valli, he requested to speak to them.

'King Ballala will be travelling past our western borders in two days. He wishes to meet Hakka Raya. The meeting is to be an hour past midday.' He passed the parchment message to Valli.

Pattu put his hand on Hakka's shoulder in a gesture of commiseration and asked him:

'Who do Mani's loyalties lie with? You the king, or with Valli?' and burst out laughing.

'I've grown used to it, Pattu! Even when the three of us travel together, the village folk will come up and talk to her as if they've known her forever. All the while, they ignore their king,' Hakka replied, shaking his head in amusement. In their line of sight was Malaa, who could hear the conversation. She was still unable to break into the group of three and had made no significant effort to do so.

They decide they will…

Early the next morning the raya's bodyguard was waiting to accompany him on the trip to see King Ballala. Hakka was joined by Bukka and Valli, as he walked out to the contingent of horses. Malaa, however, stubbornly refused to see her husband off. As she became increasingly isolated and paranoid, she was convinced Valli was playing to the audience.

'We're going to see a king and there are only twenty men?' a surprised Hakka enquired.

'It's better for Ballala to underestimate us,' his brother replied confidently.

Hakka just nodded.

'However, I've made sure that we have cover. We have ten scouts in the field and a thousand riders ahead of us. Ballala will never see them.'

Hakka looked more at ease. Glancing over to Valli with a mischievous smile, he whispered, 'You and Bukka are just the same.' With that he was off, leaving Valli staring in bemusement.

Riding along the northern banks of the Tungabhadra, they travelled southwest to Huvina where Ballala was encamped. Bukka had brought Karthikeya for the trip for a reason. They were already looking to the next stage. They were conscious that their plans were at a critical point where the brothers would have to divide to conquer. Hakka needed to get used to the chain of command, which explained why Karthikeya had joined them. Bukka asked his brother if he was comfortable having Karthikeya as his army commander.

'Maybe you should ask Karthikeya,' Hakka replied, chuckling to himself. 'Have you decided on your chain of command, Bukka?'

Bukka paused, thinking about it for a moment.

'Faraj and Chinayya would do well as my two field commanders.'

'And how many men, do you think?'

'Since my role will require moving quickly, the fewer men the better, Hakka. Perhaps three thousand men?' Bukka replied.

Hakka shook his head in disagreement.

'At a minimum, Bukka, you will need another thousand active men, and perhaps another thousand as a reserve. Even that will still leave me with seven thousand men, which should be more than enough for what I have to do.'

Insouciance

It was deliberately planned. King Ballala's military encampment was large and messy. The area was dusty and it was a sweltering day, and he had clearly chosen a time that was both inconvenient and uncomfortable. Hakka and Bukka were taken to an enclosure where they waited for more than an hour. The simple courtesy of watering the horses and providing some shade was not offered to them. By the time they were summoned to the king's tent, it was blistering hot. As they entered, a senior courtier called Chengappa lazily announced that the two brothers from Kampili were here to see the king. Ballala was being fanned as he reclined on a comfortable divan.

'You old, fat, arrogant bastard,' Hakka thought to himself.

Without making any introductions to the rest of the senior courtiers, Ballala began speaking. Some of his bodyguards stood a touch too close to Bukka.

'Who is this?' Ballala said abrasively, pointing at Bukka.

'This is Bukka, one of my generals,' Hakka announced, as he sat down in one of the chairs, mindful that he had not been invited to do so. He crossed his legs and then casually looked at Ballala.

'You wanted to see us? What business do you have in mind?'

'I have added some territory to my kingdom in the northwest region and am now heading back to Dorasamudra. Now that you are established in Kampili, it would be advisable to secure your northern border from any Musalman attacks. That should be easy, as you understand how they think since you were one of them,' Ballala remarked with a smirk.

Hakka restrained himself, refusing to take the bait. In a mock-serious tone, he sat up in his chair.

'Is there anything else the king would like to convey? I am sure he has other important business to attend to.' Bukka could tell that Hakka was mocking him. Hakka's delicate barb did not miss its mark.

Taken aback by Hakka's response, Ballala glared at him. Bukka sensed the change in the atmosphere in the tent and started to consider how he'd get Hakka out by any means necessary.

'I am now going to take my army to the Cauvery delta to finally finish off the Madura sultanate's Musalmans,' Ballala declared. 'It is time that we eliminated them from the subcontinent. The sultan of Dilli realized he could not prevail and now his old henchmen, the traitors of Madurai, need to be taken care of. Let that be a warning to you as well. While I am away, do not hatch plans for more territory. However clever you think you are as a general, I have more experience at winning wars than you do. I have a fearsome army that could cut your kingdom into pieces quite easily. Hakka of Kampili, remember that small animals run away from elephants for a good reason: they worry they might get crushed.'

When Ballala finished Hakka stood up, feigning humility, and fumbled around to gather himself. Bukka saw a revealing, self-satisfied smile on Ballala's face. Hakka offered a namaskaram and said:

'King Ballala, my greetings to the people of the Hoysala kingdom. I will now leave you to your business.' Taking a few steps backward like a supplicant, he turned and left the tent.

Small cat, big rat

Karthikeya had Hakka's mount ready. Bukka motioned him to
get the men in reserve to join them. He thought to himself:
'I'm not going to let the bastards get us from the rear.' They
were barely out of the encampment when one thousand riders
approached from two directions at full gallop. Swinging round
to join Hakka's small contingent of horses, they heard him
bellow: 'Hiyaaa! *Kathina savari* [ride hard]!'

They thundered along at full gallop and all Bukka and
Karthikeya could see was a hardening resolve on Hakka's face.
Riding hard was his way of letting his thoughts and emotions
settle before expressing his opinion.

The red sun was setting when they neared the campsite
selected by Karthikeya. Suddenly the ground began sloping
downwards, and they slowed down sharply. With the river
visible on the horizon and a forested area nearby, Hakka smiled
to himself: 'If we win this war, it will be because of Bukka's ability
to plan and organize.' After setting up camp, following Bukka's
dictum of 'horses first', they took off their saddles, rubbed them
down and led them to the river to drink. A thousand horses
being led to the waters' edge made for an interesting spectacle.
Even Hakka participated in this ritual.

After attending to the horses, Hakka engaged in conversation
with his men. Bukka watched on as his brother worked the
group. His appeal was evident as the soldiers congregated
around him. Hakka had never forgotten what it was like to be
a line soldier: an infantryman who travelled on foot. Here he
was, king of his realm, enjoying the company of his men. It was
experiences like this which would stay with the men for the rest
of their lives. 'All of this has added to the mystique of Hakka

Raya,' Bukka thought. 'He's becoming a bit of a legend in his own time.'

'Tam'ma,' Hakka shouted as he walked over to Bukka. It was evident from his garrulous state that Hakka had made his decision.

'I am ready to proceed,' Bukka blurted. 'A few more details need taking care of but we should be prepared to move very soon.'

Hakka paused for a minute.

'Three weeks and the campaign begins. Let's show Ballala what it feels like to have a huge piece sliced off the northern part of his kingdom.' Hakka was in his element, champing at the bit at the thought of teaching Ballala a lesson in humility.

Recognizing this, Bukka teased, 'You certainly like this more than sitting in the Green Palace reviewing treasury accounts.'

Everyone was quiet on the ride home the next day, busy contemplating whether their goals were realistic. The nagging question with any campaign for Bukka was whether he had missed anything. For Hakka, the ride brought clarity. He had now refined his questions, digested the detailed information Mani Iyer insisted they commit to memory, and was able to recite every last detail to himself. If his men were prepared to make the effort to get ready, then he would do the same. Once he had command of the facts, plans and details, he moved closer to Bukka.

'So,' he announced, 'we are agreed that you are going to cut across to the west to capture Halasige, and then go northwest again to secure Karwar. Once you have secured Halasige and Karwar, you'll move south down the coast to Honnavara, and secure it. From that point you will return east across the hills. In the meanwhile, I will head south along the border of the

Hoysala kingdom, and meet up with you at Jagaluru.' Bukka nodded in agreement. 'I feel uncomfortable that you have all the hard work, Bukka. If only I could be there with you.'

Bukka grinned.

'I am not sure how much longer we will be able to go on military campaigns together. It's the price you pay for expanding an empire. Have confidence that I will execute the campaign to your satisfaction.'

'It's not you that I worry about, Bukka. It's me!' Hakka confessed.

The day before Bukka left to begin his part of the campaign was frenetic. He was going over the final details, ensuring his role was perfectly aligned with Hakka's, overseeing that the supply trains were in place, certifying that the soldiers had been paid, and confirming his two field commanders were ready. It was already the middle of the summer so they had to be well prepared. On Valli's suggestion they organized pack ponies with water bags and each soldier carried a small one of his own.

At last, all the plans were becoming a reality. Bukka, his two field commanders and a small contingent of guards would leave in the morning. Four divisions of a thousand men each had already marched ahead in the night as he did not want to tire them in the blistering summer heat. Meanwhile, their informants confirmed Ballala was heading to the southernmost part of his kingdom. This would give them enough time to seize control of a large part of his kingdom in the north before the news reached him.

Aspiration meets reality

Valli had got up while it was still dark. Bukka turned on to his back, enjoying the comfort of his bed for a little longer.

Such comfort was not going to be a part of his life for a while. Usually, Valli would sit by the side of the bed and talk for a few minutes about gossip from the marketplace, progress on the new palace, and the latest embarrassment Malaa had managed to pull off. Not today, however. She briskly told him not to dawdle in bed.

Bukka ate a meal she had prepared. Both his field commanders arrived and waited in the outer room that opened to the courtyard. At Valli's request they were joined by Mani Iyer and Massoud Khwaja, the local imam, who both said a prayer and gave a blessing. To Bukka's surprise, Hakka was waiting in the pouring rain, holding his horse. He had decided to ride with Bukka to the outskirts of town.

As Bukka mounted his horse, Valli whispered softly in the ears of Tvarita, his mare, and put a huge vermillion mark on her forehead. She did the same for Bukka, Faraj and Chinayya. In an unusual display of public affection, she held Bukka's hand, kissed it, and said:

'I pray to the Long-tailed One you will come back safe, Bukka. I will pray every moment you are away.'

Mani Iyer wished him well.

'The rains are a good omen, Bukka Raya.'

Faraj gave the command:

'*Sampurna geluvu* [absolute victory],' and they rode off. As they turned the corner, Bukka looked back and saw Valli was still standing in the pouring rain.

The small incline signalled they were at the edge of town.

'Nillisi!' the command rang out. The King's Guard stopped. Hakka looked at Bukka and said:

'May Kaliamma give you her fighting spirit.' He hugged his brother and whispered, 'Come back home an emperor.'

With a grin on his face Bukka replied:

'Please do not take unnecessary risks, Hakka.' As he started riding away Bukka heard Hakka's voice behind him roaring out:

'*Yahmik Allah* [may Allah protect you].'

Bukka turned Tvarita around to face Hakka, unsheathed his sword and raised it in salute, and yelled back:

'*Allah yahfaz milki* [may Allah protect my king].'

Bukka gave his field commanders directions for the trip. Their first significant encounter was likely to be the border town of Halasige. It was about a week's march for four divisions. There were three border posts along the route, each with about a hundred Hoysala soldiers stationed.

As they marched towards Halasige, Bukka sent out small battalions to seize control of the border posts. In case there was a need for reinforcements, the battalions would provide support.

'Chinayya, send out a battalion to each of these posts, and let's mop them up as quickly as possible. Make sure that you have the right information from the scouts and instruct them to lead your lieutenants there. The surprise attack should be early in the morning. Give the Hoysala soldiers the option of surrender. I'd wager that morale is low and they are likely to give up easily. Avoid casualties and stay away from a confrontation, if possible.'

As expected, the soldiers surrendered to Bukka's men. In total, four hundred Hoysala soldiers were returned as prisoners to Anegundi, transported by the reserve group. Now came the next major hurdle: Halasige. It was two days away. As they set up camp, a scout came galloping over to Chinayya. He handed over intelligence collected from the prisoners and the reconnaissance parties. There were one thousand eight hundred soldiers at the encampment that was supposed to defend Halasige.

About a thousand were new and inexperienced recruits. Making matters worse for his soldiers, Ballala had taken most of the horses, leaving only twenty behind. Most surprising was the fact that the encampment was in an enclosed valley, with a steep hill behind them. Bukka asked for more intelligence, specifically how many archers were on watch and the size of their bows.

He was in a state of disbelief at what he saw. They had spread themselves in front of the encampment. Faraj's men came down the steep incline—effectively encircling the men inside.

Upon Faraj's signal, the kombu sounded the beginning of hostilities and the drummers raised a thunderous beat. The archers were in position and the lancers were ready to charge. All that Bukka and Faraj could see was chaos in the camp. Realizing they were under attack, the men were running in panic.

'Bukka, there are women and children in the camp!' Faraj shouted suddenly.

Bukka immediately raised his hand for Faraj's division to hold back. He rode forward and an arrow hit his breastplate. Faraj immediately rushed to have him covered. As they moved forward Bukka yelled out,

'Who is in command?' There was no response. Noticing one of the few archers inside the post, Bukka repeated his question. 'We will cease hostilities if you bring your commander forward.'

With that, the archer ran back into the camp. A few minutes later, a rotund and bewildered man came before the poorly formed Hoysala line.

'Who are you?' he spluttered.

In a forceful tone Bukka informed him:

'You are under attack by the forces of Kampili. I give you two choices: surrender, and you will be treated with honour;

or send your women and children away and we will commence the attack.'

'I will come back in a moment,' the man said as he scurried to a tent at the back. Another portly man appeared and asked the same question. Increasingly frustrated, Bukka instructed the drummers to start a beat and ordered two archers to shoot the stocky men in the thigh. 'That should wake up the lazy bastards,' he thought. Screaming in pain, the man fell to the ground and asked:

'What do you want?'

Bukka commanded Faraj to repeat the demands. The sun was emerging and it was clear that the Hoysalas grew aware of their fate. One of the men conceded:

'We will surrender.'

The Kampilis went into high gear. They encircled the camp, separated the women and children from the men, disarmed the latter and began the process of creating a temporary prison. The prisoners, under supervision, were set to work building barricades around the camp.

Bukka was frustrated at the outcome, however. First, the Hoysalas appeared amateurish in their organization and ability to defend. He was furious that he had to waste time and energy taking care of such discreditable prisoners. 'The sheer damned waste,' he mumbled. He barked out orders to Chinayya, Faraj and their officers to make sure that all of the women and children were safe. Walking back to his horse Bukka noticed Faraj smiling.

'What are you so happy about?' he growled.

'Semanya, soon you will be known as one who wins wars without blood being spilled.'

'Faraj, that may be acceptable to some but it is not something a general should be proud of. Swords get thirsty and winning swords must be fed.' Acknowledging the severe tone in Bukka's voice, Faraj did not pursue the conversation any further.

Bukka was keen to maintain the momentum, so he prepared to head for Karwar the next morning. Before they departed, Bukka called his generals and other senior officers to see the prisoners were secured with supplies in place. It was a six-day march across hilly territory but he wanted to push the men to make good time. Overconfidence and complacency were a major concern. He also enquired about the latest intelligence and whether scouts were ready. As they got ready to leave, Bukka warned them:

'Just because we have not faced strong opposition does not mean we won't in the battles ahead. Keep yourselves sharp and prepare for the worst. If you do not stay alert, we will get cut down when we least expect it. If I find anyone to be complacent or inattentive, I will immediately relieve you of your post. Now let's march.'

Bukka's daily update relayed by his couriers informed Hakka how disappointed he was in the quality of the Hoysala military machine.

'While we should be rejoicing at the ease of our victory,' Bukka wrote, 'I look forward to facing a more intelligent and fearless enemy. Maybe I should thank our stars we have not had to face such opposition.'

They marched west towards the coast. Across the hills of the Western Ghats, they made their way through a series of valleys that made the trip easy. Once at the coast, Chinayya stayed put to secure the area. Bukka, Faraj and his two divisions marched to Karwar to seize the small encampment. It was a critical maritime centre for trade in the region and Bukka hoped efforts to take the town would not bog them down. Pattu provided a few contacts with the assurance that they would provide reliable information about the civilians in that town. His only advice was:

'For now, do not disturb the traders or the trading arrangements. As long as the traders feel safe, they will not take sides. Just secure the area and the rest will take care of itself.'

Bukka cantered along to the front of the column and met Kempayya, a veteran from days gone by when they marched to Daulatabad.

'Kempayya, where is your horse? Did it throw you off because you were too heavy?' Bukka teased with a wide grin.

'One of my men is ill so I put him on my horse. Are you upset with the men, semanya?' Kempayya asked.

'I am only upset that we have not been given a serious challenge yet, Kempayya. I am concerned the younger, inexperienced troops will get complacent.'

A voice from the formation yelled:

'No chance of that, Bukka Raya! The old man never stops giving us hell. He pushes us on every day as if it were the march to Daulatabad and then trains us for the battle at Sinhagad.' The whole platoon laughed raucously. That mood got Bukka back to a state of calmness.

If Halasige presented no opposition, Karwar amounted to no more than an expedition. They moved into the city at dawn and positioned themselves around the army camp. When the kombu sounded, an officer came running out to offer terms of surrender. He immediately laid down his arms, and ran back into the camp to order the soldiers to submit. All Bukka could do was laugh. This vaunted Hoysala military machine had so far been a complete disappointment.

At Karwar, three traders asked to meet Bukka. After being vetted by his bodyguards, they were allowed to meet him. One was from the city of Hormuz in Persia; another was an Arab from the city of Aden; the third was a strange-looking man with golden hair from a place called Venice. Bukka was amazed to learn they worked for Pattu. The traders were assured that it was business as usual for them and they went away, relieved.

He's fallen ...

Recalling the events of the last two weeks, Bukka wondered if the Hoysalas were a kingdom on its last legs. Neither Halasige nor Karwar had presented any challenge.

Bukka then went south to face the Hoysalas at Honnavara, with about two thousand soldiers. Faraj was kept in reserve with the other half of the fighting force with specific instructions to support only if required. At first glance it was thought that the relatively large opposition would be difficult to subdue. The Hoysala army lined itself up for a pitched battle but it was immediately clear that they only had five horses and very few archers.

Quickly reviewing the various scenarios they had trained for, Bukka let Chinayya make the decisions. It was important the generals developed confidence on the battlefield and there was little sense in second-guessing them. Only when it seemed the execution was flawed would he intervene.

'How are you going to attack, Chinayya?'

'Semanya, my plan is to have the infantry meet them head on. The first platoon has armour, so they can take the brunt of the attack. At the engagement I will split the mounted archers to sixty on each side, to attack them in waves so the Hoysala flanks are under continuous attack. If they last this out for more than half an hour, I will send in two hundred lancers to finish the job. Should resistance continue, I will have the archers start the attack again. We will be attacking a force twice our size, semanya, but by God's grace, the battle will be over in less than two hours.'

Bukka nodded in approval. He would join the left flank of the archers and ride with them. Bukka put his hand on Chinayya's shoulder:

'Be confident, push hard and may the strength of the Long-tailed One be with you.' Bukka mounted his horse and joined Kempayya and the archers at the rear of the column.

Chinayya led the charge from the front. They got to within a hundred yards of the Hoysalas and the drums began beating to give them the timing they needed. The formation of infantrymen broke into a slow jog, chanting, '*Kampili geluvu* [victory to Kampili]'. At ten yards they broke into a faster pace. The thundering clash of metal shields sounded as they hit the Hoysalas. The cavalry and bowmen moved in to the left and right flanks.

After two runs at the Hoysalas it was clear their defences were weakening. There was no coordination or leadership. Suddenly the rear of the Hoysala column broke and men began to flee. As quick as a flash, Bukka took ten archers with him to intercept the bolting soldiers. He yelled out to the enemy:

'Saranagati (surrender)!' He repeated the call.

Suddenly there was silence on the field. Pulling his men back to a solid defensive position, he waited to see what would unfold. A soldier walked out of the column and threw his sword down and surrendered on behalf of the Hoysalas. The Hoysalas had lost nearly a quarter of their men to Bukka's twelve. It had been a bloodbath for the opposition and the battle had lasted less than an hour.

After Faraj's reserve soldiers took charge of the prisoners, Bukka and his men marched east to join Hakka. The ease of victory nagged at Bukka. Did the Hoysalas not expect any attacks? At camp that night, he sat back resting against a tree to deliberate more on the matter. He concluded the kingdom had simply run its course. While it had phenomenal resources, it was unable to use them to good effect. Besides, the momentum was with the Kampilis and he did not see how long the Hoysalas could hold out.

It was early in the morning when Bukka heard the guard dogs barking. They were roused by a scout running towards the camp.

'Hakka Raya has a message for you of the greatest urgency.' Bukka could feel his stomach turn. Was Hakka hurt? Was Valli unwell? Had Sangama fallen ill? The messenger handed over a pouch with Hakka's seal that said 'Virupaksha', which was the method he employed to sign his name. Tearing open the short note, Bukka saw something else fall out. It was the gold chain that Qutlugh Khan had given them. No one else had one quite like it. Hakka was being very careful. He read the message:

'He's fallen. Follow the scout.
Do not change any plans. Meet in less than two days.
All arrangements made for trip.'

This was both unusual and concerning for Bukka. Was it a trap? Worse still, was Hakka in danger? He interrogated the scout for an hour, examining his uniform and the brand on the horse. His own scouts repeated the action. Convinced all was satisfactory, he summoned Chinayya and Faraj. Faraj was given command of the divisions and sworn to secrecy that he would not disclose Bukka's whereabouts.

'I will be back in five days. You will get my next message delivered by Addiga who will ride with me in addition to four other scouts. No other messenger is to be trusted.' One of the soldiers saddled Tvarita while the messenger was given a fresh horse. In an instant, they were gone. As Hakka had promised, arrangements had been made all along the journey. It prompted a smile from Bukka, who sensed Karthikeya's hand in every single detail. They changed horses five times on the journey and kept up a furious pace. The plan was to meet at Holagere, the scout said.

Around sunset on the second day, they approached the outskirts of Holagere. Bukka heard Karthikeya's inimitable whistle. Like any good scout, he was well hidden. Bukka whistled back. He saw twenty men galloping towards them with Hakka in tow. They rode to an abandoned house where a camp was already set up. Bukka could tell his brother was tense.

Hakka gestured for Bukka to follow him to the trees away from the house where all of the men were milling around. He said:

'Bukka, I got information from one of Pattu's informers that Ballala was killed by Sultan Ghiyas ud-din of Madura. Without a doubt, this has serious implications—'

'Any verification of this news?' Bukka interrupted.

'Pattu heard from two sources. I have also asked our informants in Dorasamudra to confirm this. I should hear about it within a day or two, perhaps even tomorrow.'

Hakka continued with his news.

'It seems that Ballala intended to conquer the Madura kingdom of Ghiyas ud-din. They overwhelmed his main fort at Kannanur, which is strategically significant as it is the gateway to Madurai. But when the troops inside the fort were preparing to surrender, Ballala blundered. He gave them two weeks' respite to consult with Ghiyas ud-din in Madurai before making their decision.

'As you'd expect, Ghiyas ud-din raised as many men as he could, said to be about six thousand soldiers, and attacked Ballala's base. In the chaos that followed, someone identified Ballala and took him prisoner. Supposedly, Ghiyas ud-din promised to set Ballala free if he handed over a significant amount of gold, his horses and elephants. But reneging on his deal, he had Ballala beheaded and his head put on a spike outside the fort to warn off anyone thinking of a reprisal.' Hakka was agitated by what he heard, as was Bukka.

A wash and a meal was seen as the best way to collect their minds. Both of them had endured a gruelling ride. Torches had been set up in the camp as darkness descended. The bodyguards were sent out of earshot before they resumed their conversation. To Bukka there was only one question in his mind, but whether he'd be able to convince Hakka was another matter. Once they were comfortably seated, Hakka broached the matter once more:

'If this information is true, and I think it is, what should we do, Bukka?'

Bukka rubbed his forehead.

'Hakka, we should immediately conquer the Hoysala kingdom.'

Hakka's jaw dropped and he took a moment to soak in the statement. He attempted to reply but found his throat had gone dry. Reaching for a tumbler of water, he took a large gulp and regained his composed.

'Bukka, this idea is audacious.' He was wide-eyed and clearly uncomfortable. 'Do we have enough time to make sure we are making the right decision, whatever that might be?'

Bukka let the question exhaust itself like a wild horse running around the corral. Meanwhile, Hakka looked as if he was weighed down by a mountain of care.

'There are two things to consider,' Bukka asserted in a calm tone. 'First, we have already achieved half of our objective. Second, you have little option.'

Hakka sat still, letting Bukka continue but all the while shaking his head in disagreement.

'There is little to lose, Hakka. Even if we do not get Dorasamudra, we have conquered significant land which we can use to negotiate. Besides, we have already got more than we had expected when we first made our plans. Yet, I am convinced we can overwhelm Dorasamudra and, what's more, we can do it quickly.'

Hakka intently absorbed the information being thrown at him.

'You know as I do that the Hoysala kingdom is fifty times the size of Kampili. We have just twelve thousand men between us. Remember that Ballala had a hundred and twenty thousand men when he attacked the fort at Kannanur. Are you sure we are not trying to drink up the ocean?'

Bukka was unyielding in his response.

'Hakka, we could be in Dorasamudra in two weeks if we march quickly. The capital will be in a state of chaos and nobody will be anticipating an attack. Consider the fact that even with all those men under Ballala's command, they were routed by six thousand poorly trained soldiers who were all part-timers. It's quite clear that their military leadership is poor. I have seen this over the course of the last three weeks. The troops have nothing resembling the skill and training we do. The real question you should ask yourself is, can you afford not to attack? Would you rather have mayhem on your southern border? If you decide to address the problem later, it will take more time, risk more lives and, perhaps, there will be a lower chance of success. Hit now, hit hard, hit when there is chaos in their ranks and they are dealing with the news of Ballala's death. The nobles are now more concerned about how they are going to carve up territory amongst themselves. They're all internally focused.'

Bukka's argument was compelling and his passion infectious. Hakka created a mental picture in his head as his brother made his case.

'Am I to understand that we should go to Dorasamudra and stop there?'

'Definitely not, Hakka.'

'Then what comes next?'

'We put Dorasamudra under a military command. Lock it down for a month and have Shamshed come down from Anegundi to manage it as if it were a prisoner-of-war camp. We would gather all of the Hoysala guards and military into a well-defended prisoner camp and then march south. The first city closest to Dorasamudra is Kanci, the holy city. Once we capture it, we continue south to the banks of the river Cauvery and establish control. Assuming we don't encounter any problems, we could be back in Dorasamudra in two months and begin to plan the administration of the Hoysala kingdom.'

Hakka was a shrewd strategist and he'd always had the instinctive ability to offer options.

Yet he also depended on Bukka to come up with propositions that made strategic sense. This was not just a bold move; it was stunningly audacious. Hakka remained quiet as he soaked in the information and the potential obstacles.

Just then, Karthikeya approached. He had received fresh intelligence. Ballala was indeed dead and there was chaos in Dorasamudra. Hakka asked Karthikeya his opinion about the plan they were discussing.

Karthikeya was emphatic in his reply.

'It makes sense to me. When do we start?'

It was what Hakka needed. A reassurance the plan was right lifted a load off his shoulders.

'Let's sleep and discuss the details tomorrow,' Hakka recommended.

From diffidence to resolve

The sound was unmistakable. Bukka suddenly woke up. It was nearly daybreak and Hakka was not lying by his side. Darting out he found Hakka retching by a tree, loudly cursing when he could. The profanities were normally reserved for instances when he was upset. With a drink of water, Hakka sat down to gather himself.

'I'm ashamed, Bukka. This plan we've been discussing has me behaving the same way I felt before we went into battle the first time against the sultan's soldiers in Warangal. Then King Prataparuda's twelve-thousand-strong force was facing the sultan with his nearly hundred-thousand army. It was not that

I feared dying that day, but we seemed overwhelmed,' Hakka sighed.

'History will remember that battle against the sultan, Hakka. You outflanked and outmanoeuvred the enemy and they retreated. That was your first battle as a general and you are revered for the exceptional skill you displayed despite the odds,' Bukka said. 'If you were retching before the battle, I certainly did not see it.'

'Oh, I did Bukka, fortunately out of sight, or half the soldiers would have deserted after seeing their new general unable to control his nerves. I feel the same way now. There is no sense of foreboding, just a sense of being overwhelmed by the size of the challenge ahead. I have gone through every detail of the plan you laid out, while you were asleep, and I agree with all of it. I believe it is possible we can pull it off, but anyone else hearing our plan would declare us mad,' Hakka opined.

It was that time in the morning when the birds began to chirp; in the distance a rooster was crowing. They could see a small stream and that was where the brothers headed to bathe. It promised to be a blazing hot day, the way it was late in the summer before the rains came. As they walked towards the stream, four bodyguards galloped ahead to make sure all was safe. Hakka frowned. He disliked having his privacy impinged upon. Worse still, if they were successful, his liberties were only going to become more constrained. He was not a public man.

Then, using Valli as the basis of his argument, Bukka initiated the conversation:

'Hakka, remember how Valli said even Vidyaranya had been cautious before he decided to give you his blessing? He agreed to be a spiritual advisor because he was convinced that it helped the greater good. You should consider what you could do for so

many more people. Abandoning this project would also mean
abandoning a kingdom that you might help.'

Wading into the stream Hakka retorted:

'Bukka, I am not a saint; so that argument is not going to
stick.'

Walking back to their small encampment Hakka looked his
brother in the eye.

'Tam'ma, this would never happen without your
encouragement. My suggestion is we start by designing a simple
plan. We can build on it as we go along because it's the best we'll
be able to do for the moment.'

They invited Karthikeya to assist in charting the course
for the campaign. Getting intelligence was key. Karthikeya,
whose mother was from Dorasamudra, was an ideal candidate
to obtain the necessary information. Once they hashed out
a million details, they decided that they would approach the
city of Dorasamudra from the northeast and the northwest
respectively. Once they seized control, they would send out an
expedition to subdue the town of Mangalore and the Tuluvas.
Arrangements were put in place to have Malaa, Valli, Mani
Iyer and Shamshed as well as the important administrators
and the soldiers, move into the fort near Anegundi. Finally, the
campaign to get the Hoysala kingdom was under way.

Moving fast

Hakka and Bukka rode back to their own troops the next
morning. Contending with the blistering summer heat, both
were conscious of the need to manage their men and horses on
the long march to Dorasamudra. Hakka's men were ordered
to march on foot so the horses did not have to bear the weight

of their riders. They began marching in the small hours of the morning when it was still dark for four or five hours, depending on the terrain and heat. Resting in the hottest part of the day, they would not resume until mid-afternoon. Bukka, meanwhile, had to contend with traversing across the hills, which was slow. Fortunately, the scouts had set out a manageable route. It was critical to move fast to maintain the advantage. Speed and skill were all they had. Much to the chagrin of the new recruits, the old-timers kept harping about the forced march to Daulatabad.

In just two harrowing weeks, Hakka and Bukka finally met ten miles north of Dorasamudra. Hakka noticed something unusual. The horses under Bukka's command had white cloths draped over them to minimize the effect of the heat. His brother greatly admired how he cared for all his resources, men and animals alike. Although they were tired, none were worse for the wear and that was to the credit of Bukka's foresight.

The scouts did an exceptional job getting two large armies to converge at the assigned spot at the same time. They stationed the troops ten miles to the north of Dorasamudra. It was a large city, known for its architecture and the arts. Over the last few years, it had lost its sheen, however, as the aging king had become distracted and the nobles turned their energies to other projects. For all this, questions lingered about the strength of the opposition. Would they be as poorly prepared and lack leadership like the forces they had previously encountered? Had all of the talent been siphoned off to go south with Ballala? Or were their military capabilities overstated? Above all, to what extent were the noblemen quarrelling among themselves?

As Bukka and Hakka rested following their long journeys, a visitor arrived at the camp.

Karthikeya, greeting the brothers, brought in an old but familiar acquaintance: Kazi Rahim Rahmatullah. The moment Hakka saw him he started to roar with laughter.

'The magician is at it again!' he exclaimed, referring to Pattu's continued ability to provide them with critical information at key moments in their lives.

'I was doing business in Dorasamudra when I saw Karthikeya in the marketplace, Hakka Raya,' Rahim Rahmatullah revealed. Hakka's raucous laughter was something his bodyguards had never seen before. Their intense general, their king, the legend from Kampili who never lost wars, was laughing out loud and wholeheartedly.

'I am sure that this has nothing to do with Pattu, does it?' Hakka quizzed with a smile, knowing full well it did.

It did not take long for the serious business to begin, however. Karthikeya and Rahim Rahmatullah sat down and relayed all the main details about the city. Hakka listened quietly. There were six gates into the palace complex where the king's family lived. All important matters of state were conducted in the various buildings there. Three noblemen were in control of affairs but they were busy plotting against each other. The Hoysala intelligence network, meanwhile, was preoccupied with guessing where the Madura sultan might attack them in the south. They were oblivious to what was coming from the north. What baffled Karthikeya and Rahim Rahmatullah the most was the presence of just two thousand soldiers, guards and bodyguards in the capital city.

Crucially, Rahim Rahmatullah informed them of two secret passageways for members of the palace to escape the city. As useful as this was, Bukka's mind was not focused on the attack but rather life after victory. He paused before raising the question:

'Is there a nobleman or a senior official who knows how this kingdom functions?'

Rahim Rahmatullah hesitated.

'The one person that springs to mind is Ramaswamy Mudaliar. He is riding north from Palghat and will be here either tomorrow or the following day.'

'Does he know we are here?' an unnerved Hakka enquired.

'No, Hakka Raya. He heard about King Ballala's death and decided to collect some of his debts and check on his businesses at Dorasamudra.' He paused for a moment. 'Ramaswamy Mudaliar knew your armies had moved south. He wanted me to come to Dorasamudra to see how the kingdom responded to the news, so he could let you know what to expect. When he sent me here, nobody expected that King Ballala would be killed. One of the traders Bukka Raya had met in Karwar told us that the Kampili army had crossed the hills and moved south.

'But only I expected an attack by your army; no one else paid attention to the rumour. If you were going to attack, it was likely that your scouts would be around. And if it was really that important, Karthikeya would do the reconnaissance. That led me to keep watch in the market with my men. It was I who spotted him in the marketplace. I did not mean to spy, Hakka Raya and Bukka Raya.

'Ramaswamy Mudaliar might take my actions amiss. All he wanted me to do was collect information that he could give you. Please forgive me.'

Hakka walked over to Rahim Rahmatullah and gripped his shoulders affectionately.

'If you had not assisted us in Daulatabad, or helped save Bukka's life and Qutlugh Khan's life in Sinhagad, I would find your explanation less than persuasive. But you have aided us and Ramaswamy Mudaliar in so many ways. We thank you again. There is no reason to expect Ramaswamy Mudaliar will be upset.

'Now let's send a few scouts to meet him and make sure he travels safely. I do not want him in town when we attack.'

Bukka arranged to have scouts and soldiers ride out immediately with Rahim Rahmatullah with orders to bring Pattu to camp.

———◆———

It was late the next evening and all plans had been made. Orders were given for the soldiers to get one more day of rest and to prepare themselves. Bukka would enter the southern part of the town with Chinayya's division. Hakka and Karthikeya were to attack from the north. There would be five thousand men in reserve. Just as all the final touches were put in place, Bukka heard the scouts alert them to traffic coming their way. It was the party that was sent to find Pattu.

Hakka and Bukka could see Pattu approach the camp. As soon as he dismounted, he threw up his hands and hugged them.

'I always thought I gambled big and won big in my life! Now, looking at the two of you, I realize that I am an amateur. No one will expect you to do what you intend. And I know you will win.'

The brothers took him back to their small isolated quarters, ordered a meal for him and shared their plans to see if he had any suggestions. He smiled all the way through their explanation, just shaking his head in disbelief. His only comment after they finished was:

'I hope to have dinner with you in your new palace the day after tomorrow.'

The two groups were at the northern and southern ends of town in the early hours of the morning and the attack commenced. The plan was to subdue the soldiers and establish a presence at key points in the city, all the while moving on the palace. Daylight was beginning to break when the two parties reached the northern and southern gates of the palace. The attack was initially met with force at the southern entrance on Bukka's side. Progress was slow. Chinayya had his men scale up the walls. Soon the guards were facing attackers from the front and behind. Offered the option of surrender, they quickly took it and were subsequently relieved of their weapons and bound up. Bukka had reached the king's palace, and his personal quarters.

Meanwhile Hakka's team, led by Karthikeya, had pushed through the northern gates of the palace complex with little resistance. In front of Hakka was a large palace that was used for public and ceremonial purposes. It was lightly guarded and the soldiers ran at the sight of the invaders. To his left was a smaller palace where the administrative functions of the kingdom were conducted. It housed the prime minister, the minister of defence and the minister for civil affairs. It also included, as they later found out, the treasury. The building was guarded by nearly a hundred soldiers, mostly the king's guard. Fortunately, Karthikeya's infantry expected this and were able to subdue the group. They had arrived at the northern face of the royal residence.

Hakka and Bukka were at either end of the large complex. Now came the problem of removing the occupants of the

personal quarters. There was no alternative but to send men in.
Instructions were clear: attack and kill soldiers if you have to,
but be firm and respectful of everyone else when bringing them
out. After a couple of hours, the two queens, sixteen children
and about eighty women from the harem were escorted out,
along with sixty bodyguards. Finally, the city was theirs.

'How many men have we lost, Karthikeya?' Hakka enquired.

'None' was the jubilant response. 'Just a few knife wounds.
Only one is serious.'

Most of the prisoners were taken off to a camp and secured
there. Nearly one hundred people who were members of the
family were taken to a small palace on the outskirts of town.
A scout arrived with the news that all three ministers had been
apprehended and were being escorted to the central palace. As
Hakka walked towards the garden in front of the palace, he
looked at Bukka and said:

'This has been a damned disappointment. They did not
even put up a good fight. Let's take a tour of the place and
then start interrogating the ministers. In the meanwhile, call for
Pattu to join us here for dinner.' Both Hakka and Bukka were
smiling in satisfaction with what they had achieved. In less than
six weeks, they had taken control of half the Hoysala kingdom
as well as its capital, Dorasamudra.

8

In the heat of the forge

The will to manufacture outcomes

Faraj was down on one knee, looking up at Bukka. In a beseeching tone he pleaded:

'Bukka Raya, I realize the honour that you do me by asking me to be the zabitah of Dorasamudra, but my heart is not in it. I implore you to take me with you. Let me, please, be part of this next challenge. That is an honour I ask of you instead.'

Over time, his relationship with Bukka and Hakka grown deep. Their trust in him was implicit. It was precisely why they wanted him to command all of Dorasamudra and the new areas they had conquered, while they went after the rest of the Hoysala kingdom. Yet his deepest wish was to be with them, helping in tasks of most significant import. Hakka acceded to the request.

'Faraj has the same disease you and I have, Bukka. He wants to be on the battlefield. I respect him for not accepting the easy and comfortable job of sitting safely in the palace. But who would do the job?'

'I'll ask Shamshed to travel from Anegundi,' Bukka promptly answered. 'Besides, he has the experience of having managed Sinhagad under similar circumstances.' He would be in Dorasamudra by the time they left on the next leg of the campaign.

City life had resumed within two weeks of Dorasamudra being overwhelmed by the Kampili forces. The market was open, the traders were hustling their wares, and eating places and hoteliers returned to business as usual. Much to Karthikeya's consternation, Hakka and Bukka walked about incognito in the city late at night and early in the morning to get the pulse of the city. They even stopped at a kallu kadai (beer shop) to have a drink and speak with the locals. Karthikeya rolled his eyes in exasperation.

'Imagine when these people realize they were having a drink or a meal with their new kings. They are all going to have fear-farts, Faraj.'

Not to be stopped, Hakka and Bukka spoke with the locals and gathered first-hand their fears and expectations of the new regime. A trader from Kanci, who was in town to get his dues paid by the kingdom, summed it up perfectly:

'All I hear from Kampili is that the brothers are fair, taxes are low and they care for the people. Justice is fierce but true to the law. They don't spend the taxes on themselves and they pay their bills on time, unlike the Hoysala kingdom. Kampili has done well since Hakka Raya became king. I hope they do the same here.'

With a sigh of satisfaction Hakka spoke to Karthikeya.

'The risk was worth it. Besides, I have to say that the kallu we make in Anegundi is definitely superior.' Karthikeya refrained from reminding Hakka about the chaos he created at the kallu kadai when he offered to pay for everyone, and then realized they did not have any money. Bukka took off his gold amulet and handed it over as security, pointed to one of his bodyguards sitting at the next table, and let the proprietor know he was one of his servants who would come back with the payment.

Reflecting on events the next evening with Faraj and a handful of junior generals, Karthikeya simply commented:

'Hakka Raya often forgets he is the king. His common touch is what earns him loyalty.'

The junior officers used this time as an opportunity to get to know more about the royal family, knowing that both Faraj and Karthikeya had served the brothers for a long time. Faraj regaled them with stories and added to their entertainment as he spoke Kannada with an accent.

The greatest source of hilarity was the incident of a recalcitrant nobleman who refused to hand over the keys to the treasury in one of the cities they had conquered. Breaking into a laugh, Karthikeya recounted the scene.

'First, we tied him to a chair. I had three soldiers with me, as well as Faraj. The soldiers were busy sharpening a long knife and heating it on an open fire. The man was perspiring by now and asked what we were doing. I just replied that we normally cut off toes until we got what we wanted, and there were times when we had to take off fingers and ears. Then I asked Faraj if he had permission to cut the toes, and he said we'd have to stop at three and then seek permission for the rest. The man's eyes were bulging, sweat was flowing from his face, and by the time we took the hot knife to his first toe he told us everything. Funny, though, he started to scream before the knife was a foot from him.'

Karthikeya paused to reflect further on the story.

'The treasury was two levels underground,' he revealed. 'When the large metal doors were pushed open, there were eight rooms: six were full of gold and silver coins in large containers. The other two were reserved for jewels, gold artifacts, and trays of gems. I remember Bukka was stunned because we were led to believe it was a depleted treasury.'

Hakka and Bukka planned to leave in a week for the next phase of the campaign. Pattu offered to stay back in Dorasamudra until their return.

'I will do what you need as your brother but nothing in any official capacity,' he clarified firmly. Resting one evening after a day of planning for the campaign ahead, Bukka took a moment to look at the opulence of Ballala's palaces. What was more, he had two more like it at Kanci and Thiruvannamalai. Pattu added that there were treasuries there as well, which were worth inspecting.

'You look like you swallowed an elephant, Hakka,' Bukka quipped.

'The swallowing was easy because of you, Bukka, but now I am wondering how to digest it.' He stopped for a moment before laughing: 'If the digestion goes well, at the least the farts will be elephant farts: massive and thunderous.' In a sudden change of mood, he said, 'Imagine what the little tiger is going to do to me now. He is going to terrorize me and make me study accounts, charts and lists.'

Luxury and comfort were evident throughout the palace.

'Our palace, by comparison, is a modest affair,' Bukka thought. 'Valli needs to see this to comprehend the scale of what kings from large kingdoms can afford. Though I suspect she would call it wasteful opulence. She'd perhaps ask if all the children of the kingdom were well fed and clothed and schooled. That's her measure of a well-run kingdom.'

Pattu called for more kallu and leaned back on comfortable cushions in the king's quarters where they were seated. Clearing his throat, he began:

'I've looked at the rough outline of the plan for your campaign. First, you are taking a significant risk by heading out at the peak of summer. Do not underestimate Mother Nature in the heat, or the rains that will follow.

'Communications will be slow. Make sure you factor that into your plans with your scouts. While your supply train set off last week, you will overtake them and will be without them a long time. I have a list of traders along the route whom the scouts can contact. They have put together the supplies of food you'll need for the men and animals. Additionally, when you get to Kanci you will have the necessary supplies from my traders.

'For the period you are away, you need to have a few people to work on administrative tasks here, like Mani did at Anegundi when you took over there. Tomorrow you will meet with Aslam Beg, one of my fellow traders. I have asked him to meet me. Aslam is of the same ilk as Mani Iyer—a capable man of integrity and brutally honest. He will help you while you wait for Mani Iyer. Most of all, he knows the politics of the place, and possesses the contacts you can use. I hope you can convince him to take the job. He's immensely wealthy and does not need the money.'

———◆———

Hakka and Bukka looked out of a window as Aslam Beg got out of his two-horse tonga, which was black with brightly polished brass fixtures glittering in the morning sunshine. Bukka noticed how much he looked like Pattu: tall and dignified, but a few years older. Pattu came out to welcome him and they went in. The two brothers waited for them to come into what used to be Ballala's grand audience hall.

Aslam Beg entered, offered an adaab and said:

'*Tahiati lilmalk* [my greetings to the king].'

The brothers reciprocated with a greeting. Hakka got to the issue at hand.

'Aslam Beg, you are considered to be a man of great skill and unimpeachable integrity. In this hour of need, the kingdom requires your help in establishing a new administration. Please, would you help?'

There was a pause, which became a prolonged silence. Pattu was comfortable with the silence, but the eternally impatient Hakka began shifting in his seat, holding himself back with great effort. Aslam Beg composed himself and said:

'It is only recently that I found out that Pattu was your brother. With that in mind, the way I view it is that I am responding to this request from Pattu's brother and not the king. Pattu and I have been partners in business for a long time. On more than one occasion, he has saved me from bankruptcy and ruin. It is a blessing and divine gift that he has been in my life, both as a friend and business associate. Thus, I will not decline your offer. However, with all respect to you, I will do it only for Pattu and for no other reason or purpose.'

Then there was another silence. But this time Hakka was not about to let it become awkward.

'Aslam Beg, we thank you. We also insist you assume the title of vakildar of the kingdom of the Hoysalas. You will only be responsible to two people: me and my brother Bukka Raya. Of course, Pattu will advise us in our deliberations.'

Aslam Beg considered this proposal for a moment.

'I would like to speak to Pattu in private and think about this. I promise you will have my answer by tonight.' With that, he stood up and said, '*Allah yahtamu bimalki aljadid* [may Allah bless my new king].'

'*Salaa Allah lana bieunik* [may Allah bless us with your help],' Hakka responded without hesitation. Aslam Beg smiled and left with Pattu.

Pattu's advice was crucial. Aslam Beg did not want to offend Hakka and Bukka by setting out terms and conditions but knew he could get an honest and straight answer from his friend. He had one main question before taking the job of vakildar and he knew Pattu could answer it:

Would the new king of the Hoysalas promise freedom of worship for all religions in the kingdom?

How many will go?

Hakka and Bukka had started with twelve thousand soldiers in all, when they left Kampili two months ago. Now, in Dorasamudra, there were a little more than ten thousand. They'd used the other men to secure camps and outposts along the way. Now the question was, how many would they need for the final stage of the campaign, and how many ought they leave behind to secure the territory. Six thousand, they estimated, was a safe number for the army that would proceed on the campaign. If all went well, two thousand men, that is, half the reserve at Dorasamudra, would go forward to secure outposts at border towns they brought under their control. The campaign was expected to be gruelling and Hakka and Bukka wanted to make sure that the chosen men were mentally and physically strong enough to finish the job. Given the weather conditions, a sizeable infantry was preferable with two hundred horses (which nobody would ride while travelling), as well as three hundred pack ponies for water bags and supplies. The final decisions focused on the route and how much land they would seek to conquer.

As the brothers rode into the palace compound, a vast enclosed and well-guarded area, they saw Aslam Beg (who had accepted the position of vakildar) at the gateway, barking out orders. As they climbed the steps, he greeted them, holding a scroll of parchment:

'I was about to send you a message, requesting about two hours of your time.'

'Certainly, but what for, Aslam Beg?' Hakka enquired.

'Every good task starts by setting up accounts. You must be present when we do the count at the treasury. I would like this done as early as possible so we know what we have. That way we can address any issues affecting the kingdom. Besides, you ought to know what you have. From now on, the treasury will only be opened once a month, under my supervision.

'Once everything is counted today, it will be sealed. Each month, the seal to the treasury will be broken to take out money. Individual containers that are sealed will have their seals broken to remove money. If a seal is broken, I will answer to you and account for the expenditures. I will only have permission to open a few sealed containers when you are away. Any more will require either you or Bukka Raya to be present.'

An hour later, the count began with men only wearing loincloths to make sure nothing went missing. Hakka could only smile. The last instruction he left was for all of King Ballala's army, retinue and civil servants be paid for two months and his family's expenses covered. 'Once we have those expenses accounted for, Aslam Beg, you can tell us what we have.'

At the king's palace Shamshed waited for the brothers, having finally arrived from Anegundi. He'd taken a longer route to ensure the encampments on captured territory were set up and operating the way they should. He had brought a letter and two large metal containers, which a soldier carried to their quarters.

'It's for you, Bukka Raya, from Rani Valli,' he said. Bukka read:

Dear Bukka Raya, the king of my life,

My prayers to the Long-tailed One have been borne out so far. I hear you and Hakkanna are safe and in Dorasamudra. My pride for what you and Hakkanna have accomplished is without measure. Yet, through all of your campaign, I've been paralysed with concern and anxiety. I've kept myself busy through the days making sure I did not shrivel up with fear. Sangama is well but is mystified why you need to conquer more territory when you already had a beautiful little kingdom. Attempts at explaining statecraft and your objectives have not succeeded. However, she is proud of what you have accomplished. Has Appa come to Dorasamudra? I hope he is safe and well.

Do let me know where you are headed and when we will see each other. I will ride with a few men to see you in Dorasamudra if you like. From what Appa has told me, it's a regal city and I would like to visit it while you are there. Malaa has been well, though I am sure she is anxious as well.

Shamshed has brought you two treats. There is one large container of burfis, and another of laddoos—one is your favourite, and the other is Hakkanna's. Make sure that you share them and not eat it all yourselves, which you are both capable of doing and getting sick in the bargain. You have important work to do. My thanks to Fathlulla and to Idriss for having toiled to make this ready in time. You should thank them when you come back.

Once a week, I go to the Hanuman temple by the pond with Mani Iyer to ask the Long-tailed One to give you all the strength you need and to pray for your safety.

Do please continue to send me messages. It helps to reassure us. Malaa sends her prayers to the two of you.

Make sure to tell Hakkanna that we are very proud of our king. Soon we will have to call him chakravarti [emperor], and ask for an audience! Do tell him I said so … I sorely miss being able to tease him.

Ninna prithi [your love],
Valli of Kampili

Bukka gave the letter to Hakka and wandered over to the containers to open them as Pattu entered. It was still morning and he teased Bukka for wanting to eat laddoos for breakfast. Hakka insisted on keeping the letter despite Bukka's protestations.

'It's my letter,' Bukka argued. Stuffing it into his shirt, Hakka gruffly replied:

'But you have so many of them.' His hurt was palpable, so Bukka let it pass.

It was the last day before departure. The temperature was rising even on the plateau where Dorasamudra was located. While the troops had not been told their new destination, they were prepared to move. The previous evening Hakka and Bukka had organized a massive feast and participated in the entertainment.

A grizzled soldier, who had been with Hakka for many years, had asked him politely,

'Hakka Raya, why are we conducting this campaign?'

'A small kingdom like Kampili will always find it difficult to defend itself. We do not know who might take King Ballala's kingdom. Thus, we needed to secure it ourselves. Larger kingdoms can do better for a larger number of people, so this is about making sure that more people are safe and live prosperous lives, starting with Kampili and the Hoysala kingdoms.'

'Will you take over the whole Hoysala kingdom?'

'As much as is necessary,' Hakka asserted and handed the man another tumbler of kallu, conscious that the questions were becoming somewhat sensitive. He was not ready to publicize his intentions.

Bukka, Hakka and Pattu adjourned to the king's quarters. Karthikeya, Faraj and Chinayya came for their final instructions. Karthikeya was promoted to commander of the army for the campaign. He would lead the campaign and thus relieve Bukka of the burden of administrative duties. They shared some sharayam to celebrate Karthikeya's promotion and agreed to meet early in the morning at the barracks. Sitting back, being waited on by Ballala's staff, they finally deliberated on the thorny issue of how much land they should control and how far they would expand their territories. In effect, they were redrawing the southern border of the Hoysala kingdom.

Pattu had never been party to the final preparations of a campaign. Despite being accustomed to managing large enterprises, he was impressed by the thorough and meticulous planning. The logistics were impeccably arranged; the men were well drilled and prepared. Hakka asked Bukka:

'Tam'ma, where do we draw the lines?'

'Hakka, the first part is the march to the holy city, Kanci. I think we will get there in ten days. Scouts tell us there are about four thousand Hoysala soldiers there. Many have been deserting and those remaining are poorly trained. I expect that will be our first major engagement, but if it is anything like Honnavara, it will be finished quickly. The next step is more challenging.

'I recommend we push to the east to the old temple city of Mammalapuram, so we can create an opening to the eastern coast. That would take us another seven days of marching.

'We then march south along the coast to Puducherry. From there, we move west to Ballala's other capital Thiruvannamalai. They have about three thousand soldiers at the post.

'We will leave the remaining Hoysala territory south of this to any local faction that wants it, because we will move southwest to the Nilagiri mountains. Our defensive capacity will be built in those hills, supported by our reserve soldiers.

'We then circle round and return to Dorasamudra. While we would have left behind territory surrounding the Cauvery

River that Ballala had spent a lot of time acquiring, it is too expensive to defend and there are too many threats to worry about.

'So, for now, most of the southern border will be the mountain range of the Nilagiri. However, we will gain territory and have control of both coasts.'

'Tam'ma,' Hakka smiled wryly, 'we are going to do all this with six thousand men?'

'We could do it with three thousand men but we need to secure our new borders.'

Hakka took a moment to fully digest the plan.

'Sharayam,' he shouted, and one of the staff entered hurriedly with a jug to fill his tumbler. Taking a liberal gulp, he looked contently at Bukka and Pattu.

'I agree. It will work. Do you have any comments or suggestions, Pattu?'

'You have one major issue,' he said. 'Hakka and Bukka, remember that Ballala had one hundred thousand men in his army. That army has come apart and there are deserters returning home. They are reasonably well trained, with officers and generals. If you do not take care of them, you will have the same problem Muhammad bin-Tughlaq had in the Multan rebellion.

'Once the Khorasan expedition was disbanded, there were three hundred thousand soldiers who were footloose. It led to banditry, revolts and uprisings—all issues you need to nip in the bud. You may not appreciate their abilities or skills, but bring them into the fold so you can control them.'

'How do we integrate them into our way of life, and do this quickly?' Hakka said, a note of concern creeping into his voice.

They were suddenly interrupted by the entrance of Aslam Beg and his two assistants.

Aslam immediately got down to the business of the kingdom's finances.

'Hakka Raya, Bukka Raya and my dear Pattu. What we have in the treasury, after payment for all the expenses you asked for, will leave us with a surplus of about one half of the year's tax revenues. I do not know what we have at the treasury at the palace in Kanci or Thiruvannamalai. Also, King Ballala had his own lands and they produce about two hundred and fifty manns of gold a year. There is a smaller treasury in the palace and I am still trying to determine its precise location. It is supposed to be situated in the king's quarters.'

The conversation swiftly returned to the problem of integrating the Hoysala soldiers, and they asked Aslam Beg for suggestions.

'I'll have my men spread the word that back pay will be acknowledged and the soldiers will be allowed to return to their old regiments. We could do this at three or four locations away from the capital. This way we'll divide up the returning soldiers and if we have a well organized group of Kampili soldiers to keep control, we should be able to minimize any threat. I could get this done with Shamshed and give you an update via a courier.'

Furnace and fighting

A sparrow flying above might have seen six thousand men marching in five columns, with two hundred horses following them. An additional three hundred ponies had sacks on their backs, and there were sixty fierce dogs (kombais and pandikonas) that barked loudly at the end of the column. They kept watch at camp and served as the dogs of war in case they had to deal with a cavalry attack. All the while, fifty scouts scattered around kept watch.

By the seventh day, the routine of the march had everything synchronized and they were making good time to boot. With each passing day the heat grew more intense. They began the descent eastwards to the Tamil country from the plateau to the plains. They saw a spectacular vista, with the plains lying ahead of them. The vast, barren, brown landscape was visible despite the haze from the sun. Until the rains revived life, the lowlands had to cope with an intense searing heat each year. It would get worse over the next two weeks. If the gods were benevolent, the rains would come and replenish the land. Hakka and Bukka stood next to each other taking in the impressive sight.

'We should be in the holy city of Kanci in four days, Hakka.'

'I just wish we had better intelligence. I'd feel less anxious,' his brother replied with a nod.

'In a day or two the scouts will be here. Information on the route from Kanci to Mamallapuram, and from there to Puducherry should be more regular because there will be fewer obstructions to evade. For the next two weeks, I expect our travels to be relatively straightforward. Providing Kanci does not pose a problem.'

Down in the plains, the heat sapped everything. Bukka grew increasingly anxious about the well-being of the men and the animals. Walking from one column to the next, he joined the men to gauge their spirits. It made for a curious situation because nobody could tell he was coming. Bukka wore the same uniform as the men and, like them, did not ride a horse.

He talked to the men, advising them to make sure the horses were eating well and shitting well; he even wanted to know the colour of their urine. Such details were important to understanding the health of their horses: they were powerful and extremely useful, but fragile. In the evenings, he checked on the dogs. The kombai and the pandikonas were native to the region. As hardy as they were, Bukka was not taking chances. He inspected them to see if they were well and occasionally played with them when he could.

They were now a day's march from Kanci and the scouts informed them of two sets of riders coming towards them: from the west and east. 'One of them must be the scouts coming from Kanci,' Bukka thought. 'But why would twenty men be riding towards us from Dorasamudra, when only two riders form the courier?' As they got closer, it was clear they were mostly Kampili men. In the lead of the contingent was Kamath, a senior colonel who worked for Shamshed.

'Greetings, Bukka Raya. Semanya Shamshed's men intercepted one of King Ballala's generals and two other senior officers. Instead of gathering intelligence and sending it to you later, Semanya Shamshed asked us to deliver them directly to you.'

Bukka left the marching column and paused to interview the new arrivals. He was impressed by Shamshed and Karthikeya's astute method of operation: they had a rare quality of knowing how to obtain information and then to make sure it was fed swiftly to their king.

Bukka noticed that the general still had his hands tied behind him. He ordered a soldier to untie the man.

'I am Bukka, general of the Kampili army. What is your name, and what is your rank?'

'My name is Aiyappa, and I was one of King Ballala's three commanders. After the defeat at the fort, I was the only one able to get away. One of the commanders was killed during the attack by the sultan of Madura's forces. The other was beheaded with King Ballala. I have been making my way from Madurai to Dorasamudra. There were rumours that the kingdom was capitulating but I wanted to get the news to the three ministers regardless. When I was close to Dorasamudra, I was picked up by two Kampili guards and taken to Semanya Shamshed. He immediately had me bound and sent me with the horsemen, though I did not know where we were going.'

Bukka borrowed a horse belonging to one of the soldiers and went off to find Hakka who was also marching with the men. Hakka joined Bukka in sizing up the prisoners.

'Ask Semanya Karthikeya and Faraj to join us,' Hakka commanded. 'General Aiyappa, you and your two men will continue with us. However, you must decide soon: do you want to redeem yourself and cooperate with us? Or would you rather be sent back to Dorasamudra as a prisoner of war and wait until a tribunal is formed to determine your fate? I would like your answer by the evening.'

Turning to Karthikeya and Faraj, Hakka said:

'Make sure the men are fed, and if they are capable of walking, they will march with the men. General Aiyappa will be treated like a semanya. He can march with you, Faraj.' Before Aiyappa could respond, Hakka turned on his heel and walked away with Bukka.

At the camp that evening, Hakka, Bukka and the three field commanders waited for news from the scouts at Kanci. One arrived and told them that there were twelve hundred soldiers at the Kanci palace but the city was not guarded. Most of the soldiers were raw recruits, since the seasoned soldiers had gone to Madurai to join Ballala's forces. It seemed they did not anticipate an attack.

'If Aiyappa can get these men to surrender, it would save us a lot of time and effort,' Hakka declared. 'Bring him over and let us see what he can do for us.' Aiyappa was led to where the brothers were sitting. Hakka invited him to sit down.

'Trust takes time to grow. I am not going to trust you yet. But if you choose to cooperate, you can begin to integrate yourself with the forces of Kampili. So, what is your answer, General Aiyappa?'

Aiyappa remained standing, arms folded and said:

'Hakka Raya, I am grateful for being treated with respect. I do not want to be a prisoner of war. As a military man, I appreciate being in the field. While every enemy is always suspect, maybe I can earn your trust by helping you as you consolidate your position over the Hoysala kingdom. When you have control and after you find I have been useful, perhaps you can give me employment, even if that means I will carry the mark of a traitor for the rest of my life.'

'You would not be considered a traitor, General Aiyappa. Your king is dead. The kingdom was abandoned by his son who is looking for refuge elsewhere, and the Hoysalas are under attack. Should you throw in your lot with us there will be no mark against you. That being said, trust is earned through effort and loyalty. The only question for you is, are you willing to journey down that hard road?'

'I am ready, Hakka Raya. I am ready to help you rebuild the Hoysala kingdom.'

'In that case, your first task tomorrow will be to convince the troops at Kanci to surrender. It would save any unnecessary loss of life and help us move on with our more important task. Discuss how you might do this with the field commanders and let us discuss the plan in the morning. It would help if we conclude this quickly.'

All six thousand men were deployed around the palace in Kanci the following day. The heat was unbearable but Hakka was convinced that the enemy troops would fold. If Aiyappa was unable to persuade the garrison to surrender, they would use force.

Aiyappa rode out to the palace with a hundred soldiers and Karthikeya by his side. An officer from the city rode out to meet them with the Kanci army's demands. The soldiers did not want to be treated like prisoners of war. They were seeking employment, and since they were mostly from Kanci, they did not want to serve in another part of the kingdom.

'Yes, yes, and yes,' Hakka answered promptly. 'Disarm them. Though it looks like they are better suited to being guards rather than soldiers,' he observed.

Kanci was in the bag. The only adversity they had faced was the gruelling march from the plateau to the plains. The men were exhausted but what mattered to Bukka was they had held up admirably. Bukka suggested a three-day break as reward for the men and the animals.

Meanwhile, Pattu's traders asked if they could arrange the food for the six thousand men.

They were used to hosting large festivals in the holy city and Hakka's response was for them to get 'the best you have, in large quantities, and you'll be paid well'.

The palace was not large but it was well decorated and impressive.

'That fat hairy little bear did not spare expense for his comfort,' Hakka remarked.

'They've had this in the family for nearly two centuries now, Hakka. If you are not too stupid, your wealth will accumulate too,' Bukka assured him with a sly grin.

Faraj and General Aiyappa arrived, accompanied by ten bodyguards.

Aiyappa held two large sets of keys in his hands and handed them to Bukka.

'What are they for, Aiyappa?' Hakka asked.

'The two treasuries,' he answered.

The treasury was located in the corner of the palace just past the king's quarters.

Opening it was a task that took more time than anticipated. Hakka just growled:

'Call me when it's open, and no one is to go in until I am here.' Both Hakka and Bukka went off to tour the complex.

'When would we ever use this place, Bukka?' Hakka said, shaking his head.

'I have two answers. First, you are likely to have zabitahs who could use the place. Second, if you were to ask Valli, she'd make it into a school or orphanage.'

Hakka started to laugh when they were interrupted by news of the treasury being opened. Each room was half full, but it was enough to astonish those who saw it. 'How was it possible that this was a kingdom supposedly running out of funds?' Hakka thought.

'Bukka, don't invite anyone to eat with us tonight,' he instructed. 'I am getting weighed down and need to speak about it. I want to drink some kallu after taking a bath, and eat something other than millet balls and pickles.' They both decided to ride through the camp, make sure that the men were settled, and the animals were in good shape. It was already getting late. The sun had set when Hakka quaffed a few glasses of kallu the traders had procured for them.

'So, what is it that is bothering you?' Bukka enquired.

Comfortably ensconced in a large chair, Hakka gave the question some thought.

'Bukka, how are you and I going to manage all of this? I'm beginning to think about the sultan in Dilli and the pressures that must have weighed him down. At least he was trained to do this. What training do we have? I don't even know what it means to play the role of a king. I'm just a soldier who got lucky because he was surrounded by brilliant people.'

It was infrequent, but Hakka was occasionally overcome with doubt about managing the kingdom. Bukka sat back, thinking how to respond.

'Hakka, we had the same concerns when you took over as zabitah of the Kampili kingdom. Then you declared independence and became king. Of course, what we have in front of us is a huge challenge, but it also comes with ample resources, money and people.

'I think of it like the way we would capture an elephant. First, you need to seize it in the wild, which is what we are doing. Then you have to train it, which is what we will do once we are back in Dorasamudra. It will take a lot of work, but it's not something you will do on your own. Between you, me, Pattu, Mani Iyer, Aslam Beg and the generals, we will set our sights on taming the elephant. Personally, I do not think it will take much to achieve it.

'Remember, we have the resources. All you have to do is think about the standards you want to set, and have us follow. The rest takes care of itself. Simple. While I realize the responsibility is immense, you will do it in steps, and you will do it well.'

'I like your elephant metaphor, Bukka,' Hakka replied. 'I just do not want to be crushed by it.'

On the day before they left, Karthikeya had a plan. Since there was very little by way of enemy presence in the region, he recommended that most of the troops should go directly south to Thiruvannamalai, instead of the planned longer route, reducing the distance they had to travel and remaining relatively fresh.

From Kanci, one small contingent one small contingent would travel east to take over Mammalapuram, the coastal city, then south to Puducherry, and turn west to return to Tiruvannamalai.

Another unit would cut through diagonally southeast from Kanci to meet the group at Puducherry, to provide reinforcement if needed. It made sense and the intelligence Aiyappa had provided them was confirmed by what they knew already.

Hakka, Bukka and Karthikeya would go to the coast and head south, taking the long route. Faraj would meet them at Puducherry, leaving Chinayya to lead the bulk of the troops to Thiruvannamalai. It was agreed they would converge on Tiruvannamalai in two weeks, which presented the greatest challenge of the campaign.

The battle for Thiruvannamalai

Velayudan, the governor of Tiruvannamalai, was a Tamil from the Chola clan. Once the Cholas were stripped of their kingdom, Velayudan married into Ballala's family, his ostensible qualification being that he was a 'royal'. He married the king's niece and considered himself to be part of the royal family.

Of medium height, with an ostentatious moustache, his main distinguishing feature was his stomach. It bulged out significantly. According to Aiyappa, he was also known to have a high opinion of himself with little by way of accomplishments to support it.

Karthikeya's scouts came back with estimates of enemy strength. Velayudan had nine thousand foot soldiers, three hundred horses and two war elephants. Bukka's immediate question concerned the number of archers. To his surprise, there were none. About a third of the soldiers were seasoned fighters and part of the standing army. The remaining were peasants recruited by the feudal chiefs.

After Ballala's death, Velayudan's plan was to create a small kingdom around the Thiruvannamalai hinterland. Both Hakka and Bukka interrogated Aiyappa about Velayudan, his army and its capabilities. He recommended negotiating for an amicable surrender. In the few days he'd been marching with Hakka and Bukka, he had got a taste of the capabilities of the Kampilis and was convinced the Hoysala soldiers at Thiruvannamalai would be unable to hold out in spite of larger numbers. The Kampili were nimble, battle-hardened and led by extremely talented generals. If the Hoysalas did not surrender, a bloodbath was inevitable and Aiyappa wanted to save his former men from that outcome.

Both sides agreed to meet outside the town with a hundred soldiers each the next morning. At the assembly point, both groups rode up to each other. Hakka and Bukka took the initiative and dismounted from their horses. Velayudan crooked his finger to indicate they should walk up but they stood their ground. Speaking in Tamil, he repeated his order for them to approach him.

Realizing Hakka was not going to budge, he conceded. With his large stomach and characteristic foul mood, he waddled over to the middle ground. Aiyappa attempted to make introductions but Velayudan scoffed at him saying:

'I do not need to be introduced to a low-caste soldier.'

Hakka remained unusually calm and let Aiyappa proceed.

'The king of Kampili advises that you and your troops surrender so men may not needlessly die.'

'I do not listen to orders from a traitor like you, much less from this man who claims to be a king. I have a large army and will trounce whoever lays siege on my kingdom. They can go around the kingdom of Thiruvannamalai and we will overlook them trespassing. Otherwise, they will face the bloody consequence at the hands of my army. These men are no more than bandits of the lowest order who rape and pillage, and I am surprised you would have the temerity to ask for surrender.'

The Kampili party turned and walked away. Hakka reached his horse and turned and bellowed in Tamil, startling Velayudan:

'We will meet your army here tomorrow at the same time. Just make sure you accompany them and don't hide like a coward.' Hakka turned and mounted his horse, leaving Velayudan spitting mad and cursing.

It was a hot and dusty morning, and as Bukka stared at the Hoysala army in front of him, he remarked:

'They're being utterly predictable in forming a set-piece formation for the attack.'

Hakka nodded.

'How many do you have in reserve with Faraj?'

'Two thousand men and fifty horses.'

Hakka cast his eye on the field in front of him and quickly reviewed how they would manage the attack. He would stand back to make sure the coordination went according to plan. Bukka was going to join the mounted archers on the left flank and come back occasionally to liaise with Hakka. Karthikeya gave the order for the kombu to sound the call. The steady beat of the drumming began. As expected, the Hoysalas sent out their horses first, approaching at a flat-out gallop.

When they were fifty yards away, Karthikeya gave the sign. The front of the column quickly changed configuration from being a straight line facing the enemy to a deep U-shaped formation that was at least two hundred yards deep. Large shields were in place for protection within the U-shape. About one hundred archers lined themselves along the inside of the formation. They let the first wave of riders come halfway into the cup when the archers fired the first volley of their assault. The effect was devastating. In an instant, the majority of horsemen fell. The U-shape now quickly formed into a funnel so the riderless horses could run through to the back to be collected later.

Next, they let the dogs loose and the archers successfully targeted the next wave of riders. More than two hundred horses were captured and taken back to the reserves.

Bukka, in the meantime, attacked the flanks with archers on horses who raced past, shooting, and then circled round to repeat. The Hoysalas were losing forty or fifty men every time the archers made a run past a flank. The dead piled up on each side forming a wall so that the Hoysala soldiers were unable to rush out to attack the archers. In the first thirty minutes of the battle the Hoysalas had lost approximately five hundred men.

Watching over the field, Hakka realized Velayudan at the end of his column was attempting to escape with a few men. Motioning to Karthikeya to take command, he galloped towards him. Bukka saw this and followed quickly. Steadying himself on his stirrups, he loosed off arrows from his bow and downed two of the four men fleeing with Velayudan. As they caught up, Hakka flung his dagger and got another squarely in the back. Bukka swerved to avoid the fallen horseman Hakka had just eliminated and came up alongside the fourth rider. Throwing his bow aside, Bukka drew his sword, lunged over to the rider and slashed him across the neck. Bukka was sprayed with blood as he made contact.

Velayudan was isolated. Hakka hit his back with the flat of his sword and sent him flying off his horse. In an instant Hakka and Bukka captured him before he could run away. The brothers rode back to the battle with the captive Velayudan slung over his horse with Hakka and Bukka following.

When they were within a hundred yards, Hakka bellowed at the Hoysalas to surrender. A few Hoysala men ran towards them to attempt an attack. Kampili archers dropped them before they had gone ten steps. Hakka shouted again for a surrender. It was only on the third shout that the battle came to a halt.

The Hoysalas had lost thirteen hundred men compared to forty-two on the Kampili side. The carnage made Hakka retch; Bukka gave him cover with his horse so the men could not see. Glancing at his brother, Bukka thought, 'It never changes. The wretchedness of it all can never be overcome, even though you know what is coming.'

Once the prisoners were secured, they made sure the men were settled into the camp.

Aiyappa and the bodyguards escorted Hakka and Bukka to the palace where they saw a clutch of soldiers with Velayudan held captive. Hakka drew his sword and approached him with menacing purpose. Bukka knew he would not kill him. As he got closer, glaring at Velayudan, the Hoysala general dropped to his knees and begged for mercy.

'Stand up, you coward,' Hakka bellowed. He sheathed his sword and hit Velayudan squarely in the nose with his fist, shattering it.

'You are a coward, which in my book is the only low caste I know.' And with that, Hakka and Bukka walked away.

The rains came

Bukka walked into the king's quarters to see his brother seated comfortably on a carpet with what appeared to be a large number of letters brought in by the courier. Hakka looked up and laughed.

'I feel like a child trying to make sense of his lesson. Save me from this tedious business and tell me what news you have.' Bukka looked at him with a suppressed grin.

Before he could reply, a blinding flash of lightning lit up the darkening sky they saw through the window, followed by a huge clap of thunder. Then came pouring rain.

'The gods seemed to want to get the rainy business finished in a hurry,' Hakka remarked. 'They take all their buckets and empty them quickly over the span of a month. If you are lucky and they are not otherwise preoccupied, you get another round of the same thing half a year later.' He paused as he reflected on the weather. 'Anyway, what was it you were going to say?'

'Hakka Raya, it would be reasonable to say that you are now king of the Kampili and the Hoysala kingdoms,' Bukka said and went down on one knee. 'My salutations to you, my king, for a victorious campaign that lasted six weeks.' Hakka, taken aback by this, took some time to absorb what Bukka had just said. His mouth curled into a smile as he recovered, and in his characteristic gruff voice he said:

'A few things, Bukka Raya. First, please stop this nataka [drama] and get up. Second, how do you arrive at this conclusion? Third, if you're right and there are no more wars to fight, it means endless accounts and administration for the foreseeable future.'

Bukka sat down on the carpet next to Hakka.

'I've studied the intelligence from Karthikeya's men, interviewed Aiyappa and the prisoners of war, and their answers lead to the same conclusion. The only troops left to contain are in Mangaluru and some in the Tuluva kingdom. There are no more than a thousand troops altogether in these two places. It is something a new general like Chinayya can handle. That being the case, once we settle the borders of your newly acquired territory, decide on troop placements, and hash out the outstanding administrative details, you and I should be able to get back to Dorasamudra. As a reward, I asked Mani Iyer to join us there,' and Bukka broke into a loud laugh.

For a moment Hakka seemed deflated.

'Were the Hoysalas a paper tiger, Bukka? How did we get the impression that they were an adversary to revere? I am disappointed that we got this prize so easily.'

'Hakka, they were always a paper tiger. We just did not see it. Money and resources disguised their lack of purpose, drive and focus. But also remember this. We planned the campaign meticulously, we timed the operation impeccably, and we exploited the opportunity perfectly. Just because there was less blood spilled than expected does not make it less of an accomplishment. You should take the credit for making hard decisions. Let me remind you that Pattu thought we were mad to take on such a large risk. To his credit, however, he believed in us.'

The rest of the afternoon was spent with their generals, analysing their intelligence. All the while the rain continued to pour down with ferocity. As the conversation wound down, Karthikeya stated the obvious:

'Hakka Raya and Bukka Raya, should we start making plans for our return to Dorasamudra?' At that moment they realized that the campaign was effectively over.

Hakka cleared his throat to address his comrades.

'We still have one or two days' work to organize troop placements. Once that is done, we will make our departure. Now, I would like all of you to get back to camp and make sure our soldiers are in good shape, while also checking in on the animals and prisoners. When you've done that, we can all celebrate by drinking the night away since our wives are not here!'

When the generals left, Hakka changed his tone and whispered to Bukka with an earnest look on his face:

'Tam'ma, just to make sure there is no doubt, I want you to know that our victory was because of all your effort. All I did was say "yes" and "no". You planned all of this. When you saw the opportunity, you urged me to seize the initiative. You are the architect of this great outcome. All of this was only worth it because I achieved it with you.'

Chakravarti (emperor)?

'Spare no expense. Spend what's necessary. The best food, the best kallu and sharayam, and the best entertainment,' Hakka directed Chinayya.

Following Hakka's instructions, Chinayya immediately went off with Bukka to make arrangements.

Only then did Bukka realize that they had run out of funds.

'Where's the treasury?' he asked Chinayya.

'Semanya, I will find out and come back.' Within minutes Chinayya returned with the keys and Velayudan who, in his prisoner status, had his hands bound. Two dogs accompanied them.

'Why did you bring the dogs?' Bukka asked.

Chinayya smiled devilishly.

'These were the dogs that chewed up the last prisoner of war, semanya. If the general fails to cooperate, I thought the dogs could get to know him better.' They had no trouble after that. When they opened the two treasuries the contents were three times what they had seen in Dorasamudra.

Bukka's grin broadened.

'I think we will be able to pay for the celebration,' he joked.

Meanwhile, Hakka was outside, addressing his six thousand soldiers who were congregated in a large open ground next to the palace.

'You assisted in the kingdom's expansion. Our southern borders are safer. We can now experience prosperity. You bore the hardship with no complaints, showed courage even when we faced larger opposition and you have shown what efficient armies can accomplish. For all your bravery and effort, the kingdom would like to reward every one of you. To those who have fallen during the campaign we express our eternal gratitude. We will make sure their families are supported for life by continuing the salaries of their loved ones. They will also get the same rewards as you: a year's salary, two bighas of land, two heads of livestock and a small home that the kingdom will pay for.'

'Chakravarti Hakka, Chakravarti Hakka, Chakravarti Hakka! Jai Kampili, jai Hakka Raya, jai Bukka Raya!' the men roared. Asking Bukka to join him on the raised platform, Hakka declared:

'Bukka Raya is to be credited with this great accomplishment. He managed this great campaign. He has always taken care of your welfare. We are grateful to him.'

Bukka called his three generals to join him on the dais: Karthikeya, Faraj and Chinayya. He promoted Karthikeya to commander of the army, the position that he had fulfilled already; Faraj was made full general, and Chinayya was appointed to general (semanya) on a permanent basis. Amid the celebrations, Hakka warned:

'We need to be vigilant and protect what we have seized, so be prepared and protect what we have.' The revelry lasted into the night. A small army from a small kingdom had overwhelmed a large kingdom and had done so with remarkable speed.

Hakka, Bukka and the generals congregated in the palace to plan for the future.

Karthikeya spoke first.

'Semanya, we now have more horses, so it would make sense if you and a small contingent of bodyguards returned to Dorasamudra as quickly as possible.' This was seconded by all present.

The next question was dealing with the potential threat to their expanded territory.

Hakka took the lead.

'Our position leaves us facing the armies of the Madura sultanate and the Pandya kingdom to our south. They will want our hides for having sliced off a piece of their coastline. We do not know how the Reddi kingdom will react to new neighbours to the south.

'My suggestion is to leave the army in Thiruvannamalai for a month or two under the command of Chinayya. He will report to Faraj who will command a quadrilateral area encompassing the four corners of Kanci, Mammalapuram, Puducherry and Thiruvannamalai. Faraj is now ready for more responsibility. This is going to be the most hazardous region of the kingdom for the foreseeable future. Once we have given more considered analysis to the threats we face, we may supply more troops. I suspect we will have to do this. My advice to you, Faraj, is to keep alert and make sure that the men are fit and well trained. Once you lose your edge, you will lose.'

Karthikeya pitched in.

'It would make sense to leave behind sixty of the most experienced scouts as part of Faraj's new command.' Both Hakka and Bukka agreed.

'Karthikeya, this would fall under your purview of military and civil responsibility,' Bukka added.

Hakka appeared pensive as he spoke.

'Faraj and Chinayya, this is the area of the kingdom that is most vulnerable. Deploy the scouts carefully and anticipate any danger. Never be in a situation when you are caught unawares and have to react. Take the initiative. I suspect that the Pandyas, with help from the Madura sultanate, will attempt to recapture the coastline. If you encounter trouble, apply an element of surprise and speed. Lastly, this is a perfect opportunity to train and groom eight or ten officers. If, in the interest of security or the well-being of the men and animals, you have to spend more money than is budgeted, do not hesitate.'

Chinayya was dismissed. Attention then turned to Faraj. Hakka turned to him and said:

'I'm giving you this command because you have shown exemplary leadership skills and capacity to manage men. I trust you like my family. Make me proud and make Qutlugh Khan proud. I believe you can do this, so go forth and be bold. When you are in Anegundi or in Dorasamudra, come stay with us at the palace. *Jazakum Allah khyrana* [may Allah's blessings be with you].' Tears streamed down Faraj's cheeks.

Looking at each of them, he knelt in front of Hakka and uttered in Kannada:

'*Devaru nannage sakti nidali* [may God give me strength].'

Before he left, Hakka added:

'Faraj, you will live in the palace, though not in my suite. Just make sure to sweep the place occasionally!' All of them began chuckling.

The sun had not come out when they assembled in front of the palace. Faraj felt it was appropriate to have all of the troops on display to wish the king well before he departed. They presented Hakka with a guard of honour as he mounted his horse. In a break from protocol, he stood up on his stirrups and bellowed:

'I have great faith in your new commander. I have great expectations of your new general. I have no doubt you will serve in exemplary fashion until your new relief comes to join you. Be assured, all of your families will be taken care of in your absence. It will be my first task.' With his fist to his heart he added, 'May God be with you.'

The roaring began and continued until Hakka, Bukka and Karthikeya rode off into the distance.

Faraj accompanied them to the edge of town. As they parted company, he gave Hakka, Bukka and Karthikeya each a small bag containing a gift. Looking at Faraj, Hakka smiled and, said:

'*Yahmik Allah* [may Allah protect you].' Faraj responded by unsheathing his sword, holding it up and declaring:

'*Allah yahfaz milki* [may Allah protect my king].'

Hakka led from the front.

'Hiyaaa!' he shouted to his horse, digging in his heels. Turning to the rest of the contingent, he shouted, '*Kathina savari* [ride hard]!' Faraj watched as the two hundred horsemen, with the king's standard (a bright yellow pennant) fluttering in the breeze, galloped off.

Exertion was a device Hakka had always used to quell his anxieties. They travelled at a ferocious pace to battle the demons plaguing him. He motioned for Bukka to come by his side. They would head westward in a near straight line. If the rains did not slow them, they would be in the capital in eight to ten days. The days were now noticeably cooler and the land began to turn green. Soon they would be up on the plateau where the climate would provide some relief. On the first night, Hakka pulled out the little bag Faraj had given him: it was a small shell pendant on a gold chain, with the inscription: 'You carved a way to the other ocean.'

From the battle at Anegundi fort to now—through determination, loyalty and hard work—Faraj had made his way up the ranks to being one of the most capable generals and trusted confidantes Hakka had in his army.

'Do you know who is a very close friend of Faraj, other than the usual suspects like Valli or Karthikeya?' Bukka asked. Hakka shook his head.

'Mani Iyer. He taught him the Kannada alphabet while Faraj in turn taught him about the traditions of Islam.' Once in a while, Faraj would visit his friend's house where Mani Iyer's widowed sister would feed him a good Brahmin meal.

'Bukka, this is a pleasant little titbit. From now on, I fear they will be in short supply. I used to compare matters of state to being bitten by scorpions when we were at Kampili. Now I envision them as bears that are going to assault me,' Hakka said with a rueful smile.

Bukka could not stop laughing.

'How do you make these metaphors? I can assure you that you will not be facing any bears alone, small or large.'

Mop up, and clear

A day out from Dorasamudra, Hakka announced:

'I have an idea, Bukka. What would you think about living with Valli in Dorasamudra for a while?'

'If that is what you want, then that is what we'll do, Hakka.'

'If it's not a good idea, you should say so,' Hakka hesitantly replied. 'My reasoning is based on the fact that I do not believe we should change the capital of this kingdom, like the sultan experimented with his move to Daulatabad. If I were not in Anegundi or the new location across the river, it would never be considered the capital city. But there is a huge amount of work to be done here and I have no one I can trust to do it. Perhaps one of us might visit the other every month or thereabouts? It would be a few days of riding but the road is not difficult. Sangama could also be with you for some of the time. She might like a change of scenery. I say this in spite of the fact that my life will become very empty.'

'Hakka, you will have your wife with you and, God willing, you will have a family too,' Bukka responded.

'That's hardly a replacement, Bukka,' his brother glumly responded.

After an hour, he finally came to terms with the impact of his own decision. His attention turned to another pressing matter.

'Bukka, how large a standing army do you think we need to have for our new kingdom?'

'While the actual number we need might be closer to fifty thousand, about half that number of good men initially would work.'

Hakka nodded in agreement.

'Where do you think we are most vulnerable?' he went on.

'Definitely in the southeast, where Faraj and Chinayya are positioned. The east could be an issue, depending on how the Reddis react to this new development. All this is no more than clean-up operations, but we also need to be wary of the risk from the north,' Bukka responded.

'How long would it take us to get to a standing army of fifty thousand?'

'Between two and three years, Hakka. Two years if we can find talent in the troops from the Hoysala army and they are open to being retrained.'

'Well, make that your top priority. While none of our adversaries are too big, the possibility of them joining forces to come after upstarts like us is not impossible. The Madura sultanate will test us, and the Pandyas have a territorial grievance. In fact, once you've got Dorasamudra under full control, please review Faraj's territory and make sure we have enough scouts over there.'

Hakka recalled what Bukka and Karthikeya had recommended to him: a well-trained scout was worth at least fifty troops in the field. Initially he had been sceptical, but time had proved them right. In every situation they were the eyes and ears that kept him and his troops out of trouble. True, they were better paid, had access to the best horses and most often worked with senior officers and generals. But they were given the riskiest assignments. Reflecting on this, Hakka announced:

'Pay the scouts more, raise their prestige, and recruit another hundred or so. In every scenario they have been invaluable, starting from the days when we marched to Daulatabad.'

No decision could have made Karthikeya happier. He was beaming.

'Recruiting them will be easy, semanya. There are three hundred who would volunteer immediately but we would have to choose carefully.'

It was past noon when all two hundred horsemen entered the town, the hooves making an unmistakable clatter on the cobblestone streets. As they rode into the heart of town where the marketplace was, a crowd swarmed the streets to see the new arrivals. As expected, Karthikeya grew apprehensive for the safety of Hakka and Bukka. The cobblestones made it difficult to move fast and the crowd gathered quickly along the way. Soon they heard cheering and chants of '*Manege svagata* [welcome home], Hakka Raya, *manege svagata* [welcome home] Hakka Raya.' The cheering followed them to the palace, which took them half an hour to reach. Hakka lapped up the celebratory mood and waved to the crowd as he passed them by.

Making the last turn, they were on the promenade that led straight to the gates of the palace. It was intended to be a grand and impressive entrance. Shamshed had Kampili soldiers

lining the path. Hakka and Bukka recognized a large number
of the soldiers. When they were about halfway to the palace,
every one of them drew their sword, raised it aloft and began
chanting 'Chakravarti Hakka, Chakravarti Hakka'. It left
Hakka overwhelmed.

When they finally got through the gates, Bukka saw Valli
standing with Sangama, Pattu and Malaa.

'I thought I'd set up a nice surprise for you, Tam'ma,'
Hakka said and slapped Bukka on the shoulder. Bukka was
overwhelmed. It had been four months since they last set eyes
on each other.

Hakka and Bukka dismounted, embraced their mother
and touched her feet. Her expression was that of an indulgent
mother looking at her two sons who'd been up to mischief again.
Pattu stood at Sangama's side and greeted Hakka and Bukka:

'You are the first military commanders in the history of the
subcontinent whose kingdom stretches to both coasts. You've
both accomplished a mission that seemed impossible only three
months ago.'

Bukka hugged Valli, who was trying to hide her tears by
covering her head with the pallu of her saree, while Hakka
reached out and touched Malaa in a comparably less affectionate
way.

Managing success

Even the major players of international trade and the masters of
organization, Pattu and Aslam Beg, were impressed. After a two-
day rest, the senior members of the kingdom congregated for an
exhausting three-day review by Mani Iyer of the tasks at hand.
He brought two of his staff along for the meeting. The sweep

of his coverage was extraordinary, his detail was impressive, and his analysis of finances and governance was exhaustive.

'Hakka Raya,' he concluded at the end of the review, 'what I have given you all is a "thinking framework" of how everything interconnects. However, you must keep in mind a few key essentials. First, you cannot afford a war for another year, ideally two years. By implication, employ diplomacy as much as you can.

'Second, the current revenue structure only serves the corrupt bureaucrats and not the citizens. If you can impose the same system as in Kampili, then with lower taxes, you will have an exchequer that will be richer than that of the sultan, Muhammad-bin-Tughlaq. Third, you have all the resources to build a military of about thirty thousand men this year and fifty the next year.

'Finally, you must appoint governors. There are ten positions that need to be filled immediately. At least four of these critical positions must be people of exceptionally high calibre and intellect.'

The meeting ended and everyone was eager to get some fresh air and move around. Hakka wasn't ready for a break, however. He stood up and asked them to stay for a little longer, as he had some very important business to finish up.

'It was Bukka, Mani Iyer and I, with advice from Pattu, who built the kingdom of Kampili but the task was completed only because of the brilliance and hard work of one man. Since most of you will be part of my Privy Council, I would like your permission to appoint Mani Iyer as prime minister of the new, consolidated kingdom. He will be responsible only to me and Bukka. I want him to have the title of Samrajyada Ratna [Jewel of the Kingdom]. Moreover, I will endow his favourite temple or build a new one with lands for its upkeep.

'In all of my endeavours, Bukka has provided the intelligence and the organization and foresight that made success possible. In recognition of that, I would like it to be known henceforth that he is the adjunct king. He will wear the same signet ring I do and command the same honours and privileges the kingdom gives me.'

Hakka went on: 'Before we leave, I would like to award two people with honours. The honour is Samrajyada Adharasthambha [Pillar of the Kingdom]. The first person I would like to acknowledge is Ramaswamy Mudaliar. The second is Bukka Raya. The kingdom of Kampili and our new extended territories have become a reality only because of these two men. Today I have presented three people with the highest honours the kingdom can bestow, and Kampili is grateful.'

The next day Mani Iyer returned to Anegundi in his new horse-drawn carriage with his assistants. It was a true mark of respect that the royal family came out to bid farewell to Mani Iyer. Karthikeya arranged for a contingent of guards and scouts to travel with him and make sure he had a safe journey to Anegundi.

Before Mani Iyer left, he had one final question for Hakka:

'My king, I have taken an inventory of the lands, the treasure and all the jewels after every expense is considered. What would you have me give Bukka?'

'Half of all of the money, lands and treasure. He will be given a yearly grant from the kingdom that is the same as mine.'

Mani Iyer allowed a small grin to appear on his face.

'Even after dividing it in half, you are both immensely wealthy. Perhaps nearly as wealthy as Pattu!' He bid Valli farewell, sad that she would be staying in Dorasamudra for a while, and told her he would miss going to the temple with her. 'However,' he said in a sudden change of tone, 'since you ride, I expect you to come to Anegundi with Bukka.'

Pattu also intended to leave that day. He had one final bit of business to address with his brothers. Taking them to a secluded part of the palace, he had two of his men bring a large cloth-covered wooden cage. As he removed the cover, they saw six pigeons. Hakka was confused and quipped, 'Pattu, is this a gift for Bukka the animal lover?'

'Hakka and Bukka, I had these sent over by traders in the Straits of Malacca. The Chinese emperor uses birds like these to send messages. They call them "homing pigeons". Wherever you take them, you can attach a message to their legs and they will come home. In emergencies, they will cover ground faster than your fastest couriers.'

Bukka understood what he meant and expressed his sincere thanks.

'But how much do they cost? How many can we get? How do we train them? And how often do they lay eggs? Above all, how do we make sure no one else catches them?'

Pattu started to laugh at the speed with which Bukka blurted out his questions in quick succession.

Hakka interjected:

'They should be under the protection of the scouts and no one should be permitted access to them.' A weight lifted off Hakka's shoulders as he realized they could communicate in emergencies over very long distances.

Hakka learned from Malaa that her father was upset at being excluded from the military plans. It was, according to her, 'a foolhardy plan with a very small kingdom biting off more than it was capable of digesting'. Her father wrote in his letter to her, 'Your husband seems to have an incredibly high opinion of his military abilities.' Visibly upset, Malaa threw the letter in Hakka's face. She was of the opinion that her family's situation and pedigree was superior. Hakka would have sent her back to her father were it not for the fact that he did not want to create a new problem on the eastern border. To complicate matters further, he found out that Malaa was expecting their first child.

Hakka left a week later. Bukka arranged for his brother to be sent off with full military honours. Before Hakka mounted his horse, he touched his mother's feet, before taking Valli's hands and holding them to his eyes. He mumbled quietly so only Bukka and Valli could hear him:

'I will miss you both every single day that you are away.' Bukka rode with him to the edge of town. Bidding them farewell, Hakka yelled out as he was riding away:

'*Kuna malakana* [be a king]!'

Bukka reciprocated, drawing his sword, holding it up in the air and shouting:

'*Kama turid malkaa* [as you wish, my king].'

The weight of the world was on his shoulders now that his brother was gone. It was his responsibility to assimilate the Hoysala kingdom with Kampili.

9

Chakravarti (Emperor)

1346: Dorasamudra

It just took longer ...

Bukka returned to Dorasamudra from the southern border earlier than anticipated. He hoped to surprise the family. Walking over to the far end of the palace compound where they had built a small paddock for the children's riding lessons, he could see Valli at a distance. She was teaching the two girls to ride.

The refrain wafted to his ears: 'Up, down, up, down, up ... hold the horse with your legs ... sit up straight ... toes up ... make sure the reins are taut not tight ...' Meanwhile the two boys, Hari and Haftar, were outside the corral, teasing the girls.

'You were both very good today,' Valli announced as she helped the girls dismount. Shveta and Sarah were just five and Valli had been teaching them to ride for the last year. The boys, both seven, had better riding skills but it was only a matter of time before Shveta and Sarah caught up, given their competitive spirit.

'Okay, scoundrels, bring your horses in,' Valli shouted to the boys. Bukka decided to watch from afar. He asked the bodyguards to step before him so Valli would not spot him. She started the routine:

'Did you check the horse's saddle? Did you make sure their hooves were clean? Have they had some water to drink? Do the horses feel like letting you two scoundrels ride them?' The boys giggled to themselves.

They were competent riders. Valli had them trotting around. She repeated the same instructions time and again: 'Up, down, up down, up … hold the horse with your legs … sit up straight … toes up … make sure the reins tell the horse where you want to go … pull the left rein and coax with the right heel to go left. Haftar, focus and stop making faces at the girls! They'll have the last laugh when you fall off the horse.'

Valli was a firm mother and teacher yet never harsh. She let the children have their outbursts of mischief but they were obedient. Bukka knew if he approached them now, they would get distracted. On the other hand, he had been away for three weeks and a bit of a disruption might be permissible.

The stay in Dorasamudra was supposed to have lasted a year at the most. It was now nearly five years. He recalled it was when Shveta was two that Valli came to him with her idea, which he was convinced was inadvisable. Aiza, the wife of a soldier who had died on the southern front during an altercation with the enemy, had fallen on hard times. The in-laws had taken all of the benefits given to the deceased soldier's family and had turned her out. Valli told him Aiza had resorted to being a prostitute for a while, and it was when she was on the verge of putting the children up for adoption at the orphanage that Valli had come into contact with her.

'She has two children, the same age as ours. It would be an act of great charity. And she could help me raise them.'

Initially Bukka teased her.

'Is this an act of charity, or just another way of having two more children?' he had asked.

'Both, Bukka, both,' she had replied with a serene smile. Then she went on, 'I do need help doing all that I have to do, and she could help me. The minister of happiness needs an assistant.'

He asked her for some time to think about it, and they discussed it a few days later.

'Bukka, I know this does not seem like what royals do, but this will keep us focused and it should be a lot of fun.'

He relented. As always, her instincts about people and situations were unerringly right. Looking at the four of them today, apart from their names, they were siblings. Aiza lived with them now. It had taken her a while to realize that she was not a servant. They'd incorporated her into the family.

Valli noticed Bukka first and burst into a smile. The girls ran to him and he had the two of them in his arms. Valli embraced him and had to quell the boys who immediately wanted to get off their horses. Aiza offered an adaab.

'Huzoor, should I take the girls from you? They are getting big and heavy.'

'Not that heavy yet, Aiza. I suspect I won't be able to hold both before the year is out, though.'

'Bukappa,' the term by which his family called him, 'can we please end the lesson?' asked Hari.

'Ask your teacher. Let's see what she says,' Bukka cheekily
suggested.

'Please, please, please, Vallima. We'll do double tomorrow,'
Hari implored. She finally relented. It was close to sunset so
they had to go in, anyway. As they returned to the palace, all
four children were busy interrupting each other in excitement.
As Bukka held his daughters in his arms, the two boys hung on
to his shirt for attention.

'They're getting old and, at some point, we have to stop this
circus, Vallima,' Aiza advised.

'It will stop when Bukka can no longer carry them. That day
might come sooner than we think,' Valli said with a mischievous
smile, deliberately intending for Bukka to hear.

The 'monkeys', as Bukka called his children, were put to bed
after much cajoling. The bedroom was large, with Shveta and
Sarah in one subdivided area, Hari and Haftar in another. A
small area was kept for Aiza where she slept with them. Bukka
sat on the floor in another room with all his messages spread
out. As Valli entered he remarked:

'Soon, I think it will be time to move back to Anegundi.
Hakka says it's been long enough and we've managed to get
the important work moving there. Let's get ready to go back to
where we came from.'

'But what would happen to Aiza and the children?' she
enquired.

'They will come with us.'

'Bukka, will she want that?' Valli asked.

'Well, let's ask her.' Bukka called out to Aiza to join them.

When Bukka asked if she would go with them, Aiza began
to weep.

'Allah has been kind to me and the children,' she said. 'I am grateful that you thought it fit to take me and my children with you, Vallima and Bukka Huzoor. My home is with you and, of course, I would gladly go.'

They decided they would move in the coming winter, when it would be most comfortable for the children. In the verandah, Bukka looked out on the palace grounds and saw the dim lights around the city.

'Why did it take us so long?' he wondered. In his mind he recalled all that had happened in those five years. Every sinew had been stretched. They innovated, invaded, conducted diplomacy and, while continuing to redraw the borders of the subcontinent, they put the kingdom on a surer footing. Yet his soul felt like the five years were sumptuous because he had the children and Valli with him. As he smiled to himself, he realized that he was thinking of all four children, having absorbed Haftar and Sarah into his own consciousness.

Why did it take so long?

Over the last few years, Hakka and Bukka had made sure that they met every two months, alternating each trip. When Hakka came to visit, he'd typically stay for longer. The children loved him and he felt more work got done when he was away from the capital city, Anegundi. This was about to change, however. The capital was moving a few miles away to the southern banks of the Tungabhadra, and the palace and other buildings were now completed. A huge fortified complex was built for ministers and soldiers. The new city was called Vijayanagara, or 'City of Victory'. Vijayanagara would take its name on the same day as Hakka's elevation to the status of 'chakravarti' or emperor.

The mood was very different compared to when the Hoysala kingdom was first conquered. Anxiety seemed to plague them then, primarily because they felt the need to expand the military. Yet, finding good, well-trained troops, together with an effective officer corps, was challenging. Hakka and Bukka decided that no member of the family would ever be given an honorary military rank. They would have to earn it by service in the military.

They started with twelve thousand men in uniform but two-thirds of them were either positioned at the southern border or manning distant outposts. It left just a third to be divided between the capital city and Dorasamudra. Even then, it required nearly a thousand veteran soldiers and officers to recruit and train new men. Their goal of a standing army of forty thousand soldiers was exhausting, mostly because at the end of the training, a significant proportion got culled for poor performance. The mantra in those days was simply: 'find good people'. Two large academies were established: one to train new recruits, and another for officers. Hakka repeatedly sought out men in the ranks to see if there was any potential officer in the making. Three years of relentless hard work and effort were spent doubling their army. All this was in spite of the brothers having an exceptional reputation.

Mani Iyer built his own group of accountants and tax collectors. He set up a system that was to be implemented and followed in each of the ten newly established provinces. There were three deputies in each province: one to oversee revenues, another to oversee expenditures and the last one who checked to see if the two deputies were cheating the accounts. It was designed so that each one did not know what the other was doing. On one occasion when Bukka visited the Green Palace, he asked Mani Iyer how much was in each of the provincial treasuries. To his astonishment, the reply was:

'Next to nothing,' before Mani Iyer added, 'because we have centralized our treasuries to two major treasuries: the main one in Dorasamudra, and the other in Mangaluru.' Quizzed about those locations, he responded by saying, 'Both are far away from the borders and safe. Besides, we have all the land revenues coming to Dorasamudra and the trading revenues sent to Mangaluru.'

Pattu had been privy to this plan and thought it to be an exceptionally clever idea.

'He seems to be in his element, like a craftsman painting on a blank canvas,' Pattu whispered as Bukka looked on, impressed by what he learned.

Cut off their tails!

'We have exceptional scouts. We've started to use the homing pigeons, which are a godsend, but we also get information from the neighbouring kingdoms. However, we never seem to have the ability to gather all the intelligence in one go to get a full picture,' Hakka had complained a year after they had conquered the Hoysala kingdom.

'Do you want us to do more, do it better, or do it differently?' Bukka asked.

Throwing up his hands in frustration, Hakka replied:

'I just don't know what we might be missing. It worries me. I feel it's as if we were walking through the mist in the Nilagiri hills. Sometimes we can see clearly; other times the clouds move in and you are blind. Can we have an eagle that looks from above the clouds and scans the landscape?' The problem had clearly been gnawing at Hakka. 'Why can't we know what is going on the same way Pattu knows what's going on in his line of business?'

'Hakka, I know what you are saying,' Pattu calmly responded. 'However, what I know is suited to my trading business. It is different from the circumstances you face. Attaining information can be more dangerous for you since it requires knowledge of what is going on inside and outside the kingdom.'

Hakka understood Pattu's reasoning. Bukka interjected:

'Hakka, maybe what you want are spies in enemy territories who can get information on what our enemies are planning and if they intend to interfere within our kingdom.'

'But there is more to it,' Hakka responded. 'These "spies" must also be able to take action, not just tell us what is going on. If some of the large landowners are preparing a rebellion, or the Madura sultanate is plotting with some of our noblemen, then I want my men to be able to cut the tails off these nasty rodents. That way other schemers will understand the consequences of undermining the kingdom. I want these "spies" to be able to cut off tails when needed. That's what we need.'

'My suggestion runs counter to what I wish,' Pattu announced as he rubbed his forehead. 'You need someone like Rahim Rahmatullah to run the organization which you require: both spies and scouts who could manage the homing pigeons. They would not only be prepared to take necessary action but also move fast in the shadows without anyone realizing they even exist. They'd be trained to coax information out of spies they catch. I think you need a group of people who operate in the dark and are silent, and dangerous when they need to be.' Hakka leaned forward as he listened intently to Pattu outline his idea. 'I am loath to volunteer Rahim Rahmatullah, but he would gladly work for you and the kingdom,' Pattu added.

A delighted Hakka rejoiced:

'Let's just call them "ghosts": shadowy individuals who frighten people, so when people say they saw one, you can always reply: "You're out of your mind. Ghosts do not exist."'

Putting a check to Hakka's enthusiasm, Pattu cautiously added:

'Remember that it is expensive. But if you spend wisely and well, five hundred of them would be equal to a force of ten thousand soldiers. Failure to do so will mean it will all be wasted effort and money.'

In the space of three years, Rahim Rahmatullah built an organization of five hundred people who were the eyes and ears of the kingdom. He had proven to be invaluable. Bukka recalled the case of the jagirdar (landlord) of Kannur on the west coast. Barely a few months after coming to work for the kingdom, Rahim Rahmatullah discovered a plot by the sultan of Madurai.

The jagirdar, Jogeendra Urs, a former nobleman in the court of Ballala, conspired with the sultan. When the Hoysala kingdom was annexed by Kampili, Jogenedra Urs's privileges as a nobleman were eliminated, but he was allowed to keep his lands, and took an oath of fealty to Hakka Raya.

Yet, he was seduced by the prospect of untold power and wealth promised by the sultan of Madurai. After making many trips to Madurai, Jogendra Urs plotted to overthrow Hakka. Two thousand soldiers secretly made their way north along the west coast in groups of fifty and a hundred. As they travelled north, Rahim Rahmatullah's men picked up on their movement. Since the soldiers moved in small groups, it proved easy to capture them.

Once they were in custody, Rahim Rahmatullah learned they planned to attack the palace when Hakka was in residence in Dorasamudra, with the aim of eliminating the royal family. They were then planning to poison the water supply to the barracks where the soldiers were housed. Expecting to get reinforcements sent by the sultan, they subsequently intended to hold the capital. So effective was Rahim Rahmatullah's network that they were able to eliminate the threat before catastrophe struck.

When Hakka visited next, he was shown a bag. With a puzzled look, he enquired what it was for, to which Rahim Rahmatullah said:

'So I can fill it up with all the tails I cut off. I plan to have two thousand and one tails in the bag.' To Hakka this was a hilarious reference to his earlier comment of cutting off tails of rodents. Justifying the captured soldiers doing hard labour, he reasoned that 'in a war, a prisoner is treated with respect and dignity. But this was an act of cowardice.' Jogendra Urs was subsequently relieved of his lands, and put in prison where he was put to work breaking and crushing rocks. In response to this failed plot, Hakka sent the sultan a short note.

Sultan Ghiyas ud-din,

You have conspired with one of my citizens to overthrow me. The code of honour among kings and sultans is to overthrow kingdoms by confronting each other on the battlefield. You chose an underhanded method, however.

I can assure you that the next time we meet will be on the battlefield. We will be vastly more successful than your current misguided scheme was.

I remember Qutlugh Khan telling me that you were one of the least trustworthy persons he had ever known, and his judgment was based on the fact that you lacked courage and capability. I now understand what he meant: you are a coward.

Your co-conspirator sang like a mynah bird and is now spending his time in one of my prisons. It may be an alternative that might suit you.

Righteously,

Virupaksha
(Hakka Raya of the Kampili and Hoysala kingdoms)

There was no response from the sultan.

Another case involved the prime minister of the Reddis, Bhagavati Rao, a long-standing advisor to the king of the Reddi confederation. He became increasingly belligerent about a border dispute with the Kampili kingdom, thinking he could wrest away a piece of territory. Hakka summoned him to Anegundi for negotiations. Gathering information to help with proceedings, Rahim Rahmatullah pulled together a treasure trove of material.

The prime minister had been on the take from both the Hoysala kingdom and the Pandyas to the south. In addition, it looked like he had liberally dipped into the Reddi treasury. At a nettlesome point in the negotiations, Mani Iyer was eloquently able to refer to proofs he had of the prime minister accepting large sums of money. He followed it up by producing the prime minister's own accounts.

'All we ask is that you are reasonable in your negotiations. In return we will undertake to keep this information secure.' With that, the source of all the border frictions seemed to dissipate.

Bukka recalled what Pattu had said:

'Good information is as valuable as a division or two of soldiers. And sometimes, more so.' Bukka recalled another amusing episode.

Rahim Rahmatullah had reached out to him and when they met, he said:

'Bukka Raya, I have some sensitive information.'

'Rahim, all the information you give me is sensitive, so what do you have today?'

'Faraj has been seen following a black tonga owned by Aslam Beg. He seems to know the tonga's expected movements, and the passengers are always Aslam Beg's wife and daughter.'

Bukka burst out laughing uncontrollably:

'Stop! Just tell me, is the girl pretty?'

'Not pretty, Bukka Raya. She is bewitchingly beautiful.'

'Leave it. It's his life and he needs room to manoeuvre,' Bukka advised.

A few days later Faraj came to visit. He played with the children, talked to Valli and Aiza before speaking to Bukka in private.

'I need your help. I would like to meet a young woman.'

'You do not need my permission. Why are you asking me?'

'It's complicated,' Faraj admitted. 'The woman is Aslam Beg's daughter. I do not want to create a problem by approaching her and angering her father.'

The chance to tease Faraj was too good to miss. Bukka shook his head and said:

'I do not think this would work, Faraj. They are people of great standing and stature, and you are asking to meet their only child, their beautiful daughter. I presume that you want to marry her? They are likely to say you are no more than a military man who does not have much money. You know Aslam Beg is wealthy, so they may be suspicious that you might be after his money. You will also need the permission of the king because you are one of his senior officers. I think you may have created a problem here, Faraj.'

The young man stood quietly and scratched his head.

'Bukka, you have made me quite a rich man and you pay me well. I can afford a wife and a family. I would not need help from Aslam Beg nor would I want his money. Admittedly, I spoke to Valli already and she thought it was a good idea. She thought we would be a good match. So, I am puzzled why you are not enthusiastic.'

'You are one step ahead of me, Faraj. I just wanted to tease you because you seemed so earnest and concerned. If Valli says it's good, she is usually always right. Most of all, I think Aslam Beg should feel honoured that someone of your standing would ask. Whether he agrees is another matter.'

'Valli was going to speak to you about this. She says the two of you should present my case to Aslam Beg.'

'The minister of happiness is at it again,' Bukka exclaimed. 'If she is going to present your case, be sure this is what you want, because she will make it happen.'

After Valli put the children to bed, she sat down with Bukka.

'Aslam Beg and his wife are coming to dinner tomorrow. I would like you to make the case for Faraj as a suitor for their daughter, Hiba. It would be a good match.'

Bukka could only frown.

'What?' she enquired.

'I've never done anything like this. It makes me feel uncomfortable.'

Valli stood up with a quizzical look on her face.

'Bukka Raya, you are the most intelligent and brave man I know but sometimes you act like a baby on social issues. Just open the conversation and I will take it from there.'

———•———

'Of course, it would be a great idea to have Hiba consider Faraj as a suitor,' Aslam Beg and his wife Meena declared in a celebratory tone. Valli looked pleased with herself.

By the time they left, Valli was already thinking of a wedding gift for the couple. 'How about we buy them a house, Bukka?'

'That's an expensive gift, Valli!' Bukka blurted, choking on his drink.

'I thought you said we have a lot of money. Let's use some of it.'

Two months later, Hiba married Faraj at a small but beautiful wedding that took place at the Dorasamudra palace. Hakka travelled from Anegundi for the ceremony and Bukka and Valli stood in for the family of the groom. There were even two traders, partners of Aslam Beg, who came from the Gulf of Hormuz for the celebration. And as was Valli's wish, Bukka and she presented the couple with a beautiful home in the new capital as a wedding gift.

All the while, Rahim Rahmatullah stood by Bukka's side at the celebration—the man who had first told him about Faraj's romance. Another invaluable contribution to the kingdom he had made.

The tax weapon

Bukka and the family left for Anegundi as planned. Haftar sat on the saddle with him, Shveta was with Valli, and Sarah rode with Karthikeya. Hari rode with Shamshed, who had come to escort them all back to the capital. They were just two days out from the city. Hakka had sent the King's Guard to accompany them back to Anegundi. In two weeks, they would leave for the Singeri Mutt where Hakka would be anointed emperor.

This was another milestone in their lives—moving back to Anegundi. Bukka had travelled this road so often in the past five years as Hakka and he consolidated the empire-in-the-making. He thought back to the significant events of the last five years, specifically the Kerala kingdoms in the south of the country. While there had been no conflict, they were not allies of Kampili. He recalled attempts to appease them. The devious and dangerous sultan of Madurai in the south and the recalcitrant Reddis in the west were already a handful. A threat from another kingdom might prove fatal. While a military plan could be formulated, the terrain was difficult and the patchwork of kingdoms were well governed. That, in itself, could be a major impediment to a productive solution.

The Kerala kingdoms were rich. They had abundant rains with a long coastline, which provided food and a rich maritime trade. Traders came from as far away as the Arabian ports and China. The draw of pepper, muslin, cardamom, turmeric and cinnamon made it a desirable destination for the ships making the journey. Bukka understood that a military solution would only create havoc and destruction even if the little kingdoms were likely to be easy prey. He also knew that many of these kingdoms were harassed by the sultan of Madurai. Could that be an avenue worth pursuing?

While the sultan was a nuisance, he did not have the military muscle or the capacity to overwhelm the whole area. Neither Hakka nor Bukka were open to unsettling the kingdoms.

At the Green Palace, Mani Iyer made the brothers review and study the finances as part of his rigorous process. Assessing the revenues, they realized that land taxes were accumulating significant revenue. No less surprising was the money coming into the treasury at Mangaluru, which had been boosted by maritime taxes. Revenue from trade grew from about five parts in a hundred of the kingdom's revenues to twenty-five parts in a hundred over three years.

'How are we getting so much in taxes from trade, Mani Iyer?' a bemused Hakka asked.

'What trade? We are getting money when ships dock along the coastline and drop off cargo. We are just benefiting from having a long coastline.'

'But how are we accumulating so much? I am curious as to what the underlying cause might be.'

Mani Iyer took a deep breath before explaining.

'Once you conquered the Hoysala kingdom, we acquired a very long coastline and were able to tax the traders who brought goods into the various ports. Then you added the coastline in the east, which made it easier for Kampili's trade from the Straits of Malacca to come directly to the east coast rather than come around to the west coast.

'There have been some developments that need explaining. First, a lot of the trade used to go to the Kerala kingdoms, as the rest of the west coast which is now administered by us used to be ridden with dacoits and robbers. Now traders don't need to pay bribes. The result is that we have more traders doing business—both from within the kingdom and from Malacca who go to the east coast. I'd imagine that even if you were to raise taxes a little more, the traders would concede without grumbling too much.'

At this point, Pattu joined the discussion.

'I agree with Mani Iyer. I was travelling from the east coast. We got delayed by a nobleman in the Reddi kingdom who wanted to be bribed, and the argument got a bit out of hand. In our kingdom there are no bribes, no robbers or dacoits, and people mostly see the merchant activity as an opportunity to buy or sell. That explains why your revenues are growing so fast. It's well known amongst the traders that the coastline is now a safe place.'

The conversation then shifted to military plans and how to subjugate the Kerala kingdoms. Bukka began:

'I do not know any way to bring them into the fold that would be effective. It would lead to a huge loss of life and will be an administrative nightmare.' Hakka and Bukka went over the military complications that it entailed, and Mani Iyer agreed.

'I will repeat what Pattu once said about planning for success. If we invade, we would not be able to convince the population that we are a force for good. We cannot offer them anything better than what they have.'

Pattu was leaning back on a cushion and grinning openly.

'What price are you willing to pay for the Kerala kingdoms?'

Three perplexed faces looked back at him.

'I will repeat myself. What price are you willing to pay for the Kerala kingdoms?'

Hakka threw up his hands in a quizzical fashion, Bukka was rubbing his forehead and Mani Iyer was swaying back and forth in his chair deep in thought.

'What would happen if the kingdom did not get any revenue from taxes on maritime trade? Would it bankrupt the Kampili kingdom? Also, what would it cost to mount a military campaign on the Kerala kingdoms?'

With a look of intense concentration, Mani Iyer did the arithmetic in his head.

'Our finances are in good shape. Even without the maritime trade revenues we are in a state of surplus. Not much, but a comfortable margin. We could adjust our expenses if required. However, I do not know what a military campaign would cost. Still, I agree with Bukka that converting a military victory to a lasting peace would be difficult, if not impossible, to achieve.'

Hakka added his concerns to the discussion.

'When you talk about a price, Pattu, are you thinking of bribing people so we could overrun the kingdom? You know that we have never chosen such dubious methods and I am not prepared to start now.'

'I propose to use another weapon: just make a change in your taxes and it would have the same effect as waging a war on the Keralas. It's a simple and honest way of waging war, Hakka. There is nothing underhanded.'

Veins in Hakka's face were pulsing. The effort of trying to contain himself was beginning to exert pressure on his patience. He looked intensely at Pattu, as if pleading with him to stop the teasing.

'Pattu, please explain your idea to me. A simple military man finds the ways of your world difficult to understand. What is this war you are talking about and how does this work? How do you wage war without a sword?'

Pattu paused to formulate his proposition in the simplest terms.

'Hakka, I know that the Kerala kingdoms depend heavily on maritime taxes. In fact, I know that without revenues from trade or a reduction in those revenues, the kings would go bankrupt. Their land revenues would be unaffected but are not enough to keep their expensive lifestyles afloat or pay for their courts and military.

'Now suppose Kampili cut the maritime trade taxes to nothing. Where would the traders go? Most of them would come to the Kampili ports. Thus, the Kerala kingdoms would be faced with no trade revenue and, when that well runs dry, they are going to be at the mercy of anyone who comes calling. When they are starved of resources you can offer them redemption: they can become your subjects, pay you an annual tax, and you could even maintain your army on their territory. Then you can turn on the tap by raising your taxes and they can do the same. Not one arrow shot, not one life taken. Just one change in the tax.'

Mani Iyer immediately saw the potential of such a move. Swaying in his chair, he kept muttering:

'A new way to fight a war, a new way to fight a war—no bloodshed, no harm to the citizens. A tax war. Hmmm ... this is a very shrewd way to fight an alternative war and subjugate territory; a new way to fight a war. This is an inspired idea; how elegant—it does not get better.'

Bukka absorbed the ramifications of the plan: from the costs to the expense to the time it would take to bring the Kerala kingdoms to heel. In a flash he realized that it was a subtle and very powerful weapon—provided it worked, of course.

Hakka needed more convincing. He understood the point about starving the Kerala kingdoms of their revenue and how it would force them to negotiate.

'If it were not for the efforts of Mani Iyer and Rahim Rahmatullah in building our resources and ridding the countryside of the thieves, Pattu's proposal would not work. Yet Pattu anticipated our advantage and for that we are grateful to him. But what concerns me is, how long will it take to accomplish this.'

'Two years,' Mani Iyer said after a moment's thought.

Pattu then offered his prediction:

'Hakka, I think it will not be longer than a year. In fact, it might even be accomplished in six months. The kingdoms are very shrewd trading families and they know they cannot address such a problem by military means. So, they will have to beg for peace and they will do it quickly because, like all traders, the Kerala kingdoms are supremely pragmatic.'

'Taxes are a very powerful weapon. A useful way to wage war peacefully,' Hakka observed.

Dénouement

Couriers carried the news of the tax cut the next day to the governors and tax collectors. Initially, it did not appear to have any immediate impact.

'Maybe the traders are deaf and do not hear us clap,' Hakka remarked gruffly. It was only when Hakka visited Dorasamudra that he noticed a significant increase in traffic. His bodyguards took longer clearing the way in the city. On a whim, Hakka pushed his way through the bodyguards to speak to the visiting traders. There was a melee as Hakka began talking to a few of those on foot with carts packed with wares. Where were they from? Had they come to this market before? After he arrived at Dorasamudra, he called for Aslam Beg to learn more about the increased traffic and whether there was an increase in traders. Sure enough, it was confirmed that policing was more difficult due to the influx of new traders.

Eating establishments were full, finding a place to sleep was challenging, and people had begun renting out rooms in their homes to address the problem and make some money too.

'Perhaps this will work,' thought Hakka.

Bukka regularly checked his intelligence reports and looked for any information he could find about circumstances on the ground. Rahim Rahmatullah demonstrated his skills by gathering information on how traders in the Kerala kingdoms were facing bankruptcy, while nobles and the royal families asked the likes of Pattu for loans. Indeed, many of the prostitutes were now planning to move north to the kingdom of Kampili because business was better there. Despite the progress in just four months following the tax change, Hakka's impatience could not be quelled. He'd regularly ask: 'When will we hear?' Bukka understood his brother's frustration, but only time would tell.

Just then, Karthikeya and Rahim Rahmatullah noticed a squadron of soldiers riding from Kozhikode on behalf of the kings of Kerala. They wanted safe passage to deliver a message to Hakka at Dorasamudra. Aslam Beg met them at the palace to receive the message as per official protocol.

To the Exalted and Gracious King Hakka Raya,

This is a joint message from the kings of the Kerala kingdoms, your neighbours and friends. There is an issue that has caused much confusion in our kingdoms as a result of changes implemented by the Kampili kingdom. We request and beseech you to meet with us so we can present our case to you. Will you meet us halfway in a gesture of friendship? Perhaps we could meet at Mangaluru on a date that is convenient.

Your neighbours and friends,
The kings of the Kerala kingdoms

It was six months to the day since Pattu made his prediction. He was right, yet again.

Decisions were made, plans agreed upon and a rigorous period of study and practice were organized for Hakka as well as Bukka.

'This is a war that will be won with words. This is a meeting that will need you to be cognizant of your goals, keeping in mind that a small change in any of the details will affect you and the kingdom. By the time you leave for Mangaluru, you must know every detail of their finances, their backgrounds, the factional politics there and what you have to offer,' Mani Iyer instructed. 'Like the gods, you must become omniscient. You must be seen as being omnipotent. You must have the guile and craft to convince them that what you propose is in their interest.'

For the large part of every day, the brothers recited their budget, reviewed the geography of the Kerala kingdoms, and practised the interplay between each other in the form of a presentation. Mani Iyer continued to lead the preparations.

'Hakka you are going to be the benevolent and sagacious king, while Bukka will behave like a hard-nosed general who is insistent on finalizing every last detail. You know what your starting positions are in the negotiation. However, you can concede on certain matters to achieve the final goal. Bukka will disagree with you in a strident tone and you will play the role of the wise older brother.

'Remember, a lot of this is nataka, nataka, nataka [drama, drama, drama].'

At the end of the brothers' final presentation, Mani Iyer glanced over at Pattu for his reaction. Pattu was deeply impressed. His only laconic comment when he finished was, 'Be warned, they will want you to marry their daughters.'

Hakka grinned.

'I am fearless, Pattu. For the sake of my kingdom, I would gladly consort with as many of the beautiful Kerala women as required.'

After a few final touches to their presentation, the brothers prepared themselves to travel south. Mani Iyer and his staff were to leave a week early. For his security, a hundred of the King's Guard accompanied him. Three of his assistants also joined him so they could continue to work in his horse-drawn carriage. On the morning of his departure, Hakka and Bukka wished him a safe journey. As Bukka inspected the guards, he overheard a young soldier say:

'This tiny man is the prime minister of this great kingdom? Why are they making such a big fuss about this little chap?'

'Sainika [soldier],' Bukka said to the young man, 'this man is invaluable to the well-being and the progress of the kingdom. The reason we make such a fuss about him is because his dedication makes all our lives vastly better. Remember, great men come in all sizes and shapes, and from different cultures.'

Aiyappa, the Hoysala general who had been captured years ago, led the contingent taking Mani Iyer—his first high-profile independent assignment—to Mangaluru. Just before they left, Hakka called to Aiyappa:

'It is of utmost importance that you protect Mani Iyer. Do not compromise his safety and make sure he is comfortable along the way.' Mounting his horse, Aiyappa gave the order and the convoy moved off. As the carriage rolled past the brothers, Mani Iyer shouted out:

'Make sure to keep preparing! And may the Long-tailed One give you both strength to study.'

Hakka turned to Bukka and remarked:

'I cannot imagine what we would do without the "little tiger". There are only two people in the world who tell me what to do, and he is one of them.'

Hakka and Bukka departed a few days later, discussing their respective roles and arguments, which they had practised with Mani Iyer. The meeting with the kings of the Kerala kingdoms was to take place over the course of two days. The plan was to present them with an ultimatum on the first day. On the second day, they hoped, they would secure their prize of unconditional fealty by the kingdoms. One of Ballala's former palaces had been chosen as the meeting place. Guarantees were provided for the safety of the kings and their entourage. Soldiers escorted them from their borders to the secure site: it was strictly business. Bukka ensured every courtesy was provided and that two divisions of soldiers (ten thousand altogether) were in plain sight. Though not meant to be threatening, it had the effect of sending a clear message of power.

The kings were led into a large durbar (meeting) area where Mani Iyer informed them that Hakka would hear their proposals. It would be followed by his own presentation. Hakka walked in with much fanfare, with Bukka by his side. Sitting on the floor at the head of an oval, he raised his hand as his audience hushed into silence.

'I am here to listen to your grievances. Please proceed.'

The prime minister of Calicut was nominated to make their case. A courtly old man, he stood up to address Hakka:

'King Hakka, you have attacked our kingdoms. You have brought havoc to the trading business. You have destabilized the relationships we built over decades with traders from different parts of the world. Many people are driven to penury because of your kingdom's actions. We argue that it is not legal, or at least it is not an appropriate course of action from a neighbour of ours. We have never coveted territory, or brought any military action against the Hoysalas.'

Hakka immediately interrupted the prime minister to remind him he was dealing with the Kampili kingdom.

'My apologies, King Hakka, but the fact is that you need to immediately change your policies.'

Hakka looked at him in the eye and said: 'Or else?' An eerie quietness descended on the room.

The prime minister stood up and repeated the litany of complaints again. Hakka stared at him piercingly.

'You did not answer my question. But let me ask you another: if you and I are selling coconuts in the market in Kozhikode, and I lower my prices, is that illegal?'

'Of course not,' the prime minister replied.

'Then how is the reduction in trading taxes in Kampili illegal? How is it different?' Hakka asked.

'When you reduce taxes, you take away our business. Acts of illegality will have consequences,' the prime minister replied in desperation.

'Do you realize you are contradicting yourself, prime minister? What I do with my taxes is not any of your business. Maybe you should lower your taxes too? That way your coconuts would cost the same as mine. Nothing stops you from doing that. And what exactly are you threatening us with?'

In a state of panic the prime minister had run into trouble and made the mistake of threatening war. Hakka scanned the room.

'You are not a military man, but I am. So let me tell you that with my force of forty thousand of the best soldiers in the subcontinent, your kingdoms do not present an obstacle. Even if you were to attack me, I could retaliate with greater conviction. All the while, I will bleed you dry every day as the trade comes to the Kampili coast. Worse still, that nasty sultan in Madurai will identify a weakened confederation and take advantage of the situation. Need I remind you what he did with Ballala? He broke his promise, stole everything from Ballala, and then had him beheaded. The straw-filled head of Ballala was left hanging from the ramparts of the fort for days.'

'What is your point?' the shaken prime minister asked.

Hakka stared at him impassively before feigning a yawn and scratching his crotch. Then he furrowed his brow, looked at all the kings and cleared his throat.

'The way I see it, you do not have a choice. I suggest you graciously accept to become my wards and sign a treaty of accession to the Kampili kingdom. All of your problems would therefore be solved.'

A loud murmur spread throughout the room.

'And what happens if we do not accede to this demand?'

Bukka jumped in: 'We continue to bleed you dry. We know exactly how much the trade taxes mean to you. In a few months, I am sure that the sultan of Madurai will come calling. He is not someone who believes in niceties. His method involves pillage, rape, destruction and mayhem. By that stage it will be too late to come to your assistance. It would be a shame to see all these fine prosperous nations crushed and reduced to nothing, especially since none of the kings in this room will survive.'

Hakka stood up as if to show a disinterest in the conversation. He looked at Mani Iyer and commented loudly (so his audience could hear him) that it was a waste of time. As he turned to the kings he announced:

'I expect you to come here tomorrow morning ready to sign documents of accession, pledge fealty to me as your new king and then return home in the knowledge that your kingdoms will be safe in my care. We will meet at the same time.'

He left the room.

As he walked out, the noise of chatter rose. It was still early in the day, and the question now was if and when there might be a breakthrough. Would his veiled threat and vague reassurance be enough to convince the kings? Only time would tell. Mani Iyer repeatedly reminded Hakka that the kings were driven by self-interest. With revenues drying up, they had few options. Land taxes were already high and the implications of raising them only made their dilemma more difficult. Added to the mix was their vulnerability to the sultan of Madurai, who had already harassed and bullied them in the recent past. Mani Iyer concluded:

'If they are thinking clearly, they will call for more details of the deal. I will wait to see if their emissaries reach out. Only then are we likely to have the issues resolved.'

Hakka and Bukka made themselves unavailable by riding to the coast. On their return, Mani Iyer informed them of new developments.

'They had a number of questions. I was able to answer most of them in your absence. The primary question is how much independence they would be allowed to manage their kingdoms. I told them that while they would be responsible to the king of Kampili, they should realize that Hakka is fair and keeps his word. I warned them of the consequences if they failed to resolve the matter and that it was in their kingdoms' interest to take the deal and secure their future.'

'Do you think they will accept?' an excited Hakka asked.

'They are shrewd men. Unless they have a hidden agenda, they will grudgingly accept. While it will be a victory for the Kampili kingdom, it will take time to smooth out all of the smaller issues of governing and tax collection. Some of this might be messy, but it will not be difficult to deal with.'

A call for an audience with Mani Iyer came a little later. It was the prime minister who wished to continue discussions. A busy night was anticipated. Sure enough, he did not return until the early hours of the morning.

At the formal meeting the next day, the Kerala prime minister started proceedings by saying they required more time to study the proposal. Hakka, clearly impatient with the delay, stood up and bluntly replied:

'If you are going to agree, you will do so now. Otherwise, this opportunity will no longer be available. There is no time for long-drawn-out deliberations.'

The sound of rustling echoed around the room. Then, slowly, one after the other, the kings stood up, performed a namaskaram and handed over a signed document of accession. To mark the new partnership, Hakka organized a banquet as their new king and welcomed them into the fold.

The recalcitrant Reddis

Bukka came back to the present with a start and looked around. The trip from Dorasamudra to Anegundi was taking a lot longer than usual, he thought. With the children and the horse-drawn carriage, it seemed they were moving more slowly.

He realized just how fast he travelled when he was alone. Patience was needed around the children all day long. He enjoyed them, and they were well behaved, but it still required a great deal of effort. He paused to think of the care and consideration Aiza and Valli provided. Had he lost the ability to relax and enjoy family life when he had the opportunity? Or was he distracted by work since the Hoysala kingdom had fallen? Valli noticed the look on his face and asked him to stop grimacing.

'Shveta thinks you've put on a funny face and it won't go away. Relax, Bukka, enjoy yourself. We do not always get to travel together.' She was right and for some time he listened and replied to the chatter of the children as they rode down the road. One by one, the children grew tired and were put into the carriage to sleep, with Aiza to keep an eye on them. Valli and he talked about setting up their new home. Finally, they fell silent and rode in companionable silence.

Bukka's thoughts returned to matters of state—tasks that remained to be finished, and issues they had faced and resolved. He could not resist casting his mind back to the contretemps with the Reddi kingdom a year ago.

His brother had called him to Anegundi to help deal with a problem.

Despite Hakka's marriage of political convenience, Malaa had proved to be a source of perpetual trouble. Her younger brother, Kumar, had aspirations of succeeding his father. He was thin-skinned, with a large ego and no accomplishments to back it up. He drank and gambled using public money. He was a known schemer and liar, and he had a talent for stirring up trouble. His family status resulted in his being appointed governor of the southern region of the Reddi kingdom, which adjoined the new and enlarged Kampili territory. What was a fraught relationship with Kumar only became worse.

In the space of a year, Kumar's soldiers attempted several raids on Kampili territories. Initially, Hakka merely told his father-in-law to rebuke his son but went easy on Kumar. A ridiculous parade of manufactured evidence was presented whenever complaints were made.

Everything fell on deaf ears as the raids increased, stealing cattle and setting homes on fire. It served no purpose other than causing a nuisance. With time, the raids became infrequent because the Reddi soldiers suffered severe losses in the skirmishes.

However, one raid that changed it all was when they set a village on fire and raped the female inhabitants. As the reports came in, Hakka was informed that additionally, about thirty children had either died in the fires or were put to the sword. Bukka could take no more and admonished his brother for what happened.

'I realize that this is a sensitive situation for you, Hakka, but we are not upholding our promise to safeguard the people of the kingdom. This is a wrong that must be set right.' Bukka removed his sword and dagger, and put them at Hakka's feet. 'My king, please relieve me of my command. Under the current circumstances, I am not serving your people accordingly and should be replaced.' He touched Hakka's feet.

Hakka bent down, picked up Bukka's weapons and handed them back to him.

'Perhaps your king should be stepping down for failing in his duties, Bukka. I am ashamed that I let this drag on so long. Let's discuss this tomorrow and put an end to it once and for all.'

Malaa was listening closely from behind the curtains and suddenly burst in.

'Bukka, I see that you are trying to manipulate Hakka again about the Reddi kingdom. Perhaps you should stop bullying, harassing and creating havoc for the Reddis. You must realize that they are more powerful. The small kingdom of Kampili is no match. It is time you acknowledged that my father's generosity and graciousness has saved this little kingdom.'

Bukka scowled at her. Over time she had become a replica of her mother; arrogant and obstinate, her loyalties were resolutely with the Reddi kingdom. He summoned strength from the Long-tailed One, before summoning the strength to offer a more measured response:

'I am grateful to you for your thoughtful advice. However, I serve only one king,' he said brusquely and departed.

'The only way this charade will end is if the two-faced Komati Vema is taught a lesson and the Reddis are left with nothing more than a tiny estate for recreation,' Hakka announced to his senior generals. 'I propose that we cut away half or two-thirds of their kingdom as punishment. I want Kumar captured so I can have the pleasure of parading the rat before his father and sister. I will lead the campaign with Bukka Raya. Let's get moving.'

Two weeks elapsed and Bukka was still working hard creating a plan with his four senior generals: Karthikeya, Faraj, Chinayya and Aiyappa. He let Chinayya and Aiyappa take the lead so as to gain experience in planning and executing a campaign. Only seven thousand soldiers were required, two thousand of whom would be archers. A supply train was dispatched within two days of Hakka approving the plan. Karthikeya and Faraj were to provide reserves if needed, but the Kampili army had never relied on reserves.

'We fight for the king's honour. Don't forget that for a moment. May your minds and swords be sharp,' Bukka reminded his generals.

'We will follow the divisions as they make their way through the villages to make sure to win support and to seek out any spies and saboteurs,' Rahim Rahmatullah assured him. 'We will also start following Kumar Anupayukta. I'll make sure that we have an abduction plan in place.'

It was going to be a long ride to the border. If anything, it seemed like a reprise of the initial Hoysala campaign. Waiting at the entrance of the palace, Bukka was surprised to see Malaa accompany Hakka to his horse, for she usually didn't bother. She looked at the brothers disapprovingly and said:

'I know what you have planned. It is an ill-conceived and vengeful act. This will come to no good. The Reddis are more powerful and righteousness is not on your side. Find a way to come to terms with Anupayukta who has always had your best interests at heart, though you seem unable to comprehend his kindness. You still have time to change plans.'

Hakka ignored her as he mounted his horse. The head of the King's Guard gave the order to commence the march to which Hakka replied:

'May God give you his blessings.' Then he bellowed, '*Kathina savari* [ride hard]!'

Other than reviewing battle plans and discussing logistics, Hakka remained quiet and seemed distracted. Travelling within Kampili was now such a regular ritual that each of the rest stops was well appointed. They were small houses, well-protected and off the beaten track. Resting up with a drink, Hakka appeared to be in a contemplative mood.

'Bukka, do you know the most difficult period of my life?'

'When you were a line soldier, I presume?'

With a wry smile, Hakka admitted:

'It's all these years that you and Valli have been away. It feels like I am serving a sentence for a crime I did not commit.' There was a long silence. 'Conversing with you and Valli are such an important part of my life. I feel hollow when you are absent. While I accept Malaa will never be part of the family, I am not even able to be with my own sons, who are Hari and Haftar's age, to play with them, to teach them.' He paused and stared blankly ahead. 'Only when there is love and affection does purpose take on any meaning. The underpinning of dharma [righteousness] is love. Everything else matters little.' He sighed.

'When I come to Dorasamudra, the kotigalu [monkeys] are all over me and I am awash with love for them. I pray we get back home safely so you and Valli can join me in the new palace. It will be fun to have your dogs, your kotigalu and my little sister back with me.'

Hakka's mood had lightened at the thought of Bukka, the children and Valli soon being near him in Anegundi.

'How are the children progressing at riding?' he asked.

'Well, all of them are doing well, though I think the girls are a lot more competitive than the boys,' Bukka said. 'They have no time for the ponies and want to ride horses like the boys do. Valli lets them and they seem to be managing well. Much of it is instinct, but Valli is extremely good at teaching them. It's funny when you hear her giving lessons—the same instructions I used to give her when she started out. Anyway, I think I am ready to take the boys on a long trip to see how their stamina holds up and to see whether they can handle the open terrain.'

'Just make sure that you have someone riding by their side, leading their horses,' Hakka advised.

'I will, Hakka, I will,' Bukka said with a smile.

Hakka and Bukka rode together to Tirupathi where they joined Aiyappa's divisions at the foothills of the sacred city. Chinayya had already moved his divisions to Sullurpeta.

In the first stage of their campaign, Hakka would move northeastward from Tirupathi to Venkatagiri, Gudur and then onward to Nellore on the banks of the Penna river.

Bukka, along with Chinayya's army, would hug the coastline and move straight up north, directly to Nellore where he would link up with Hakka.

The plan was to then consolidate forces and move directly to Guntur, the final point of the campaign. The Krishna river would form the northern boundary of the empire they were in the process of establishing. The scouts provided useful information on the location of enemy troops, which had only one encampment at Nellore on the banks of the Penna river. Hakka smirked.

'Nobody realizes the importance of a permanent and well-trained army. Instead, peasants are pressed into military service and thrown at the enemy with little effect. In times of relative peace, they are sent back home.'

Scouts kept lines of communication open between Hakka and Bukka. As was usual with a Kampili attack, it was swift and decisive. There were stray attacks by small pockets of enemy soldiers but many either bolted or surrendered. Hakka's forces travelled north to Kalahasti while Bukka kept close to the coast. Having seized Kumar Anupayukta's palace at Venkatagiri, Hakka sent a cryptic message to Bukka:

'Palace with many fine women and surprisingly lots of young boys. A man of many talents.' Bukka was amused; his brother's sense of humour had returned. Hakka continued north to Gudur, the state's capital city, managed by Narasimha Reddi. He was a Komati Vema acolyte and a co-conspirator of Anupayukta, who helped him stir mischief. Scouts informed Hakka and Bukka that the opposition had five hundred troops but were ready for an assault. They had prepared an ambush along the main road leading into Gudur. Part of the road went through a ravine about a mile long. The Reddis had positioned their soldiers, many of them archers with poisoned arrows, on the upper reaches of the ravine in anticipation that Hakka's men would march through.

On the approach to Gudur, Hakka instructed his men to separate in flanking movements to surprise the Reddi soldiers on top of the ravine. As a feint, Hakka had two hundred soldiers approach the ravine. As they marched into the ravine, the Kampili swordsmen and archers attacked the ambushing Reddi soldiers from behind. Within minutes the opposition were either wounded or killed.

Two hundred Reddi soldiers attacked the advancing column from the northern end of the ravine and found the tables turned, with Kampili soldiers above and before them. One of the Kampili commanders shouted to the Reddi soldiers to surrender as they were trapped and outnumbered. One hundred soldiers were captured; another fifty were severely wounded.

The troops marched on Gudur that afternoon and took it without any opposition. For most it had not been too taxing a day and they settled down in camps around the palace of Governor Narasimha Reddi.

Making use of the luxurious accommodations, Hakka was enjoying a much-needed rest. A knock on the door interrupted him. It was Karthikeya, who'd come to fill them in on the location and reports of the scouts.

'Might I present a gift?' he asked.

Hakka waved him on:

'Go ahead, just make sure it's a good one,' he joked. With his distinctive call, Karthikeya summoned three of his men. They brought in Anupayukta with his hands tied like a petty criminal.

'I am a rajkumar [prince] and demand to be treated appropriately,' Anupayukta shrieked.

'What would that involve, Rajkumar? I know, let's have him tied to a tree outside and make sure he is well guarded. Tomorrow he can be transported back to Anegundi where he will be tried for the murder of more than thirty children and the rape of countless women,' Hakka replied sarcastically. 'Please, Karthikeya, get him out of my presence.' Anupayukta was dragged out, screaming. Karthikeya told them Anupayukta had been trying to escape dressed as a peasant in a bullock cart. However, he'd forgotten to remove the expensive rings on his fingers and when he was questioned, the Kampili soldiers realized he was no ordinary peasant.

All that remained was to capture Nellore. Estimates from the scouts indicated the governor was determined to hold his own with the aid of about a thousand soldiers.

When Chinayya's divisions joined Aiyappa's divisions, Hakka met up with Bukka to discuss some information the scouts had given him about troop strength in Nellore.

'Bukka, if we don't give Governor Gajapati Raju a chance to reconsider, he is going to face decimation. His troops are poorly trained; they barely have one hundred horses. Gajapati Raju is an old warhorse, but now he's a feeble old man.'

Karthikeya was dispatched to arrange a meeting with Raju. They met the next day. Hakka gave him an ultimatum:

'We will attack. It's clear you are outnumbered, Rajugaru.'

The old general prevaricated, claiming he did not have the authority to surrender. Hakka declined his request for a two-week truce to send a message to the king. To find a resolution to their stalemate, Bukka suggested:

'Rajugaru, do not surrender. However, we do not want a military engagement and loss of life, either. We would like this to end in a dignified manner. It would not help to take you prisoner along with your men. Let us give you the chance to retreat across the Krishna River to the other bank, which is the state border. From there you can proceed wherever you wish as long as you promise not to attempt an attack.'

Hakka was startled at the proposal. Yet it gave them what they came for, while a military victory would only exacerbate Reddi grievances.

'I'll give you my answer in the morning.'

'No,' Hakka insisted. 'You will decide now. Cross the river this evening with your troops and you can send anyone you want to collect your belongings. From there you will march directly with your troops in a withdrawal to Guntur. We will give your family safe passage in the morning. And realize that we will be close behind you all the way to the banks of the Krishna.'

The old man was broken.

'I kept telling Komati Vema not to keep taunting the tiger,' he muttered. 'I warned him that Kumar Anupayukta's actions were dangerous and asked him to find a suitable peaceful arrangement. I even gave him the blunt truth: the opposition has a well-trained, battle-hardened army and when they come for us it will be the end. And here we are!'

There was a protracted silence, before Raju raised his voice once more.

'Will you permit me to take what is in my treasury? Otherwise, I will be penniless since my lands will from now onwards be in enemy territory.'

Hakka consented.

'Yes, you may, and you may keep you lands too. However, you must make arrangements in advance with the governor of the region before you enter the territory.' The two sides finalized their arrangements. Hakka and Bukka rode with Raju to the river's edge and witnessed him get on the ferry. He was followed shortly after by the Reddi troops making their retreat.

In a leisurely march north, Hakka and Bukka reached the banks of the Krishna River, following Gajapati Raju, his retinue and troops until they crossed over to the other side.

Anupayukta was tried and sentenced to a life of hard labour. The judge declared that death in war was an acceptable consequence, but the death of innocents without a declaration of war constituted murder. Malaa's entreaties were ignored. Anupayukta's sentence meant the Reddi were finally neutralized: two of Komati Vema's children were in what was now enemy territory, he'd lost half his kingdom and the blame was laid at his feet because of the unnecessary provocations by his son.

———•———

'Bukkappa, Bukkappa!'

He was shaken out of his reverie. It was the angelic voice of Sarah shouting. She decided to ride with him on the last part of the journey to Anegundi. Standing behind him on the saddle, with her arms wrapped around his neck, she gave a review of all that was going on. Since she was the shortest of the four, Sarah was the perfect height to whisper into his ear.

'Bukkappa, look to the right, look at all those people.'

Bukka saw the Tungabhadra river where they would cross to get to Anegundi. There must have been at least a thousand people waiting on both banks with a large contingent of the military and the king's guards.

'It's Hakappa over there!' Hari screamed in excitement. Bukka realized that the king had come to receive him. Valli rode up next to him.

'I was hoping it would be a quiet homecoming,' he remarked with a wry smile.

'Bukka, sometimes I truly think you and Hakka imagine you are still soldiers in the army. Remind yourself that is an indulgence you can no longer enjoy,' Valli said. Next, she admonished the child. 'Sarah, hold Bukkappa tight or else you will have to ride in front of him. I do not want you falling off and crying like a baby.' Bukka grinned and grabbed Sarah and put her on the saddle in front of him. Meanwhile Shveta rode with Valli.

Soon they had reached the waiting group. Bukka and Valli dismounted as they got to Hakka, who stopped his brother from touching his feet.

'When you left on the campaign to defeat the Hoysalas all those years ago, I asked you to come back an emperor. Today, you have achieved it.' The brothers embraced as the people watched and cheered.

Jai chakravarti!

The small town of Sringeri to the northeast of Anegundi was famed as the home of the pre-eminent religious school where Vidyaranya once taught. This was where Hakka was to be formally anointed emperor of Vijayanagara. It was a beautiful December day, the sky was a deep blue, with a gentle breeze blowing, and the sun was glowing but had tempered its warmth. Preparations at the Sringeri 'matam' sounded like a swarm of bees busy at work. There was a mass of people congregating around a huge structure with a platform and roof. Present on the stage were a hundred Brahmins reciting from the Vedas, headed by Vidyaranya. Hakka and Malaa sat facing them, with Bukka and Valli sitting the behind.

Also on the platform were the children, Pattu, the generals, and all ten governors of the various states of the empire. The Kerala kings who had come to show fealty to Hakka Raya, the emperor-to-be, sat near the platform.

The ceremony began at daybreak and lasted six hours. It was preceded by a week of celebrations that Vidyaranya had conducted. Today was the culmination. A large fire burned in the homa between Vidyaranya and Hakka. At the end of the ceremony, Vidyaranya asked Hakka:

'Do you promise this day as emperor of Vijayanagara to uphold the principles of dharma [righteousness] forever?'

'Yes.'

'Do you understand that you are bound by an oath to this supreme principle until the last day you are emperor of this land, whether you die or are succeeded?'

'Yes.'

'And does the person who will succeed you at a point of your choosing in the future know of his designation as your successor?'

'No, he does not,' Hakka replied.

'Are you ready for me to ask him if he will be bound by the principle of dharma when he does succeed you?'

'I am.'

'Then I will ask Emperor Hakka Raya's future successor whether he will be ready to be bound by the principle of dharma on succession. Will you, Bukka Raya?'

Bukka had been enjoying the ceremony sitting next to Valli, following along with the chanting. Through the corner of his eye, he could see the children sitting with Pattu, Aiza and Faraj. He was caught off guard by Vidyaranya's question.

Leaning over, Valli whispered:

'Bukka, stand up and do a namaskaram to Vidyaranya Guru, and to Hakka. Quick, stand up and stop dreaming.'

Bukka stood up. He walked past the fire to face Vidyaranya and vowed:

'I solemnly swear and take the oath to uphold the principle of dharma as successor if that is what my emperor demands of me. I ask for your blessings and the blessings of my brother to serve him and this kingdom as well as I mortally can.' With that he prostrated himself in front of Vidyaranya, walked over to Hakka, prostrated himself again, and did a namaskaram. Staring his brother in the eye, he said: 'Bless me that I may have the strength, wisdom and fortitude to serve my emperor who reigns over the land of Vijayanagara.'

Vidyaranya next consecrated a coat of arms for the new empire. On a background of turmeric yellow, it featured the sun, the moon, a dagger and Varaha [the Boar], an avatar of the

god Vishnu. He presented it to Hakka, marking the end of the
ceremony.

Hakka and Malaa, followed by Bukka and Valli, prostrated
themselves in front of Vidyaranya and Andal. Departing from
the platform, Bukka put his hand on Valli's shoulder and said:

'Hakka and I may have won the wars, but it is you who
brought anugraha [grace] to this land.'

Valli broke down, with tears streaming down her face, and
made no attempt to hide it either.

Book 4

Anukrama: Succession

10

And the river flows on …

1357–69: Vijayanagara, Mangaluru, Vijayanagara

Suryasta (sunset)

Except for the two lamps in two corners of the room, it was dark. Looking out through the window on to the verandah, Bukka could see just a hint of light, indicating that soon it would be daybreak. He was sitting by the side of the bed and could hear Hakka's breathing was laboured and raspy. But at least he was getting some rest, unlike most other nights when the pain would overwhelm him and eliminate any possibility of sleep. It had been a week since Hakka's accident and illness, and he seemed to be losing ground with every passing day.

Valli had kept a nightly vigil, assisted by Aiza and two attendants. As a result, she had been getting increasingly tired, not realizing that at some point the body would break down and she would no longer be able to keep going on willpower.

Bukka had insisted she get a good night's rest and he sat by Hakka all night long. Malaa, however, had barely spent any time by his side or done anything to help. She'd never forgotten the humiliation her family had suffered at the brothers' hands.

Strange, he thought, how it had started. Hakka and he were coming back from a long ride along the river after having checked on repairs to a fort. The convoy had bodyguards in the front, and Hakka was busy talking to some of the young cavalrymen, regaling them with stories from the past. Karthikeya was riding alongside him, and they had another contingent of bodyguards following.

There was a narrow ditch that each of the horses was jumping over, and Bukka noticed that Hakka nearly lost his balance as his horse jumped across. What rattled Bukka was that Hakka was about the best horseman he knew. Karthikeya saw it as well.

'Something is not right, semanya,' he said to Bukka, using the term he had always used to address Bukka. 'I've seen horses lose balance, but I have never ever seen the chakravarti look unsteady.' Hakka was known for being an exceptional soldier and a gifted rider. Whether it was on a long ride or manoeuvring in battle situations, anyone watching him would marvel at his style and skill. Then suddenly he slumped forward in his saddle and slid off sideways, falling hard as if he had no control of his body.

In a trice, Karthikeya had jumped off, two of his bodyguards had immediately moved to lift him off the ground, and Bukka was by his side. They were barely an hour away from Vijayanagara. Karthikeya shouted swift orders to the bodyguards.

'The guard post is twenty minutes away, ride there and bring the carriage and make sure you bring some water. Two of you ride to the palace immediately and inform the household to be ready for the chakravarti and have them get the vaidyan.' Bukka was cradling Hakka, supporting him from behind so he could lean against him. It was clear that he had lost consciousness. Within the hour they had him back at the palace, in his own bed.

Pratapa Sharman, who had been Hakka's physician since the days of the campaign against the Kolis at Sinhagad fort, was attending to him. He knew his physical condition well and Bukka was glad he was at hand. He asked to be left alone for a while.

It was nearly two hours later that he emerged from Hakka's chambers. Bukka looked at him and knew the news was grim. Pratapa Sharman spoke up but found it difficult as his voice broke with emotion:

'His condition is bad, Bukka Raya. It is not the accident that is the cause of his illness; it is his illness that caused the accident.' Pratapa Sharman looked at Bukka and Karthikeya, as well as Mani Iyer who had joined them.

'He is now suffering from two conditions. The first is that somewhere in his body he is losing blood, and there is no way of telling where. And the second is that his blood seems to be poisoned.' He noticed Bukka about to speak and he immediately interjected by saying, 'No, he has not been poisoned from the outside, but bad things are happening to his blood—sometimes your blood goes bad like food goes bad. About two months ago one of his old battle wounds in his leg had opened up. It is possible that it might be the reason, but that is only speculation.'

Bukka felt as if he were going to be ill. He held himself together and managed to get a question out:

'Is there nothing we can do? And in this condition, how long does he have?'

'We will get the opinion of another hakeem and vaidyan to make sure we are not making a mistake,' Pratapa Sharman said. 'However, I think this condition is not difficult to diagnose. Unfortunately, there is little we can do other than keep him as comfortable as we can. Finally, even though he is a very strong man he may last a week or two, but not longer.' Bukka went to the side of the verandah and threw up. A palace attendant ran to help him get cleaned up. Just as he sat down, he saw Valli running down the verandah, followed by Aiza and the girls. They had been at the other end of the city, working at an orphanage, as they normally did three days a week. Haftar had heard the news and had brought them back.

'Haftar says Hakkanna [Hakka my big brother] had an accident,' Valli said. She looked at Pratapa Sharman and asked for his evaluation.

'Valli, come sit by me,' Bukka said. She looked puzzled and startled.

'Shouldn't we be taking care of him and why are we standing around here? Unless, you are telling me ...' She read their faces and sank down to the floor, heaving and trembling. Bukka stood up, walked to her, held her by the shoulders and said:

'He is not dead. But he is grievously ill, Vallima.'

She held her dupatta to her face. She half rose, holding Bukka's arm, and asked Pratapa Sharman, 'Can you cure him, and if not, how long does he have?' She was now holding Bukka with one hand and Mani Iyer with the other.

'Two weeks at the most, Rani Valli,' Pratapa Sharman said gently. She crumpled, and went down on her knees sobbing.

Aiza helped her up, and she walked her away. Within a few minutes, she had washed and changed and was back. Calling out to Pratapa Sharman to follow her, she sat down by Hakka's side and asked for the diagnosis and for ways she could help. If helping Hakka was all she could do, she was going to muster every resource within herself to do it, and get organized to make sure it happened. In a minute there was frenetic activity as she gave a flurry of instructions following the physicians' advice.

It was curious, but Hakka was lucid for a few hours every afternoon. He would drift into a clear and conscious state, while later in the evening it was as if the curtain closed for the day. Making a note, Bukka wanted a few people to speak to him while they had a chance. He sent the girls and boys to spend a little time with Hakka alone. Pattu and Mani Iyer came every day and managed to bring a smile to his face. His favourites, Karthikeya and Faraj, and Chinayya and Aiyappa visited. He spoke to Aiza when she was with Valli, tending to him. Malaa did not come, nor did Hakka ask for her.

A few days later Hakka was unusually talkative after they had spent time with the Privy Council and Pattu. Then he wanted some time with just Pattu and Bukka. He asked for help to sit up.

'I am feeling a lot of pain and do not think I have very much energy left, so I will be brief. Pattuanna, this family has been blessed because of your caring and concern and your dedication to its well-being. You built every one of us up, and never ever questioned the path we took. Both you and Valli will be the sounding board Bukka will need, even if only for a while. And Chakravarti Bukka Raya, this empire will benefit from your reign. I expect history to mark you as a benevolent and exceptional ruler. Use the boys now in the role you used to play. You ask the questions and have them give you the answers. And you should know that your abilities, judgment and courage have been the reason we were able to build what we did.' Then he asked for Valli to join them.

She came rushing in, wondering what might have gone wrong. Or should she fear the worst? When she was sitting by his side he said:

'You brought grace, happiness and beauty into my life and our lives. I have always admired your audacity and courage. And for Bukka and myself, you have been our conscience.' He held her hands and kissed them.

'Hakka, you are a very rich man. You have lands and lots of gold. How do you want me to parcel it out?' Pattu asked. Hakka replied with a weak smile:

'Half to Bukka and Valli, and the rest you should administer to my wife and son in ways you see fit.' With that the curtain closed for the evening as his eyes shut.

Bukka decided to stay with him that night. Unusually, even the physicians said he was sleeping well. It was dark outside and it began to rain. And unusually, the wind began to blow hard, and thunder rumbled frighteningly. The lightning made daylight out of darkness. Six or seven times he cowered at the intensity of the thunderclaps.

He noticed that one of the lamps had gone out. He stood up and looked at Hakka. It was clear that he had moved on.

Faraj and Karthikeya, his two favourite generals, and the King's Guard led the cortege to the river. Ramanatha, his son, lit the pyre and soon all they could see was a huge fire that consumed Hakka's body. Harihara, Bukka's son, tapped him on the shoulder and pointed upwards. People were packed on both banks of the river, standing there to pay their respects; respect for a man who began his life as a foot soldier, who built an empire, who was a legend but never forgot his humble beginnings. Hakka always looked to see what a person was made of, whether they were king or peasant. In the course of his life, the legend and the stories had grown. Bukka was shaking as he noticed the mass of people in attendance. The only thought that came to mind was, 'The myth and legend surrounding this man was not far from reality.'

Once the crowds dissipated, all that was left were the embers of a huge fire and the glowing memory of a great man.

Bukka sat on the sand with Mani Iyer, who was softly reciting verse after verse of the Bhagavad Gita, hoping in some way that it might give Hakka's brother some solace. As darkness descended, Karthikeya, Haftar and Faraj came to Bukka to accompany him back to the palace. For the next seven days it rained hard and it seemed as if Mother Nature had come to collect his ashes.

Malaa sequestered herself and only Valli could see her. For the rest of the inner circle who had been with Hakka over the years, it felt as if they were suddenly enveloped by a debilitating silence. Mani Iyer came every morning and insisted on sitting with Bukka, Valli and the children for a few hours, reciting from the Bhagavad Gita. He translated the chants and hoped it would give them all some perspective on life and dealing with bereavement.

Exactly a month after Hakka's death, Vidyaranya visited Bukka and Valli. He sat with them but said nothing for an hour. Then he suddenly began chanting softly the 'Vishvarupa Darshanam' from the Bhagavad Gita. He said:

'Life must carry on, and grief cannot consume. Succumbing to grief is a form of indulgence and not appropriate, especially for one who is expected to follow the path of dharma [righteousness]. The empire that you, your brother and your wife built needs to be tended to. And just as Arjuna returned to the prosecution of the war against the Kauravas from a state of paralysis, you must now draw on your strength to administer to the needs of the people of this empire.' Looking at both of them he said:

'The people depend on you to find the strength to serve. It will be the best form of solace you can find to overcome your grief.' He put a hand on each of their shoulders, smiled and walked away. Mani Iyer returned the next morning to accompany Bukka to the Green Palace. As he rode out, he noticed Hakka's horse from the Emperor's Guard with his saddle reversed, marking the observance for a fallen soldier.

It took Bukka and Valli nearly a year for their wounds to partially heal. The pain, however, lingered in their broken hearts.

Back in the saddle

Bukka was back into the routine of rising early and training every morning with the troops. He decided that he would now take the boys along with him. Both were sixteen and he would soon have to decide how the remainder of their education would proceed. Together with the girls, they had been taught languages and mathematics. Haftar was never the student Hari was but he could never be faulted for neglecting his tasks, either. When it came to military skills, the two boys were exceptional. If anything, Haftar had the edge on Hari. Both were excellent riders and in a short period their swordsmanship abilities had reached the point that Karthikeya, their teacher, could no longer keep up with them. He called some of the younger and quicker officers to spar with them.

Malaa refused to let Ramanatha participate, claiming that the young man was delicate and had skills better attuned to administration. To be fair, Bukka felt, he was competent in this field. Ultimately, however, he was being handed a life of indolence and indulgence, and it clearly showed. While the three boys were barely a year apart in age, Haftar and Hari were strong and sinewy. Ramanatha was severely overweight and could barely ride. He refused to take part in any of the activities that Bukka's children did. The girls were as good as their brothers at riding and on a recent trip to Dorasamudra, all six of them (Bukka, Valli and the four children) rode all the way and back, which was a first for the girls. As teenagers always do, they often got into trouble, but the four of them managed to stay on the right side of Aiza, who was the disciplinarian.

The question Bukka was wrestling with was whether to train the two boys as officers, and especially if they should go away to a training camp for six months as was usual for officer training. Their identity would pose difficulties—they might get preferential treatment or get bullied; there could be security issues. Karthikeya came up with a solution. He was going to Mangaluru to evaluate the commanders located along the southern border. The assignment would take him about six months to complete. He suggested that the boys be enrolled anonymously in the officer-training camp in Mangaluru and he would supervise their progress. Bukka agreed immediately. It was a safe and sensible plan. Valli, however, was worried and unhappy at the idea that they would be away for so long. They would be incommunicado and while no one would know their identities, this brought her as much concern as it did solace. For Bukka, it was important since it was the only way they could be tested impartially.

It was a long six months. A pall descended on the palace as all four women missed the boys. Valli spoke up one evening:

'It is so quiet, Bukka. I never realized that they made so much noise.' Hari and Haftar tended to be loud at the best of times but they were also always accompanied by three dogs and an annoying parrot that would never stop squawking. Besides they constantly teased the girls and bantered with them.

'I never thought I would miss the noise they make,' Valli confessed.

'Even the dogs barely bark or misbehave without them,' Aiza added. 'And quite honestly, the girls have just shrivelled up and gone quiet.'

Bukka chuckled to himself.

'When they are here, you complain, and when they are gone you complain. Just wait, the moment they come back, both you and Aiza will nag them to comb their hair, to put away their riding clothes, and forbid the dogs from sleeping on their beds. You'd better get used to this as they get older.'

Irony

Karthikeya rode to Mangaluru with his two charges. When they reached the outskirts of the city he stopped at a barber's shop and told Hari and Haftar to follow him in. Upon entering, he asked the barber to shave the two men bald. Hari looked at him quizzically, to which Karthikeya replied:

'Under no circumstances do I want anyone to know who you are. If you are going to graduate as officers, you are going to do it on your own merits. From now on, Hari, you are going to be called Hussein. You are both from Honnavara and your parents are farmers and traders. It is on Shamshed's recommendation that you are being sent to train as officers. You will not deviate from the story.' Then, with a crooked smile he said, 'Let's see if what I have taught you so far will help you graduate.'

Both Haftar and Hari laughed.

'If we fail, Karthapa,' Hari said, 'it's because you did not teach us well.'

The school was located in the woods, close to the shore. Every six months, a group of thirty or forty students enrolled. At the end of six months usually about half the class graduated. Of the two schools in the empire, Karthikeya thought this was the better one and the reason was the commandant. Kempayya was a stalwart of the march to Daulatabad and a favourite of the emperor. Now a colonel in the army of the Vijayanagara empire, Kempayya had a sharp eye for talent and was unrelenting in his training. He was known to be fair and honest; he had dismissed students from prominent families, who could not take the pressure. With forty other soldiers and staff to help him, he had become a legend when it came to training officer recruits. When Karthikeya rode into the school, Kempayya noticed the two young men and immediately expressed his objections.

'First, semanya, they seem a little on the young side and might not be able to take the stress. Second, you know I do not like officer recruits coming here on the recommendation of senior officials. While I have a lot of respect for Semanya Shamshed, I don't like these situations.'

Karthikeya appeared distracted.

'I have to leave now. Anyway, if they cannot perform, kick them out. That is your prerogative. No one has ever questioned your judgment.' He turned his horse, briefly looked at Hari and Haftar with a hint of a smile and rode off.

The two boys were brought to a long hut with twenty beds. Kempayya showed them around and gave them all the equipment that came with their new situation. He said:

'This is where the favours end. I couldn't care less if you were the sons of the emperor: I will give you the boot if you deserve it. The empire needs the best, and if you can't qualify, go back to your father's trading business.' He turned on his heel and left.

There was no one else around so Haftar looked at Hari and said:

'Hussein, if we get kicked out, how in God's name do we go home? We do not have a mohur to call our own.'

'We have only one option then—not to fail,' Hari responded.

That evening an additional eighteen recruits filed in. They were all older and some looked a little rough. It gave them license to pick on the two young boys. One wanted the bed that Haftar had chosen. Haftar refused to move and in a soft voice he informed him that it was his.

The conversation soon became heated when the man called Haftar a 'little boy sold in the market for pleasure'. Haftar responded by asking, 'Do you even know who your father is?' The man swung out at Haftar. Ducking to avoid the blow, Haftar responded with a punch on the aggressor's nose. In an instant the man was down on the ground wailing in pain. Suddenly everyone stood back. Unfortunately, Kempayya walked in and for the next week the two fighters were punished with extra physical exercise and reduced rations.

After three weeks of training, something seemed amiss to Kempayya. Whatever he asked of Haftar and Hussein, they managed to do very well. He pushed them and they never caved. Their attitudes never turned surly. In fact, they helped the other recruits and were always respectful. Though they were gregarious and always joined in on the fun, no one ever seemed to find any information about their backgrounds. Yet they seemed to know each other very well; almost like brothers. It was not until they started to ride that Kempayya's suspicions were truly aroused.

The only two people he had ever seen riding with such command and grace were the emperors.

Through the training sessions, Rahim Rahmatullah's men kept feeding Karthikeya information on the progress of Hari and Haftar. The reports indicated they were doing well and enjoying themselves but it seemed that Kempayya remained suspicious. It was reported he said, 'If they were not so young, I'd say they already were high-quality officers. I wonder if Semanya Karthikeya is playing a trick on me.'

After the six months the two boys had become the most popular among the recruits.

Unusually, more recruits passed Kempayya's muster than normal because Haftar and Hari frequently helped and taught their colleagues. On the last day, Kempayya informed them where they would be deployed. Haftar and Hari got the most prestigious appointment: with the King's Guard.

Karthikeya came later that day and quizzed Kempayya about his choice.

'Why the King's Guard?'

'They are both exceptional students and if they are in the capital city they will be noticed and given more training.' Karthikeya nodded in agreement. Kempayya's curiosity got the better of him.

'Who are they, semanya?'

'If you really want to know, Kempayya, Hussein is actually Harihara and in all probability will be our next yuvaraja.'

'I knew it, I knew it, I knew it!' Kempayya shouted gleefully. 'Well, semanya, thank you for the honour.'

Karthikeya pulled a long parchment letter and a large leather pouch of mohurs from his pocket. He handed them to Kempayya.

'The emperor is grateful to you for doing him the honour of training his sons to be officers. When I suggested your name, he agreed that they should train with you.'

Kempayya stood there in shock, trying to take it all in.

Hari and Haftar prepared to leave. They thanked Kempayya for being their teacher and touched his feet. Kempayya was unable to speak. He stood watching the contingent of horsemen bearing the Vijayanagara standard ride away with the two young men. Shaking his head in disbelief, he repeatedly said to himself:

'I've dealt with two generations of the Sangama sons, and they're both exceptional.'

Even the parrot's squawking

The month's Privy Council had been uneventful but Bukka managed to take care of some critical business. The borders were well preserved although the north still presented problems. He commanded Shamshed to gather more intelligence on Daulatabad. Rumours had circulated that the Dilli nobility were trying to strengthen their presence there. It had all the hallmarks of trouble brewing once more.

It was the sixth year that the rains had been plentiful, so crops and land revenues were doing well. Trade continued to prosper as the traffic to the east coast was busy, while the west had significantly more volume of outgoing trade. In the south,

Bukka conceded he would have to take on the sultan of Madurai. He asked Shamshed to plan a fact-finding mission following Karthikeya's return. Time was on their side and Bukka saw to it that they should make maximum use of the opportunity to prepare thoroughly. Mani Iyer was in positive spirits as all ten provincial governors were marching to his orders and the surplus in the treasury was the highest they had ever been. The only issue debated was whether they should reduce land taxes.

The council meeting lasted longer than expected. At last, Bukka was back at the palace and settled in his favourite spot on the verandah overlooking the river. With a glass of sharayam in one hand and a sheet of parchment in the other, he began to read the report on 'Hussein' and Haftar from the officer training school. A smile creased his face as a growing sense of pride overwhelmed him. His mind wandered and he thought about the four children. The girls were accomplished. Valli had clearly put her imprint on them. He often wondered if he should break the mould and have them trained to be administrators, perhaps even governors of provinces. He made a note of it and felt it needed greater thought before proposing it to Valli. Then he had a twinge of regret that he could never get Hakka's boys to become part of the group. They were so different from his 'monkeys'.

His thoughts were interrupted by the squawking sound of Haftar's parrot, followed by a crescendo of dogs barking. Soon he could hear the children. The boys must have returned. Once the excitement had died down, they would eventually saunter over to see him. It had been reassuring to have the dogs in their absence. Yes, he needed to get a new crop of dogs. After Hakka, he had not replaced his last two kombais who died of old age. It was time to get a few puppies. He knew he would not get any protests from Valli. Even Aiza, who was initially fearful of dogs, had grown to love them.

He suddenly heard footsteps. He turned around. There were the two young men in uniform. They saluted and asked if they might 'present arms'. He nodded and they went through the military drill flawlessly. He remarked:

'When you come to see the commander-in-chief and emperor, make sure you are wearing a clean uniform.' He roared laughing, for clearly they had rushed back to Vijayanagara and come straight to him. He held out his arms and hugged the boys. He noticed they were more muscular and tanned. The girls, who had followed with Valli and Aiza, poked fun at their 'stupid-looking haircuts'. The boys proudly showed Bukka, Valli and Aiza their badges as commissioned officers in the King's Guard. Valli ordered them to wash up and they obediently went off.

'They did well,' Bukka glowingly stated as he passed the report to Aiza.

'I'm glad, but I hope you might think of having them at home for a while before you dispatch them out again,' Valli said sternly in an effort to convince her husband.

The process must begin

Mani Iyer asked to see Bukka in private. It was not the usual social visit, which Mani Iyer had taken to making more frequently after Hakka's passing. Valli and Bukka joked between themselves that he came to cheer them up. They enjoyed his company. Mani Iyer had a subtle sense of humour and was full of news from around the empire. He arrived at sunset and brought Valli some prasadam from the temple. He settled down on the floor on a cushion even though Bukka invited him to sit with them.

They talked for a while and then Valli asked the boys to come over. He broke into a big smile when the boys walked in.

'I gather the two of you were very successful with your training.'

'We got through,' the boys said and chuckled.

As Mani Iyer inspected them, he commented, 'They certainly made you stronger. It's really obvious. They must have kept you out in the sun too because you are now the colour of jaggery.' Prompted by Valli, they offered a namaskaram and asked for his blessings. Mani Iyer wished them well and reminded them to visit the imam in town and get his blessings as well.

Taking Valli's cue again, the boys excused themselves and departed. Mani Iyer then settled down to business.

'It is an auspicious day and I wanted to raise an important issue with you both. It is time, my emperor, that you begin to make plans for your successor. The yuvaraja will need time to learn the military and administrative functions. All of this takes time, so you should think about getting this process started soon.'

Valli seemed confused. 'Why am I part of this conversation?'

Mani Iyer cocked his head in her direction and remarked:

'Because you know a lot about the business of being an emperor. Your brother was an emperor, your husband is an emperor, and you may well be called upon to train and serve as the next emperor's mother. It makes sense to include you in the conversation, Samrajini Valli.'

'How do you see this process unfolding, Mani Iyer?' Bukka enquired.

'Bukka, every good succession must be valid and legitimate. Public opinion must coalesce around a choice. Additionally, there must be a valid test that lasts a period of time so people can see how those chosen handle responsibility and adversities. They will be closely guided, observed, and tested by stalwarts of the empire. Finally, it might be advisable to inform Guru Vidyaranya of this process so he might offer his benediction and judge who guides you in making the decision, Bukka. His involvement will provide a stamp of approval.'

Bukka thought about this critically important process. He crouched over and in a quiet tone asked Mani Iyer: 'Who else have you spoken to about this?'

'No one else, Bukka. However, the last time Vidyaranya passed through Vijayanagara, he mentioned that there was an obvious candidate to succeed Bukka Raya. Yet he felt that a strenuous and demanding process would need to take place to establish legitimacy.'

When Mani Iyer left, Valli looked searchingly at Bukka. There was a strained silence and Valli asked:

'What plans do you have, Bukka?'

Bukka carefully thought about how he was going to answer the question. Now was as good a time to face the issue head on. Bukka asked Aiza to join them and to sit down, as well.

'Soon we will have to start the process of deciding who will be the yuvaraja, or my successor. An empire cannot go on without that decision being made. While I was Hakka's second-in-command, it ensured the certainty of a fall back. Now there is a vacuum. If we are going to choose who will be the yuvaraja, it can only happen, to my mind at least, if both Hari and Ramanatha are put to a test. That test will be one that gives them both a challenge but they will have to be sent away for a long period of time. Right now, I have not decided what the test will be, nor do I know when it will begin. But I daresay the sooner the better.

'The reason I asked Aizama to sit down is because if Hari goes, Haftar will want to accompany him as well. While I am fine with that, and I have always considered Haftar as my own, I can only make the decision to send Haftar if Aizama is willing.' Bukka looked at Aiza and searched for her response. He could see her wipe a tear.

'Huzoor, if you think it is something Hari must do, then so be it,' she said in a clear voice. 'You must decide whether it is also good for Haftar to do the same thing. Hari will be emperor someday by God's grace and my only wish is that the two are not separated.'

There was a silence in the room as Bukka looked at the two women. Valli had tears in her eyes. Quickly regaining her composure, she announced:

'If that is what Hari must do, and if Aizama is willing to send Haftar, then please send Haftar. I will be at peace knowing the two boys will be together. When do you plan to send them away, and for how long?'

Bukka stayed quiet as he gathered his thoughts.

'They will leave in a few months and the length of their deployment could be for two or three years.'

At this point Valli began to sob.

'Bukka, are you not being too harsh?' she asked.

In a gravelly voice he replied:

'You are an empress and might be the mother of the next emperor. These are the sacrifices you must make. There is no alternative for a robust succession. We must know which of the two princes is better suited for the responsibility. There is no other way than testing them.' It was clear he had made up his mind.

My name is Haftar Imtiaz

It was clear to Bukka that the choice for the next yuvaraja (heir apparent) would either be Harihara or Ramanatha. He was torn by two issues. First, what would the ramifications be if Harihara were chosen? Second, how would Haftar react to not being considered? Haftar was not his natural-born child but should he be treated as such? Bukka let Valli know his concerns. He was surprised at how pragmatic she was about his dilemma but it also meant having a difficult conversation with Aiza.

It was the day after the New Year celebrations and the kingdom usually shut down for a week. Bukka was at home with the children. Pattu came to visit; he had finally moved to a new house in the capital and was marking it by planning a celebration in his new home, and had come to invite the family for it. After Pattu left, Bukka resolved that he would speak to Aiza and Haftar. He made sure that Valli was by his side.

Bukka asked for Aiza to join him and Valli in their private apartments in the palace. He invited her to sit down with them. Clearly uncomfortable, Bukka decided to get to the point right away.

'Aiza, soon the empire will have to announce my successor, as we talked about earlier. When Hakka was still alive, he commanded that it would be the best-qualified son in the family who would succeed me. However, he insisted that it was to be the direct children of the brothers. I just want you to know that despite viewing Haftar as my son, he will not be among the children considered.'

Aiza sat beside Valli on the floor. She was quiet for a moment as tears started to well up. Wiping her eyes, she got to her knees, turned towards Valli, held her feet and sobbed:

'Please forgive me. I am truly very sorry.'

Valli gently raised her and held her face in her hands. 'What are you sorry for, Aizama? Why are you sorry?'

It took a few minutes for Aiza to regain her composure. She wiped her tears with the long end of her saree.

'My Samrajini Vallima, and Bukka Raya, my chakravarti, when I was a lowly prostitute, you lifted me up. You brought me into your home. My children became your children. This *niematan 'aw waqt samah* [grace of Allah] is puzzling to me but I pray every day and thank Allah for your kindness and affection. I ask your forgiveness if you thought I'd even expect that my son be considered for such an exalted position. I am deeply sorry for my behaviour. I am deeply sorry if Haftar Imtiaz has behaved in such a way.' She began sobbing uncontrollably, again.

Valli reached out to hold her, whispering softly:

'The one who should be crying is me, Aiza. Haftar is my son and I've raised him as such. Why should one son, because of birth, be preferred over the other? It is a strange set of circumstances that Hakka Raya ordered us to follow. Haftar unfortunately is a victim of this rule. So, forgive Bukka and forgive me.'

Aiza had composed herself. 'I hope that Haftar has not said or behaved inappropriately, Vallima?'

'If he had I'd have corrected him myself, Aiza, as I have in the past,' Valli smiled.

The little scene had shaken Bukka. He asked Aiza if he could tell Haftar about the decision.

'Of course, Huzoor. But why do you even want to waste your time with it?'

'Because, Aizama, he is and will be my son, regardless of this decision.' Bukka asked for haftar to join them.

Haftar walked in and he could see Vallima still holding Aiza, and there was palpable tension in the room.

'Is everything okay? Have I done something wrong?'

Bukka smiled and invited him to sit down. He sat on the floor next to Valli. Bukka delivered the news in a quiet tone, to which Haftar replied with a big smile. Putting her hand on his shoulder affectionately, Valli asked why he smiled.

'I never once thought I should be considered for such a high honour, amma.'

'Why did you say "should"?' Valli asked. Haftar put his arm around her shoulder, as he frequently did, and began to laugh as he looked at Bukka as well.

'In most ways Hari and I appear the same but there are a few notable differences. He is more astute than I am and sees things in ways that I cannot. His ability to grasp complicated ideas is wonderful. While I can manage people with a degree of competence, his abilities are even greater. I think those differences are important when someone is to be emperor. On that basis I should not be considered for such an exalted position. But please, promise me that you will not tell him I admitted this. It will embarrass him.'

Bukka smiled in admiration for the young man who had a clear sense of self and spoke so eloquently. Reclining again on his divan, he asked:

'If you cannot be considered for chakravarti, what would you be?'

The answer was swift.

'When I am at the peak of my career, many years from now, I want to be like Karthikeya. I will strive to be a scout and be with Hari when he goes out on campaigns. I'd like to be there for him as Karthikeya has been for you, Bukkappa, and was for Hakkappa as well. For me, it would be a fine accomplishment.'

Bukka could see why Valli secretly favoured Haftar. Bukka remembered when he once teased her about it, she said: 'When you say something to him, he understands immediately. I just wish the other monkeys were as mature.' As he got up to walk out to his usual spot on the verandah, he couldn't help but notice Aiza beaming with pride.

Building a test

The only way Bukka felt he could be fair was by being patently unfair. Giving the same challenge to both men would not, in his mind at least, be enough. He had to give Hari a tougher test and if he succeeded there would be no argument. But then there was the issue of how hard he should make it for Hari. It had to be plausible, it ought to be perceived as a challenge that was distinctly harder than that given to Ramanatha.

He spent a few weeks going over reports of the state of the empire and its borders with Rahim Rahmatullah and Mani Iyer.

When he arrived at the Green Palace, Bukka handed his horse over to one of the guards.

'Make sure the horses are stabled, as this gathering might take long, Nagendra.' He walked up the stairs smiling to himself: this was Mani Iyer's kingdom. He was ushered into the large, well-lit room where the Privy Council gathered. All the members were in attendance and he greeted each of them. There were four ministers present: defence, civil affairs, revenue and justice. Karthikeya was present as marshal of the Vijayanagara army, as was Rahim Rahmatullah, who was the minister of information (external and internal). Mani Iyer chaired the meeting. Pattu had excused himself on the grounds that participating in the discussion was a conflict of interest (since Hari was his grandson). Pattu knew that his informants would keep him updated about the two contestants' progress. His only comment to Bukka when he had invited the family to his new house had been: 'Bukka, in the interests of neutrality, do not be harsh and unfair.' Bukka had nodded, knowing exactly what he was talking about.

Bukka seated himself and signalled to Mani Iyer to proceed.

'Today's council is called to discuss the succession to the imperial throne. It has been decided that two members of the royal family will be considered for the position of yuvaraja: Ramanatha and Harihara. As a starting point, over the next few days, the Privy Council will convene without the emperor to conduct a long and thorough interview with each of them. This will be followed by a longer evaluation.'

The councillors listened as he continued:

'Chakravarti Bukka has indicated that this evaluation should last three years so we can thoroughly monitor their progress. When they take their posts, they will be accompanied by two senior officers of the empire who will act as mentors and evaluators. One will be from the army and nominated by Karthikeya; the other will be an administrator who will be nominated by me. They will be with the candidates throughout the period of the evaluation. We realize that it is a great sacrifice for the four members, but the choice of who will be the next emperor is critically important and we appreciate the service to the kingdom in advance. Finally, I will ask Chakravarti Bukka to give us his ideas on the assignments that each of these young men should undertake.' He turned to Bukka.

'I recommend that Ramanatha be sent to Mangaluru as governor. His military advisor will be General Aiyappa and his civilian advisor will be Vedanta Menon, one of the prime minister's deputies.' Most heads of those sitting on their diwans nodded in satisfaction. Karthikeya, however, was concerned because Ramanatha was being given an assignment that was more than easy. Mangaluru was peaceful and well run. He feared what was in store for Hari.

Bukka then turned his attention to the second candidate.

'Harihara will lead a battalion of four hundred men to the north. He will establish a new state between our current borders currently at the Tungabhadra river, and the River Krishna in the north. As you know, this region nominally belongs to the Bahmanis but has been neglected by them. He will bring it under his control and secure the new border. For that, he will have to raise an army, build an administration, raise revenues and fund the state. Apart from providing four hundred men as the core of the army and the resources for preparations, there will be no further assistance from the empire during this period. For his military advisor, I recommend General Chinayya. For his civilian advisor I nominate Gnyanadasa, who is also one of the stalwarts of the prime minister's cabinet.'

A murmur rose in the room.

'What is the source of concern?' Mani Iyer asked.

Shamshed, the minister of defence, stood up.

'Chakravarti, you are putting Harihara in an almost impossible situation. I am taking the liberty, chakravarti, of saying that you are asking a young soldier to do what two intrepid and experienced brothers did not accomplish. While this is no-man's land, the Bahmanis to the north of the Krishna river are better equipped and ruthless. All he will have is four hundred soldiers. I fear the outcome. Please consider giving him more resources, at the very least.'

Bukka cleared his throat.

'Shamshed, you said two brothers had not accomplished this task. To make this fair, we'll have Harihara's brother, Officer Haftar Imtiaz of the King's Guard, accompany him on this assignment.' Bukka looked over to Mani Iyer. 'Let us get the final details completed so the meetings with the two candidates can be organized as soon as possible. I would like them to begin their assignments next month.' Everyone in the room took a large gulp. The assignments appeared lopsided and unfair.

Everyone in the room wondered what their emperor hoped to accomplish. Karthikeya rubbed his chin and was deep in thought. He always knew Bukka to be fair and to give everyone an even chance. Smiling grimly, Karthikeya thought to himself, 'At any rate, there is something I can do to make this a little less unfair. As the marshal of the army, I can give Hari the best men to help him succeed. He has two of the best advisors already, and he'll have Haftar with him too. If there is one person who could pull this off, it will be Harihara.' As he knew so well, Harihara possessed many of the stellar qualities of Bukka and Valli. And with that his spirits lifted a little.

Ramanatha and Hari were summoned to the Privy Council. Each faced an intense grilling for a whole day. Every member wanted a measure of these two young men and they all recorded their opinions.

Pattu sat in on the sessions but remained quiet. Though Bukka appeared to have handed out a tough assignment, he was convinced Hari could do it. Hari was meticulous, thoughtful and fearless, just like Bukka. But he also had the qualities that made Valli such a remarkable woman. He had the common touch: he could draw people to him and get them to trust in his leadership. With Haftar and the two advisors, he would surely pull it off. It was going to be tough, however. He completely dismissed Ramanatha and his prospects. While Ramanatha had a lot of Hakka's abilities, they had never been drawn out or truly tested. In his case, privilege was not an advantage he had used. It had been wasted.

On the final day of the Privy Council's deliberations, Ramanatha and Hari were asked to attend. Bukka informed them that one of them would be chosen as the yuvaraja after three years of intense scrutiny. He first announced Ramanatha's assignment and asked if he had any questions. Ramanatha remained seated and in an informal tone, enquired:

'Bukka Raya, will I have the rank of governor with all of the attendant privileges?'

Bukka answered in the affirmative, but remained terse so as not to be seen as favouring any candidate.

Then he called Hari, who stood up and saluted him as an officer in the emperor's army. Bukka gave him his assignment and asked if he had any questions.

'Yes, chakravarti. When do I start?'

11

It's the Doab!

1370–73: Vijayanagara and the Doab

What's he really after?

Once the candidates had been assigned their tasks at the Privy Council, all the members left. Mani Iyer told the two young princes that they would receive documents to study and asked Harihara to present himself at the Green Palace the next morning. The young men departed as well. Mani Iyer called messengers and sent Ramanatha reams of revenue, judicial and military documents. There was much less for Harihara to work with: just a few maps and old intelligence reports.

Karthikeya stayed behind to speak to Mani Iyer. He still felt troubled about Hari. Mani Iyer was the best person to share his worries with.

'What is the chakravarti up to? First, he sets up a test that is unequal. If he wanted Ramanatha to succeed, he could have just said so and we would not have to go through this trying process. Then he gives Harihara, though very capable, an unusual assignment. How will the Council on the Succession even know how to test him or evaluate his performance?'

If there was a person in the empire who had dedicated his life to the brothers, it was Karthikeya. Bukka's and Valli's children knew him and his wife Sharada very well, and since they did not have any children, there was a deep bond between them. Mani Iyer appreciated that he would find this difficult.

Mani Iyer began to sway back and forth again.

'Karthikeya, Bukka has to honour the memory of his brother by making sure that the chosen one is beyond any reproach. Even though there will be a recommendation by the Council on Succession, he wants the outcome to be clear-cut in public opinion too. The last part is this—Bukka knows that Harihara is extremely competent yet wants to test him all the same.

'Keep the complete picture in perspective, Karthikeya. Think about the two people in question and the challenges ahead of them. Ramanatha has been assigned a governorship. The prospect of great outcomes is not high as it already is a well-administered state. The bigger challenge for Ramanatha, who is supposed to have administrative abilities, will be to stay consistent, focused, disciplined. Otherwise, the whole framework will unravel. So, it is his personality being tested.

'In the case of Hari, the chakravarti has decided to give him a task that is full of risk but with the possibility of great outcomes. Remember that in all these years while we were focused on securing our empire, the Bahmanis too were dealing with their own consolidation and the succession of Bahman Shah by his son Muhammad. Therefore, the Doab has been ignored and no one truly laid claim to it, other than the presence of the

Bahmanis at the fort at Raichur. They perhaps presume that
the territory belongs to them, but they are not paying much
attention. If Hari moves cleverly and quickly, he can succeed.'
Then he added:

'Our emperor is extremely shrewd. Now that the succession
is being openly discussed, it will give him a chance to see many
people in a very different light. Will they choose sides? How
will they work to give both princes an even chance? What effort
would they make to guide these young men? In other words,
how will they work to make this a smooth succession?'

'Well, yes. But this assignment still does not make sense.'

'It makes all the sense in the world. He wants Harihara to
go out and secure the Doab in the next three years. If he can
accomplish that, then his claim to succeeding his father is clear.
There would be no questioning that outcome. And this is why
he has made this test so unbalanced. The gods would smile at
such an outcome.'

Karthikeya spluttered at Mani Iyer's remarks.

'The Doab! You do realize that the Doab, the area between the
rivers Krishna and the Tungabhadra, encompasses a significant
amount of territory from west to east. It is a monumental task.
Neither Hakka nor Bukka did that when they were just eighteen
years of age. This is preposterous. Maybe I should plead with
Bukka to reconsider this.'

Mani Iyer smiled and continued to sway gently.

'Do nothing of the sort, Karthikeya, as this is also a test for
the two of us: how well will you, the marshal of the Vijayanagara
army, and I, the prime minister, help these two rajkumars
accomplish their tasks?

'Remember, Karthikeya, when Hakka wanted to get an
answer from Bukka, he would keep on posing questions

relentlessly. He did this because it was the only way he could uncover the many layers of Bukka's thinking. Rani Valli had learnt the same thing about him. During our walks to and from the temple, she has told me his thinking is like a parcel—you have to carefully unpack all of it. And if you carefully unpack this decision, you will see that he is testing us, testing an enemy, testing his son and in the meanwhile testing to see if his nephew has the constancy of purpose to manage a state effectively. And while he knows the answer, he wants to be sure if all his assumptions are true.'

For a moment it seemed like Karthikeya's life flashed in front of him. Thinking of Bukka in every battlefield situation outwitting the enemy. And here he was, at the most consequential decision of his life, bringing the same keen strategy into play. Karthikeya conceded to the point being made.

'I agree and that only tells me we have a lot of work to do in the next month.'

'Fortunately,' Mani Iyer replied, 'both Chinayya and Gnyanadasa are exceptional and will help pull this together. I know that both Harihara and Haftar will get along well with them. All we have to do is make sure that they have the right direction, point out the pitfalls, and give them the resources they need. Then I will pray to the Long-tailed One for their success.' He added, 'Karthikeya, come here tomorrow morning and we can interview Harihara. I've sent him some material to study. Let us see how much he has been able to understand. While he is still young and might not have the same finesse with which the emperor plays his game of chaturanga, it is quite likely that he will beat his father.'

The moment the messenger gave Harihara the material from Mani Iyer, he recognized he faced a dilemma. Should he

share the information with Haftar? Thinking about it, he felt
he had to start to make decisions like this. Besides, both Hakka
and Bukka discussed and debated issues with Mani Iyer and
Karthikeya, and sought their opinions. Haftar was going to be
his advisor. He was pleased with his decision since Haftar could
see through people and their stratagems better than he could.
With the dogs following him, he walked to the end of the wing
of the palace, where Haftar began putting plans in place for
their assignment.

Do you realize?

Harihara showed up for his meeting with Mani Iyer the next
morning. When he walked into the room, he was surprised
to see Karthikeya, who invited him to sit down. Mani Iyer
launched into his interrogation.

'Do you know what is required of you to accomplish the
assignment?'

Harihara thought about it for a moment and stated:

'Add the Doab to the empire.'

Quizzed about how he would find the resources, he
immediately replied, 'Taxes,' but then added that he would
need the expertise of Gnyanadasa as he was unfamiliar with the
precise details of the system.

The next question was from Karthikeya: how many men
would he need to recruit for the military during this period?
This was the hardest one of all.

'I may be wrong but I will not be able to raise an army large
enough to defend against all-out attacks from the north. The
best one can accomplish is to build an army that uses attacks
to slow down and harass the enemy. If that reasoning makes

sense, it would be about three thousand soldiers.' Karthikeya contained a smile.

The last question came from Mani Iyer: 'How will you proceed with all of this?'

Harihara gulped before commenting: 'Slowly.' Both Mani Iyer and Karthikeya burst out laughing. Harihara blushed. They reassured him that he was on the right track.

Collecting his thoughts, Harihara said:

'I will start in the west drawing a straight line from Vijayanagara to Bagalkot, the town on the Krishna river. If you think of the Raichur Doab as the blade of a dagger, then my move to Bagalkot will be traversing the widest part of the blade. I will move eastward from there, building administration, recruiting soldiers, and collecting taxes. I will have to build loyalty to the empire and that will require giving people security and succour in whatever ways they need it.'

Karthikeya stopped him. 'That leaves a gap between Bagalkot and Karwar. How will you handle that?'

Harihara paused.

'The Bahmanis have their capital at Gulbarga, which is north of Vijayanagara. If they try to attack our capital, our very large army at Karwar will be able to attack their western flank. Meanwhile I shall slow them from the east, attacking their flank and rear. But maybe there is a flaw in my thinking, so please excuse me.' Karthikeya nodded and asked him to continue.

'In the first two years the focus will be on recruiting, training soldiers and administrators, and covering the territory of the Doab, that is, the area between the two rivers. The final year will be dedicated to establishing observation camps, methods and ways to harass an army that might attack from any point along the length of the Krishna river. I realize full

well that the group I train can only stall rather than defeat a
large army. Yet, if there are smaller groups that plan an attack,
we should be able to stop them. Finally, the third year will also
be spent coordinating with the marshal of the Kampili armies
to coordinate how the empire's army will be deployed to thwart
a full-scale attack.'

With a serious look on his face, careful not to give away his
delight, Mani Iyer said:

'Let that be your plan, Harihara. For the next week you will
spend some of your day with Gnyanadasa and me, detailing
how the taxes will be raised and administration established. For
the remainder of the day, you will work closely with General
Chinayya and Karthikeya on military plans and recruitment.
You will be given some resources, of which there will be an
accounting, and you will be responsible for detailing how
they were used. I will see all of your accounts from the various
territories. May the gods give you their blessings in this
endeavour; do not stray from the truth. While you will make
mistakes, have the humility to admit them and then learn from
them. You are dismissed, Harihara.'

Once he was out of earshot, Karthikeya looked at Mani Iyer.

'Is he more like Hakka or Bukka?'

'Like Hakka in his speed at understanding the situation
but like Bukka in being meticulous. He has the honesty of
Valli in admitting what he does not know and is not ashamed
of it.'

Mani Iyer called in a scribe and began noting all the
information he would collect on the interaction with the
rajkumars over the next three years. He would freely share
it with the other members as well. He had every intention of
faring well in the test the emperor had set for him as well.

You cannot take the dogs!

A strange breeze was blowing through the capital since the announcement of the beginning of the succession, though the palace itself had its own upheaval to contend with. All of it seemed to be emanating from the wing where Bukka and Valli lived. Valli was deeply upset that the boys would leave so soon and be away for so long. Of course, she understood the rationale but could not accept Bukka's decision to heap such a strenuous test on Harihara and, in consequence, Haftar. She found herself getting irritated with all that was going on and sensed that their departure would gouge something big out of her life. When all four children were around, there was always commotion and laughter every minute of the day. The last time the boys left for their training for six months, she had felt she had lost everything. This time, Bukka's strange plan had them going away for three years and she was unable to get him to reconsider his plan.

It was her agitated state of mind that prompted an argument with the boys.

'No, you cannot take the dogs with you,' she asserted with a tone of finality. Fortunately, as she was haranguing the boys, Bukka walked in with two puppies in his arms. 'The army will not permit them to take the dogs, Bukka, did you realize that? The poor things, who will feed and take care of them.'

'The monkeys will,' Bukka replied, 'the way they have all these years. You taught them to take responsibility and they have.' Frustrated, she stomped out of the room. Bukka, in one of his clownish moments, tiptoed out of the room as well, carrying the puppies, which had the children laughing.

'I heard that,' came Valli's voice from down the corridor.

The departure brought more tension to the palace. The girls would not stop harassing Bukka about his decision. They even questioned his need to have a test last three years.

'In this case, the answer is so clear. How could you not see that? All that Ramanatha does is eat too much, drink too much and run around with women all the time. That is not what emperors are made of,' Sarah argued. Even Bukka's deep patience with the girls was being tested.

Meanwhile, Karthikeya handpicked the men who would accompany Harihara and Haftar. He made sure the contingent had forty scouts, many young loyal men wanting to make a career for themselves and eager to serve a possible future emperor. Gnyanadasa chose several accomplished administrators and plans were in place for them to leave in a day's time. Haftar was appointed scout and would be trained by a senior member. The route was carefully chosen: they would follow the Tungabhadra west to Gadag and then north to Bagalkot on the Krishna river. When Mani Iyer enquired about the logic of it, Harihara replied: 'The route lays out the first district that I intend to work from and the district headquarters will be at Bagalkot on the banks of the Krishna river.'

On their last day, they made it a point to visit Malaa to ask for her blessings. All she managed to say, in a typical grudging manner, was how difficult a task Ramanatha had been given. Valli dragged the boys off to the Hanuman temple and then to the mosque. The whole family ate dinner together but there was little chatter. Valli was adamant that Mithran, who had been the boys' bodyguard since they were young, should go along. The emperor was in no state to argue with her.

A fog of gloom descended on the palace that morning. Harihara and Haftar said their goodbyes but it seemed like everyone was coming to see them off. At the entrance of the palace were assembled the four hundred cavalrymen and scouts going with them. The boys hugged their sisters, touched Aiza's and Valli's feet, saluted the emperor and touched his feet as well. Mounting their horses, they called out to the three dogs. Haftar headed the company, shouting:

'To Gadag and Bagalkot. Ride with pride.' The company galloped out of the gates with the dogs barking loudly as they ran alongside. Harihara was somewhere amongst them. Valli quickly walked back to the palace in tears, with one of the girls on either side, followed by Aiza. The emperor stood at the entrance watching until the last horseman was out of sight.

To Bagalkot

Riding to the eastern city of Gadag, and then north to Bagalkot, would normally have taken four days. However, Harihara decided he would examine the terrain, the better to learn the territory, have extended conversations with his two advisors, after stopping at the major villages and meeting their leaders, rather than rush to the north. One of the men hired by Gnyanadasa served as his scribe and carried key documents. He made notes of the names of village heads, the vegetation in the area and every last detail of the territory. General Chinayya planned sites for them to camp in the evenings with functioning field kitchens.

Harihara knew some of the men from the King's Guard and worked on getting to know the others he had never met before. While there were some grizzled veterans, most were young, with a few years' military experience. Getting to know Harihara was important for them as well. Haftar, meanwhile, was given a crash course in being a scout. An old veteran, Achaiah, had been sent along by Karthikeya to teach and train Haftar. Harihara barely saw him during the day when they were riding, as Haftar was ahead of the pack or behind it. The pace was slow enough that the dogs were able to keep up. Kaloo was young and tired more easily, so when Harihara saw her long tongue hanging out as she trotted by him, he'd move away from the riding group, pick her up and put her in front of him. His other two dogs, Kelsa and Kopa, were able to handle the pace at which they were moving.

Camping for the evening, Harihara made sure to set his own standards. The troops saw him remove the saddle of his horse, Burfi, which Hakka had given him as a gift and named after his favourite sweet. He would brush her down, clean out her hooves and water her. If they were at a river or a lake, he would give her a bath. He made it a point to let the troops know just how important the animals were and, like Bukka, wanted to make sure they were cared for.

At Bagalkot, they set up camp by an old farm. There were two old houses, a grove of mango trees, and the vegetation was lush. Harihara suddenly realized that the soil was dark brown, unlike the red-ochre colour south of the Tungabhadra river. It struck him how rich the area was in terms of the soil and crops. It became clear that all of the vegetation and the colour of the soil were due to the rivers.

That led to his question for Gnyanadasa: would tax revenues be higher if the land was more fertile? He started to ask questions and the pace at which he posed them to both Chinayya and Gnyanadasa slowly began to grow. Chinayya smiled to himself. 'More like the uncle than the father, who is a lot more deliberate,' he thought to himself. He enjoyed the young man's enthusiasm and demeanour. Harihara was a year older than his own son and he found him respectful and fun-loving in equal measure. Haftar, by comparison, was a little more reserved but very quick to learn as well. Karthikeya was right: they would be excellent students and easy to work with.

On the first morning at the camp in Bagalkot, once the morning exercise routine and washing of the horses was finished, Harihara asked if he could meet with Gnyanadasa and Chinayya. Once they were seated in a room in one of the old houses, Harihara was about to begin when Gnyanadasa raised his hand.

'Rajkumar, there are a few criteria in our role that you must be made aware of. As we start out on this three-year assignment, both Chinayya and I will teach you in the first year. In the second year, we will advise. And in the final year we will only consult, when asked. When we have disagreements, we should all debate them, consider the alternatives and find the best solution with regard to what is best for the empire. After all, this is ultimately an initiative to expand and secure the borders of the empire.'

For four days they spent every waking hour in that room formulating a plan. The two teachers were the ones questioning Harihara, and providing answers when he did not know.

Gnyanadasa taught Harihara about crops, taxation, judicial systems and the cost of building. Chinayya offered advice on methods of recruiting, training, deciding which soldiers to retain, and how they would get paid. It seemed as if they never left his side and Harihara was usually deep in conversation with them when they rode to villages to introduce taxes, recruit men, hunt down dacoits, and begin administering justice in the name of the empire. On occasion they would stop along the journey and pose a serious question to Harihara. For example, they asked him: 'Do you think you have the funds to pay your soldiers?' He was left flatfooted in attempting a response.

Chinayya smiled and said: 'Unpaid soldiers usually desert, rajkumar.' Then Gnyanadasa chimed in and asked if he could estimate what the revenues would be the first year, and if it would cover his expenses. Harihara once again struggled to come up with an answer. It was demanding but he began to slowly understand the logic of their reasoning. He used more of the information he was picking up and applied it to his answers. Haftar went through the same process.

At the end of six months, they had recruited four hundred soldiers and were confident they would get to a thousand by the end of the year. They visited each of the forty-three villages in the newly formed district at least three times. Harihara memorized the names of the village leaders, the crops they grew, the yields, the prices in the market, and the various taxes for the various crops.

Then he reported to the emperor, the prime minister, and the marshal of the army every week. They presented questions for him and offered suggestions.

They recruited a thousand soldiers in the first year and covered half the territory of the Doab and brought it under the tax administration. They travelled east on a five-day march, bringing the territory into the Vijayanagara fold all the way south to the Tungabhadra. The second year involved going farther east, continuing along the banks of the Krishna river to the city of Kurnool.

Late one evening, as Haftar was drifting off to sleep, Harihara said:

'I think maturity is creeping up on me, Haftaree.'

'In your case that is difficult to imagine because maturity is unaware of your existence, Hari.'

Harihara could hear Haftar giggling at his own joke.

'Seriously, I now understand the pressures and stresses that Bukkappa faces and the demands that are put on Vallima and Aizama.'

'Hari, stop showering yourself with rose petals. You just miss them. The next thing you'll say is both of our sisters are sweet-natured girls,' Haftar said.

'But they are,' Harihara responded.

'This proves my point, rajkumar. So, let's just get some sleep,' a weary Haftar replied.

Raising the 'monkeys', Bukka and Valli, and then Aiza, never gave them too much free time. They were kept busy, given chores and made to work. Then the boys had gone to officers' training camp, with its gruelling routine. Now there was this last year and what they had experienced. Harihara even confessed to Haftar: 'I think even my bones are tired.'

It was a month before the end of the first year and the demands of the job got even busier. Taxes were collected, tabulated and counted. A new headquarters had to be chosen for the following year, and the final test for the last two hundred recruits needed to be completed. Harihara was summoned by Gnyanadasa and Chinayya, who appeared pleased by the progress. Taxes were higher than estimated, with only a few delinquent farmers. Gnyanadasa revealed the numbers and had two large bags of gold mohurs with him. 'This is what we have left behind after all of our expenses, rajkumar. What do you plan to do with it?'

Harihara laughed and said, 'It belongs to the treasury.'

'But we haven't been paid!' Gnyanadasa appeared downcast for a moment.

Harihara stood up to bow in a deep namaskaram, apologized profusely, took the two bags and handed one to Gnyanadasa and another to Chinayya. Puzzled by his actions, Chinayya asked the young man, 'What about paying yourself and Haftar?'

Harihara thought for a moment and answered:

'If we are on an assignment for the emperor, then I hope someday he will pay us what we deserve.'

Learning to juggle

In the second year they moved their headquarters to Jalahalli. It seemed as if the work was a hill that got steeper and harder to climb as they went on. Both the teachers stepped back and Harihara was left to rely on the experience he had accrued. He felt the weight of leadership. While he hit his targets, he realized his teachers possessed skill and experience that had made the first year so smooth. He just felt he was constantly making mistakes, pulled in all directions to the point that he could barely think problems through. Late one afternoon, when he was on the verge of exhaustion and overtaken by anxiety, he walked down to the river and sat on the bank. How could he manage all of this? Maybe he'd have to admit defeat. Then he heard footfalls behind him. It was Gnyanadasa.

'I appreciate that you are feeling overwhelmed. I know that you are now questioning yourself. I also realize if you do not learn the lesson I am about to teach you, you will not be able to manage your responsibilities and tasks.' A long silence followed. Harihara turned his head to him and asked:

'You said you would become my advisor in our second year. What advice would you have that I might use? Because I do not see how I can handle this any more. I do not have the skill or experience that you or General Chinayya have. Is there some magic potion I need to take to get all of this done?

Otherwise, I need to be like the god Vishnu and have many hands, and omniscience with infinite capability.' Harihara looked distraught.

'Rajkumar, you cannot do all of this by yourself. You need to find good and competent people to whom you can assign your tasks. Give them clear guidance. Check on their progress regularly. Help them when they have a problem and hold them responsible for the outcomes. Should they do well, give them due acknowledgement and reward them. If they make mistakes, counsel them, teach them and encourage them to perform better,' Gnyanadasa advised.

'How do I find these people? How do I know what they can do?' Harihara asked tiredly.

'Think of the emperor and his brother. Think of all the people they surround themselves with. There are the generals like Karthikeya, Faraj, Aiyappa, among others. Then there are the administrators like Mani Iyer the prime minister, Aslam Beg the vakildar, Rahim Rahmatullah and all the governors. So, despite the fact that Bukka Raya and the late Hakka Raya are exceptional people, they found great people, and they gave them responsibilities. As a result, some brilliant people have provided them with guidance and were rewarded in turn. There is no other way. So go out and find capable people, and if you need the help of your advisors, they will be here when you need them.'

Gnyanadasa stood up, put his hand on Harihara's shoulder, and turned to leave before commenting:

'Your success will depend on the quality of the people around you. Never be apprehensive of their ability. However, measure their honesty and loyalty to you.' He then walked away up the path. Harihara sat there, looking out, trying to absorb all of it. The only thought that crossed his mind was: 'Why does the obvious sometimes seem so sublime?'

He sat there for a while when he heard the gravel of the pathway crunch behind him again. He was sure it was Haftar. Sure enough, a mocking voice came from behind:

'It looks as if you are trying to convince yourself that you are not up to the job.'

Harihara smiled wryly and spoke without turning around.

'Haftaree, the requirements of this job at times seem obvious but just when you think you have understood it, it becomes so much more complex. And when that happens, I just feel overwhelmed.'

'It is a hard job you are training to do but it can be made easier if you have the right people to help you. Perhaps you are trying to do it all. You cannot do it and neither do you know how. Just imagine how you want everything to be and then put everything in place.

'In fact, the best lesson is one that Vallima taught me. When she wants to decorate a place, or build something new, she says, "Try and see the picture in your mind. Imagine as much detail as you can in that picture. Find all the resources around you and get the help of the best people to work on it." But it's funny— she'd always add, "Just don't be lazy and think of the way things are; think of the way they might be and how they could be better." Those are the words of our mother.

'Yet keep in mind that most of your duties will require you to solve big and hard problems. While I was not as good as you in arithmetic or algebra, you would always say, "do not get overwhelmed; think of it as a puzzle." It's the same in this scenario you face. Remember when we learned how to ride; it was hard at first but once we got the hang of it, it became something we enjoyed doing. Like Vallima helping us to ride, now we have teachers who are doing the same. Get up on the horse and go where you want to; guide the horse; treat the horse the way Bukka and Vallima showed us. Once you get moving, you will trot, canter and then you will break into a gallop.'

Harihara was amazed.

'Haftaree, you save me from myself. Joking aside, this has helped me understand the situation. Now tell me, have you found some good people we can promote to help with the tasks at hand?'

Harihara had two men he could count on: Haftar and Mithran, his bodyguard. Mithran knew everyone and, while he did not speak much to others given his sceptical view of people, he was astute when it came to judging character. Harihara thought about a story Vallima had told him about Mithran. When they returned to Anegundi from Dorasamudra, Bukka assigned a bodyguard to each of the children. When Mithran was asked if he would guard Hari—he was circumspect. Bukka asked what the issue was, to which Mithran replied: 'If he is a good person and he commands my respect, I will take the job. Otherwise, you will have to find somebody else.' Valli asked how he could find such qualities in a twelve-year-old. His terse response was: 'You can look into someone's eyes and watch the way they move and speak, and tell if they are honest. I will spend an hour with the boy and inform you of my decision. Please forgive me, chakravarti, but I will be responsible for your child and I must be motivated to take care of him under any circumstance. One cannot be motivated unless one respects the person.' The story made Harihara smile as he noticed Mithran standing by the stables keeping watch over him with the three dogs.

It was Haftar's comments that shed light on his problem. He could see most of what he wanted to accomplish, whom he could ask and what could be achieved.

Trot, canter and gallop

In deciding on the names of people to trust, Harihara had Haftar and Mithran join him to offer their opinions. The names were subsequently run past Gnyanadasa and Chinayya. He announced those who were going to take on responsibility for the new state he was building.

Madappa, a wiry man from the Coorg hill country, was in charge of the recently trained recruits. Though he had a great deal to learn, he had the drive and passion of a leader and was fearless in everything that confronted him. Then Harihara had a young assistant, who had been hired at Bagalkot, appointed to help him with administration. A magician with numbers and possessing an encyclopaedic memory, Bikram Seth came from a small moneylending community from a coastal town near Gove. Haftar became his second-in-command.

Suddenly Harihara felt as though he were not the only one pulling at the oars but calling out to the oarsmen to pull harder to reach their destination. He still went to his two senior advisors to keep them informed and asked for guidance on occasion, but after that he went ahead and managed all the tasks that were expected of him. He had come out of the mist and could see what he needed to accomplish and how he wanted to do it.

In an interesting twist, the questions he had for Gnyanadasa and Chinayya became more complex. The first one he asked was if a farmer or a trader paid taxes to the empire, what did he get in return? The next was, 'Shouldn't people clearly know about what they should expect?' The third testing question featured justice and security, specifically how the empire should go about helping to improve the people's well-being. Harihara said they should ensure that the farmers got better prices at harvest. He suggested building homes for destitute women and children, taking a page out of Valli's book. The conversations began to get heated and the debates more complex. It seemed the young charge was developing faster than anticipated.

Late one afternoon, Chinayya and Gnyanadasa were walking along the banks of the river, discussing what they would present in their weekly assessment to Mani Iyer and Karthikeya. Chinayya remarked:

'As Harihara began to take most of the responsibility off our shoulders, we anticipated a lighter workload but he's suddenly asked loads of deep questions that have me completely out of my depth.'

'I think he's just getting started,' Gnyanadasa said. 'Soon, I think the only contribution I can make will be that ephemeral quality called wisdom. Bukka was always the faster of the two brothers. The pace this young man is setting is going to make Bukka seem like a tortoise!'

Fervour and a fever

'Mithran, where is Burfi?' Harihara asked as he stood outside their home in Jalahalli.

'In the stable, rajkumar,' Mithran responded. It was out of character that Mithran was not waiting for him with his horse. Holding down his growing sense of impatience, Harihara looked at Mithran. It seemed he had no intention of moving or mentioning that he might have forgotten.

'Why did you not bring him out, Mithran?' Harihara asked a little more pointedly.

'Because he is not going out today, rajkumar,' Mithran answered in a voice he had used with Hari many years ago when he was much younger. Before Harihara could say anything more, Mithran said:

'The vaidyan said you needed to rest for a week after you and Haftar suffered from fever. It is only three days, and you still have four days left. You have worked continuously for the last one hundred and sixty-three days without rest, which is perhaps why you fell ill.'

'I do not care about the vaidyan, Mithran, and I have work to do,' Harihara responded sternly. Mithran waited for a while, by which time Haftar joined Harihara at the door and enquired what the matter was.

'You have to rest another four days and then, if the vaidyan says you can work, we will get to work. Harihara, I am only following orders,' Mithran said.

'Whose orders?' an exasperated Harihara asked.

Mithran looked immovable as a boulder.

'The samrajini and Aizama. I am to protect you from harm which includes from yourselves as well. That is all I am doing.'

'And when did they give you these orders, Mithran?'

'Before we left, I promised the samrajini and Aizama that I would make sure to take care of the two of you. If you were to pull rank on me, I have their permission to send a message by the courier through General Chinayya. That is what I promised them and I have every intention of keeping that promise, Haripa and Haftaree.' He had reverted to the names he used for them when they were young boys and he needed to reprimand them. 'Do not doubt that for a moment.'

Mithran cared very deeply for the young men but they were his charges and as far as he was concerned, it mattered little that one of them might be on the verge of becoming emperor. He had his orders and nothing was going to change that. Then, sensing Harihara was about to give in, he asked him in a softer voice if he wanted something to eat or drink.

Harihara returned to the house in a huff.

'I can't believe how he sometimes treats us like we are little brats, Haftaree.'

Haftar shook his head. 'We're lucky he did not smack us the way he did in Dorasamudra. I can bet you anything Aizama and Vallima have given him full authority to do what it takes if he thinks we are crossing a line. What's more, he is so damned strong he can take on the two of us. Let's rest up, because you and I have no alternative.'

Later that afternoon Mithran returned with the vaidyan, who informed them that they could walk to the river and bathe if they wanted to. Only after a good bath did it fully sink in that they were at the halfway mark; it had been eighteen months since they left home. They also realized they now had recruited nearly three thousand soldiers, and the administration for the second region had been set up. Harihara had worked at a frenetic pace and falling ill was the result of exhaustion. It was a small price: they were ahead of schedule.

In the evening, Mithran walked in.

'The vaidyan says it would not hurt you to have a few glasses of kallu and a good meal.' Harihara and Haftar laughed and invited him to join them. Mithran looked at them, barely cracked a smile and said, 'Perhaps, if I can find two soldiers to take my spot for just this evening. You must celebrate because it is the halfway mark of your assignment and soon you'll be back home.'

The rest gave Harihara a chance to review all he had achieved. Moreover, since he had spent a few full days with Haftar, he could speak to him and use him as his sounding board. It was only then he realized that a large part of his assignment had military objectives and he had only laid the administrative foundations. The new focus was on the enemy to the north and finding what it would take to thwart the enemy should he decide to cross the Krishna river and head south to Vijayanagara.

Dull, diligent and dangerous

'What are your enemies' motives? How do they train? What are the methods they use on the battlefield? What are the politics they face back home? And who are their enemies?' This was a refrain that Harihara heard Hakka discuss when he was younger, and Hakka would tell them stories or even try and give them a quick lesson in statecraft. Now Harihara had a clearly defined enemy and set about filling in the pieces.

The Bahmanis to the north were a rebellious residual of Muhammad-bin-Tughlaq's empire. After a skirmish was put down by Emperor Tughlaq there was another uprising, but this time the emperor was in Lakhnauti putting down yet another rebellion. Many nobles in the Bahmani kingdom were from the court in Dilli and this new entity was ruled by Sultan Ala ud-din Bahman Shah. He had ruled for more than a decade and died the previous year. He tried to attack the Vijayanagara kingdom twice and failed on both occasions: beaten back once by Hakka and then by Bukka. He moved his capital further inland to Gulbarga, which was in the middle of the Bahmani kingdom.

From Harihara's viewpoint, it meant any Bahmani army would be north of Vijayanagara and would have to cross the Doab to the capital. The way he saw it, the few years of peace were a result of Bahman Shah's death. His son, Muhammad I, had just ascended the throne—a 'dull, diligent and very dangerous person' according to Rahim Rahmatullah. The four days of forced rest gave Harihara a chance to compile the necessary information about what he needed to do over the next eighteen months.

Once Muhammad was comfortably ensconced, there was every indication that he would begin testing the Vijayanagara defences. It was clear to Harihara that the best he could do was build a force that was able to detect the movement of the enemy and then harass its flanks and attack it from the rear. Three thousand men would certainly not hold off an army of fifteen thousand—the rumoured strength of the Bahmani army. That task would fall to the emperor, who could easily mobilize twenty to thirty thousand soldiers of his standing army quickly if he had forewarning. There were two tasks Harihara was faced with.

First, he needed to organize a strategy that severely harassed a slow-moving convoy of soldiers and their supply train. It required taking the initiative and coordinating his efforts with Karthikeya to make sure it had maximum impact. Second, he would work with Rahim Rahmatullah to find out how he might set up a system to transmit information about the enemy.

In a fit of self-doubt, Harihara wondered if he might be overstepping his mandate. Was he supposed to be taking on such initiatives, or were his directions more modest? He decided making a mistake and overstepping his mark might be better than hiding from a bigger problem. He resolved to stop doubting his judgment and encouraged his advisors to offer their views. Chinayya nodded as Harihara went through his explanation, even though the young man acknowledged having an attack of self-doubt.

'Growing happens in spurts and is a process that is uneven,' Chinayya reassured him. 'So, what you are facing is exactly what we expect you to wrestle with. Go ahead and take the initiative. That is what you were charged to do. The emperor asked you to go north and secure the borders and what you are considering is the kind of initiative that is expected of you.'

Harihara returned to the house where he decided that any 'dull and diligent enemy' was a dangerous enemy. Karthikeya might be the marshal of the army and nominally his superior, but the man who gave him his assignment was the emperor. He needed to pay heed to the spirit of what was asked of him. He called for the scribe to write a letter to Karthikeya, with copies to be sent to Mani Iyer and Rahim Rahmatullah, the minister of information.

Kurnool and onwards

Kurnool would be the headquarters for the last of the three areas in the Doab that Harihara had planned to bring into the ambit of the empire. He'd been stationed there for eight months already and, according to schedule, he was expected back in Vijayanagara in four months. The administration of the area was set up in a methodical process. He had recruited an additional six hundred cavalry, so that his forces numbered four thousand. The newly recruited army would secure a border that took about fifteen or eighteen days to traverse.

Finally, Harihara put a framework in place should the enemy choose to attack. He set up a squad of fifty ponies that were used to communicate with the various outposts. Each outpost was, at most, a day's ride away from the next. All were situated in locations with excellent visibility. Should the enemy attempt to cross the river, the nearby outposts would know within the day. Furthermore, the capital would know the same day if carrier pigeons were used, or within two days if couriers were employed. The attack and harassment of an approaching enemy had been planned. He trained two hundred archers who could attack from hidden locations.

Four thousand men and a thousand horses could do a lot of damage to a slow-moving army and a long supply train that had to cross a river.

It was only in the last month that Karthikeya arrived to review the front line and examine the effectiveness of the communications and the scouts. He went to every location unannounced and was pleased to see their efficiency. Finally, he decided to check the defences of Kurnool. He rode towards the camp late at night with a contingent of approximately two hundred horsemen.

Karthikeya was confident that he would be able to surprise the camp. After they had rested up and were an hour away from Kurnool, he had a nagging feeling they were being followed. Suddenly, out of nowhere, three hundred horsemen had surrounded him and his men. Then he heard the unmistakable whistle signal of a Vijayanagara, scout and the distinctive voice of Haftar in the distance. Karthikeya ordered his own scout to signal back.

Haftar rode out to meet them. He saluted Karthikeya, dismounted and approached his horse.

'How long have you known we were here?' a bewildered Karthikeya asked. Haftar modestly revealed that he and his men had been tracking Karthikeya for the last two hours.

'I have mixed feelings about this,' Karthikeya said as he dismounted his horse. 'Either you have all been trained very well, or my contingent let their guard down.'

Karthikeya stayed for a day to review Harihara's plans with Gnyanadasa and Chinayya in his company. What was so impressive were the resources they had pulled together, the configuration of the defences, and the strong sense of identity of the army. Harihara and Haftar had become extremely competent officers with great self-assurance since the last time they met Karthikeya, which was when they left Vijayananagar on their assignment.

Karthikeya met Gnyanadasa and Chinayya privately and commended them on the exceptional job they had done. Gnyanadasa in his typical laconic way confessed:

'They have been doing all this on their own for the last year and a half. They've improved on everything we taught them. To be fair, the credit is all theirs.' This lined up with all the reports Karthikeya got from them and Harihara. Just before he left, Karthikeya spoke to Harihara and Haftar:

'The emperor sends you his regards, and looks forward to spending some time with you when you are back. Please be wary and safe.' Karthikeya did not deviate from the role of the commanding general and, in return, they saluted and bade him a formal goodbye as was befitting his rank.

It left Harihara and Haftar a bit puzzled but they chalked it up to Karthikeya not wanting to show any undue favours to them.

12

To the Tungabhadra

1372–73: Alampur in the Doab, and Vijayanagara

The Bahmanis attack

It was only a matter of time before the Bahmanis woke up to the fact that the Vijayanagara forces had established themselves in the Doab. Spies relayed information back from Raichur, the only encampment of the Bahmanis on the Doab.

They reported high levels of activity. Cavalry had arrived from Gulbarga, raising their numbers to two thousand. The Bahmanis took interminably long to get supplies and logistics organized before moving towards Alampur, the tip of the Doab in the southeast, which was a six-day march by Harihara's reckoning. When they were a day away, Harihara finalized his plans with General Chinayya, who agreed with the tactics. Harihara would draw them in and then hit them hard. He had to be careful about his timing as the Bahmanis had the distinct advantage of having twice as many horses. The plan focused on neutralizing this advantage. Meanwhile, the scouts were feeding him critical information.

They expected the attack the next morning. Harihara prepared the men by declaring that their reputation as soldiers would be determined by the outcome of this battle.

'Proceed with pride and maintain the honour of the Vijayanagara army, which has not lost a single battle under Hakka and Bukka,' Harihara told his men. Now it was their turn to show what they were capable of and to prove to the rest of the empire that the soldiers recruited in the Doab were as good as their compatriots. Then he had them move into position.

By the time the Bahmani cavalry made their appearance, it was nearly eleven in the morning. They homed in for the formation of infantrymen that Harihara had set up on the plain near the river. Coming from the west, they somehow paid no attention to the sharp escarpment to their right. It was nearly a cliff face, between fifty and a hundred feet in height.

Harihara was in front of the ranks of the foot soldiers. Fifteen hundred men were on the field, with others in reserve to hit the rear of the Bahmani column, waiting for his signal. Next to him was Mithran, who always rode by his side, and whose preferred weapon was a spear that he employed with devastating effect. Harihara reminded Madappa, one of his newly minted officers, to follow the plan. Timing was crucial.

'On my command, we will make our move.'

Haftar was with the cavalry in hiding behind the escarpment. Another new officer, Chengappa, was on the escarpment, along with two hundred archers, keeping low.

Harihara had made them practise this manoeuvre several times until they counted down the seconds in their heads.

When the Bahmani column was half a mile away, he called for the drumbeat to begin. Mithran quickly dismounted, got a packet of vermilion out of his pocket, smeared some on Burfi's forehead and then on Harihara's sword. He held Harihara's sword hand and said:

'Kaliamma will steady your sword and give you victory today.'

Mithran was a veteran of multiple engagements, having been Bukka's bannerman, but he was acutely aware it was Harihara's first major engagement and wanted to make sure he kept his nerve. When the Bahmanis were a quarter mile away, their horses broke into a full gallop. Harihara's infantry stood its ground, waiting, while the drumbeat went on.

'All according to plan so far, Madappa,' Harihara said to reassure him, raising his voice above the drums and the approaching thunder of hooves. The men began the chant of 'geluvu, geluvu, geluvu [victory, victory, victory]' to keep their timing.

The temptation for a cavalry who only saw foot soldiers was to hit the front hard and then get to the flanks. It was the favoured technique of General Yusufzai, who was commanding the Bahmanis, according to Rahim Rahmatullah's spies. By now the cavalry had too much momentum to be able to stop easily.

On Harihara's command, his men began counting backward: 'Five, four, three, two, one—one step back—raise the stakes, secure them—move back into the formation.' They moved flawlessly. The Vijayanagara infantry rapidly moved back in step, following the gradually sped drumbeats. Harihara could see the eyes of the horses bulging and the shock in the faces of the cavalrymen as they saw what was in front of them.

The Bahmani cavalry hit the large sharp stakes set in the ground, facing them like giant spears. The first fifty horses rushed into the spikes along with their riders, while the next two hundred slammed into those ahead of them. There was mayhem on the frontline and it seemed the Bahmanis' leader was lost in the charge.

Harihara signalled Haftar, and the archers on the escarpment stood up, took aim and launched a volley of arrows. They repeated it again and again. The Bahmani riders on the right flank were hit. Meanwhile the infantry charged the Bahmani column.

Harihara commanded the war-dogs to be let loose on the rear of the Bahmani cavalry, causing panic. Mounted archers, hidden with the dogs behind the escarpment till now, attacked the rear. There was chaos in the enemy ranks.

The Bahmanis spotted a possible escape through a ravine in the escarpment, which could easily accommodate three or four horses abreast. It appeared to be a suitable route for retreat. Harihara let them do just that. Once they began to ride into the ravine, which opened up into an open field, they were unwittingly bottled up where they were faced with cavalry ahead of them as well. Behind them the infantry closed off the exit.

As Harihara rode to see how developments unfolded, a Bahmani cavalryman made a run for him and lunged with his sword. Mithran severed his hand in an instant and another of Harihara's cavalryman rode to Harihara's right side to give him cover, accidentally hitting his right leg hard. Mithran, whose eyes bulged with ferocious focus, screamed, 'Death is your friend,' and beheaded the man before he hit the ground.

The game was up for the Bahmanis. Harihara saw a man bearing a white flag ride towards them. He offered to surrender. In this first engagement, the Bahmani lost nine hundred men with another two hundred wounded, while the rest were taken prisoner. By contrast, Harihara lost just nineteen men and roughly one hundred soldiers were wounded, mostly with broken bones. What seemed like ten minutes actually lasted two hours. It took three days to secure the prisoners, clear the battlefield of the dead and bury or cremate them.

The relentless training was the winning ingredient. It helped everyone overcome any anxiety they may have had in their first major battle. Mithran had counselled Haftar and Harihara earlier on what it felt like on the battlefield when the enemy was advancing and how to quell one's nerves.

'Go into the battle to win, Harihara and Haftar. Never show fear, though it is good to feel it. Let fear be the fuel that pushes you. You need to have a hundred eyes and make sure you see all sides of the battle. If you push onward, the men will follow and do the same. You must show a desire to crush the enemy. And remember, there is no room for doubt, because if you do not kill the enemy, he will kill you.' Mithran's straightforward talking had not changed since they were young boys and he taught them how to use a sword.

Haftar had smiled when Mithran had walked away after the pep talk, and had glanced over at Harihara and whispered:

'He has first-hand experience having been by the side of two of the best-known generals of all time. He knows how they operated. Yet there are other times he thinks he is still talking to twelve-year-old boys.'

Harihara had nodded his head in agreement.

'True, he's earned the right to advise us; though, as you say, he does switch between treating us like officers and treating us like boys.'

The last comment that night was from General Chinayya, who had observed the battle from the escarpment where he was situated with the reserve battalion.

'I have nothing more to teach you, Harihara. Your training, timing and execution were faultless. And your strategic sense is a lot like that of Hakka Raya and Bukka Raya.'

The path of the arc

Despite being in a deep sleep, he felt the dog lying by his feet tensing up. Its breathing grew shallower. He immediately woke up and saw Kaloo, his four-year-old kombai, her head up and listening carefully, getting ready to move towards the entrance of the tent. While hostilities against the Raichur encampment of the Bahmani had ceased five days ago, he trusted the animal's instincts. In spite of his guards encircling the tent in two concentric circles, it was enough to alert him that something was amiss. Reaching for his sword by the light mattress on the floor, he got to his feet slowly due to the wrenching pain in his right leg after his lancer had smashed into him during the battle of Alampur.

Hobbling over to the entrance of the tent he could see Mithran.

'Is there something up?'

Mithran turned and smiled, and in the dark one could see only his gleaming teeth. The rest of him blended into the dark night.

'Kaloo must have woken you. The noise was much too far away for you to have heard it inside the tent. The courier was getting ready to leave for the capital with the mail, including reports of the battle and your letter to the emperor. One of the horses must have been upset with the way the syees [groom] saddled him. It neighed and kicked him.'

'Is he okay?'

'He'll live, by God's grace.' That was about as loquacious as he would get. Mithran had more time for animals than people because he felt most humans were deceitful.

Harihara walked back into the tent to get some more sleep if possible.

Kaloo brushed up against his left leg, sensing that his right was hurting. She was his favourite for a reason. She was able to respond to every circumstance and anticipate events in an uncanny way; she was gritty, fearless and had the will if not always the stamina to keep up with him on a long hard ride. That being said, she was also full of mischief.

He was tired and drained. Even his feet were tired. He knew he was not going to be able to rest, though Haftar was sleeping like a log. Perhaps he would sleep as he rode. Burfi, his horse, was trained well enough to follow the pack. As a shiver consumed him, he felt something shift perceptibly. It was like his mind was being moved to another situation. A new situation he feared he could not control like he had the last three years.

His memories attacked him like a swarm of angry bees—the rush of every emotion he had ever felt seemed to wash over him. He wondered if he were ill. He had not hit his head anytime during the last two weeks. He forced himself into a pranayama routine. He could feel Kaloo's breathing by his ear, which soothed him. And with that, gradually, came the answer to the cause of his anxiety. After three years, he was going home.

If his sense of time was right, it would not be long before he heard the soldier blowing on the kombu to announce the start of the day at the encampment. He had asked that this be a little delayed to give his men some rest—not too much.

With his hand on Kaloo, he carefully arranged his thoughts. The orders that Bukka had given him kept ringing in his head: 'Establish the state on a stable footing and secure its northern borders. You have three years to accomplish this task.'

Then his mind drifted to the ride home—a journey that would take roughly three weeks, twice what it normally would be to get to the capital city of Vijayanagara. Minister Gnyanadasa and General Chinayya were instructed to go directly. He was going to backtrack over ground they had secured over the last three years. He would trace an arc westward along the banks of the Krishna river, starting from the west at Jalahalli and then on to Bagalkot. From there he would move south towards Gadag and onward to Vijayanagara: the capital of the empire that his uncle and father had built.

He would have typically travelled with twenty men and a few extra horses to make good time, but General Chinayya refused to allow it. This was still new territory and the Bahmanis might have ideas about a reprisal after the capture of Raichur. Chinayya was a senior general in the imperial army and Harihara was a major in the King's Guard, so he followed Chinayya's counsel. There would be scouts in the advance and rear, and both he and Haftar would ride with a contingent of a hundred cavalrymen.

A short while later the kombu sounded to awaken the men. Kaloo started licking his arm and face so there was no sleeping after that. Having eaten with the troops, many of whom would be riding with him, he turned the corner past the small encampment where his commanders and administrators had their tents pitched. His departure had been announced. The army gathered, roaring and cheering the victory against the Bahmanis at Alampur and Raichur. It was the last thing he expected. Four thousand troops made an awful lot of noise and now they expected him to address them.

'The Bahmani assumed they were better than us and we defeated them. This territory is now part of the Vijayanagara empire and adds to the large and prosperous state of Gotak, which we have built over the last three years. All of you, with your loyalty and your love for your emperor, Bukka Raya, are responsible for this victory. We are fortunate to have been led by General Chinayya.' He paused, calling for a moment of silence in remembrance of their fallen brothers-in-arms. 'We need to make a solemn promise their families are all taken care of: wives, children and elders. Each of you has given fearlessly to the effort and it is now time for your emperor to take care of you. There will be a bonus of the spoils and money from the treasury at Raichur for each of you. I've been summoned by the emperor and will be back once I get my orders from him. In the meanwhile, stay alert, follow your orders and make sure we do not give back what we worked so hard to get.'

A rumble rose from the back. It was a chant: 'Yuvaraja, yuvaraja, yuvaraja!' This refrain went on. He raised his hand in an effort to quiet them, reminding the troops that there was no decision yet about who was to be the yuvaraja. The emperor was Bukka Raya and he asked them to pray for his long reign and good health. Being called crown prince left him a little shaken, however. More than that, it was unexpected. Where had this come from? Was it spontaneous?

Westwards

After last-minute instructions were given to the commanders of
the camp and the head of the district, he mounted Burfi, called
for Kaloo, Kelsa and Kopa, and set off. He rode out front to
avoid being covered by the dust kicked up by the riders. It was
a grey day, which was some consolation for the long hard day of
riding ahead of them.

He enjoyed the next three days of travelling with Madappa,
the commander of his company, Mithran and Haftar among
others. Such occasions enabled him to loosen up and even
allowed them to ask searching questions, talk about themselves
and tell bawdy jokes. Nor was he spared from being the butt of
relentless teasing.

'Rajkumar, if only you spent half the time thinking about a
woman rather than the dogs, it might make you happier.'

'I do not know of any woman who is willing to take half of
anything, do you, Madappa?' he responded.

The banter continued but they rode fast and made good
progress. Evenings were given over to some kallu and roasted
game the advance party had hunted. He sat with all of them
around a huge fire, drinking and eating until he stood up to
signal the evening was over. Madappa was constantly checking
with scouts to make sure there was no suspicious activity.

Kaloo kept up for at least half the day and then she would
start to fall back. Then he would change horses and ride bareback
with her lying in front of him. She managed to balance herself,
though he never broke into a gallop when she was riding with
him.

They got to Jalahalli on time. Over the three years it had
become the de facto capital of the new state. As they rode up

the main thoroughfare his heart skipped a beat. How did they know when they would be arriving? It seemed as if the whole village had turned out. What had changed? Haftar was able to read his mind. He said:

'Success, Hari, draws people out. You've given them success, safety and prosperity.'

The men were given a few days to rest before the next leg of their journey. He wondered if he should leave Kaloo behind. Just then he received a summons from the emperor requiring his presence at court on the last day of August, but it did not indicate how long he would be required to stay. If Kaloo could not handle the trip, she could ride with him or one of the couriers would bring her with them. He resolved that all three of his dogs would ride back with him. Besides, Vallima surely wanted to see them.

During his stay at Jalahalli he dealt with issues of supplies and pay for the military. Decisions were required on taxes and collecting them in the new territory. Informants provided him with updates on enemy activity or suspicious happenings. Accounts were checked, building projects were appraised and judicial issues were debated.

Harihara started his day early, exercising at the military encampment. Harihara and Haftar were always looking for the best swordsmen to spar with. But when the competition grew intense, Mithran was always hovering around. Once he even suggested tying a rope around a sparring partner so he could pull him away in case it got dangerous. Harihara had to ask him to accept the risk as there was no other way to keep their skills sharp.

After training it was back to the encampment to check in on the horses, feed the two war elephants, and ensure all the war-dogs were cared for. The process came to Harihara naturally and he was in his element. While he was away at battle, two Arabian mares had been bought at great expense. They were beautiful horses. He wandered up to them, fed them lumps of raw sugar, a few fresh green leaves and then some grain. He touched their noses and flanks, rubbed all four legs and exulted at the beauty of the animals.

They had travelled a long distance by sea and land and Harihara wanted to make sure they were healthy. His reasoning behind purchasing them was to improve the quality of horses in the cavalry. He peppered the horse doctors with scores of questions and ordered that they were not to be saddled until he got back from Vijayanagara, and he wanted them well fed and exercised. Then he realized that when the monsoon came, the thunder and lightning might frighten the horses. He ensured that the paddocks were padded and asked that a syees be assigned to each of them to make sure they were not alarmed.

Two of his assistants doused him with water and helped him bathe in plain sight of those around the stable. Harihara changed into a loose shirt and a pair of light cotton trousers that were tight around the calves and loose around the thighs for ease of riding, exactly what his cavalrymen wore. He wore a wide belt and anchored his sword on his side. Had it not been for the jewelled sword it would have been difficult to know he was royalty in the line of succession.

He returned to the encampment where his men were eating their first meal of the day. The fragrances from the kitchen were rich: coconut chutneys, rice pancakes, mutton curry and millet balls. While he never grew to like millet balls, he had grown to accept that they were necessary for sustenance, especially on long trips.

Harihara was hungry. He ate heartily. Calling for the head of the kitchen, Dodappa (roughly translated as 'big man'), he thanked him for the meal and for training the cooks. Dodappa wore a simple pair of pajamas and had hastily put on a cotton shawl when summoned. The compliments had him beaming. Harihara gave him a purse of coins as a reward for his endeavours.

Harihara made his way back to his manai (home), wandering through the bazaar with his small bodyguard contingent. He wanted to see whether the vegetable and grain market was well stocked. At the end of the long street, he saw tradesman who were key to his success: blacksmiths, locksmiths and cobblers. Then Harihara stopped at a vegetable stall and saw Kaliamma, the old woman who still tended to her job.

Everyone said she was a soothsayer but, in his eyes, she was just a strong old woman who refused to give up her independence. Stopping before her, Harihara dismounted and he was greeted by a smile.

'Rajkumar, I have been thinking of you the last few days.'

'I am sure you did, Kaliamma, because you knew I was in town,' he teased.

'Of course, I knew. I was the one who sent all the vegetables to your house for dinner tonight. But that was not why I was thinking of you. What I have to say is for your ears only.' It was her way of saying she did not want any of the four bodyguards to hear her, yet they were loath to move away. Harihara instructed them to move back.

She breathed heavily and spoke with her eyes closed.

'You are destined for greatness, rajkumar. Trust in your instinct, do not be modest because everyone should know how capable you are. If you are overly modest, it will be the downfall of us all. May you be well, my yuvaraja.'

'I am only a rajkumar, Kaliamma.'

Before he walked away, he left a small pouch of coins at her feet, gave a salutation to the emperor, and walked back to mount his horse. A crowd gathered around. He smiled, looked at everyone surrounding him, listened to a few petitions, wished them well, and let them know he had an appointment to keep. The crowd gave way shouting, 'Jai rajkumar!'

The rest of the day was spent discussing tax revenues, law and order and administrative matters. To his satisfaction, all three districts were peaceful and on time with revenues.

When Harihara was at home in the capital, lunch tended to be a protracted affair with Haftar. Having had a good meal, he played with the dogs. Often, merchants came to the house and he bought small trinkets for his mother and sisters, and had them sent by the weekly courier to the capital.

In the evening Harihara met the treasurer, Bikram Seth. The harvest was good, trade was on the rise for the third year, and despite having spent money on military campaigns, equipment and bonuses for the soldiers, there was still a significant surplus.

'How did that happen?'

'Rajkumar, you never spend any money,' was the prompt reply.

The sun had nearly set when Harihara got home. The dogs had returned with Haftar from a long ride. He went off to tend to his horse, while Kaloo, Kelsa and Kopa settled down, having drunk what seemed like a gallon of water each. Harihara pulled off his shirt for it was warm, and asked his major domo to get him some kallu from the little coconut grove behind the manai. The taster drank a large glass in front of him and sat by his feet. Mithran was just behind him and to make sure he waited half an hour before he had a drink, just to make sure.

While he waited for his kallu, he played with the dogs and threw a coir ball towards the well for them to fetch. Kelsa (meaning work) and Kopa (upset) bounded off but Kaloo (black) would not move from his feet. Beckoning her over, she would not look at him, sensing she would be left behind.

'Kalooma,' he called to her, 'you will go with me. The trip back is going to be hard, so get ready.' Her ears perked up, her tail wagged and she was standing straight with her mouth open and alert. How in god's name did a dog understand?

Finally, Harihara got his glass of kallu. It was a long day on top of a long few months. He drank it down and asked for another. Taking a sip he sat back and invited Mithran to have a drink with him. With replacement bodyguards in place, he put down his sword and lance and asked formally:

'With your permission, may I join you, rajkumar?'

Harihara nodded and gestured to his servant to serve Mithran. There were six bodyguards in close proximity. More could be seen in the outside perimeter of the house.

Haftar entered with a big smile on his face.

'Why are you smiling, Haftar?' Harihara asked.

'Because I have not seen you this comfortable in a few months, maybe a year. Besides, without your shirt on, you look like a landlord with his dogs at his feet and his henchmen drinking with him. Be assured that all of the security is in place and you should truly relax.'

Harihara called for a glass of kallu for Haftar. It was just the three of them. They had known each other for a long time, tied by bonds of experience and trials. Mithran and Haftar had given every ounce of their skill and ability to make Harihara succeed over the last three years. It seemed trite to praise them.

It would have insulted them. His confidence in them was what mattered most.

They ate grilled meats and bread, drank fresh kallu, which was tasty but not too potent, making it easier to drink more than they should. It was time and he would delay this no more. Harihara gestured with his hand and the major domo entered.

Mithran was asked if he could still stand up. Wondering if this were a test, he immediately jumped up, to the amusement of Harihara. The major domo brought a large tray of clothes with a string of flowers on top. Standing up, Harihara stated:

'This will be short and I am not going to make too much of this because I have had a bit to drink.'

Handing over the tray to Mithran, he announced:

'Today I am making you an officer and a member of the Imperial Guard.' The import of this was not lost on Mithran. His eyes welled up. He was an enlisted soldier; to be given a commission in the Imperial Guard was an honour that he had never expected.

In gratitude, he made the gesture of a namaskaram.

'Rajkumar, may I always serve you and have your trust.' Putting away the tray, he fell to the ground and prostrated himself.

Harihara knelt down to draw him back to his feet.

'Mithran, remember that officers do not do that,' he said, smiling.

They heard the noise of horse's hooves clopping on the ground.

'For you Haftar, I have one of the Arabian mares that was sent to us. I also want to let you know that you are formally appointed my margadarsi, or advisor.' This was a critical position at court that was not only esteemed highly in close circles but also throughout the kingdom.

There were only a handful that held this post. They were the emperor's agents without portfolio who were assigned to take on sensitive and dangerous assignments.

Haftar put his glass down, stared blankly at Harihara and said:

'Tam'ma, I hope you are blessed with all that your ability and potential warrants. Our reward will be to be by your side.' The first thing he did was to go over to the mare and caress her. Harihara was content with the evening's proceedings: two fine men had been, in a discreet way, appreciated and recognized in ways they would prize most.

He then asked to be alone. One final glass of kallu was needed to think about the remaining tasks on his last day in town. Harihara thought hard about how he would not be his own master once he returned to his father's domain. He would be just another player in court, albeit a significant player. Decisions would get complicated with competing voices and relationships getting in the way. He was satisfied with where he was in life. But all the rumours and intelligence, and the way everyone around him had started to behave, suggested change was afoot. And changes were not always for the better.

The three dogs were suddenly up and ran off to meet a visitor. It was someone they knew. Harihara saw the shadow emerge and, as he expected, it was Sayeeda. As he stood up to greet her, he was struck yet again by her obvious grace and her presence. But that was not the only aspect which made her attractive. She was more than ten years older than him, a Muslim woman, who was a widow. He had not tried to make sense of this relationship. Every moment Harihara spent with her he cherished, and savoured the memories of it long after. He wondered if their relationship might get poisonous in the future and grew anxious that it might put her in more jeopardy than him. That concern was for another day. It was the present he revelled in, and she stayed with him that night.

The last day was similar to the previous day in terms of duties that needed attention, except now it went five times faster and with a huge range of issues that required Harihara's consent. When he finally settled down to eat his dinner after sundown, he thought about the scores of people he met and tried to sort out the information he had gathered and impressions he had formed. Haftar ate with him but was equally quiet. There were mounds of fish, rice and venison, as well as the vegetables that Kaliamma sent. Harihara ate well and insisted Haftar do the same. Rations on the road would be basic on the route they had mapped out.

Sitting in the garden after dinner, he decided the dogs would accompany him on the journey. He gave his housekeeper final instructions and Haftar laughed.

'Vallima and Aizama would be proud of your housekeeping skills, tam'ma!'

'Haftar, it is the job of a prince and a king to be a good housekeeper.'

Haftar smiled widely and said, 'Tam'ma, I know you believe what you just said.'

The final stretch

He came round the corner past the stable, and in the darkness he could discern a team of horses with men milling around them. The smell of droppings was pungent and the chatter of the cavalrymen was muted though there was a sense of excitement in the air. They were all part of a new regiment that Harihara had raised after he had arrived in the state three years ago.

Now most of them were capable and experienced cavalrymen. The best he had. They were going to be his bulwark and provide a clear example of what he had accomplished. Harihara was early but the moment they realized he was approaching, the men shouted a salutation: 'Jai nayaka!'

One hundred men were chosen to ride with him. They wore a tan uniform of light riding trousers and a loose shirt with the king's insignia and epaulets to distinguish them as cavalrymen from the most recent state, Gotak, added to the roster of the empire and the new cavalry regiment, 'The Alampur Horse'.

The bannerman raised a new sign aloft. It had a white background with a black dog's head. Kaloo ought to be happy. Underneath were the words: 'Loyalty, Integrity, Bravery'. There was much to be happy about, but these small touches made Harihara feel a sense of accomplishment. The priest, a small man with a booming voice, appeared. He asked for silence from the troops. Then he noticed Harihara in the background and immediately changed his tone.

'Rajkumar, pardon me for being rude.'

'You were not rude, shastri [priest], you were only getting a group of unruly soldiers to listen,' he laughed. 'Please proceed. Just make the incantation short.' The priest quickly said a prayer to Ganapathi, the elephant god and remover of obstacles: '*Vakrathunda mahakaya ...*' and ended with '*Eeswaro rakshatoo*'. He then broke a coconut and put a vermilion mark on each forehead.

Harihara thanked the priest before asking the mullah to come forward and give him their blessings. Kadar, a handsome young man who was the muezzin, came forward and in short order went through his prayer: '*Bismillahir rahmanir raheem ...*' and concluded with '*Alhamdulillah*'.

When the proceedings came to a close, Mithran called the men to order. They were inspected by Haftar and Mithran. Harihara was invited to join the formation. Mithran, who was now the nominal leader of this contingent, stood at the head of the squad and bellowed: 'To the Tungabhadra!'

They rode out in formation from the outskirts of town as the sun was coming up. Harihara was eager to make good time for the next four hours, before resting for a similar period, and then ride another four as the sun set on the horizon. It was to their advantage that the days were long. As they broke into a canter, Harihara was impressed at the horsemanship of the men. Haftar and Mithran had chosen the best to accompany their leader. Once they set a good pace, they could see the scouts ahead and knew the direction they were taking. There was a strong sense of symmetry to the formation. Mithran and Haftar fell in on either side of him. The horses quickly found their stride as the men settled into their saddles and the dogs found a clear area next to Harihara's horse, happy to be out in the open and easily keeping pace.

When the sun became blistering hot, they broke off for lunch and found shade until the heat receded. At the end of a long day's ride, the men built small fires and set up camp.

The summer sun blasted down every day, as it did on the plains of Karnataka. Harihara stopped the contingent at noon. He saw to it that the horses and dogs were given some water and made sure the men were handling the heat and had enough water. Most of the men in his contingent came from the plateau and the searing heat was a new experience for most of them.

He overheard one soldier talking to Kaloo: 'We'd better get you an umbrella, darling, or you are going to boil in your black coat. You are not like Kopa in his white suit. He can handle it.'

When Harihara noticed him, he smiled and said he did not mean to insult the dog.

'I don't think she took it that way. She's just waiting for you to get her an umbrella,' Harihara said as he erupted into laughter, joined by the soldier.

The summer was at its worst. Despite this, they had made good time and were not far from the capital. The king's scouts had spotted them in the distance so the capital started preparing for their arrival the next day. Aizama sent large baskets of food to add to the excitement. Harihara settled down with his men at the end of the day, and reminded them of protocol and discipline—all eyes would be on them in the capital. He did not expect this trip to last longer than two weeks. Restraint would be the key word.

Harihara shared his baskets of food with his men. So much for Aizama's estimation of their appetite! He spoke with Mithran and Haftar and lay back with his head on the saddle, convinced this was the best team he could have assembled. There was nothing more he could do to prepare for court. His father had sent him out with the rank of a major and three years later he remained at that rank. His uniform of the field was what he still wore and he made sure the simple identifiers of rank and unit were visible for all to see. Harihara went over all the issues he anticipated being quizzed about and the rationale behind the decisions he had made, specifically finances, tactics and the inevitable criticisms that would entail.

The next day at dawn they started on the last leg of their journey.

Within the hour, they were at the crest of the hill and ahead of them was spread a sight that he had not seen for three years. On the banks stood the capital of the empire of Vijayanagara. The fortifications were impressive and the scale of the complex was huge. It was meant to intimidate its enemies. The city seemed three times as large as before.

'Rajkumar,' Haftar called out from behind, 'the city we left is now populated with three times as many people.'

'While we heard of all of the changes that have taken place, we are no doubt going to be surprised. Pleasantly, I hope,' Harihara said.

They were met by a large contingent of the King's Guard at the banks of the river.

Harihara identified himself to the officer.

'I am Harihara, major of the battalion of the Alampur Horse, along with my contingent of cavalrymen.'

'The nature of your business, sir?'

'To see Emperor Bukka Raya.'

The formalities over, the officer got off his horse, greeted him and said: 'Welcome home, rajkumar.' They crossed the river and the officer commanded the gates of the city to be opened and instructed a runner to inform the palace of their arrival.

Harihara and Haftar were unable to fathom the extent of the change. Harihara asked the officer to lead them as the streets seemed unfamiliar. The entrance to the palace was different. There was a new courtyard to the right of the palace and as the gates opened, the officer indicated they should all ride in with him. They rode in, four across, into the courtyard. The King's Guard followed and swung to the left and lined up at the side. Further down the courtyard was a palace building with a large door where the emperor, Valli, Aiza, Sarah and Shveta stood on the wide steps.

Harihara presented himself to the emperor in the formal manner:

'I, Harihara, major of the regiment of the Alampur Horse, of the Imperial Army, present myself and this contingent to you, chakravarti.'

Mithran boomed: 'Present arms!'

It could not have been coordinated better: the ringing of one hundred swords unsheathed in unison. Then he commanded: 'The greeting.' In one voice they shouted:

'Jai varaha! Jai Bukka Raya!'

The emperor motioned for his son to dismount and opened his arms wide. Harihara put his sword down, prostrated himself in front of his father, and gave a namaskaram, before finally embracing his father.

'You are early but I somehow expected that,' Bukka said.

General Chinayya and Gnyanadasa were also in attendance and the emperor gestured to them to come forward. Bukka then ordered Mithran to come forward too. He dismounted, knelt down at the emperor's feet, put down his sword and repeated the words, 'Jai varaha, jai Bukka Raya.'

The king addressed Gnyanadasa and General Aiyappa.

'The empire and I are grateful for this assignment you have completed with distinction. Now, join your families and we will meet formally at the durbar next week.' In a softer voice he told them that they would meet before then.

Bukka looked to Mithran.

'I thank you for bringing my sons back safe. Your loyalty and service are unmatched and we are grateful to be in your care. Congratulations on your promotion.'

Mithran dismissed the troops. The horses turned and filed out of the courtyard, followed by Mithran at the rear. Harihara and Haftar were left facing the king who promptly put his arms around their shoulders.

'Welcome back, my sons. You've been gone a long time.'

Behind the king were the four women in their lives: Valli stood there trembling in excitement as much as relief, holding on to Aiza, both with tears in their eyes. To the side stood Shveta and Sarah, who were beaming and waiting to run over to their brothers. Gradually, the clatter of the hooves receded.

The emperor now turned to being a father. He smiled and moved the two boys towards the door where all four women waited impatiently. Haftar and Harihara walked up to Valli, and touched her feet. She pulled them upright and held them in a long hug.

'It's been so long! It's been one thousand one hundred and twelve days since you left: three birthdays, three Deepavalis and Dasarahs and Eids.' She sobbed as Bukka came and put his arm around her.

They then turned to Aiza, touched her feet and were gathered in her embrace. She started sobbing as well.

'Both you and Haftar look so different,' she said affectionately.

Then it was a reunion of the monkeys, which was never without lots of noise and shrieking.

Valli and Aiza led them into the palace. Aiza asked them to take off their headdresses. When they did, all she could say was, 'Do you both ever comb your hair?' All of them burst out laughing. Ever the fastidious one about her children being well groomed, she continued: 'Don't forget that there are expectations of you.'

Bukka grinned. 'We'll buy them a comb. I think I can afford it.'

Bukka's right arm did not seem to be functioning fully. Moreover, his right leg was stiff and he seemed to have an awkward gait. The fevers that Harihara read about in Valli's letters were true. Bukka also appeared much weaker. Fortunately, he'd been a very strong and vigorous man in his youth and had a reservoir of strength.

The new home looked huge to Harihara and Haftar: stately but very comfortable. It was certainly not ostentatious. The boys sat on cushions and drank some cool water. Aiza's hair was nearly all grey and Valli had streaks of grey. The girls were transformed. No longer the brats, no longer the younger sisters who wanted to do everything they did and then try and do it better. They both sat there looking like the personifications of grace, much like Valli. For the moment, they all simply sat there, absorbing the joy of being back with each other.

13

The council will meet

1373: Vijayanagara

Being back home

Bukka gave his protégés a day to recuperate. Were it not for Valli, who scolded him for being impatient, he would have summoned them sooner. He tried to put on an imperial sulk but soon gave up and spent the evening enjoying his time with the children, joined by Valli and Aizama.

Dinner was a riot of flavours and smells, served hot on what was already a hot and humid evening. It was exceptional fare, the sort Valli and Aiza would conjure up. Bukka complimented them but was surprised to hear Valli—not one to give praise easily—say, 'A lot of this was Sarah and Shveta's doing.' The laughter grew raucous and they teased the girls about whether they knew the difference between flour and sugar. Valli smiled:

'Hari and Haftaree kanna [my dears], you both *think* you can cook; they *actually* can. In fact, the girls are as accomplished cooks as riders. So, overall, I think they come out ahead of you.'

Bukka chuckled:

'The boys have lost favour already and they haven't been home long!'

'Who taught them?' an incredulous Harihara enquired.

'The same person who taught the two of you: Aizama, of course. They have even learned every trick in the book from Idriss and Fathlullah. By the way, you should stop over and visit them after dinner as they would like to see the two of you.'

Everyone bombarded Harihara and Haftar with questions, which they had to answer in turn or else they could not have eaten. The conversations carried on late into the evening.

Bukka and Valli smiled as the siblings relentlessly teased each other, occasionally interceding when it got too rambunctious. There were not many occasions in his life that Bukka had felt so happy.

The emperor planned to meet with his confidants as soon as possible to get a first-hand account from General Chinayya and Gnyanadasa of the last three years, and then interview the boys. Their report was critical.

The two generals visited the next evening. The sun was setting. Led down the long verandah by the bodyguards, they were in awe of the new palace. It was much larger and statelier than the old one.

They arrived at the entrance of the wing inhabited by the emperor, expecting one of the chief attendants to usher them in. No sooner were they there than they heard Bukka's characteristic booming voice: 'Chinayya, Gnyanadasa!'

The emperor approached them briskly, hugged them, and then stood back to look at them.

'I don't feel guilty, after all,' he said. 'The two of you look as though hard living conditions have done you good!' He thumped them on their backs and added: 'Unless you have been living a secret life of comfort that I am unaware of.'

The men walked into Bukka's new private quarters. Few people were given the privilege of calling the emperor by his first name. Even then, it was blended with deference. Chinayya and Gnyanadasa didn't need to keep their reserve in Bukka's presence. The shared experience of battles, losses and wins, shared intimate conversations, great joys and wrenching disappointments had bound them together over the years. That elusive entity, loyalty, had been tested over the years as well.

As the three old friends retold old stories, Valli gracefully slipped in to greet them. She told them about her meetings with their families in their absence and reassured them that all had been well. Valli saw that the attendants brought enough food and drink before excusing herself. As she prepared to leave, she wondered if they might have to be carried home, seeing the rate at which they were drinking. She smiled as she left the emperor's quarters, happy in the knowledge that old friends were back together.

Bukka sat on a large divan with cushions, resting back. His friends were on either side on similar divans but at a slightly lower level. They took the initiative to raise the topic of Harihara. The emperor certainly would not do so.

Gnyanadasa downed a gulp of kallu and launched into talking about the lurking issue.

'Bukka, you sent us away for three years because you wanted Harihara to have the benefit of advice and for Haftar to be trained as a scout. We realize you want us to scrutinize Harihara's potential, but this has put us in a very awkward position.'

Bukka's heart skipped a beat. What was it about Harihara that had been exposed? What weakness, what deficiency? His mind was whirling with endless possibilities.

Then it was Chinayya's turn to chime in.

'Bukka, the problem with Harihara is that he is a very modest man. Modesty of a form similar to his mother's. Our concern is his lack of awareness of his own abilities and incredible skills.'

'And what do you think?' Bukka asked Gnyanadasa.

Before he could answer, there was rustling at the door. Valli walked into the room. She could tell that they were in the middle of something sensitive. She immediately turned to leave but Bukka called to her in his deep, booming voice.

'This is something that you should hear. It's about Harihara and Haftar. Come and join us.' She gave him a searching look. 'Come and sit with us,' he repeated by way of encouragement and reassurance. He held out his hand and motioned for her to come sit beside him. She pulled up a cushion and sat by the base of the divan next to Bukka.

'Vallima,' Chinayya began, in the warm tone of a close relative or friend, 'Bukka wanted our estimation of Harihara and his potential. We were just about to talk about him.' Valli, worried about the assessment, attempted to get up.

'Valli,' Bukka said, 'let's hear this together. It's too important for only me to hear about it. Besides, whatever Chinayya and Gnyanadasa have to say, let's hear it as parents. Then the affairs of state can take over.'

Chinayya got up and walked across to stand before them. He took off a ring, which had the seal of the 'Emperor's Commander' and laid it at Bukka's feet. 'It's best I hand over all symbols of authority. Once I provide my summary to you, my assignment is over. Gnyanadasa will speak for himself and add to what I have to say. He's a smooth talker while I'm a rough soldier, so he'll do it better. He may survive this meeting, even save my sorry soul.'

To fortify himself, he walked to his divan, took a long swig of kallu and faced Bukka.

'Chakravarti, my Emperor Bukka Raya, what I say is heartfelt but it is also based on my estimation as a military man who has been by your side for many years.'

He paused, waiting to find the right words, though he wondered if the alcohol and tiredness had finally got the better of him. Holding his hand up to his eyes as if to wipe a tear, in a soft voice, he finally presented his assessment.

'Bukka, Harihara is better than you or your brother Hakka in every single way but one.'

'What?' an incredulous Bukka asked. Chinayya swayed a little, as though he were ready to faint.

Valli stood up, held him by the arm and guided him to his divan. She poured him a glass of water and fanned him—it was stiflingly humid, a precursor to the rains. Chinayya recovered and started to speak.

'Three years ago, you sent us with two eighteen-year-old men. In the case of Harihara, the objective was to test him and let you know if he had the grit, gumption and mental capacity to succeed you as the next emperor of Vijayanagara. You gave him a task that was amorphous and undefined, even to us. You asked him to organize a frontline state where there was none. To complicate matters further, you did not give him resources of any consequence. We understood you did this on purpose, but what Gnyanadasa and I were impressed with was how Harihara was able to adapt to such a vague set of orders. Most perfectly capable people would take half a lifetime to do it.'

Gnyanadasa thought he would take some of the burden off Chinayya. He took up the tale where his colleague left off.

'Bukka, Harihara's ability to listen to advice, ask searching questions, argue and present his case, are skills such as few have. I'll let Chinayya talk about his military abilities once I finish, but in three years he created and transformed Gotak into an effective state that is now part of the empire. I have never seen it done so quickly and effectively. He also has an ability to engender loyalty among his men. And he knows his numbers, Bukka. Ask him about any number pertaining to Gotak's revenues, and you will get a clear and succinct answer.'

Chinayya, clearly feeling better, resumed his explanation.

'In the early skirmishes with the Bahmanis, I took the lead in planning the battlefield. However, all of the early fights were minor. By the end, Harihara was a more accomplished battlefield commander than me. In the last campaign against the Bahmanis we fought two thousand cavalrymen, which was double the size of our own cavalry. It was a massive engagement. Though he consulted me in advance, every single detail was stage-managed by Harihara. You have read the reports that describe it all in detail: the strategy, the plans, the training, the actual battle and its stupendous outcome. In sum: the leader was killed and a large number of the cavalrymen and eight hundred fine horses were captured. We lost just a few men. Harihara subsequently recovered documents, loot and treasure from the opposition's encampment located a few miles away.'

Continuing with his report, he stated: 'What made it work, Bukka, was his attention to detail and his ability to lead from the front. The state of Gotak is going to have many prisoners to feed but in exchange has a huge amount of free labour, not to mention very fine horses—they are even better than those in the stable here in the capital, which makes this one of the most profitable campaigns in recent times.'

Chinayya sat back and gurgled in delight.

'Bukka, you've never seen anything like this. It was a sight to behold. It will be a lesson that we will teach for years. And all of this from a twenty-one-year-old! I could have never conceived Harihara would pull this together the way he did.'

Valli grew agitated.

'Chinayya,' she asked respectfully, 'is he devious?'

'Vallima, not in the least. He is an exceptional general and there is not a devious bone in him, excepting when he is dealing with an enemy.'

'Then where does the reservation come from?' a puzzled Bukka enquired. 'You say all this but you also say there is one dreadful defect. What is it? What cancels all this praise? What am I to be told that is so terrible, friends?' He was troubled. Valli looked around to ensure the attendants were out of earshot.

Gnyanadasa took the initiative to reply.

'Bukka, I am not sure that he is ambitious. He attends to the assignments he is given and he has the physical and mental ability to achieve them. But I am not sure that he has the necessary ambition to be emperor.'

'Do you mean he might turn down the opportunity to succeed me if he was offered it?' an increasingly irate Bukka asked.

'No,' responded Chinayya. 'The point is that you would have to make that decision and tell him it is his duty to do so. He will not fight for it.'

The information brought Valli to tears born of mixed emotions: concern that her son wasn't ambitious, and happiness and pride that while brilliant and capable, he was not grasping and greedy as so many princes were. Bukka reached for her hand and invited her to sit beside him. But she declined; it was not appropriate, especially in front of Chinayya and Gnyanadasa whom she'd known since she was a child.

Instead, she said, in an attempt to lighten the sombre mood of the conversation:

'It's ironic that I never imagined I would be a queen, much less an empress; my husband never expected to be emperor; and now we have a son who is not interested in succeeding him.'

To this, Chinayya responded: 'And for that, Vijayanagara is blessed, chakravarti and samrajini.'

The drinking was not going to stop, despite Valli admonishing the attendants to stop filling their glasses. So, she decided to try a diversion. First, she asked Malaa, the first queen, to pay her respects to the two visitors. However, Malaa was busy with her coterie playing dice, and dismissed the invitation: 'The soldiers and clerks can wait.' Valli sighed and thought, 'At least I gave her the chance to be involved.' Then she called Harihara, Haftar, Sarah and Shveta to go pay their respects in an effort to distract the older men from their sombre mood and the kallu. As a group they could challenge a circus for entertainment value.

The children interrupted the serious conversation and within minutes the atmosphere changed dramatically. Bukka had the two girls on either side of him, Haftar stood next to him and Harihara sat where Valli had been.

That evening Harihara was the butt of all the jokes. The girls chimed in with excerpts from the letters he sent home to his mother. Little remained secret between the four women in the household, but then, little ever got out.

Sarah and Shveta mocked Harihara and Haftar by singing little ditties about them. It had Bukka, Gnyanadasa and Chinayya in stitches. The boys got in on the act and told stories about each other. However, the two young women were working with fresh material, both rumour and fact, so both Harihara and Haftar were outclassed.

Valli and Aiza escorted them next door for dinner. They sat on cushions on the floor, excepting Bukka, who sat on a chair at a table—furniture that was not common. It was a long, beautifully laid-out room, grand in its proportions but lacked pretension of any sort. On an evening like this, Aiza and Valli served them. Valli made sure the two young men and Bukka got the bulk of her attention. One needed it, and the two others had been deprived of it for a while.

When dinner was over, it was clear that Bukka was growing a bit weary. He retreated to the sitting room with Chinayya and Gnyanadasa. With his arms on the shoulders of his two friends he informed Valli, 'We'll be next door if you need us.'

They stood in the archway opening to a large verandah looking out onto the garden. Being a floor above, they had a perfect view of the Tungabhadra river.

'It seems we have enjoyed exceptionally productive years; my friends, I thank you for your services.'

'Bukka, it is gratifying to see how Harihara has become such an exceptional individual,' Chinayya said. Bukka still had his arm on Chinayya's shoulder.

Perhaps it was the alcohol, or perhaps it was simply the reaction to missing his two close friends and his sons, but Bukka persisted with the debate about Harihara.

'Would both of you just give me a simple answer to my question? Does he have what it takes to succeed me?'

'Bukka,' he responded, 'the first thing I would say is that Harihara is and will be a better administrator than you. Second, by my measure he is an excellent general, though strangely you still have him at the rank of major. But third, Harihara is straight-talking, honest and loyal, while the court is more devious when it comes to making deals. Also, all the governors and petty rajas under your dominion owe you in many ways, and these debts are personal. If Harihara should succeed you, little of this will transfer over to him. That will slow down the efficiency he is accustomed to.'

The conversation went into a lull as the three men sat down on their diwans in the gentle cooling breeze.

'Bukka, Hakka handed the empire to you because he knew you were an exceptional administrator and were responsible for many victories. Yet he was the one who handled the court. Still, he knew you would be capable of growing into the job—and you did. That is where we are today. Harihara will grow into his job.'

Bukka sat back with a sense of satisfaction.

'You do realize that he had two of the very best teachers. You let him grow. I compared the weekly dispatches that each of you sent to what Harihara wrote to me, and it was a distillation of what you would tell me. The only thing he never talked about were the two beautiful women he met.' There was an outburst of laughter. 'Have either of you seen these women?'

'Of course, Bukka,' Chinayya replied. 'Harihara was discreet but never tried to hide anything. We ate dinner with them a few times.' He turned to Gnyanadasa, pointing at Bukka. 'Do you remember, this was just the way he was with women, except a little more graphic, until he met Valli? Full of questions and always on the hunt! In that way, Harihara is different from you, Bukka. He seems to have stable relationships with these women. Not one-night stands, though he could afford that luxury.'

'So, is Syeeda the better looking of the two?' Bukka asked with a mischievous smile. The discussion went on until late at night.

When it was time to leave, the two old friends embraced Bukka before making the official salutations to their emperor.

Bukka motioned for the bodyguards to accompany them out. As if from nowhere, Valli appeared. She held him by his hand and gently helped him back to his suite. He changed his clothes and she made sure he was comfortable in bed. Before she walked away, he asked:

'Where are you off to now?'

'The monkeys are making the most of this reunion. Harihara and Haftar sent Aiza back to her room because they wanted to drink. You should see them. You'd think they were two drunkards, Bukka. Now I am worried they will challenge the girls to drink.'

'Valli, I am sure Aizama can handle it. Besides, they are all not children anymore.'

'Bukka, they drank a lot when they were away.'

'Your spies are better and more reliable than mine,' he replied with a smile. 'I am sure you know the colour of Syeeda's dupatta the last time she saw Harihara!'

'How dare you,' she said in a half-serious tone, suppressing a smile. 'I hardly know what my son is up to. He writes more regularly to you than to me. You never did let me go and visit him and now I seem to have the empire's best spies monitoring my sons.' She made sure he was comfortable, and as she was walking out she whispered: 'Green and gold.'

'What?' he yelled from his bedroom.

'The colour of Syeeda's dupatta,' she said, smiling, as she walked away to check on the mischief next door.

Mothers' joy

Valli walked down the long verandah before turning to her right where she had set up a new suite of rooms for Harihara and Haftar and looked in to see all was ready. The large wing had been built after they left. She took considerable pride in how bright it was, while at the same time it looked comfortable and stately. She was suddenly interrupted in her thoughts by the noise of three dogs barking loudly.

In the melee of the young men's homecoming, she had forgotten about the dogs. She could hear the sound of singing coming from another nearby room. The barking came from the same direction.

'Harihara, Haftar!' In an instant Haftar emerged from the noise.

'Were we not permitted to have the dogs?' he enquired. Valli paused for a moment. They'd always had animals with them. The only time she said no was when they wanted to have a pet monkey.

'You may have them here so long as they do not wander into Bukka's area or Queen Malaa's quarters. Let me meet them.' Haftar called out to the three dogs who came bounding out, furiously wagging their tails in excitement. He instructed them to sit, which they dutifully did, waiting to be touched and to smell her. They remembered her instantly. Valli stroked their heads and as she knelt down by them, they rolled over to be rubbed on their tummies.

'Vallima, you are leading them on. You'd better stop or they will not leave you in peace.' She kept petting them and called their names, particularly enamoured with Kopa. When she stood up, she held Haftar by the hand and walked into his new suite. The dogs started to follow them in but he pointed at them and they stopped by the door.

When Valli walked in, Sarah, Shveta, Aiza and Harihara immediately stood up. There was a full-scale reunion in progress, and even Aiza was part of it. Looking at the four children she had raised with Aiza, she choked up with a sense of deep gratitude and pride. Clearly, they had all been drinking, something she was not accustomed to seeing. Occasionally, she and Aiza would sneak a drink or two to celebrate, but that was a state secret. Even Bukka did not know.

The four siblings were now adults. Valli sat between Haftar and Harihara, then smiled, before putting her arms around them. As silence descended, she announced: 'Where is my drink?' All of them started to laugh and the slight constraint evaporated. As she expected, the three women were drinking fresh kallu. 'Good,' she thought to herself, 'the girls should be able to handle it.' In a stern voice Valli made it known that Shveta and Sarah were only to drink when they were with her or Aiza. They both had wicked smiles on their faces.

Turning to Haftar, she said: 'Maga [son], we are so proud of all that you've done over the last three years. I heard that you now have an elevated and prestigious position at court.'

'Vallima, I appreciate your comment but the focus should be on what Harihara has accomplished. My achievements are no more than a reflection of that.'

She pulled him closer and, as he moved sideways towards her, she kissed him on his head. 'May Eeswara's blessing always be with you.' She held him close to her side, amazed at how much the two young men had grown. They were even more muscular and clearly hardened over time, exuding a quiet confidence that comes with accomplishment. She'd seen this a few times in her life. Men and women in powerful positions, who had achieved a lot, wore it lightly but it was reflected in their confidence. The two young people she sent away had come back as men with much to their credit.

Aiza's eyes were welling up. It always amazed her to see the extent to which this queen, nay empress, thought of her children as her own. Nor was it an insincere gesture. Jewellery and clothes for Sarah came before Shveta. The standards she set for the two were never different. Valli repeatedly said she was blessed with two girls. As for the boys, or rather men, now, Haftar was always told he was a prince with all the opportunities and resources at his disposal. His horses were just as good as Harihara's, as were his clothes, and he studied under the same teachers who tutored Harihara.

At the end of the evening, Valli led Harihara and Haftar into their suite.

'What is this place?' the aghast but excited Harihara and Haftar asked.

'This is where you will be from now on in the new palace.'

'Vallima, it is luxury beyond what we are used to!' Haftar replied in astonishment. 'Huge rooms, washing areas, attendants, and imagine, mattresses. I'm not sure I'll able to sleep. If we dare get used to it, life on the frontline will be miserable.'

'No,' she interjected. 'You will have something to look forward to when you think of coming home.'

She pulled them both close to her and whispered in their ears how she was overwhelmed by her blessings. Aiza walked in from behind with a lamp on a tray. She collected the soot from the lamp and smeared it upward across their foreheads, remarking: 'May the evil eye never fall upon you both.'

Private consultations

Every two months, the calendar of activity contained days when the emperor did not hold durbar. Today was one of those days. The rains would soon begin and there were some crucial decisions to be made. Bukka's day had already been long and it was only late afternoon. The minister of finance and the minister of public works discussed matters of state. He kept a close watch over the two of them since they had access to large sums of money and he wanted to keep them accountable. Even with intelligence, it was difficult to know if the minister for public works was not lining his pocket. Today, Bukka decided to replace the minister due to poor results and even less dependability. It would be announced when durbar commenced next month.

Following this, he held a meeting with his most important official, Mani Iyer, who now held the highest rank in court. When the durbar was not in session, Mani Iyer frequently came to see Bukka. Yet, he realized that this particular visit was likely to be more than just a discussion of state revenues, foreign affairs, promotions or a review of the empire.

Bukka sat in the verandah—his favourite place in the palace—which looked out on the river, and saw the dark clouds rolling in. 'A premonition?' he wondered. The rustle of the bodyguards who accompanied Mani Iyer interrupted his thoughts. He waved them away as Mani Iyer walked down the long verandah with the emperor's aide-de-camp.

Mani Iyer bowed low in a namaskaram to greet his sovereign: 'I am at your service and I pray Eeswara will confer his blessings on you and our empire.' Bukka smiled and gestured to him to sit down.

'Chakravarti, what affairs would you like to cover today?' At the end of the verandah, Bukka could see Mani Iyer's assistant with a large package of materials in case Mani Iyer needed to consult them. Unless there were seals that had to be affixed, they were rarely needed, as Mani Iyer had every last detail committed to memory. Bukka informed him about his decision to change the minister for public works.

'I am glad you agree,' Mani Iyer said. 'All the public works are a demonstration to the empire of the care and attention that you pay to the needs of the people. It needs a person of great integrity and caring to be the administrator.'

There was a short pause and Mani Iyer let the emperor take his time to raise the next issue. He knew exactly what was on his mind and how hard he was wrestling with it.

'Mani Iyer, the question of succession is not really about who will replace me; rather, the problem is, how it will unfold.'

Another protracted silence ensued.

'Would you like something to drink or eat, Mani Iyer?' Without waiting for an answer, Bukka called for water for both of them. Mani Iyer never ate anything that was not cooked at his own home.

'I was looking at the rolling clouds coming in, Mani Iyer, and it felt like an omen.'

'Chakravarti, they come with the season, as does the inevitability of succession. Being prepared for the monsoon and for a succession ensure that the negative impact is minimal. Besides, empires need to be nourished, like the land, with new leadership.'

'But how and when do I make the decision and announce it?' a distraught Bukka asked.

Mani Iyer closed his eyes, held his hand together in a namaskaram and recited from the Bhagavad Gita:

Strive constantly to serve the welfare of the world;
By devotion to selfless work one attains the supreme goal of life.
Do your work with the welfare of others always in mind.

'This quotation from the Bhagavad Gita does not guide one to an answer,' said Bukka, exasperated.

'It does, chakravarti,' Mani Iyer insisted.

'What part of it do I not understand?'

'The welfare of the empire commands you to make a decision in the best interest of your subjects. Being selfless requires you to move into the background as a newly anointed chakravarti assumes control at some point in the future. It implies that you will face the consequences of the decision for the greater good. Delaying the decision will only give those with an agenda time to scheme and plot.'

'It seems as if you know who it should be.'

'Chakravarti, the answer has always been clear and obvious. Your successor should be Harihara.'

'Mani Iyer, I am intrigued how confident you are about this decision, especially given that you were Rajkumar Ramanatha's spiritual teacher.'

Mani Iyer collected his thoughts and said:

'Some in the world, chakravarti, believe their station in life owes them the accompanying benefits. They would not be able to handle the absence of benefits and comforts. Yet the inner self needs a balance to be effective; it needs empathy to understand the hardships of others, particularly when you are raised with every privilege; it requires that you have the ability to test yourself; it finally requires the humility to learn and the courage to admit shortcomings.'

'And these qualities Ramanatha does not have?'

'No. Emphatically not. These are flaws that will have dramatic implications for the empire and its subjects, should he be chosen to rule.'

'However,' Bukka said, 'you could argue that he does have a stately presence and has the presence that people might respect.'

'Superficial, chakravarti. I respect you for your accomplishments and the way you come to your decisions. I respect you for what you hold dear. One of those attributes is the love of your people. My respect for you in no way depends on your stately presence,' Mani Iyer sternly responded.

'How can you arrive at the conclusion that he does not have a deep-seated love of people and sense of duty?' Bukka continued with his line of questioning.

'Chakravarti, I never could inculcate a love of others in Ramanatha. He always sought to see what I was looking for and tried to please me. Not once did he show a genuine search for this important quality. There was, and there still is, a constant need for self-indulgence. It also leads to another shortcoming,' Mani Iyer revealed.

'Which is?' Bukka asked, as he leaned forward.

'Being susceptible to flattery.'

'Excuse me, Mani Iyer, but I need to stand. My leg bothers me when I sit on the floor for a long period,' Bukka said as he moved awkwardly to stand up. He grimaced at one of the nearby guards who hurried forward to help.

'Then let me stand as well, chakravarti. Perhaps walking back and forth on the verandah will help your legs and mine.'

As they began to slowly pace to one end of the verandah, Bukka resumed their conversation.

'I do not understand philosophy as well as you do but is the lack of compassion the only flaw in him? Is that the chief disqualification in your estimation?'

Mani Iyer pondered the question for a moment.

'No, it's not the only shortcoming but most of the other failings I can think of are the result of this flaw.'

'Are there any others that you can think of, Mani Iyer?'

'Excessive self-indulgence and an increasing lack of self-discipline.'

As they reached the end of the verandah, they could see the Tungabhadra river. The rain clouds were looming and soon there was likely to be a downpour. In a day or two, the life-giving rains would finally come down and bathe the dust and mud off everything, leaving a carpet of green.

'Have we made preparations for the rains?' Bukka asked.

'Every important protection you suggested, in addition to the council's recommendations, have been put in place. Supervisors have travelled all over the empire to check, and the network of informers confirmed preparations are finished. Most importantly, all grain supplies are in granaries high off the ground and will be protected from the rain. The military is secured in all locations for the monsoon; the routes have been prepared so couriers will be able to make their way back and forth, even when river crossings are difficult to make.'

'Have all people along the river been moved away from the banks in case of flooding?'

'As of yesterday, chakravarti, all people have been moved to high ground,' Mani Iyer confirmed.

Bukka smiled in satisfaction.

'It's ironic that we wait for the monsoons and the bounty that it gives us, but Mother Nature is not always gentle when she manifests herself, so we have to prepare for her exuberance as well. I want to make sure that we keep a close watch on flooding and provide relief when it is needed. The poor and the old will be vulnerable. The last two monsoons have been manageable but I worry we might not be as fortunate this time,' Bukka said, concerned about the potential for natural disasters.

For the next twenty minutes, Mani Iyer listed out the details of what had been done to prepare for the monsoon: the names of every minister and district head, locations of surplus grain, public buildings that would serve as shelters. He listed the locations of all the lookouts along the river monitoring its level. He even knew the fording paths for couriers who carried information to the capital. After all these years, it never failed to impress the emperor.

Bukka had tried to give this little man, his confidant and trusted advisor, the highest civilian decoration for three years, but each time, Mani Iyer got wind of it before it could happen. A line he frequently used was:

'I am but a priest who serves his God, his emperor and the empire. That is enough honour for a priest.'

'Excessive indulgence is what we were talking about before I changed the topic,' said the emperor. 'What do you hear now?'

There was silence as they kept walking back and forth. Bukka needed time to brace himself and Mani Iyer wanted to be both honest and positive. By the time they reached the other end of the verandah, he offered his opinion.

'Chakravarti, the excesses are only growing: they involve temptation of women, liquor and gambling, and a total inattention to managing the state that he was supposed to govern. I remember your orders to Harihara when you sent him north. I understood your intentions and, to a certain extent so did Gnyanadasa. Any young man would have been at a loss for what to do. Yet, Harihara appreciated what was in the best interest of the empire. He considered how these goals might be accomplished and achieved them where others might not have. Of course, like any young man, he indulges himself but at the same time you see a sense of moderation, consideration and discipline in him. Yes, he drinks and has a few women who keep him company occasionally but that is the extent of it,' Mani Iyer said delicately as Bukka chuckled at the priest's stringent standards.

'He has lived on his own resources,' Mani Iyer continued. 'Harihara has set an example of integrity and honesty that all officers and administrators should follow. I need only remind you of the contrast. Ramanatha undid a lot of the work we put in to building his state. He will find it very difficult when the "Council on Succession" quizzes him. I imagine they will not be forgiving.'

'Have there been any scandals?' Bukka asked with trepidation.

'Yes, chakravarti. And that brings me to the point I wanted to make: he will be late coming to Vijayanagara. He has been trying to clean up the mess and that has taken him more time than expected. His excuse will be that affairs of state delayed him.'

Bukka started walking again. This time he placed his hand on Mani Iyer's shoulder but did not need the physical support. Mani Iyer spoke again.

'Chakravarti, the only choice you need make with regard to succession, in my opinion, is when and not who. The empire will grow and flourish when Harihara succeeds you. Everything else is insignificant.' He did not embellish, nor did he stray from the facts. Honesty was critical to his thought process. Besides, he'd given Bukka his opinion on the most important question of the day.

Bukka turned to him and said:

'Prathama manthri (prime minister), my advisor and my friend, I will think about what you have said.'

Mani Iyer then stared directly into Bukka's eyes.

'With your permission, may I convene the Council on Succession?'

Bukka thought about it for a moment, mulling over the ramifications. Then, accepting that life was moving in a strange new direction, he said:

'If you believe you have all of the necessary information, please proceed. I will endorse or reject the decision of the council. But the Council on Succession should meet after the monsoon. We also need to inform Guru Vidyaranya before any final announcements are made, and seek his advice and, if possible, request his presence when the decision is made and the announcement is made. In fact, it would be appropriate for him to make the announcement at the durbar, if we can. I will, or you can communicate this to him and wait for his response.'

The aide-de-camp led Mani Iyer and his assistant out. As he left, Bukka wondered, 'How does a man who barely weighs two sacks of rice have such energy, drive and focus? He barely eats anything of substance. There are no earthly pleasures he indulges in and his only allegiance is to the principle of what is right.' Well, he did have an indulgence: Mani Iyer loved music.

Bukka reminded himself to invite a few accomplished musicians and dedicate an evening to his loyal prime minister. Only a few of his close friends and the immediate family would attend. That would be the best way of recognizing his effort.

'Well, Mani Iyer, I will get you drunk on music!'

He sat on one of the divans that was set against the verandah wall, from where he could see the expanse of the river. He asked for a glass of buttermilk and smiled at how this had all started when he was with Hakka and Qutlugh Khan in Dilli.

When big decisions had to be made, Bukka sat by himself and mulled over the information he had been provided. There were questions to consider. Why was he so hesitant to make a decision on succession? Why was he giving Ramanatha such a wide berth?

I hereby call the council to order

Mother Nature had been gentle this year. Her munificence has been delivered with minimal disruption. And in one area in the new province of Gotak, where there had been flooding, they had been prepared for it.

The Council on Succession was convened early in the morning two days before the first durbar of the year. The advisors who had accompanied the two rajkumars on their tasks were present. Pattu, despite strenuous objections, did come but only as an observer. The ministers, General Karthikeya and Rahim Rahmatullah were present as well.

Once they were all seated in the Green Palace, Mani Iyer called the meeting to order.

'You have all received reports relating to the progress of the two rajkumars over the last three years. These include the individual assessments which members of the council submitted as well. Since we are aware of the record in great detail, what I suggest is to propose the name of the yuvaraja (the heir apparent). Emperor Bukka Raya has made it clear that he intends to abide by the decision of this council. However, the deliberations of this council will remain secret and need we be reminded that the future course of the empire is being laid out by each and every one of us. We have to live with our choice. The only question before us is who will be chosen: Rajkumar Ramanatha or Rajkumar Harihara?'

Mani Iyer paused for a moment.

'To reiterate the gravity of the decision and to make sure that we are all blessed with the perspicacity and wisdom we need, I asked Guru Vidyaranya to join us.' Everyone nodded in agreement. Mani Iyer signalled for Vidyaranya to enter the room.

Graceful as always, Vidyaranya did a namaskaram and sat at the head of the horseshoe arrangement of seats.

Vidyaranya addressed the audience.

'I have been invited by Mani Iyer to attend this deliberation. My role is not to be a participant but to offer my good wishes and blessings. May the strength of your gods be with you as you make this very important decision. Please proceed, Mani Iyer.'

A silence descended on the room before Mani Iyer spoke.

'I propose that we present our opinions and if there are disagreements, we can consult the reports to evaluate the rajkumars.'

Everyone nodded and muttered in acceptance of the proposal. Prabhakar Reddi, the justice minister, asked to speak.

'We all want to make sure that this decision is fair. Over the last three years I do not know of any council members who might have been partisan in the process. If it were not for the fact that I have absolute trust in our emperor, I would say that the evidence being presented is totally biased.' Everyone sat up when he made this statement. Prabhakar looked around and smiled. 'Let me explain what I mean by my statement.

'First, of the assignments handed out to the two rajkumars, one was a reasonable challenge and the other seemed next to impossible. To me, there was a high degree of unfairness at the start. And now we see that the final result is totally lopsided. Any judge, unaware of the proceedings, might ask if such evidence was manufactured. We do know that this is not the case. Accordingly, there is little doubt in anybody's mind about the choice of successor. I propose, prime minister, that we proceed to the conclusion and just ask for Guru Vidyaranya's blessings.'

Mani Iyer had a hint of a smile. He put it to the floor to see if the proposal was acceptable. The councillors nodded. Mani Iyer was invited to provide the name of the successor.

Mani Iyer stood up. Facing Vidyaranya, he proclaimed:

'The unanimous recommendation of this council is that Rajkumar Harihara is to be anointed yuvarja (heir apparent).' Vidyaranya looked at him as if he had known the answer a long time ago. Scanning the room, he responded:

'Your decision has my blessing.'

Mani Iyer reminded the councillors that he would take the decision to the emperor, accompanied by Vidyaranya. Each man was sworn to secrecy about the result, as the announcement would only be made at the durbar in two days.

14

Let the durbar commence

1373–74: Vijayanagara on the eve of a succession to the throne

A panoply of colour

The blowing of the regimental horns was the signal that the emperor was on his way to attend the durbar. Outside the Durbar Hall and in the square before it, one could see the panoply of imperial grandeur, its pomp and pageantry. Royal elephants lined the avenue. They were draped with the colours of their regiments across their backs, and each had a large bell hanging from its neck and the crest of the empire as an ornament on its head. A mahout stood by each elephant's foot in the uniform of an infantryman. The only thing setting him apart was the shiny brass ankh he used to guide the elephant.

Nearer to the Durbar Hall was the cavalry of the Suttige (hammer) Regiment, dressed in a bright yellow uniform, with their horses draped in similarly coloured saddlecloths. The men wore black-painted metal helmets matched with equipment that was black too, making the contrast dramatic. Mounted on their horses, each had a sword at his side and held a long lance bearing the emperor's standard as well as the regimental colours on pennants that fluttered in the autumn breeze. It was a vivid and majestic sight.

Bukka rode with the Suttige Regiment when going into battle. It was the first regiment that Hakka and Bukka had established when they came back from Dilli to Anegundi. They were experienced and battle-hardened soldiers. Veterans were usually invited every year to the first durbar of the year as an acknowledgement of their service and it was clear that quite a few Suttige veterans were missing a limb—a poignant reminder of the price of building the empire.

The emperor's journey from the palace to the Durbar Hall was made on an elephant down a long promenade lined by crowds on both sides. It gave the townspeople a chance to see him and he, in turn, could wave to them.

The emperor's elephant, Bhima, a fierce young bull, was big and powerful. He was dark, almost black, and had long, curving tusks. The red cover on his back only made him look more dangerous. The company of the King's Guard who surrounded the elephant were also in black uniforms and red helmets, and projected the same aura of fierce power.

They turned left and into the avenue leading to the Durbar Hall. The horns sounded again to tell the participants at the durbar to take their places. The emperor first saw the two lines of elephants, and after them, the horses of the cavalry that stood lining the street and the perimeter of the square. Kempa Raju, the mahout, knew the routine. He slowed Bhima down to give the emperor a chance to greet some of the soldiers along the way. Emperor Bukka Raya recognized a few of the mahouts and called out to them by name. When they approached the cavalry, he knew every one of the cavalrymen of his regiment.

Just before Bhima halted to face the entrance of the Durbar Hall, the horns sounded again. Bhima slowly sat down, a manoeuvre he managed with ease for such a large animal. Bukka, who declined to use steps to dismount the elephant, climbed over the edge of the howdah and, gripping it with both hands, lowered himself to within a foot off the ground so that he could land on his good foot. Getting off the elephant was not as easy as he made it look. With his recent illness, it was reassuring to the troops of his regiment to see him pull it off.

Mani Iyer was waiting nearby.

'Welcome, Chakravarti Bukka Raya, to the beginning of the durbar for the year,' he announced loudly in his pleasant baritone for all to hear. The durbar was a duty that Mani Iyer felt came close to being sacred, and he took every bit of the ceremony of the opening day very seriously. Bukka, accompanied by Mani Iyer, walked in.

The Durbar Hall was a long, well-proportioned space, awash in natural light, and very stately. The rough grey granite was plastered and whitewashed with lime, which made it bright. A long aisle down the centre led to a platform at two levels. The first was reserved for the emperor's Privy Council and important dignitaries who might be visiting, alongside invited members of the royal family. At the second, higher level was the throne, a large stone chair covered with upholstery. There was a lectern for the prime minister, Mani Iyer, at the first level. Bukka had designed this setup to emphasize that the prime minister was running the Durbar and would be conducting the business of the empire.

Jostling ...

Ramanatha, the older rajkumar, wandered over to one of the two empty seats beside his mother. However, Mani Iyer quickly admonished him and commanded him to join the other nine governors of states, who were seated at a lower level, near the first platform.

'Why, may I ask?' an ignorant Ramanatha enquired.

'Because, governor, that is where governors are seated,' was the acid response from his former teacher, Mani Iyer.

'Does being a governor remove my privileges of being a member of the royal family?' Ramanatha asked with an arrogance that sat ill when addressing his former teacher.

'In my administration you are one or the other. Since the emperor will arrive shortly, I advise you to join your fellow governors as befits your station for this durbar.'

Ramanatha was not used to being told what to do, much less by a mendicant who played the role of prime minister. This was another score that had to be settled, he thought. For now, however, defying this man was not prudent. He would not have tolerated such an insult in his state. He was literally the crown prince. It was just a matter of time before they announced it.

A fuming Ramanatha waddled over to the lower level. Anyone close enough would have noticed that he was bloated way beyond his earlier portly size. They could see his face was puffed and his eyes were red and bulging. Was this stress or excessive indulgence? Looking for a natural comparison, distracted eyes searched for the other rajkumar, Harihara.

The attendees searched the crowd for Harihara. He was not sitting with the generals but was standing behind them in a military uniform and blending in with the rest of the onlookers. He appeared noticeably tanned, tall, and to those who remembered him from three years ago, even more muscular. His hair was short and he held his helmet under one arm. The only reason he could be easily spotted was because he was holding his lance with a pennant no one had seen before: it was white with the outline of a black dog. His uniform markings showed the rank of a major.

A few rows ahead stood Haftar, who was facing an uncomfortable truth. He was originally going to stand with his military unit, close to Harihara. However, Mani Iyer's assistant spotted him and reminded Haftar that he was a margadarsi, or a special agent of the empire. He was expected to stand close to where the governors congregated. This created two problems.

First, Harihara was farther behind with the mid-level officers. Second, he had to confront the impetuous Ramanatha.

'What are you doing here, Haftar?' Ramanatha said; his voice was dripping with disdain and bore just a hint of menace.

'I was asked to stand here, rajkumar.'

'Protocol seems to be a mess and will need to be attended to soon after the durbar has concluded,' Ramanatha announced imperiously. He knew full well that his comment would not draw a response as all the members of the emperor's council were out of earshot. If Mani Iyer had overheard it, it most likely would have drawn a searing comment or an official reprimand.

'Silence as Chakravarti Bukka Raya enters the durbar,' the master of the durbar loudly announced.

Bukka walked at a moderate pace, his face inscrutable. He followed the bodyguards with Mani Iyer at his side. He made his way to the platforms, stopping at the first to offer his namaskaram to his council of ministers. It was merely ceremonial, but was a public acknowledgment of their importance to the empire. He called out all six by name before smiling when he addressed the seventh, Mani Iyer.

'With your permission, I will ascend to the throne,' Bukka said. Not many heard it but those within earshot knew it to be an inside joke, as he always asked permission of the prime minister to take his seat. Yet it was the emperor who assigned the management of the durbar to Mani Iyer as his prime minister.

'Your prime minister and the durbar are honoured to have you attending the opening ceremony for the year,' Mani Iyer said, smiling, participating in this standing joke between the two of them.

The emperor looked at his family. He noticed Malaa wearing a blazing red saree. Always attracting attention, he thought to himself. To her left was Valli in a moss-coloured saree, muted but vibrant. She sat a good head above all of the women, gracefully erect, with the pallu of her saree covering part of her head in a gesture of modesty. Malaa's mouth was red, as she had been eating betel leaves, and she might well have been wearing all the family's jewellery she could find. The contrast with Valli was striking. Two empresses, one his deceased brother's wife and the other his own, yet from two different worlds with two different worldviews. He looked at Malaa and Valli, where his gaze stayed for an instant longer. Behind them were his two girls: Sarah and Shveta. He realized that now they were even taller than Valli. Aiza sat beside them. The two young women had appropriately serious faces but their eyes were twinkling.

Bukka sat down on his throne, intent on pressing on with the business of the empire. He nodded at Mani Iyer. Taking his cue, the prime minister stood at a lectern right in front of where the Privy Council was seated and looked out at the audience before turning to face the emperor.

'May I have the permission of Chakravarti Bukka Raya to commence with the durbar?'

The emperor assented. In the crowded Durbar Hall, the anticipation of important news grew.

The tension builds

Mani Iyer began by thanking the gods for a bountiful monsoon that had not caused any problems around the empire. No property was damaged nor had lives been lost and for that he was grateful. He then spoke for ten minutes and provided a report of the state of the empire in the past few months and an outline of the planned proceedings for this season's durbar.

His notes were on the lectern but he stood at an angle so he could see the emperor and the audience simultaneously. When he spoke of serious matters such as proposed changes in the laws or the economy, he would frequently pace back and forth. Today was yet another master performance from an unassuming man of great ability. His voice boomed so those at the end of the Durbar Hall heard him clearly. Every fact and detail was at his command. As usual, towards the end of his peroration, he came to the subject of new appointments and assignments in the empire. It started with the junior appointments and gradually moved to the more senior posts.

As he addressed the junior appointments, Mithran's name was proposed for a commission in the King's Guard. For the time being, however, he would continue in his current assignment with the newly formed regiment, the Alampur Horse. It was rare for a promotion of a junior officer to be mentioned at the durbar. To those in the know, of course, he was the rajkumar's taciturn and fearless bodyguard. Mani Iyer read a short citation that praised his outstanding service alongside General Chinayya and Minister Gnyanadasa during their recent mission to the northern territory. While Mithran glowed at being publicly commended, he wondered why there had been no mention of the rajkumar. The roll call moved to other appointments and commendations. It was all very routine and boring; people's thoughts started to wander towards lunch.

As proceedings turned to senior military officers, Mani Iyer declared he had two announcements to make. First, he called for General Chinayya, the commander of the Northern Forces, to approach the lectern. Chinayya was at the rank below Marshal of the Army Karthikeya.

Chinayya was first commended for his work over the last three years on the frontline. He was awarded the 'Samrajya Ayudha' ('Weapon of the Empire'). There was cheering from the military men at the back of the Durbar Hall. Chinayya received a scroll from Mani Iyer along with a chain and a pendant made of solid gold from Bukka. The honour came with a large bonus of money and land.

Chinayya saluted the emperor with a closed fist held to the heart. As he stepped back, he was asked to wait. To the surprise of everyone Mani Iyer read out another citation.

'As of today,' he proclaimed, 'the new marshal of the army is General Chinayya.' The whole durbar burst into applause. Chinayya was a popular and respected man.

Chinayya replaced General Karthikeya, who was now promoted to minister of defence. Karthikeya handed over his ceremonial sword and the emperor presented Chinayya with one as well. It was made from the finest urukku steel, better than a Damascus steel sword.

As Chinayya prepared to leave, Mani Iyer indicated that he still had some business to complete. Chinayya hid a smile as he saw Valli in his line of sight. He could tell what was coming even if she did not. General Karthikeya came up and spoke:

'The Emperor's Council and I recommend making Haftar Imtiaz, currently a major in the Northern Command Scouts, a colonel for his exemplary service to the emperor and the army. He is to also assume the title of margadarsi and joins the hundred margadarsis who take on important and dangerous assignments for the empire. As colonel, he will become the regimental commander of the newly formed Alampur Horse regiment, replacing Major Harihara.' The announcement was popular: loud cheers were heard from the military standing in the durbar.

Haftar marched up to collect his new insignia and a signet ring that identified him as a margadarsi.

Harihara chuckled to himself. It would make for a good ribbing over kallu this evening. He would egg on their sisters to tease Haftar for doing him out of a job.

Valli's heart was racing. She had not expected this for Haftar, though the emperor hinted at something else in store. Valli's only request to Bukka had been to never separate their boys. Bukka had grunted and reminded her that they were not children any more and that they had obligations to the empire.

General Karthikeya was not done yet.

'It is with great pride that I announce the promotion of Major Harihara of the Alampur Horse to the rank of general in the emperor's army. He will assume the command of the

Northern Forces effective immediately. Could Harihara please present himself.'

Valli could barely breathe. She should have been happy but was merely numb. She had not seen this coming, though she often wondered why he was under-ranked for the responsibilities he had been asked to assume. Harihara had borne his load without complaint. Making a mental note, she vowed to do an aarti later that day for the boys.

Harihara composed himself and drew a deep breath as he approached the aisle. The cheering in the Durbar Hall had now grown into a roar. 'So much appreciation being shown by the crowd despite his being away from the capital for three years,' a pleased Bukka thought to himself. 'And this despite the fact that he has not tried to ingratiate himself with the military, the ministers or the court, unlike Ramanatha, who had been doing so incessantly. What is it about him that makes him so popular when he is so unassuming?'

The chanting in the hall grew louder:

'Rajkumar Harihara, Rajkumar Harihara, Rajkumar Harihara.' The generals, ministers, and even the council stood up to clap and cheer, but Bukka remained seated. Even more conspicuously, Ramanatha remained seated in his chair as well.

Harihara saluted General Chinayya, who handed him his own sword and the staff carried by a regional commander.

'Congratulations, general,' Chinayya boomed. 'This promotion has been a long time coming. May your service to the empire continue to be exemplary as it has been under my command.'

As he turned, Harihara caught Bukka's eye and there was just a hint of a smile. Valli was visibly proud, while Aiza and the girls were beaming. Malaa looked stonily ahead. He had barely taken a few steps when the generals in the enclosure invited him to join them. They pointed to Chinayya's chair. Cheering started again: 'Yasasu, yasasu, yasasu [success, success, success]!'

As the noise rose to a crescendo, Mani Iyer, who was normally a stickler for protocol, stood at the lectern with a broad smile.

Mani Iyer called for the cheering to stop. But it only grew louder.

Bukka raised his hand and silence fell. He nodded to Mani Iyer to continue.

'Our final appointment is to the seat of minister of public works, as the incumbent has requested retirement for personal reasons. The new member of the Privy Council is the previous governor of our capital city, Minister Gnyanadasa.'

Cheering broke out as he took his place.

Finally

'We have one very important piece of business to complete before we conclude our proceedings today. May I proceed, chakravarti?' said Mani Iyer.

Bukka consented.

'I now request all members of the durbar to stand out of respect for our guest.' With that Mani Iyer skipped down the steps to the entrance. Bukka stepped down a level and invited Valli to join him. She was puzzled, unsure what was happening. He asked Malaa to also join him but she looked away. The anticipation grew as everyone craned their necks to get a glimpse of who was at the door.

It was Valli who was the first to see. She burst out, 'Guru Vidyaranya!' and ran to welcome him. She smiled as she bent down to touch his feet and offered a namaskaram. Bukka caught up with her to welcome their guest.

Mani Iyer led Vidyaranya to the lectern. Addressing the durbar, Mani Iyer announced:

'You are all aware that Guru Vidyaranya has been the spiritual guide for the royal family since the time of Emperor Hakka Raya. Today, a special council commissioned by the emperor and blessed by the guru, has asked Guru Vidyaranya to make an announcement.'

Vidyaranya strode to the lectern and faced the crowd. His rich, dignified voice filled the hall.

'Emperor Bukka Raya, in keeping with the late Emperor Hakka Raya's command, asked the Privy Council and military commanders to form a "Council on Succession". This council has been working for three years to evaluate the candidates and select his successor. The chosen person will be the yuvaraja until the emperor chooses to hand over the reins of the empire to him.'

Vidyaranya paused as the crowd began to murmur in excitement. Bukka raised his hand for silence.

'In keeping with the rules laid out by Emperor Hakka Raya, it will be—'

Ramanatha suddenly stood up while Malaa perceptibly shifted forward in her chair in expectation. Vidyaranya went on:

'It will be his nephew, Harihara. Rajkumar Harihara is named yuvaraja and will succeed Emperor Bukka Raya.'

Mani Iyer gave the sign and the horns began to blow, the elephants outside started to trumpet, while the temple bells rang out in celebration.

'Harihara, please come up,' Vidyaranya said. By now the raucous crowd could not be kept quiet. Harihara prostrated himself in front of the guru, then touched the feet of his father and mother. He then turned to everyone in the Durbar hall and offered a namaskaram. Valli covered her head, sobbing uncontrollably with happiness. The girls ran up with Aiza and led her out.

The last view

Mani Iyer escorted Guru Vidyaranya out to his carriage and returned to accompany Bukka and the new yuvaraja out of the hall. Bukka called Minister of Defence Karthikeya and General Faraj to join them. As they stood beside the elephant outside, the noise grew even louder. People poured into the streets. Bukka vaulted himself onto Bhima, followed by Harihara, Karthikeya and Faraj.

Harihara sat by his father, riding with him on the elephant for the first time. He saw the cavalrymen saluting them with their swords drawn. The elephants were all kneeling as a mark of respect to the yuvaraja.

Bhima started out in his brisk gait on the way back to the palace. Over the increasing noise, Bukka said to Harihara:

'From today, your advisors will also be Karthikeya and Faraj.' He added, '*Narju 'an tazadahir almalik alshshabu* [may you prosper, young emperor].'

Karthikeya and Faraj, veterans of the march to Daulatabad, laughed when they saw Harihara's bewilderment. Faraj leaned over to him and said:

'Whenever Hakka and Bukka were heading out for a major battle or doing something important in the years following

Dilli, they would always use the little Arabic they had learned from Qutlugh Khan to wish each other well. Those good wishes were pretty effective, don't you think?' They all broke into renewed laughter.

Bhima turned into the promenade that led to the palace. Bukka and Harihara waved as they passed by the jubilant crowds who cheered after them.

The elephant bearing the present and future emperor of Vijayanagara passed into the palace courtyard where their family waited; the great doors swung shut. For today, the gates were closed to the world.

Glossary

Word	Language	Meaning
-appa	Tamil/Kannada	Suffix used with a name, indicating affection
-ji	Hindi	Suffix used with a name, indicating respect
-ma	Tamil	Suffix used with a name, indicating affection
adaab	Arabic/Urdu	A salutation used by Muslims in India
adhikarigalu	Kannada	A term for a superior
ajji	Kannada	Grandmother
al-mujahia fi sabil Allah	Arabic	Directed in the cause of Allah
al'ahmaq		

Word	Language	Meaning
Allahu akbar	Arabic	God is great
almuminin bihaqin	Arabic	True believers
alnnayib	Arabic	Deputy governor
amhi atmasamarpana karato	Marathi	We surrender
amma	Kannada/Tamil	Mother
ammi	Urdu	Mother
anna	Kannada/Tamil	Older brother
anukrama	Kannada	Succession
appa	Kannada/Tamil	Father
aqidah	Arabic	Islamic term meaning 'creed', a part of the theological framework of the religion
arambha	Kannada	Beginning
archanai	Tamil	An offering of prayer to a god at a Hindu temple
ashva	Sanskrit	Horse/Knight
badshah ke yahaan	Urdu	To the emperor's place
Bajrangpali	Hindi/Sanskrit	Refers to Hanuman, a Hindu god in the incarnation of a monkey
basith	Arabic	Messenger

Word	Language	Meaning
begum	Urdu	A term of respect when speaking to or referring to a lady
bhai	Hindi	Brother
burfi	Hindi	A sweet confection made with sugar
Chetana	Kannada	Spirited one
chakravarti	Kannada/Tamil	Emperor
chaturanga	Kannada/Sanskrit	The game of chess
chiwda	Urdu/Hindi	A savoury mixture eaten as a snack
Diwan-i-Aam	Urdu	Audience at court for commoners
Diwan-i-Khaas	Urdu	Audience at court for nobles
Doab	Persian	Literally, land lying between two bodies of water—used for the landmass between the Ganges and Jamuna rivers
doordrishti	Kannada	Foresight
Eeswara	Kannada/Tamil/Sanskrit	God
Eeswaro rakshatoo	Kannada/Tamil/Sanskrit	May God help us

Word	Language	Meaning
falnarkab	Arabic/Urdu	Let's ride
Fiqh		Fiqh is Islamic jurisprudence. Fiqh is often described as the human understanding of the Sharia, that is human understanding of the divine Islamic law as revealed in the Quran and the Sunnah.
firangi	Hindi	Slang for foreigner
gaja	Kannada/ Sanskrit	Elephant/Bishop
gaurava torisi	Kannada	Show respect
gharana	Urdu	School or tradition of North Indian classical music in which a student is trained; from 'ghar' meaning house
gulli-danda	Hindi/Tamil/ Kannada	A simple team sport played in India, in which a short piece of wood is struck with a stick

Word	Language	Meaning
Hadith	Arabic	A collection of traditions containing sayings of the Prophet Muhammad which, with accounts of his daily practice (the Sunna), constitutes the major source of guidance for Muslims apart from the Quran
hafiz	Arabic	Honorific for a person who can recite the Quran from memory
hakeem	Urdu/ Arabic	A physician
halwa	Urdu/Arabic	A sweet confection
Alhamdullilah	Arabic	Praise be to Allah
Hanuman	Sanskrit	The monkey god in Hindu theology
Hanuman nannage sakti nidali	Kannada	May Hanuman give me strength
haraam	Arabic	Refers to anything that is prohibited in the Quran or would result in sin when committed by a Muslim
haraami	Hindi	Bastard

Word	Language	Meaning
hijada	Urdu/Hindi	Transvestite
homa	Sanskrit	A sacred fire used in Hindu religious practice
hoshiyaar	Arabic/Urdu	Beware
huzoor	Urdu	Sir
iqta	Arabic/Urdu	The area governed by a governor
irali bidi	Kannada	Let it be
jagarukaragiri	Kannada	Please be careful
jai	Most Indian languages	Hooray/to cheer
jai Vignahartha	Marathi	Hail Ganapathi the god with the elephant head
janaab	Urdu	Sir—a salutation
jauhar	Hindi	Mass self-immolation by women in parts of India to avoid capture, enslavement and rape by invaders
kabaddi	All Indian languages	A team sport
Kali Devi	All Indian languages	Refers to the Hindu goddess Kali known for her ferocity in battle
kallu	Kannada/Tamil/Malayalam	A drink made of fermented palm sap
kanakkupillai	Tamil	Accountant

Word	Language	Meaning
karshayam	Tamil	An ayurvedic potion
keḷamaṭṭada jeevana	Kannada	Lowlife—an insult
khan	Urdu/Arabic	The highest rank in the court of Muhammad-bin-Tughlaq
khazana	Urdu	Treasury
konish	Persian	An elaborate salutation made to the emperor at court
kumkum	All Indian languages	The vermilion powder that Hindus use to make a mark on the forehead
Linga	All Indian languages	The physical representation of the god Shiva
Long-tailed One		A reference to Hanuman
Makhduma-i-Jahan	Urdu/Arabic	Mistress of the World
malik	Urdu/Arabic	A general in Muhammad-bin-Tughlaq's army
mandapa	Tamil/Kannada	A gaily decorated enclosure used for weddings or religious ceremonies

Word	Language	Meaning
Mann	Persian/Urdu/Hindustani	Mann (rhyming with done), also called maund, was a traditional Persian measure of weight, equal to about 37 kilograms
mashaik	Urdu/Arabic	A religious patriarchs
mutt	Kannada/Tamil	A centre of religious learning in the Hindu tradition
meladhikari	Kannada	A senior officer
mudaris	Arabic/Urdu	Teacher
mudaliar	Tamil	Frequently used term to refer to a proprietor, or someone belonging to a southern Indian community who are well known as traders
muealim	Arabic	Teacher
munde	Kannada	Ahead
muqti	Arabic/Urdu	Governor
Musalman	Hindi/Urdu	Someone who is a Muslim
museid	Arabic/Urdu	Assistant
muezzin	Arabic/Urdu	The person who makes the call to prayer at a mosque

Word	Language	Meaning
naib	Arabic/Urdu	Governor
namaskaram	Tamil	Greeting someone by folding your hands in front of you—the same as namaste
niemat Allah	Arabic	May Allah's blessings be with you
nillisi	Kannada	Stop
nishthavanta	Kannada	Loyalty
oopar dekhiye	Hindi	Look up
pakora	Hindi/Urdu?	A fried savoury snack
panchakaccham	Tamil	A variation in the way a dhoti is worn
parvagilla	Kannada	It's okay
patashalai	Tamil	A religious school
peta	Urdu/Hindi	A milk sweet
prasaadam	Tamil	What is handed out at the end of prayer at a temple: could be a flower or something edible
Qawwal Baccho Gharana	Urdu/Hindi	The oldest school or tradition of North Indian classical music
qanuni	Urdu	Enforcers of the law
rafiq	Urdu	Companion
rajya	Kannada	Kingdom

Word	Language	Meaning
ratha	Sanskrit/ Kannada/Tamil	Chariot/rook in chaturanga/chess
sahiba	Urdu	Lady
sampurna geluvu	Kannada	Complete victory
samrajya	Kannada	Empire
sanbusah	Persian	A savoury stuffed and fried pastry—like today's samosa
sastrigal	Priest	One of the ways someone like Mani Iyer would be referred to as he was the priest of a temple
sawf nufuz	Arabic	We will win
semenya	Kannada	General
Shaitan	Arabic	Satan/the devil
Shaivite	Kannada/Tamil	One of the major sects of Hinduism, worshippers of Shiva
shamiana	Urdu/Hindi	A decorated tented enclosure used for religious ceremonies or other celebrations
shaqiq	Arabic	Brother
sharaab	Arabic/Urdu	Liquor
sharayam	Kannada/Tamil	A distilled alcohol

Word	Language	Meaning
sharbath	Urdu/Hindi	A sweet drink
shastri	Kannada/Tamil	A priest
shloka	Sanskrit	A prayer
sigri	Urdu/Hindi	A small coal-fired heater
sipahi	Urdu/Hindi	Soldier
Subhanallah	Arabic	Glory to God
Sultaana	Arabic	My sultan
sumangali	Most Indian languages	A married or newly married woman
Sunnah	Arabic	The way of the prophet
tam'ma	Kannada	Brother
tammagalu	Kannada	Brothers
Tayi Durga	Kannada	Mother Durga–a reference to the goddess Durga/Kali
thailam	Tamil	An ointment
thankgi	Kannada	Younger sister
thanthe	Kannada	Father
ulema		A body of Muslim scholars recognized as having specialist knowledge of Islamic sacred law and theology
ummal	Arabic	Tax collectors

Word	Language	Meaning
urukku	Telugu/Tamil	A special steel forged in medieval India renowned for its strength and flexibility
vaah-vaah	Urdu	Bravo/bravissimo
vaidyan	Tamil	A physician
vakildar	Arabic/Urdu	Master of ceremonies
Vedas	Sanskrit	A reference to the four holy books of Indian scripture
Ya eazizi almaelim	Arabic	My dear teacher
Yaraan-e-miafaq	Arabic	Sincere friends
yurshad	Arabic	Guide
zabitah	Arabic	Governor
Zahir-ul-Juyush	Arabic	Commander of the Imperial Armies
zamindar	Common to many Indian languages, perhaps originally from Urdu	Landlord

Source Materials

Aiyangar, S. Krishnaswami. *South India and Her Muhammadan Invaders*. Maven Books, 2018.

Aiyengar, S. Krishnaswami. *Sources of Vijayanagar History*. Forgotten Books.

Asher, Catherine B. and Cynthia Talbot. *India before Europe*. Cambridge University Press, 2006.

Chandramouli, Anuja. *Muhammad Bin Tughlaq—Tale of a Tyrant*. Penguin, 2019.

Darrett, J. and Duncan M. *The Hoysalas: A Medieval Indian Royal Family*. Oxford University Press, 1957.

Debroy, Bibek. *The Mahabharata*. Translation. Penguin, 2010.

Haleem, M.A.S. Abdel. *The Qur'an–A New Translation*. Oxford World's Classics, 2004.

Karnad, Girish. *Tughlaq*. Oxford University Press, 1972.

Mahalingam, T.V. *The Administrative and Social Life under Vijayanagar*. University of Madras, 1940.

Pillai, Manu S. *Rebel Sultans: The Deccan from Khilji to Shivaji.* Juggernaut, 2018.

Sastri, K.A. Nilakanta. *A History of South India from Prehistoric Times to the Fall of Vijayanagara.* 4th ed. Oxford India Paperbacks, 2019.

Sewell, Robert. *A Forgotten Empire: Vijayanagar.* Forgotten Books.

Smith, Tim Mackintosh, ed. *The Travels of Ibn Battuta.* Macmillan, 2000.

Stein, Burton. *Vijayanagara.* Cambridge University Press, 1993.

Sundaresan, Indu. *The Twentieth Wife.* Washington Square Press, 2002.

Talbot, Cynthia. *Precolonial India in Practice: Society, Region and Identity in Medieval Andhra.* Oxford University Press, 2001.

Acknowledgements

My debts in getting this story off the ground are significant. Meenakshi Alimchandani, you gave me the confidence to proceed with this story-telling endeavor. Your advice and direction were significant. Harini Narayan and Krish Murti, I am grateful to the two of you for reading a crude first version and giving me your reactions to the various personalities—it reassured me that it was a story worth telling. Anuja Chauhan and Vatsala Raghavan helped me get this manuscript into the right hands so it might get serious consideration. *Dhanyavad.*

And Mark Empey, I hope you see this, and see your handiwork all across the manuscript. Adam Bender, your experience and your suggestions helped me with the logistics of getting on with it.

I will always be indebted to Mita Kapur, at *Siyahi*. A deeply perceptive reader, I have come to respect her sure touch and clear-headed professionalism. It has been a privilege to have her on my side. She truly is *eximius*.

Padmini Smetacek who helped me edit this book was a joy to work with. She truly was deft in the way she brought consistency and clarity to the narrative and helped sand down the rough edges. Padmini, you practice your craft with poise and elegance. To you, a thousand thanks.

Swati Daftuar, my commissioning editor, was the motor force behind getting every bit of the production of this book taken care of.

Mily and Govi, you were my cheering squad. Your enthusiasm, curiosity about the history of the period and patient indulgence gave me all I needed to get this story written. Neither of you ever did waver in your belief that it was a story worth telling.

Mily, your deep love for animals has made its way into the narrative. I was not even conscious I was doing it. And Govi, thanks for reading multiple versions of the manuscript and debating the history of the period with me. It helped more than you might imagine. And Pax, your calm, affectionate and furry presence saw me through many doubt-filled days.

About the Author

Buchi was born in India and spent his early years there. After completing his post-graduate education, he completed his Ph.D. in economics in the US. For the next ten years he was an academic, on the faculty at three institutions in the northeast of the US. He subsequently moved into Banking.

Buchi now lives in New Jersey with his wife, and his dog Pax, his writing companion. He has a son who serves as his advisor on all matters historical.